HOUSE
OF SECRETS

BY JAMES A. MOORE
AND KEVIN MURPHY

A novel based on the Vampire: The Eternal Struggle™

Collectible Card Game from Wizards of the Coast

WHITE WOLF
PUBLISHING

House of Secrets is
A product of White Wolf Publishing.

White Wolf, Inc. Executives
Mark Rein•Hagen and Stewart Wieck, Owners
Stephan Wieck, President
Wes Harris, Vice President of Marketing
Michael Krause, Vice President of Sales
Richard Thomas, Vice President of Production and Design
Ken Cliffe, Director of Development and Editing
Benjamin T. Monk, Jr., Controller
Rebecca Schaefer, Warehouse Manager

Cover Illustration: Harold MacNeil

Cover Design: Michelle Prahler

Printed In Canada

Special thanks to Bonnie Moore for everything, especially putting up with my unusual work hours; Inge Moore for being a great Mom. Thanks also to Kevin Andrew Murphy for making our joint effort a pleasure and to Rick Hautala, Richard Chizmar, Tom Monteleone, Marcus McClaurin, and Charlie Grant for the encouragement. Last but not least, thanks to Stewart Wieck and Staley Krause for the opportunity.

— James A. Moore

Thanks to Fran Zandonella for the emergency computer loan, Ray Pimentel for the German, Judy Tarr for the Latin, and Marie Laveau for the wish at World Fantasy. And to my mother, Christine Murphy, for help with the German and everything else, this book is lovingly dedicated.

— Kevin Andrew Murphy

Wednesday, April 21, Miami — Praxis Seizure: Miami

Waking up was a slow process normally, but the sound of honking horns and the occasional shifting of his weight made it hard for Kurt Westphal to stay comfortable. Eventually he sat up and shook off the day's draining effects. He was thirsty, but there was no crisis. "I'm awake now, Jackie."

The traffic in Miami was hellish, but no worse than what he was used to back home in Berlin. He rolled down the window for a better view than the heavily tinted glass would permit. Outside the limousine, the night was as clear as crystal and the temperature was remarkably cool. Kurt always expected the southeastern parts of the United States to be humid and outrageously warm, but now and then he was pleasantly surprised. The weather almost made him feel like he was back home in Berlin.

"Good evening, Mr. Westphal. We're almost there. I've double-checked, and the Presidential Suite will be ready for us when we arrive." Jackie Therman's sultry voice carried through the thick, black glass barrier that separated him from the driver's seat.

Kurt stared at the moon outside, scanning the landscape

and orienting himself. "There" was the Miami Hilton in this case. Not perfect accommodations, but the best he could manage on such short notice. "There were no problems getting me through Customs?"

"Just the usual. They wanted to check the body for contraband. I showed them my diplomatic courier card and slipped 'em a little on the side for their troubles. End of problem."

He shook himself mentally. The very idea of spending time in a coffin was repugnant, even if he did sleep through the majority of his confinement in the narrow box. Still, having diplomatic immunity made the trip far more tolerable. In human society he was a diplomatic courier. Among the Kindred's vampiric society, he was an Archon, assistant to the Ventrue Justicar, Democritus. His power was equivalent to that of a federal marshal in the United States. People listened when he spoke up. Important people. He never needed to worry about the car being stopped and inspected while on the road, just so long as the German Embassy license plates were in plain sight. "There has got to be a better way to get around than in a casket."

"Well, we could take the Concord, but that idea seems to bother you even more."

"Yes. Well, at a certain height, Jackie, there is not even a prayer of cloud cover should the sun creep around the edge of the world. As you know, I have a problem with my delicate skin."

"Delicate, my ass." She chuckled throatily, and he was reminded how much he loved the sound of her voice. "You have skin like steel, except when a little bright light creeps past the curtains."

"You have the mouth of a street urchin."

"I am a street urchin." The glass barrier between them rolled down, and Jackie looked over her shoulder as the limo rolled to a stop in front of the Hilton. As always, her pleasant smile made him almost forget that she was a well-trained killer. "I'm just a street urchin who knows how to dress. We're here, boss."

She slipped from the driver's seat of the massive car and stepped quickly to the side door. Seconds later, she was helping the valet with the luggage, and Kurt was standing to one side, admiring the way her body moved beneath her chauffeur's uniform. Her voice was one hundred percent efficient professional when she spoke again. "The rooms are ready, sir. Shall I meet you there?"

"That would do well. Also, call on Mr. Winter at his home. If he's not there, leave a message that I wish to meet with him."

"Very good, sir." Kurt didn't wait around as she climbed back into the monstrous vehicle and carefully maneuvered away from the main entrance of the hotel. By then he was already half the distance to the front desk and pulling his billfold from his custom-fitted Armani jacket.

Five minutes later, he was in the Presidential Suite and setting up his laptop computer. Jackie let herself in and grabbed the phone without a word being spoken. Despite their friendly banter, she never bothered him when he was at his computer unless there was an emergency. Her voice became background noise while Kurt checked his e-mail messages on four different networks to make sure there were no last minute changes in what was required. There weren't.

"Have you contacted Winter?"

"Yes, sir. He'll be in the hotel bar of the Marriott down the street within the hour."

"Well, then, I suppose we should be on our way." Kurt opened one of his three briefcases and pulled several bundles of hundred dollar bills from inside. He placed the rest in the safe that the Hilton provided. Winter was very efficient, but he could be persuaded to change sides in any situation if his price were not met, and exceeded. Kurt hated using Winter, but there was no real choice in the matter. There simply wasn't enough time to use anyone else.

By the time Uriah Winter showed at the bar, Kurt had been waiting for almost two hours with Jackie. Jackie had changed into more comfortable clothes and Kurt into a less formal suit. They could have been a couple on a date, and that was exactly what Kurt wanted people to think. Winter came dressed in blue jeans and a muscle shirt with a long great coat slung over one arm. His white hair was slicked back against his skull and dragged into a tight ponytail. His perpetual sneer was firmly in place, and Kurt had no reason to believe he wasn't carrying a weapon of some sort in the folds of his coat.

"Hello, Uriah. Why don't you have a seat?"

"How the hell are ya, Kurt? Haven't seen you around here in a few years."

"Yes, well, we all have our own work to do, don't we? Mine required that I spend most of my time away from your lovely city."

Winter lit a cigarette, patently ignoring the No *Smoking* sign, and slid into a chair at the table. The waitress paused a moment, looking at Winter's cigarette and the smoke curling away from it, then took in the dangerous- looking man himself. She blinked, smiled, and asked if she couldn't get him anything. He ordered an imported beer. The only one actually drinking was Jackie, but when Winter's Heineken showed up, all three had glasses sitting in front of them. Appearances had to be maintained.

"So, what can I do for you, Kurt?" Winter's tone made the casual question sound vaguely insulting, which, Kurt was sure, was exactly what the man intended. Winter never hesitated to make certain that everyone knew he was in control of the situation, no matter what the situation might be.

"I have a list of items and people I need acquired. I will need them all by seven p.m. tomorrow. I will need this taken care of with discretion. Do you understand me?"

"What are you trying to imply, Westphal?"

"I seem to recall that the last time I offered you a commission, there was a problem with a large automobile and several automatic weapons. You are the only person I spoke to on the matter. What do you think I'm implying?"

Winter grinned ear to ear, revealing even, white teeth in a barracuda's smile. "*Caveat emptor*, old buddy. Besides, there're plenty of people gunning down Germans in this city. Don't you read the newspapers?"

Kurt reached across the table and grasped Winter's arm in a crushing grip. Winter stared at him levelly, but a trace of pain still showed in his expression. "I will not play this game with you again. Do you understand me? I know how you work, and I will not allow you to ruin my plans a second time."

"You don't want to go there, Kurt."

"You do not want to take me there, Uriah. You want to finish the task properly this time, or I will make it my personal mission in life to see you destroyed. Do I make myself clear?"

"Like glass." Kurt released his arm, taking great satisfaction in the way Winter was suddenly favoring the limb, rolling his wrist in circles to assure himself that nothing was broken.

"Good. Now then, considering the short time you have and the large list of needs, I am perfectly willing to triple your normal fee." He could all but see the dollar signs in Winter's eyes. "If you need more than that to successfully achieve your goals, we can discuss it later. After you have procured what I need."

"Payment up front, Kurt."

"Not a chance in Hell, Mr. Winter." Winter's eyes flashed briefly, but he remained seated. "You will receive exactly one half of your usual fee up front. More than generous when you consider the expense of having my suit replaced after Anvil and his friends decided to pay me an unexpected visit last time, don't you think?"

Winter flicked his cigarette across the room and grinned with obvious satisfaction as it landed in a middle-aged patron's coffee cup. The balding man stood up, scowling and looking for the source of his unexpected additive, but calmly sat back down when Winter winked at him and blew a kiss in his direction. Kurt waited patiently as his contact lit another cigarette and kicked his worn boot-heels up on the scarred surface of the table between them. Kurt gestured with one hand to prevent Jackie from kicking the chair out from under the Caitiff. She pouted, but complied.

"Yeah, Kurt. I guess it'll do." Winter stood up with unsettling grace, smoke creeping from his mouth and nostrils as he did so. His voice dropped lower, growing deadly and filled with threat. "But if you ever threaten me again, you'd do well to remember that I have friends too."

"You do not have friends, you simply have associates you have not yet betrayed for money." He nodded to Jackie, and she slipped a manila envelope from inside her jacket, letting Winter see the compact machine gun that rested against her side at the same time.

Winter took the money and smiled. "I'll see you tomorrow."

"Be good, Uriah."

"Be careful, Kurt."

Kurt watched as Winter walked away, pausing only to drop his second cigarette in the new cup of coffee sitting in front of the middle-aged business man and to rub the man's bald spot like he'd rub a Buddha's stomach for good luck. The man flinched, looking directly down at the spoon he used to stir his coffee and started blushing furiously. No one laughed, except Winter.

Jackie shook her head and sighed while Kurt watched the retreating figure with amusement. "What are you smiling at? He all but threatened your life."

"Nonsense. If he'd actually wanted to hurt me, he'd have kept his mouth shut. Uriah only cares for two things — himself and money. It will take a substantial amount of the latter for him to risk the former by betraying me a second time."

"You're too confident for your own good."

"Of course I am, dear. That's why I keep you around." She smiled at that, her blue eyes twinkling and setting off the fiery accents in her dark red hair. "That, and you are a pleasure to look at."

"Flatterer."

"Who's next on the list?"

⇒⇐

"How have you been, Grendel?"

The handsome young man smiled back, apparently grateful and surprised that Kurt had offered his hand. His particular clan of vampires were not often greeted warmly. Grendel hid his true appearance behind a sheath of illusions, but Kurt knew what he truly looked like and knew also that a handshake would please the Nosferatu. They shook vigorously.

"I'm fine, Mr. Westphal. It's good to see you again." The voice sounded rusty, like an old iron gate being forced open. Knowing Grendel's penchant for listening and not speaking, Kurt wouldn't have been surprised if it had been months since the vampire said more than five words.

"How can I help you today, sir?" The vampire's voice echoed as it bounced off the sewer walls. Much as Kurt hated being in the sewers, he hated even more the idea that the Nosferatu might take any offense if forced to meet elsewhere and decided not to return the old favor he was about to ask. He straightened the tie around his neck and smiled, despite the sludge running into his shoes. Just his luck — the place they'd arranged to meet was flooded well past his ankles. As if the stink itself weren't enough.

"Well, I have a favor to ask."

"Anything. You know that."

"I understand that Anvil and his little group of cronies are looking to seize power here in Miami. I was wondering if you could tell me anything about that."

Grendel nodded, looking around the area carefully. Finally satisfied that no one else was around, he whispered, "Tiberius heard all about it. They didn't see him, but he was there when they discussed the situation. They think Gilbert Duane's a little too crazy, even for a Malkavian. They're gonna call for a Praxis seizure tomorrow night at the meeting of the primogen."

"Hmm. Did they list any examples as to why he's not competent?"

"You mean aside from him being a Malkavian?" Grendel flashed a nervous grin, apologizing even as he made the joke.

"Now, Grendel, we both know Gilbert's competent. If he wasn't, he would not still be the prince of Miami after forty years." Kurt shrugged. "A good point, nonetheless. But was there anything else solid?"

"Well, they were saying that Natasha Volfchek has him wrapped around her finger and that she's the one really running the town." Grendel looked ready to back-pedal and run. Kurt smiled reassuringly. Volfchek was Ventrue, just as Kurt was. The implication was that the Ventrue led the city and used Duane as their pawn.

"What utter nonsense. I spoke with Natasha only last week, and she assured me that there was no such situation."

"Well, she does hold a lot of clout with him. That's a given." There he went again, stepping back, as if to make certain he had running room. After years of dealing with each other, Grendel apparently still had trouble believing that Kurt meant him no harm. Kurt suspected Grendel had spent most of his life before the Embrace running from one threat or another.

"True, but clout is something that all of the primogen have, not just Natasha. No, I suspect that Anvil is probably interested in more power than he has and, like as not, a bigger share of the drug moneys here in town."

"Well..."

"Really, Grendel, who has the most to lose if Anvil and his group of bully-boys take over? Gilbert has made it very clear that he likes the Nosferatu and considers them allies. Have you ever heard similar remarks from Anvil or from any of the merry little group he runs with? Or have you heard the same old comments about Sewer Rats and the same old threats of mouse traps and poisoned bait?"

Grendel stared at the ground at his feet, his jaw muscles working and his eyebrows knitted close together over the bridge of his nose. "Well..."

"I want you to do me a very big favor, Grendel. For the sake of both our clans. For the sake of everyone in Miami, really." He placed his hand on the man's shoulder, and Grendel glanced up, pleased by the contact. "I want you to talk with Chester DuBois for me, and I want you to arrange a meeting."

"Oh, I think I can do that, Mr. Westphal."

"Thank you, Grendel." The man ran back into the sewer from which he'd stepped earlier, nodding and mumbling to himself. The figure of the handsome teen cast a misshapen shadow the wall, revealing Grendel's deformities for any who cared to look. In seconds, even the sound of him moving through the water was gone.

>€

Jackie and Kurt wasted substantially less time waiting for Chester DuBois' arrival than they had waiting on Uriah Winter. The Nosferatu elder of Miami didn't bother to disguise his features like Grendel did. He showed himself in his natural state, his blue skin and deformed body clear evidence of his particular clan. Jackie stepped back slightly, but Kurt stayed where he was and extended his hand for a shake just as he had with the other Nosferatu. DuBois accepted his hand and nodded his acceptance of the gesture. He stared intently at Kurt, his eyes focusing from different heights in a face that belonged only in nightmares. Within minutes they were discussing all of the details about the meeting the next night. Kurt learned that Anvil had imported a new man for the position of prince, a bruiser by the name of Crusher. He'd never met the man, but he had heard tales of Crusher's ferocity. This was not what the Ventrue Clan wanted for Miami, and Kurt intended to make certain the Brujah did not succeed in their attempted coup. DuBois made mention of an unexpected bonus and asked the two to wait just once more while he made arrangements for an early meeting the next night.

They spent the remainder of the night and a good portion of the early morning hours waiting, but it was worth the patience and the rewards were tremendous. Later, after the deal had been struck, all the plans had been solidified, and he was finally able to get back to the Hilton, Kurt showered vigorously, imagining the raw contaminants that had touched his body. The Nosferatu really were the most revolting creatures he could think of, but their domiciles were even worse.

>€

The weather had turned foul sometime before Kurt awoke for the evening. His best shoes were beyond repair despite Jackie's best efforts, the Mariott was far too crowded for his tastes, and to top everything else off, Uriah Winter was late. Kurt had started to contemplate the best ways to destroy the clanless little whelp when he finally showed up with a small group of dressed like any of a dozen youth gangs from coast to coast in the U.S. Jackie looked displeased by the turn out, but Kurt just smiled.

"Hi, Kurt." Winter's voice was saccharine at best. "Sorry I'm late. You know how it is — you get hung up in traffic, and then it all goes to hell." The smirk on his face made a lie of his words.

"It's not a problem. This time. Perhaps in the future I should take my business elsewhere." Apparently Winter got the hint; he put on a straight face. "Now then, let's get down to business, shall we?"

Kurt sat down with the other vampire and the leader of the pack of humans and started talking. Within half an hour, all the details were settled, and the first part of Westphal's plans were set into motion. He climbed into the limousine a few minutes later, worrying about the wasted time.

From the driver's seat, Jackie called out with a total disregard for formalities, "Where to, boss?"

"Back to the hotel and quickly. I'm supposed to meet with Natasha Volfchek. She does not like to be kept waiting."

"Since when do you care what any of the primogen of any given city think? Especially when she's one of your own clan?"

Kurt chuckled at that, shaking his head and smiling at Jackie's reflection. "I only care when the difference is between winning and losing, or when the individual in question has the right connections. In this case, both factors are worthy of consideration. Natasha and I did not part on the best of terms, I'm afraid. She took offense to my opposing her at the last regional vote. You may disregard your enemies from time to time, Jackie, but never ignore the wounded feelings of a dear friend." He paused for a moment, making certain that he looked appropriate for the meeting less than two hours away. He didn't have time to change into a more formal outfit, but what he had on would have to do. "Especially when the friend in question is on very good terms with your sire."

"Okay, I'll trust your opinion on that one."

"Besides, she'd be furious if she showed up before me. She is supposed to keep me waiting, not the other way around."

They pulled up to the hotel only a few minutes ahead of

Natasha Volfchek and were in place so that she could still feel she had the upper-hand. They met her and her entourage in front of the Hilton; there was no need to get comfortable inside, not when they'd be leaving almost immediately. Natasha was a lovely woman, aristocratic and regal, but not to the point of appearing too pompous. Her hair was coifed just so, and the blue evening gown she wore was understated. With her were four men, three humans breaking a light sweat in the humidity and one additional Kindred. Kurt had never seen the humans before. The vampire was Robert "Jazz" Wentworth, a powerbroker with slightly less money than God. Jazz smiled broadly as Jackie opened the door for Westphal. Natasha's face was completely impassive.

"Natasha, you look as lovely as ever." Kurt kissed her cold cheek. "Democritus sends his regards, dear. He also asked I invite you to a little to-do at his place in Atlanta. Just a gathering of good friends, nothing too formal."

The frost melted slightly, and Natasha even managed a slight smile, almost as broad and flamboyant as the one on the Mona Lisa's face. "It's very nice to see you again, Kurt. How have you been?"

"Better, now that I've seen you. I really must apologize for staying away so long. I've been in Berlin for the better part of the last year. What with the mess going on over there, it's all but impossible to find any free time these nights." He mentally breathed a sigh of relief. If she was holding any grudges, they were against his sire and not him.

He turned to Wentworth and flashed a brilliant smile. "Jazz, you old bastard! Good to see you again."

"Likewise, Kurt. How's the grand life back in the Old Country?" Kurt gripped the hand Jazz offered and pumped three times sharply before releasing it. "Old Gustav and Wilhelm still arguing?"

"Naturally. I don't think those two will ever see eye to eye about anything. Jazz, you are still the only man I know that can wear a bow tie and not look like an elderly schoolmaster. How do you do it?"

"It's not what you wear, old boy, it's how you wear it." He smiled charmingly and shot a quick wink to Natasha. "Or in the case of dear Natasha, how best to show off your natural attributes."

Natasha actually smiled at that one, and Kurt hastened to agree with Jazz in his assessment of her natural charms. Had the compliment come from anyone less cultured than Jazz, it would have sounded dirty instead of flattering. "Listen, we have a little time before the festivities begin. Perhaps we should take the scenic route and discuss how best to handle Anvil and his little friend, Crusher?"

When both agreed, Kurt ushered Natasha towards the limousine's door, careful to maintain just the proper distance and to stay half a step behind her the entire way. The humans with them, apparently bodyguards to Natasha and Jazz, climbed into a dark sedan and followed close behind the limo. By the time the three reached the office building where the primogen was planning to have their meeting, all had smiles of agreement on their faces. Throughout the entire trip, Jackie never said a word.

⇒€

The glass towers of the Waterford Building were impressive, especially up close. The heavy glass reflected light from every part of the city and sent it dancing across the night sky. The architectural design was but one of many by a young new star of the design world, Carlos Rodriguez, better known to the Kindred of Miami as Masika, the Toreador elder of the city. Unlike most of the buildings he had designed and built, this one was also his property. He'd been offered a king's ransom for the building on several occasions, but always refused the bids. More than just an office plaza, it was also a museum of modern art and part of the Elysium, neutral territory for the vampires that ruled in the area.

Masika was dressed fashionably, but with less formality than the Ventrue. Nonetheless, he was as proper as any of Kurt's own clan in how he handled his affairs and even brought a collection of his own blood dolls for everyone to enjoy. There were limitations to being Ventrue, the most annoying of which was the need to feed on the blood of only one particular type of person. Some could only feed on the wealthy, some could only feed on the blood of children. Kurt felt he could live with his limitation, so long as the world had attractive young women in ready supply. Kurt had always preferred dealing with the humans willing to offer their blood than to hunt down his own prey, so he appreciated the gesture.

The second basement below ground was furnished impeccably and had every possible modern convenience — plush office couches, heavy marble coffee tables and a state-of-the-art stereo system all surrounded by oak-paneled walls and resting on a set of priceless Persian rugs. The most powerful Kindred in the city gathered together in the office space and chatted amongst themselves casually. No retainers were present, and even the blood dolls would be asked to leave before the business of the night got started.

Kurt spent a good portion of the time before the meeting of the primogen talking with Gilbert Duane, once again having to remind himself that the man was supposed to be insane. Duane's pleasant African accent was almost musical, and Kurt found himself listening to every word the man said as if it were of great import. The faint accent reminded Kurt that Gilbert Duane was originally from Africa, but had been in the States since he'd been brought over in a slave ship. It was a mark of the Malkavian's insatiable curiosity that he'd allowed himself to be captured and hauled in an overcrowded ship to the Colonies that later became the U.S. He remembered the one time they'd discussed the matter: Duane had explained the methods the slavers used to transport their goods — literally stacking their bounty like cord-wood and hoping that a decent percentage survived the long journey — and had pointed out that feeding in such a situation was remarkably easy.

While both of them knew that Duane's political career was on the line, neither mentioned the matter even once. Duane was dressed in ratty blue jeans and a flannel shirt, tennis shoes that had seen their best days a few years back, and a scarf wrapped around his shaven scalp. He looked for all the world like a rap musician, and there was nothing about him to indicate that he had been manipulating Kindred and kine alike for the last forty years. In honor of the formal occasion, he'd purchased a new silk tie which he carefully placed around his neck. His dark brown eyes were expressive, and Kurt could tell he was not happy about the situation, despite the jovial attitude and boisterous jokes.

Almost two hours passed in pleasantries and carefully worded insults before the primogen of Miami prepared to get down to business. Despite the unexpected visitors, there was room enough for everyone. In addition to Kurt's own surprise appearance, there was an as yet unidentified Nosferatu sitting beside Chester DuBois. Both looked human, but their shadows were out of sync with their forms and water stains covered the couch where they sat. Simply put, no other clan wallowed in the sewers. Kurt had no doubt they were Nosferatu.

Masika sat by himself, perched at the edge of the full-length bar that covered one wall of the room. On the couch closest to the door, the two Nosferatu sat, both wearing false faces and dressed in formal clothing. Sylvester Simms, the elder of the Malkavians, sat on the next couch, apparently having a completely lucid conversation with his shadow. Beside him, a stunning woman with red hair and slightly vulpine features sat with her arms crossed, obviously impatient for the meeting to begin and be over. Basilia was the primogen of the small Gangrel contingent, but that did not make her much more civilized than the others of her ilk who loved nothing better than creeping through the woods. Anvil sat with another Kindred, a heavy-set man with a short shag of brown hair growing from the top of his head. He was massive and brutal-looking. There was no indication that he was anywhere near as intelligent or friendly as the slave who once ruled the city. So this was Crusher, the would be prince. The two wore matching cocky sneers to go with their ratty street clothes. Anvil tossed his long brown hair away from his forehead and pulled at one side of his mustache, obviously deep in thought despite the grin he affected for everyone present. Natasha, Jazz and Kurt sat close by, but just far enough away to make it clear that they were not chumming around with the riff-raff. Lastly, alone in the corner with his chin resting on the balled fist of his right hand, Lazarus of the Clan Tremere sat in a plush chair. He made no noise and stared intently at the two Nosferatu.

For the vast majority of the meeting, very little happened that interested Kurt, and he simply watched the elders of Miami go through the motions of maintaining friendly order in a hostile city. There was little or no love lost between any of the participants, but most at least acknowledged each other civilly and maintained the illusion of working together and being sociable. Anvil spent a great deal of that time pointing out the flaws of the present prince and making certain that everyone knew how he felt about the man.

Finally, after listening to three hours of what basically came down to dealing with the anarch and Sabbat threats and balancing the budget, Jack "Anvil" Calloway said what everyone in the room knew would eventually be stated. "I think it's time to seriously consider losing Gilbert Duane and replacing him with someone more capable of handling the city."

Gilbert Duane himself leaned against the wall nearest the main door to the room. He was silent, but the small smile on his face made it clear to Kurt that he did not expect Anvil's vote to go through. Despite the street clothes he wore, it was obvious enough to Kurt that he was a man used to being in a position of authority. When he spoke, his voice was deep and resonant. "Given that I am the one being questioned as to my ability to rule, I shall abstain from the vote at this time. I do, however, reserve the right to place my vote later."

Basilia was the next to respond, her voice filled with the threat of a growl. "Who would you have replace him, Anvil? And I hope you mean someone other than Crusher, because if that's the best you can offer, I vote against."

Crusher stood up and took a step her way before Anvil grabbed him by the arm and all but threw him back onto the couch. "Why is that, Basilia? Afraid he might do something to hurt your precious parks?"

"No," she snorted. "I'm afraid he'll start trying to think for himself instead of working as your number one supporter." Anvil glared, but knew better than to try something in a place of Elysium; violence in the places acknowledged by all Kindred as inviolate would certainly turn the vote against him. "He's bad enough now. I'd hate to see what he might try to pull if he actually got an idea." Next to her on the couch, Simms started cackling to himself and whispering urgently to his shadow.

Masika looked around the room, smiling politely and asked, "Does anyone else feel concern over whether or not Prince Gilbert can hold the city against the threats from other sources?" He paused while he waited for a response and finally shrugged. "I'll second Anvil's suggestion." He waited a moment and finally continued. "I think the rising crime rate, the violence against foreign tourists, and the increasing population of indigents can all be traced back to when Gilbert Duane seized control from his predecessor. His control over the police forces and his ability to accurately assess a situation properly is questionable at best."

"I'll agree with that." The voice came from behind almost every person in the room. Lazarus had spoken from deep in the shadows. The Tremere wizard stood up and walked slowly across the room, looking at Masika briefly and then moving his eyes over to Anvil and Crusher. "I believe we could do far worse than Crusher. He at least is strong-willed enough to make a decision without consulting a Ouija board — being dead does not mean being omniscient, a fact that still escapes the prince — or having to ask his reflection for feedback." He smiled then, and the Kindred in the room focused on him. "Meaning no offense to Gilbert Duane or his clan, he is perhaps too unstable to maintain the forces necessary to control the city. We have the Sabbat threats from Orlando to consider and from Cuba as well. We cannot possibly hope to hold this city against infiltrators with a madman on the proverbial throne."

Lazarus stepped over to where Simms was apparently listening to noises that no one else could hear and stared down at the Malkavian elder. "How can we even hope to hold back the influx of Setites and Samedi from Haiti if we do not have a capable leader for the troops? Are we expected to do everything ourselves, Sylvester?"

Sylvester Simms glanced up at the serpent-headed cane in Lazarus' hand and then looked at the Tremere himself. "I should hope not. I have better things to do with my spare time." Kurt cringed inwardly, dreading what was rapidly becoming a full-scale battle instead of the minor difficulty he had actually expected. Still, the matter wasn't half solved yet.

Before Lazarus could continue, Chester DuBois spoke for the first time since the meeting had begun. "I don't think Sylvester has been paying enough attention to fully understand what it is you're after, Lazarus." He turned to Sylvester and spoke clearly and slowly. "Sylvester, do you understand what Lazarus is asking you to agree with? He wants Crusher to become the prince, and he wants Gilbert to step down."

Sylvester Simms looked up at Lazarus with a wide, feral smile and boomed laughter across the room. "And you call me crazy? Please, if you want to remove Gilbert, at least replace him with a thinking animal. I'd sooner see Elmer Fudd in the White House."

"Do you have a better suggestion, you moron?" This last from Crusher, who cracked his knuckles audibly as he spoke.

"Yes. Elmer Fudd."

"This is serious, Simms," Anvil all but growled.

"So am I. Crusher is a nice young lad, but he hasn't the common sense of a farm-bred turkey." He gestured wildly, narrowly missing Basilia with his left hand. "The boy would stand out in the open sunlight if someone didn't remind him to come inside."

Basilia raised her voice before Anvil and Crusher could decide to start screaming. "That's two against and three for. Let's hear from the rest of the primogen.

Natasha Volfchek looked directly at Anvil and smiled icily. "I abstain."

Every single Kindred in the room turned to stare at Chester DuBois, who glanced at the Nosferatu beside him and shrugged. "I vote against the change."

"That means a tie." Anvil, Kurt noted, was very efficient at stating the obvious.

"Nonsense, Mr. Anvil." The voice was very deep and sounded heavy with phlegm. "I believe I shall vote on this as well." The heavy-set Kindred stood up. "I am Sheldon, Justicar of Clan Nosferatu, and I also vote against this change of leadership." He stared hard at the Brujah contingency, his bulbous eyes glowing with barely contained contempt. "I have heard rumors aplenty about the ways in which the Brujah of this city mistreat those of my clan. I do not see why any sensible Kindred would condone such behavior, nor do I see the mentality behind your clan's actions as a solid reason to add any potential assistance to your cause."

The cultured voice continued on as the squat, bloated mockery walked about the room. The fine velvet jacket and ruffled shirt he wore were almost made laughable by his grotesque features. The long, tusk-like incisors in his mouth, the folds and wrinkles of fatty flesh and the uneven wisps of white hair around the back of his skull all seemed inappropriate for the man whose mellow words reached Kurt's ears and presumably, the ears of the vampires that sat watching him intently. Kurt gave credit where it was due; despite the misshapen inward-turning right knee of the Lord of the Clog, the Nosferatu managed to pace with barely a limp and speak before his impromptu court with a quiet authority that demanded respect.

"Additionally, despite my preference to wait until I have all the facts before speaking of such matters, I will make it known to every member of the Camarilla in this room that I am pursuing a line of investigation into the hideous death of not one but two members of my clan who had made Miami their home. They were diablerized, their lives drained from them and their bodies left to burn in the sun's light. I refer to none other than Heronimus Bloat and the childe he created, one Peanut McGinty. Their only known crimes being that they were Nosferatu, I feel a deep and passionate need to vindicate their deaths. Had the two not been found within minutes of the crime's completion, we'd have never had any evidence at all. Their bodies were already well- decomposed when they were located.

"While I feel that the guilty parties are known to me — and there is more than one, I may assure you — this is neither the time nor the place to accuse all members of the group that committed the aforementioned atrocities." Sheldon carefully sat himself back on the couch next to Chester DuBois, who gazed at him with an expression of raw adoration. "Just the same, in consideration of the attempted manipulations by Mr. Anvil, I should point out that 'Crusher,' as he prefers to be called, is one of the primary suspects in this investigation."

Several cries of outrage, some genuine and many false, erupted about the room. Lazarus looked from the Justicar of Clan Nosferatu and the elder of Clan Brujah, pausing only once to stare intently at Crusher, who did his best not to be noticed. When the clamor had died down, he spoke softly but with authority that none in the room could ignore, "I hereby rescind my previous vote."

Masika stared harshly at Anvil, pausing briefly to glare at Crusher. Kurt decided that more than was immediately obvious was conveyed in his words. "I also wish to change my vote from a 'Yes' to a 'No.'"

Anvil looked ready to fly into a fit of rage, but held himself back with obvious effort. No one spoke for several seconds, and the tension in the room continued to mount. Finally, his voice heavy with threat, Anvil looked to the Justicar. "And do you have proof of this accusation?"

Sheldon chuckled, the bubbling sound emanating again from his lungs. "My dear boy, one has but to look with eyes that can see to notice the black stains in your associate's aura." Masika and Lazarus murmured their agreement. "This brings up the question of whether either of you are fit to occupy your seats as primogen of this fine city, Anvil." Sheldon's voice dropped several octaves as he spoke this last.

Anvil fairly leaped from his seat, trembling with barely restrained fury. "Who the hell do you think you are, you bloated sack of shit?!"

Sheldon was utterly unfazed by the outcry. "I believe I am the Justicar of Clan Nosferatu. I believe I am a man capable of ruining you. Do I make myself clear?"

Kurt stood up and walked away from the couch, casually placing himself between Anvil and the Lord of the Clog. The Brujah elder had taken three steps forward, his teeth bared and his hands balled into fists. Kurt stared hard at him for a dozen human heartbeats before he finally turned and stalked back over to his own seat. Kurt was relieved, as he wasn't quite certain if he could take the brute in a fair fight. Not that he'd intended to play fair. From the corner of his eye, he'd seen Basilia, Masika and Lazarus all preparing to intervene. He had no doubt at all that they'd have been on his side in the argument. Masika's voice rang with suppressed outrage, "Do I need to remind you that this is Elysium?"

Anvil glared in return.

Finally Sheldon spoke again, and this time there was a certain amount of satisfaction in his voice. "In light of the investigation, I have spoken with Don Cruez, Justicar of Clan Brujah. He is in agreement that all aspects of this investigation should be handled carefully and that, as a temporary measure, another member of the Brujah clan should be placed in the position of clan elder in the city." As he spoke, Sheldon stood and walked over to the main door of the large meeting room. "Ladies and gentleman, may I present Tura Vaughn of Clan Brujah, your new associate during these troubled times."

The woman who stood in the doorway was dressed outrageously in leathers that barely concealed her impressive figure. The smile she presented to Anvil was far from congenial.

➤❖◄

Once the formalities were finished, the various elders started breaking from the meeting to go their own ways. Outside the meeting hall, Sheldon spoke briefly with Kurt and the other Ventrue who had been present at the meeting. There was some talk of the current situation and then Kurt offered a round of hearty thanks. Sheldon waved away the gratitude and pointed out that they were now even for what had occurred three years earlier in Cleveland.

Anvil slipped close to the Archon as the conversations continued, hissing in his ear, "This was your doing, wasn't it, Westphal?" Kurt merely smiled in response and allowed Anvil to pull him a small distance from the others. "You want to watch yourself, Ventrue. You're making dangerous enemies pulling these little stunts of yours."

"You wouldn't be threatening me, would you, Anvil?"

"I don't need to make threats. I'm just letting you know. You're causing more trouble than you're worth." The greasy-looking man sneered, peeling his upper lip back to reveal heavy fangs and pale pink gums. "I'll be seeing you later."

Kurt remembered the muzzle-fire and blood from his last encounter with Anvil. If it hadn't been for Jackie showing up when she did and bringing reinforcements.... He let the thought go, but he remembered the lesson he'd learned that night. The ousted Brujah elder did not take well to losing, and he had no doubt there would be unpleasantness before the night was over. He thought briefly about his discussions the night before with Uriah Winter. If the man decided to betray him a second time, there was no guarantee that he would survive the night. Hired help was always a gamble, but twice the gamble when dealing with a cut-throat like Winter.

"I think you should leave now, before I'm forced to call Tura over and have her give you a spanking." He looked at the woman standing a few feet away, the play of her muscles as she shifted, the way what little she wore clung to her, accenting rather than hiding her statuesque body. "Not," he added, "that being disciplined by the likes of Tura would have to be a bad thing." He paused again, calculating how far he could push the Brujah before the conversation ended in conflict. "You lost this little round, Anvil. Take it like a man for a change." He turned away from the angry Kindred, heard his ineffectual sputtering sounds, and walked towards the group he'd been led away from.

Gilbert Duane was on his way out the door, but mouthed the words *I'll see you later* in Kurt's direction as he left.

Crusher and Anvil slipped away into the storm that finally erupted outside, just as Kurt knew they would. Later, after the Justicar had left the area and the other members of the primogen had vacated the premises, Kurt thanked Masika for his hospitality and escaped in the comfort of his limousine. By the time the sun rose in the sky, he intended to be well away from Miami. The thought was pleasing.

It came as no surprise when Anvil, Crusher and several other members of the Brujah decided to attempt an attack. They showed up on motorcycles, preferring the speed and efficiency of the powerful bikes to the security and comfort of armored cars. It would be impossible to fend them off without stopping the limousine or exposing himself to the firearms they waved like swords over their heads. The Malkavians were called insane, but the Brujah were all but suicidal in their maneuvers. Time and again, they'd completely surround the limo, slowing down until Jackie had to either risk bumping into them or literally running them down. She never slowed, fully prepared to crush one or more of them. Kurt watched as she calmly reached into the glove compartment and removed a decidedly illegal machine gun. She also threw three boxes of ammunition on the seat next to her, pausing once to steer the limo towards the right, where Anvil was trying to drive his Harley Davidson and fire a sawed-off shotgun simultaneously.

The Brujah swerved to avoid the collision, narrowly missing one of his clan-mates in the process. Both of them screamed obscenities that Kurt could barely hear through the bullet-proof glass. The slick roads were more of a hindrance to the cycles than they were to the limo, and even Anvil seemed to realize the potential problems that he and his group of thugs could get themselves into.

Jackie opened a box of ammo with the word "glasers" scrawled across its front and pulled out a fully loaded ammunition clip. She was nothing if not prepared for combat. She let go of the wheel for a brief moment as she locked the clip in place. "Betcha I can blow him off the seat without hitting the gas tank, Kurt." Her tone suggested she was thoroughly enjoying herself, and as if to prove the point, she gunned the engine and struck the back wheel of Crusher's hawg. Bike and driver wobbled dangerously and then fell in a sliding, sparking mess. As wreckage faded into the distance, Kurt saw Crusher standing up, wounded but not seriously.

"I never place bets that I won't win, dear."

"You spoil all my fun."

From one of the on-ramps, another group of motorcycles roared onto the interstate, bearing a group that Kurt had never seen before. All of them wore T-shirts with the legend "Slashers" printed across the fronts, and as one of the gang gunned the engine on her bike, Kurt could see that their matching jackets bore the same caption across the back. His guess was that they weren't there to help him. Whoever they were, they were with Anvil. The muffled cheers from the gang that already surrounded the car was all he needed to prove the point. Jackie's smile faded, and she reached into the glove compartment again. Kurt doubted anyone could have been more shocked than he was when she pulled a hand-grenade from the compartment. "Jackie, you cannot be serious."

"Hey, it's my job to protect you. Sometimes you manage to get some tough enemies."

"No reason to be defensive, dear. I trust your judgment. Still, one would think those hard to come by."

"Are you kidding? This is America! If you've got the cash, you can get the weapon."

"Stay away from the nuclear arms, won't you, dear?"

"Well, okay. There are a few weapons that are inaccessible..."

A loud series of thuds slammed into the side of the limousine, and Jackie cursed under her breath as she yanked the steering wheel hard to the right. The Slasher doing the firing dropped her weapon as she and her bike were lifted from the ground and tossed through the air. "I think they're serious about tearing you up, boss. Maybe you should get under the seat."

"Nonsense. Here comes the cavalry."

From the on-ramp they had just passed, a small battalion of cars ranging from rusty Cadillacs to battered Mustangs came thundering onto the road. The driver in each car was seated and wearing a seat belt. All the passengers were sitting on the edge of their windows, exposed to the wind and rain. The faces varied from clean-cut and serious to wild-maned and grinning, but every single person perched on the seven cars was aiming a firearm at the motorcycles that surrounded the limousine.

What could easily have become a massacre was brought to a complete standstill by the arrival of Uriah Winter, Sylvester Simms, Gilbert Duane and a dozen heavily armed people. Anvil was a fighter, but he wasn't, to the best of Kurt's knowledge, suicidal. He and his pack of rowdies fled into the night with no more damage done save to their collective pride. After the entire herd of cars had pulled over, Gilbert Duane offered his thanks for everything that Kurt had arranged, and Kurt in turn said that all of the thanks due belonged to Natasha Volfchek. The prince of the city smiled in response, a wistful look coming over his features. Kurt continued for several minutes about the potential threat that Anvil presented. He strongly suggested making certain that Tura Vaughn felt welcome in Miami.

Morning was only a few hours away when Kurt handed a fully loaded briefcase to Winter. The Caitiff smiled thinly and took the money. He didn't bother counting the bills, but Kurt knew he would before the sun was up. The amount paid was excessive, especially when Kurt considered how little the Caitiff had actually done, but he was certain Winter would think twice before setting him up for a fall in the future. Money, not fear, seemed the only route to securing the mercenary's loyalty.

There was one final meeting before the night could be called finished and that one took place at the hotel, even as Jackie was loading the limo with all of their supplies.

Jazz Wentworth talked in urgent whispers and handed a

heavy sheaf of papers over to the Archon. "This one's big, Kurt." Jazz sounded mildly worried, which was extremely rare in Kurt's experience. "Democritus would rather it be handled quickly and discreetly."

"What's so important about this one?" Kurt examined the photo of the young woman pinned to the dossier. He could not imagine why she would be overly important. She was attractive enough, true, but she was not recognizable to him, and that normally meant she stayed out of the heaviest levels of politics. "I know all the Archons and most of the hit men. Who is she?"

"If our sources are accurate, she is very important to Etrius."

The name almost made Kurt flinch. Etrius, one of the most powerful Kindred of Clan Tremere, the number one threat to the Ventrue's consolidated power in the Camarilla. "Is she his childe?" Kurt looked to Jazz and waited for an answer.

Jazz finally shrugged, "I don't know, Kurt. I don't look over the files I'm to give you. You should know that by now."

"Well, then," Kurt was rapidly growing annoyed by the lack of solid answers, "what the hell am I supposed to do when I meet her?"

"Democritus didn't say. He said you should call him when you get to Los Angeles."

"Well, this is wonderful. I'm following a woman who *might* be important to Etrius. And to make the matter even more unusual, I'm following her into the Anarch Free-States." He shook his head and grimaced in disgust. "Do you know what they do to members of the Camarilla they find spying in the Free-States, Jazz?"

"No, but I imagine it's unpleasant."

"Neither do I, but I suspect you are right."

Kurt silently folded the papers and slipped them into his overcoat. By the time he'd said his good-byes and slipped into the luxury vehicle, Jackie had finished securing his possessions.

"Where to this time, boss?"

Kurt sighed and slipped his shoes off. The dawn was coming soon, and he hated resting with anything heavier than socks on his feet. "We're off to Los Angeles. Driving this time, thank God. It seems there's a little trouble brewing for the Ventrue in the Anarch Free-States."

He reached into the pocket of his overcoat to retrieve his pipe and tobacco pouch. True, dawn was approaching, but sweetened leaves smelled wonderful, a reward to himself for finishing his assignment. He filled the pipe bowl, and Jackie passed him the limo's cigarette lighter, already glowing. He lit his pipe and returned the lighter, inhaling the sweet fumes with the satisfaction of a job well-done. You could hardly be Prussian and not smoke something.

He removed the folded papers from his coat and flipped a few pages through the pile before finding a second, clearer photograph. The pale blonde woman that stared back from the picture was lovely. He regretted that they would be enemies in the coming battle.

"So, you are important to Etrius, are you, Miss Ilse Decameron?" He stared at her face, memorizing every aspect revealed in the photo. The written files revealed more than he would have expected. She was also allegedly one of the Tremere's best undercover operatives, specializing in gathering information. "Well, we shall see who learns the most about whom. Why are you important to Etrius, Miss Decameron? More importantly, why are you important to the Ventrue?" The black and white image did not answer, nor did Kurt expect it to. He tended to speak aloud when thinking about his next case, a habit that he had yet to break himself of. "Time will tell. Time will tell me everything I need to know."

Friday, April 23, Hollywood — The Camera Eye

Night and Hollywood. The neon sparked and sizzled, granting the boulevard new life in the fading twilight, and Ilse Decameron stepped out of the shadows of the Egyptian Theater. With a directorial flourish, the floodlights came on one by one, banishing the shadows and illuminating the lotus columns, making the grime and chipped tiles vanish in the glory that was Hollywood. Only a bit of flash and dazzle, but that was all that was needed. It worked, and as far as Ilse was concerned, that was the test of true magic.

She placed the Iron Key back on the chain around her neck, a key that fit no lock in the mortal world as the charm required, and slipped it back inside her turtleneck to where it rested safely and comfortably between her breasts. Ilse paused to adjust the neck strap so that the camera outside the sweater did not press too hard, then reached into the bottom left pocket of her vest for her cigarettes. Wicked habit. She'd sworn she'd give it up the day she died. Well, *that* was a vow she'd broken for a good seventy years, almost to the day, but it wasn't as if it were the only broken promise on her conscience. She thought about swearing to give up the habit upon her Final Death, but then she'd caught glimpses of wraiths in her camera eye, and some of them were smoking yet. Better not to tempt fate, and everyone knew what the gods thought of oathbreakers anyway.

She saw the glow of the lighter through closed eyelids. The fire was less frightening when you played with it blind, and much more dangerous. The thrill of danger, but safe in her hands. That had always been part of the allure. In death as in life, the more things changed the more they stayed the same. She let the warm smoke curl lazily over her tongue.

It was somewhat less than what humans thought of the Kindred, come to think of it, and she took another drag, letting the smoke nestle inside her lungs and warm her dead flesh. It helped to take the edge off the Hunger, and while it was becoming no longer socially acceptable to smoke, drinking blood had never been socially acceptable.

People were already queued up for tickets to whatever the latest film was, and Ilse smiled as she saw their auras, as pretty and varied as the lights of the boulevard. She took another puff and stepped back, raising her camera. "Smile!" she called. A flash and the image was captured. It might prove useful, and it was always pleasant to practice her Art.

The ancients believed that the third eye had the power to see things beyond the ordinary, and with lens, lid and iris, what else could the camera be considered? The Path of Imagery, and the associated thaumaturgic rites she'd developed, made it so that the myths were true, or at least possible, and the art of magic and the art of photography merged, like the doubled image of a stereoscopic card. Spirit photography — the art of capturing that which lay beyond the pale, fleeting images that vanished so quickly that even the most sensitive could scarcely catch a glimpse before they were snatched way. Even the heightened senses of the Damned could hardly hope to match a camera's arcane arrangement of lenses and crystal, especially when it was infused with the power of vampiric Thaumaturgy and even more so when an artifact like the Monocle of Clarity was attached to the end.

The new Pentax was a joy to use, much better than the bulky apparatus she'd started with in the Silent Era, even before her fall into darkness, and it was good to return to the canyons and hills; she'd been away far too long. Hollywood magic on a Hollywood night for a Hollywood vampire. Nothing escaped Ilse's notice, not once she got to the dark room. Slivers of souls caught in the camera eye... and every soul had its price.

Ilse wandered out onto the boulevard, skirting streetwalkers and dodging punks, capturing the occasional image. She made her way down the Walk of Fame, wondering. When you walked among the stars above, were there pushers and pimps, tourists and runaways? Celestial bag-ladies? As a parallel for the heavens, the boulevard left something to be desired.

Someone had played "Loves me, Loves me not" with a copy of *Dianetics*, and the pages were scattered like breadcrumbs down the Walk. Ilse made her way along till she came to Larry Edmund's. The door was open to let in the night air, and the store was brightly lit and as clean as a fresh script. She dropped her cigarette with the dozen or so littering the ground outside, crushed it with a twist of her foot, and stepped inside.

The screenwriting store catered to all types, professionals and has beens, aspiring writers and wannabes, college students and housewives. And vampires, or at least tonight. In the far corner, where he said he'd be, was Smudge. He'd probably had a real name once, but all that was left was a sullen look, a leather jacket and a smear of blood at the right corner of his mouth. It was always there, like the stain on his soul, a black smudge over the red of hurt and anger. Ilse touched her pocket, making sure it still contained the photographs, then slipped down the aisle to where he sat on a footstool, paging through a book.

"Hello, Smudge."

He looked up from beneath his fringe of thinning blond

bangs, eyes wary, then carefully shut the book, holding his place with one thumb. Ilse took quick note of the title: *The Battle of BRAZIL.* "You got 'em?"

"Of course," Ilse smiled. "The question is, do you have what I want?"

"I checked out the Chinese girl, if that's what you mean."

"And the man?"

"Seen 'im. He's meetin' her again tonight." He paused and licked his lips, nervous, but not erasing his trademark smudge. "Can I have 'em?"

"Perhaps." She unbuttoned the pocket, but did not take the envelope out just yet. "Do I have your loyalty?"

"I got dreams too, you know." His voice was barely above a whisper. The look in his pale blue eyes was that of a child, a hurt and frightened child, but one so badly scarred that he just might strike back. "Nobody thinks much of me, but I got dreams too. I'm gonna be somebody, and ain't you or anyone else gonna stop me."

"Is that what you told Mickey Phoenix?" Ilse dropped her voice even lower, silent to all but the sharp ears of the dead. "Or Doug and Kirsten Berry? They're gone now. You're still here. Be thankful for that." She flipped open the envelope and fingered out the top two photographs. One showed a huge blond man, baring his fangs for all to see — along with a T-shirt that advertised *Fangs by Phoenix.* The second showed a couple with a crazed look in their eyes, the woman fat, the man cadaverously thin, both pale. There was an inset shot on the man's tattoo, possibly the worst Grateful Dead tribute in the history of the art for the singular reason that under the malformed red and blue lightning-bolt skull were the words: *Greatful Dead.*

Ilse fanned the pictures and handed them to Smudge. "As I said, they're dead, in soul as well as body. Truly and permanently so. You're still here."

"They were Sabbat," Smudge whispered. "They were gonna

bury me in the ground and leave me for the worms to eat. They said so."

"Tell it to the Justicar!" Ilse snapped. "I don't care. I don't care whether Mickey Phoenix was a fox-crazy Malkavian or a Ventrue with a twisted entrepreneurial sense. I don't care whether the Berrys were Toreadors into kitsch or Ravnos out to embarrass the clan. Do you understand? I don't care. Diablerie is forbidden among our kind, no matter who or what you are, no matter how vile or deserving the victim. It is forbidden by all but the Sabbat, and you know what value they put on life. You can hide here in the Free States for a time, but the Anarch Barons don't take any more kindly to diabolists than do the princes of the Camarilla. And until you decide you want to enjoy one last sunrise, Smudge, I own you. Body and soul."

Ilse pulled out the last picture and handed it to Smudge. It was a close-up of him, a good likeness in good lighting, over which were the pale reds and golds of his aura like ghost flames, tarnished by a large dark smudge. "The stain isn't on the camera eye. It's on you, Smudge. It's on your soul. And you and I both know what it means."

"I ain't nothin'," Smudge said, his voice small, pleading. "I ain't anyone at all. If I vanished tomorrow, no one would care. No one would know."

"That's exactly why I do care, Smudge. You're the perfect agent. And besides," — she took a moment to ruffle his hair — "remember what you said: you're going to be someone someday."

There was a faint smile across his face, a shy puppy's grin and a need to be needed and loved, and it stuck into Ilse's gut like a sickled knifeblade. She closed her eyes for a moment. This was crueler than hunting, crueler by far, and she didn't have the taste for it. But taste had nothing to do with it, only survival and orders. She had her orders, and it was time she carried them out for the good of the clan.

She opened her eyes and winced again, inwardly this time, for she saw the look in Smudge's eyes, and it spoke of love, love for any attention at all, no matter how cruel or inhumane. Smudge had been ignored, and no matter what vile or wicked thing she did now, she was paying attention to him, and for that Smudge was grateful.

Slowly and carefully then, so as not to frighten the young Caitiff, Ilse moved her hand to her vest's penholder and withdrew one of her finest magical implements: Aaron's feeding razor. The artifact had been crafted in the seventeenth century, but the silver was still preternaturally bright, and with a gentle thumb on the catch, the blade revealed itself, shining and blemish-free. She raised it to catch the light, then lowered it carefully and nicked herself once on the ring finger, the left one that led to the heart's blood. A drop of her vitæ seeped into the well of her nail, the end notched with the razor.

She licked the drop of blood from the razor's tip, then folded the magical implement and slipped it back into place. Hunched over so that none but Smudge could see, Ilse took out her compact and a square of vellum cut from the skin of a black lamb. The young vampire watched, fascinated.

Ilse used her nail as a quill, quickly sketching out the Sator Square, line by arcane line, each word five by five:

```
S A T O R
A R E P O
T E N E T
O P E R A
R O T A S
```

"For privacy," she answered the unspoken question. She sucked the drop of blood from the tip of her finger, allowing the nail to seal closed, then pried open the back of the compact and slid the square in behind the mirror. She squeezed it back together, then opened it properly, setting it on the top shelf of the corner bookcase, mirror exposed but charm hidden, as would be they to any who saw them.

Ilse glanced about to make certain that there was no one else in this corner of the shop, for the Mirror of Hathor would only hide them from those who had not seen its making. But there was no one down either aisle, so Ilse turned back to Smudge. "House Tremere requires the Kiss of Fealty. Where other times you would have to drink thrice of my blood on three separate nights before the ancient power of the Blood Bond took hold and made you my slave, both heart and mind, by this Kiss you pass three nights in one and take the Bond now, becoming my Thrall as I become your Regnant."

She took out her razor again and unfolded it with a sharp flick, then slashed her left wrist quickly, dark blood beading up along the line of the cut. The pain was as bright as the blade, and she clenched her fist at the burning white sensation. She held her wrist before him. "I cannot force this upon you, Smudge, for it is a grave thing, and by charm and honor, it must be of your own free will. Do you accept?"

In answer, Smudge grabbed her wrist, kissing it, sucking it, his tongue probing the edges of the wound like a lover. A thrill ran through her as he continued to suck, tongue thrusting, lips caressing the delicate sides of the wound, fangs tearing it wider. She felt the blood drain out of her and the spell take hold.

She reached down and, with a swipe of the razor, scored Smudge once across the forehead. He hissed in pain against her wrist and whimpered softly, but did not protest. He wanted this too much to cry out. Dark blood stained his brow, and she placed her hand over it, the wet warmth spreading across her palm and the handle of the blade. "Willingly given, willingly taken, with this blood I bind you to myself, and with this mark I mark you as vassal of Clan Tremere. I am your liege, Smudge, and my will is yours."

The adoration in his pale blue eyes spoke of more than mere Blood Bond or even the charmed power of the Kiss of Fealty, and Ilse felt the knife twist in her gut again as two blood red tears trickled from his eyes like some miraculous portrait of one of the Holy Innocents. He was hers to command but for the asking.

She was weak from loss of blood, pale and shaking. "Kiss it better," Ilse said. With great love and sensual passion, Smudge licked the wound, more to lick away the blood than for true healing. The razor wounds would take longer to heal than a bite. She willed the cut to partially seal, like a paper cut, to prevent further blood loss. Ilse felt another shiver run down her as he continued to lick the delicate skin of her wrist free from blood.

With a fluid motion she raised her hand, licking Smudge's blood from the razor and her palm in turn. The sweet taste slid down her tongue with a savor like fine cognac with a drop of wormwood underneath, Smudge's sin and the blood and shadowed souls of the Sabbat he'd murdered a bitter spice that matched the mad auras of his victims from the pictures she'd taken. Yet theirs was the only Kindred blood Ilse tasted, aside from her own, the Caitiff's vitæ free of Bond or allegiance to any others.

She folded the razor away then, sliding the implement back into place on her jacket, and took the miserable Kindred's chin between her thumb and forefinger, tilting his head up to face her. She paused a moment, watching the bloody tears trickle down his cheeks, then leaned down, kissing the mark on Smudge's forehead. When it continued to seep, she gently reminded him to at least close it for now. He nodded, and in a few minutes, a threadlike red line was all that remained. "There," she said, smoothing away the saliva from his skin with a brush of her fingers, "all better now. Now wipe away your tears, Smudge, and listen to me."

Obediently, the young vampire brushed away his bloody tears with the back of his hand leaving two smudges across his cheeks, one darker than the other. The knife in Ilse's gut went in a little deeper as she realized that his trademark smudge came not from his victims but from his own tears.

Tears of pain and grief, lust and longing. She hated herself now more than ever, but what was done could not be undone, though she'd still do what little she could to salve her conscience.

"You, Smudge, are now my vassal and will serve me, and through me, Clan Tremere. You are a wretched Caitiff no longer, for though you are not of our blood, our blood flows through you, and you are adopted into our House. Let no one speak to you of your base origins, for though they are lowly, you serve the greatest of the vampire clans, we who were made what we are not through God's curse but through our own desire and will. We will teach you the skills you need to survive." Ilse paused, letting her words sink in. "Even magic, if you prove yourself worthy."

It was the standard carrot-and-stick speech as kindly put as she could make it, but its effect on Smudge was profound, and blood poured freely down his cheeks. Ilse searched her pockets for a tissue, finally letting him mop his face with her lens cloth.

"Thank you," Smudge said, and Ilse knew it was for more than the makeshift handkerchief.

"Don't thank me," she said. "Don't ever thank me, Smudge." She gathered up *The Battle of BRAZIL* from the floor where it had slipped from his fingers and set it back on the shelf, moving another book to hide the three bloody tears staining the cover.

She sat down then, leaning back against the bookcase, weak from the magic and the loss of blood. Smudge took her hand with great tenderness, and Ilse looked away, not wanting to see the look in his eyes. "Well, Smudge," she said, "now that we're on more intimate terms, tell me a couple things. First off, where is the man I mentioned going to be meeting Jing Wei? And second, where in this town does a girl go now for a quick bite?"

>€

Hunger sated, Ilse had the cab drop her off at Gladstone's in Malibu, the northernmost tip of Baron Fortier's demesne and the southernmost claw of Lupine territory. Politics and boundaries had changed, especially since the Anarch Revolt, but the terrain was still familiar from her mortal life, even though the buildings had changed.

Gladstone's sat at the wilder end of Sunset Boulevard, lording over its section of the Pacific Coast Highway in a manner truly Californian. Ilse wandered into the patio area, rife with drunken college students, actors, waitresses in pert skirts and waiters who handed patrons leftovers wrapped up in colored foil elaborately twisted to form swans, crabs and pink and silver parrots. Ilse wished that she still ate, if only to walk home with one of the pretty things, then instead just snapped a picture.

It was a great pity Malibu was contested territory. Gladstone's was made for the Masquerade. Here a seagull savaged a forgotten shrimp salad, there a beer could be conveniently spilled over the railing to the beach and rocks below. Perfect — Flash and glitter and more food than any person could be expected to eat. The mood was high, the pulses were bright, and if the wolves were guarding a jewel like this, well, something had to be said in their favor.

It would be an hour till Jing Wei would show, or at least so Smudge had said. As for why Jing Wei would have picked such a perilous point for a rendezvous, Ilse couldn't say, unless her blood-sister from Hong Kong had decided that privacy was at a premium, and the jewel of Lupine territory was the last place likely to be frequented by a nosy Nosferatu or Malkavian. Even if the wolves were here tonight, they could hardly be expected to try something around so many of the common rabble whom they doted on, especially on a crowded Friday night. In truth, if ever there were a place made for a peace conference, Gladstone's was it, and that fact made it de facto Elysium — no hunting permitted — and the perfect spot to set a mortal at ease who was nonetheless aware of the Kindred and their proclivities. On second thought, Jing Wei's choice was very calculated and canny. The girl might be much younger than Ilse, but she bore watching. Which was why Ilse was here tonight. Partially, anyway.

The man who awaited Jing Wei wasn't in the outer portion, so Ilse moved towards the indoor section of the restaurant, only to have her path blocked by a tall man in a pink polo shirt, who seemed to suffer from the unfortunate delusion that Malibu was Cape Cod, judging at least from the khaki shorts and Topsiders.

"Excuse me, madam," he said, and Ilse had to revise her opinions. The man's English had a certain Euro-American flair to it with a faint, underlying German or Austrian accent, Ilse couldn't tell which, but well-educated and well-traveled, and Kindred as well, judging by the faded aura and the heart Ilse could not hear beating within his breast.

"Yes?" Ilse smiled up at him, one hand on her camera.

He smiled back at her, white teeth even, the perfect Nazi recruiting poster except for the dark brush-cut hair. "You took my picture over there. I must object to that."

Ilse didn't recall doing anything of the sort, unless he'd managed to get into the background of her picture of the leftovers, in which case he'd be blurry and out of focus and Ilse would have trouble distinguishing him from the seagulls, so she couldn't see what the bother was. "I'm sorry, sir. I won't do it again."

"I'm sorry as well, but I must ask for your film. I dislike being photographed."

Ilse blinked. Not only Kindred, but paranoid. "My apologies. If you'll just give me your name and address, I'll be sure to send you your picture and the frame of the negative."

"You do not understand," the man said. "What I object to is not so much the photograph, but that it is held by a woman of your talents."

Ilse smiled. Why, yes, Gladstone's was perfect for the Masquerade, public enough to keep him from doing anything overt and chaotic enough to cover her own actions. "I'm sorry, sir, I don't quite follow you. What possible objection could you have to your portrait being shown by Clan Toreador?"

His smile grew sharklike. "I have no objections to Clan Toreador, Fraulein. However, a photograph in the possession of Clan Tremere makes me nervous. I must insist." He reached for her camera.

This bozo really was paranoid, because even if she were so inclined, sticking pins in a blurry group shot was about as difficult as throwing darts in a high wind and just about as dangerous. Like as not, she'd end up voodooing the leftovers in someone's refrigerator.

But he was still reaching for her camera. "I'm sorry," Ilse said. "I must refuse. Smile!" She raised the camera and hit the button, blinking to hide her eyes from the glare.

Her Germanic Kin had no such luck. Flashed at point blank without expecting it, he responded exactly how any Kindred would — falling victim to sudden Rötshreck, the Red Terror. He screamed at the light and stumbled backwards, fangs bared, and knocked over a waiter and his tray, going down in a tumble of salads and seafood.

Then he glared at her, and Ilse clutched her camera to her chest, feeling her dead heart turn to ice. Raw fear crystallized in her veins at the sight of his blazing eyes and gnashing fangs, paralyzing her with a horrid fascination, With an act of will, she wrenched her head away from his dread gaze, looking at the ground beside him where she saw...bread. An ordinary loaf of bread. It was instinct, the smallest of the Movements of the Mind, but a glance sent it flying to cover the European's terrible face and horrifying shrieks.

He screamed and thrashed even harder then, steaming chowder pouring out around the sides of what Ilse suddenly realized was not a loaf of bread, but a bread-bowl. With it his face covered, he was suddenly less terrifying, and Ilse felt the ice in her veins begin to melt — then freeze again with a new stab of dread at the thought of a mortal having witnessed what she had, the power of a vampire's blood rage and growing fury. Somehow, she had to preserve the Masquerade, act as if nothing were happening beyond the ordinary, nothing unusual at all. Ilse moved forward, raising her camera, and took a picture for her scrapbook, but she wasn't the only one. A fat woman picked up the idea and jostled her as she raised her own camera into position. Soon a flock of camera-wielders gathered like gulls around a forgotten salad.

Ilse backed away from the vulgarity of Hollywood vultures. Tourists could be such morbid creatures, and there was laughter from those who she guessed had only seen such scenes in movies and hadn't yet realized that a man might be seriously injured by such an accident. If, in fact, he were still mortal, but that was beside the point. She hoped the German would be able to conquer the Beast before he got the chowder off his face, and she wondered briefly what clan he might be to display such fierce power. Toreador? Brujah? Ventrue? Anything was possible, even Setite, for she'd heard that the Sand Snakes had made a nest in the canyons of Southern California, and she knew they could display the same overwhelming Presence that the better clans did. And their terror of the light was legendary.

Ilse hadn't time to speculate and made her way into the restaurant, hoping she could find the man she sought before the Kindred outside could recover and follow.

The asphalt floor was strewn with rice hulls and peanut shells, the wood dark and dimly lit, beamed and timbered like a medieval inn. A crowd milled about before the bar, chatting and laughing over the raucous music.

And there he was.

"Paul," Ilse breathed.

It had to be him. He wore a stranger's face, but the eyes were the same. Paul's odd, unmistakable, magical eyes. The right was as blue as the ocean water she remembered from her living days, the left as green as leaves in springtime, both flecked with sparks of gold and magic. A magician's eyes, the things that had drawn her to Paul in the first place and the feature that had endeared him the most — those beautiful, mismatched eyes that could change expression in a moment, laugh and sparkle at a chance remark or blaze with anger as fearsome as a vampire's. In her long death and short life, she'd only seen eyes like that once, and now here they were again, in a stranger's face.

Right now, the look in those eyes was faintly disconcerted, troubled by something, but the man who wore them scanned each person as they came in. He locked eyes with her for a moment, a brief flash of interest in those so familiar eyes, but then he looked away, showing no sign of recognition.

It was the second time that night a mere look had wounded her, but this knife was in her heart. It was Paul, it had to be, alive and well as he'd always been. Paul, who as far as she knew, had died but once.

Ilse paused, her hand coming halfway up to her mouth as she took in the stranger who seemed so familiar. Paul's odd eyes were deep-set beneath brows so fine as to be invisible, separated by a nose that came straight down from the man's forehead like the guard of a medieval helm, lending character to a long, blandly handsome face framed by fine, moon-pale hair, straight and neatly combed where Paul's dirty blond locks had never gone the same way twice. Where Paul had been small and almost endearingly scruffy, this man was tall and well-dressed, a London Fog overcoat folded over one arm of a fine quality charcoal gray suit set off by a silk tie subtly brocaded in blues and golds. The colors matched those of his aura, softly patterned gold and blue, the blue a brilliant azure of ingenuity and cleverness, the gold a holy glow of kindness and honor. Not Paul's aura, not exactly the same, but similar in color and weave and texture, as if they were two swatches cut from the same tapestry, two souls fashioned from the same cloth. And as with Paul's, the man's aura was mage-bright, as vivid in its life and intensity as a vampire's was pale and faded.

It was a mage she'd been sent to find, but Ilse had never thought...

She looked back to the man's eyes, Paul's eyes, and fell back to when she'd seen them last, over sixty years before... the day Paul had died, first, last, and final death. 1929, the beach and the pier. "I love you, Ilse. I always will," he murmured. "No, don't." He grabbed her hand, staying her from cutting her wrist and giving him drops of life-giving vitæ. "Let me go. I'll be back, I promise."

Then the last of his precious blood ran out of him. The light in his eyes became twice as bright, flaring for a brief moment like the last burst of a candle flame hovers over the wick in a final mote of brilliance before vanishing into soot. And then the light was gone, leaving his beautiful, mismatched eyes as clear and lifeless as a pair of crystal pebbles. "Paul..."

Her vision blurred, and she suddenly swam back to the present, eye contact breaking as the man before her shook his head and smiled. "I'm sorry, I believe you have me mistaken for someone else." The voice was British, cultured, friendly, the voice lighter than Paul's, more melodious, but still holding the basic underlying tone. Yet there was no sign of recognition, not in voice or smile or in either mismatched eye.

"You—," Ilse stammered, coming closer, searching his face. "I'm sorry. Your eyes — I knew someone who had eyes like yours."

He grinned. "Well, then, they have my condolences. I wouldn't wish the David Bowie look on anyone."

Just the same sort of thing Paul used to say, the same humor. "He's dead now."

The grin turned into a grimace, and the mismatched eyes became sympathetic. "Well, he still has my condolences, for what it's worth." There was an uncomfortable silence, then the man set down his glass of sapphire gin and put out his hand. "I'm Carl, Carl Magnuson."

Ilse shook her head to clear it and remembered her manners. "Ilse," she stammered, accepting the handshake, "Ilse Decameron." She stopped then as the mismatched eyes broke away from hers sharply, and she followed the look back over her shoulder.

The German vampire stood in the doorway of the restaurant, seafood chowder covering his face but for his snarl and his glaring eyes. "My goodness," said Carl's voice behind her. "I've heard of chowderheads, but this is ridiculous."

Ilse turned back around, and locked eyes with...Carl. Carl Magnuson. "Please," she said quickly, "we're in danger. You must trust me. I'm Jing Wei's blood-sister, and we must leave."

Carl continued to gape at the chowderheaded vampire. "You've got that bloody well right. Please, lead on." With one hand he grabbed his drink and with the other absently flipped a bill onto the bar.

The other vampire took a step forward, and Carl touched his spare hand to the signet ring on his hand with the glass, the blue liquid tossing like the waves of the ocean. "*Ignis magnificus, veni y illuminatum occulos mios,*" he murmured

In shock at the appearance of the Undead Chowderhead of Party Beach, one man dropped his drink at the same moment an ember fell from a woman's cigarette. There came a shattering sound from the floor, and a moment later a ball of sapphire flame roiled up, mixed with the scent of one-fifty-one rum.

Ilse turned her head in time, avoiding the Rötshreck the German was no doubt suffering again, but then she had been warned by the mortal mage's words: *Magnificent fire, come and illuminate my eyes.*

She grabbed him by the sleeve and pulled him into the depths of the restaurant, mazelike in its complex of pillars and booths. "Have you been here before?"

"Bloody unlikely. First time in L.A."

"Good. I've never been here either. With luck, that will be enough."

Carl didn't question the remark. With her free hand, Ilse reached into her turtleneck and pulled forth the Iron Key, pressing her thumb into the ornamented head until blood ran down the shaft.

Round one pillar, then another, Ilse led the mage, searching for a forgotten, shadowy corner. The route was different each time, and the path always had to be come upon by lost ways. "Dark. We need dark."

"Allow me," said Carl, followed by, "Fiat Noctem."

Let there be night, the charm spoke, and its magic took hold. The lights winked out on the cigarette machine, plunging the far end of the hallway into darkness.

"I have a way to get us out, but it might not take you. Can you manage on your own?" she asked.

"Trust me, I'll find something," she heard him mutter in reply.

Ilse took the lead, thrusting the Key into shadow and feeling its bloody teeth take hold in the nonexistent lock. "House of Secrets, House of Shadow, House of Fear, open your door to me. Open the doorway to the forgotten, and allow those of your blood to enter."

The lock clicked open, and Ilse stepped through the door into mystery, pulling Carl after her.

And he passed. He had passed the test.

Only a warlock of the blood of House Tremere could pass by that ritual through the doorway of their ancestral chantry. And here he was, a mortal mage of House Tremere, a living man of the bloodline that had sold itself, its magic and its heirs to the darkness in exchange for power and the immortality of the Damned. She had found that pearl beyond price — a man who was at once a mortal of the blood of the House and a mage psychically aware of the possibilities of the universe. One who was as they were before Tremere's circle had drunk from the Unholy Grail of innocent blood and taken for themselves the Mark of Caine.

Ilse felt the blade twist in her cold heart, for she had led him into the lair of the Damned, and she was certain that Carl Magnuson, whatever his name now, was in truth a man she thought she had lost and whom she had never ceased to love.

➤⬧

The unlit chandeliers sparkled darkly, late nineteenth century elegance, and the parquet floors were inlaid with elaborate *voudoun vever* patterns, ebony in maple. Cold blue flames cast long shadows from the fireplace, mixing across the patterned floors with the moonlight from the night garden. Ivory angel's trumpet and blood-red bougainvillea twined their way round the glasswork of the open French doors, moonlight seeping through the vines and angled panes.

Carl walked behind her, the parquetry creaking with each step, breaking the silence of the blue flames and pale moonlight. "What place is this?"

Ilse looked about. "I believe we're in one of Mammy Pleasant's parlors. That or Lady Sarah's. They work together a good deal now and have refurbished most of the newer wings. And the style's different from what Houdini would do."

"Well, yes, the room isn't filled with water, for one, but that's beside the point. Where are we?" Carl gave her a sharp look, one that demanded an answer.

"The House of Mystery," Ilse said. "The Tremere ancestral chantry. It exists neither here nor there, but in the places between, the forgotten corners and the lost ways. There are permanent doorways in a few spots in the mortal world, but most exist only for a second, in the places of darkness and shadow."

"A pretty speech," Carl said. "Did you rehearse it?"

Ilse would have blushed if it still came naturally, but only felt the knife twist in her heart again. "Well, yes. Initiates expect it, and it's nicer to have something prepared, since they always ask questions anyway."

"I'm not planning on becoming an initiate. I've had my fill of that rot already," the mage said, taking a step in and examining the Yoruba spirit figures Mammy had left out on the mantel. "I made that much clear to Jing Wei."

Ilse paced around behind him. He reminded her so much of Paul — the way he moved, the tilt of his head, the timbre of his voice. And, of course, his eyes. "I...hope you don't mind me bringing you here."

"So long as it isn't like the Hotel California or the Home by the Sea, I don't really much care." He reached out and touched his finger to the surface of the mirror behind the bone carvings, with an expression of wonder so like Paul's that Ilse felt her dead heart flutter once, like a moth trapped inside a clenched palm. She clutched her hands to her breast, catching her breath as she had only once since she'd died, when Paul had died, over sixty years before.

"Fascinating...I knew the Tremere had preserved much of their magic when they left mortality, but I didn't know they'd managed to keep hold of one of the Shade Realms as well." He paused and grinned at her via his reflection. Ilse put down her hands and attempted to act as if nothing were wrong. "Sorry, Magick Newspeak there. I mean the Shadowlands, Betwixt and Between, the Out Of, the Dreamworlds, Looking Glass Country, Dimension X, all the rest of that rubbish. Which is it that you call them?"

"I — I'm sorry. I only know of one, this one, the House of Mystery."

"I'm sure it goes by other names." He turned, leaning back against the mantel. "I've already heard you mention a couple."

Ilse nodded. "The House in the Shadows, the House of Secrets, das *Schrёckenschlöss*, Rambledown, the Dark Manse, the Midnight Palace, the Castle of Ten Thousand Rooms, the Labyrinthine Hall. But we don't tend to advertise. It doesn't like that much."

He smiled, eyebrows bouncing once. "Has a personality, does it? Don't worry, most of them do." He wandered off towards the night garden, pausing at the threshold and looking out into the moonlight. "The better ones, at least. I fancy you didn't so much build this place as find it?"

Ilse came over next to him and placed a hand on the branch of the angel's trumpet, the gray bark cool beneath her hand. "Yes. It's far older than House Tremere, at least to judge by some of the rooms. Lady Sarah thinks she's found part of the Palace of Cnossus."

"The original Labyrinth, eh? Any minotaurs?"

"Not so far as I've seen," Ilse touched one of the tree's delicate white bells, "but there are a lot of rooms, and no one has ever explored them all, not even Lady Sarah."

She paused, releasing the blossom and glancing up at Carl, his hair twice as pale in the moonlight. "It's easy to get lost in the passageways. Some Tremere…"

His odd eyes twinkled. "Have never been heard from again?"

Ilse nodded.

Carl grimaced. "Let me guess — They were the ones who were always sticking their noses where they weren't wanted, right? Poking and nosing about and breaking things?"

Ilse nodded again. "How did you know?"

Carl shrugged. "Stands to reason. Can't have a House of Secrets without allowing it a little bit of privacy, and anyway, I've heard stories about this place. If a door's open, feel free to go in, but if it's locked, it's locked for good reason, and you'd do better not trying to force your way in, right?"

"Just that. How…"

"Please, you allow the House its secrets, leave me a couple. Us mages need them." He grinned. "All I'll say is that I always thought Bluebeard's wife was a prize idiot." He cocked his head, still grinning, poised on the threshold of the night garden. "But anything else you think I should know?"

Ilse looked out towards the garden and the dark hedgerows. "It's always midnight here."

"Cinderella time. Hollowers must just love it, eh wot, love?" He smiled and started down the tiled steps, and Ilse had to catch herself on the rough branch of the angels' trumpet. Love. It was just an expression to him, just another word to an Englishman, nothing more, no significance beyond a bit of comfortable informality. But from a man with Paul's eyes…

Her fingers slipped, and she stumbled down the steps.

"Steady, love," the mage said, catching her. "Steps are slick, and there's no end of poky, spiky things 'round here to stick yourself on. And that would be a nasty way for one of you Tremere girls to tie it off, skewered on a garden gnome." He laughed, but without malice, and his voice had fallen into a more lilting pattern, some regional accent Ilse didn't quite recognize, but she could tell that it meant that he was becoming more comfortable with her. Grateful for small favors, Ilse took his arm and allowed him to escort her down the garden path.

It was truly lovely midnight, full moon overhead casting lacy shadows through the branches of willow and cypress and their trailing veils of Spanish moss, moonwort and asters in the open patches, fluttering with white moths and pale butterflies, all glowing in the moonlight. From the trees to the right came the call of the nightjar, deep and throaty, while from the left came the lovely trilling song of the nightingale, point and counterpoint, a duet of opposites.

They turned a corner of the path, and the human mage laughed. "Eh, now I like that. Someone's got a sense of humor, they do." Carl pointed to the knoll in the center of the garden where two low pillars stood, one with a Victorian gazing globe, the other with one of Lady Sarah's sundials. They came over next to it, and Carl traced the legend with a finger and laughed again — I KEEP ONLY SUNNY HOURS.

He turned to face her, and Ilse had to let go of his arm. She stumbled a step back, but recovered nicely, attempting to disguise it as coyness, making her way round the gazing globe and placing her fingertips on either side. The glass was cold as night, as chill as her own heart. She looked across at him, standing there, one hand on the sundial, the bronze glinting feebly in the pale light. Sun and moon, man and woman, sundial and gazing globe, living and dead, the two halves of the whole. It must have struck him as well, for he asked, "Always midnight then? Never noon?"

"Never," Ilse said. "Thankfully for us, but the moon and seasons still go through their changes, or half of them, anyway — summer to winter, full moon to dark. The waning cycle."

"So this is where it got to..." Carl mused, not explaining himself.

Ilse glanced down and saw her own shocked expression reflected in the silvered glass, green eyes wide beneath blonde hair, white skin even paler than normal.

"Sorry, couldn't resist," Carl said, and Ilse looked up to see him contemplating one of the white butterflies which had come to rest on his finger, its pale wings as spent and tattered as a Froud faery's. It was dying, as was everything in the garden, the flowers full blown and fading, the nightjar and nightingale near their last days despite the dishes of her own blood Mammy fed them. "There's supposed to be a land of perpetual springtime somewhere, where the sun never sets and no flower ever fades. But then I suppose you wouldn't have much use for a place like that."

"Have you been there?"

"No, but I talked to a werewolf once who said he had. Lying bastard, but it was an interesting enough tale — not that I'd ever be able to see the truth of it, mind. He said the

Summer Country would only admit those of the blood, and I didn't have it, so I'd have to take his word for both." He cocked his head, smiling. "So is this like that?"

Ilse bit her lip. Quick, so very quick. Just like Paul. "Yes," she said and nodded slowly. "Only those of the blood of House Tremere can enter the Midnight Palace." She paused. "At least I think so. That's the way the Rite of the Iron Key works, and it's the only way I know."

Carl laughed. "Bloodlines. Always seemed a sloppy place to me to keep keys. Wait a couple generations, and any bastard can get one."

"So you knew you were of House Tremere?"

"Knew it? Listen, love, that's why they kicked me out of the Order. Nice neat little Hermetic types didn't like the thought of staining their lily-whites with vampire blood, even if it came by way of living folk ten times removed. So they tossed me out on my ear, just because they didn't like who I had for kith and kin, and I think, eh wot, might as well look up my old relatives, they were the ones who got me into this fix in the first place. So here I am, one way or t'other. Lad from Lancashire goes to London, then ends up with vampires in another world by way of L.A. Makes as much sense as anything."

He looked about the night garden, only the tallest spires and widows walks of Rambledown visible beyond the cypresses and their hanging moss. "So, when do I get to meet the family?"

Ilse was taken a bit aback. "Um, whenever you want, I suppose. We'll have to find them. Master Harry would be best. He's my sire."

"You mean he's your da, your king, or is there some other business to it? Because I'll be frank, the only time I hear that word often is when I'm around the Royal Kennel Club or the West-End Whippet Fanciers, and I don't think that's what you mean."

Ilse nodded. "I mean he's the Kindred — vampire, if you will — who made me what I am, giving me the gift of the Embrace. He's also my master and has taught me most of what I know of the Arts."

"Well, the second sounds familiar enough, and the first I can guess, since you Tremere seem as fussy about talking about how you get more of your kind as living people are of talking about how they get more of theirs, even if it seems a fairly simple and straightforward business. I think I prefer to remain in the dark as to the exact particulars, because I'm still rather fond of the light." He set the dying butterfly gently onto the bronze tip of the sundial.

"But I'm also rather interested in meeting the rest of my relatives, so lead on, good lady, if you please." His speech had turned courtly and amused, self-consciously formal, a spark dancing in each eye just like with Paul when he was enjoying himself. Ilse took Carl by the hand he extended and led him down the far path, under the trees and over the brook, careful of the rotted planks in the footbridge, to the small oaken door beneath the yew hedge.

This door opened onto one of Lady Sarah's staircases, the small switchbacks with the many steps that seemed to lead nowhere, but were actually one of the fastest ways of navigating the Mystery House.

Carl took the steps three at a time. "There a charm to how you use these?"

"I think so," Ilse said. "Unfortunately, it's Lady Sarah's, and she's very private about its workings, so it's between the Manse and her. The main trick is to catch it in a good mood."

Carl hopped down the steps, swinging around the polished wooden orbs atop each newel post as he came to it. "Be tempted to play Mary Poppins except there's a few too many of these in the way."

"You seem to be taking well to it."

"Shouldn't I? After all, you said it was the old family

house." Carl looked back and smiled, so much like Paul that it hurt. "Anyway, you haven't been to Doissetep. They've got madmen running around the halls with broadswords and bunny slippers, and I don't exaggerate. And when those broadsword-wielding, bunny-slippered madmen are also the archmages who run the show, well, you can see where I might find this refreshing."

Carl rounded another newel post, but the orb twisted in his hand this time, and he lost his balance, catching himself on the railing before he could fall down the stairwell. With a click, a panel opened in the opposite wall, leading into the Red Hall.

It was one of the older sections of the House, the grand banquet room of a seventeenth century Viennese hunting *schlöss*, with a long table down the center of the room. Lynx, pheasants and other smaller trophies were set at intervals along its length with the heads of deer, elk, wild boar and the other larger game mounted on the walls to either side. The Hall's name came from the blood-spattered battle standards hanging in the vaulted ceiling and the red crystal oil lanterns that were placed about the room, suffusing the chamber with a ruby glow.

Carl stepped in, Ilse following his lead, and she heard the almost noiseless click of the panel sliding to behind them. The mage didn't seem to notice, or if he did, didn't care.

At the far end of the table, facing the rampant remains of some fierce black wildcat, sat two figures, an elaborate porcelain tea service set out before them, tinged pale rose by the light.

"How lovely, Ilse, dear," said Lady Sarah. "You're just in time for tea."

"Yes, yes, child," said Mammy Pleasant. "And bring your gentleman friend in too. We want to see him for ourselves. The House has been tellin' us all about 'im, but it's one thing to listen to the walls creak and another to see somethin' with your own eyes."

Carl looked at her, and Ilse realized that the introductions were hers. "Mammy, Lady Sarah, let me introduce Pau — Carl. Carl Magnuson. Of...?"

"Of, until lately, the Order of Hermes, but no longer, I'm afraid. So I suppose that just makes me of House Tremere."

Mammy Pleasant laughed, high and light, echoing and carrying to them down the length of the banquet hall. "Ooh, girl, you've got yourse'f a charmer there, that's for sure! A real charmer, an' a proper English hoodoo man, an' they don't come cheap. No, they don't! Jing Wei's gonna throw a hissy fit when she finds you've gone and grabbed her play-pretty." She slapped her knee and laughed. "Now you bring him over here so we can get a better look at 'im."

Lady Sarah laughed as well, but respectfully and properly. They were like two sisters, two old women wrapped in shawls and lace and fine muslin, white in black and black in white, jiggling and giggling together like a pair of magnetic dogs on a magic mirror.

They made their way down the hall, Carl glancing up at the heads of the deer and boar who seemed to watch them with glittering red eyes. "Carl," Ilse said, drawing his attention back down to the table once they reached its end, "may I introduce Lady Sarah Winchester, chief architect of Rambledown." The tiny old woman nodded, hunched into her chair with her teacup like an apple doll in Victorian widow's weeds, "and her companion, Mary Ellen Pleasant, head of housekeeping."

"Call me Mammy," said the old black woman, her dead skin still shockingly dark against her white dashiki and her lace cap and shawl. "I run the show, and I'm a whole theater in myself."

Carl bowed low, coming back up with a smile. "I'd say I was charmed, except I'm afraid that would commit me, so I'll just say I'm pleased to make the acquaintance of you both."

"He is a charmer," Lady Sarah agreed. "What did I say, Mary? You owe me your tarot cards *and* a bottle of holy water."

"Well, there's the truth." Mammy chuckled, slapping her knee. "Sit down, you two. Sit down. Pull up a chair, an' make yourselves comfy. Have a cup of tea. Well, at least you, Ilse. I don't know if your young man would care for our blend."

"Oh, who knows, Mary?" Lady Sarah said. "It's not Darjeeling, but he might care for it anyway."

Mammy pushed at her playfully. "Oh stop it, Sarah! You're terrible!" she cackled. "But it's not Earl Grey neither!"

Lady Sarah giggled and poured a cup from the bone china pot, the rich red of blood changing midstream to steaming brown tea. "Have a cuppa," she said, her Mayflower accent turning mock-British, setting the cup before the empty chair at her right hand. "Bet it's been a while since you tasted hot tea!"

Carl took the chair to the left of Mammy Pleasant. "I believe I'll pass on the tea, but thank you, anyway."

Lady Sarah set out another cup of fine bone china and pushed it towards him. "Oh, it doesn't have to be tea. Would you like coffee? I can do it. Abracadabra, presto-chango, hey-ho, we've got coffee!" She held the teapot, poised.

"I daresay you ladies could manage Turkish delight if I were but to ask, but I'll pass all the same. Ilse and I were just looking for...?" He trailed off, looking askance at Ilse.

Ilse took the seat Lady Sarah had offered her, not wishing to offend the hospitality of the old blood-sisters. "Master Harry." Ilse picked up her cup. "Do you have any idea where he might be?"

The two old women looked at her and burst into renewed peals of laughter at their latest private joke. Ilse was used to it. The old blood-sisters had an endless number of amusements, ranging from Blood Bound poodles to enchanted stereoscopes, and the Tremere council didn't care overmuch what they did so long as they kept the Castle of Ten Thousand Rooms running smoothly and in a good state of repair. And happy.

Mammy at last wiped the tears of blood from her eyes and

stared, her eyes wide and goggling. "Oh, I daresay Massa Harry must be *somewhere* around here." Then she collapsed onto the table, howling and pounding it with the flat of one hand.

Ilse decided to humor them, not that they seemed to need much more. "I suppose I'll get the cream of the jest eventually."

Lady Sarah's eyes went just as wide as Mammy's. "Oh, would you like cream with your jest, Ilse?" She raised the teapot.

"Yes, thank you, Lady Sarah," Ilse said and held out her cup as the old sorceress used the Magic of the Smith to transmute the blood into pure cream, swirling into the tea in her cup and changing the brown from dark to light, while Mammy Pleasant pounded the table and gasped out, "Jest cream! Jest cream!"

Carl chose to act as if nothing were amiss and sat there, inspecting the rampant black wildcat, testing to see if the claws of its taxidermized paws were still sharp. They were, and he put his finger in his mouth, sucking away the blood before anyone could offer to do it for him.

Ilse chose to just take a sip of her tea and savored the taste of full-bodied orange pekoe flavored with bergamot and violets and sweetened with fresh cream. It was an illusion, of course, for the tea was still in its essence blood, but there were reasons why the old sisters' tea parties were such popular affairs, despite the silly, girlish manner with which they comported themselves. "Where is Master Harry? I'd hoped to find him, but the House led me here instead." Ilse took another sip of her tea.

"Isn't this a lovely cake?" Lady Sarah asked, ignoring the question. "Mary helped me bake it." She lifted the crystal cover of the cake plate and revealed a large, heart-shaped piece of dark cake, decorated with more of Mammy's *vever* patterns. "It's chocolate *lebküchen*," she said. "My own special recipe."

"Rowwrrrr!" The wildcat pounced onto the cake plate, knocking the cover out Lady Sarah's hand and spilling the teapot, blood staining the white linen. The cat screamed again and raked its claws across the cake, a splinter of wood flying out, a toothpick, which landed on the table before Ilse. The cat gobbled down the *lebküchen*, growing larger and larger until it stood the size of a panther. It lapped up the spilled blood from the table, then bit the teacup from Lady Sarah's hand and swallowed it whole.

The giant cat snarled at the two old women with bloody fangs, then leaped between them, landing on the floor and turning in a flash, darting between them and under the table. The chairs down the length of the Red Hall's grand banquet table rattled and shifted, jumping back one after the other as the creature raced down the length, until at last the master's chair at the far end jumped back a full foot, the great cat coming up in it, facing them, its paws on the table, mouth open in a horrific snarl —

Then the paws came up behind the cat's ears, and the beast's face came away, the mouth still snarling. Dark eyes laughing under dark curly hair, Master Harry set the mask aside and nodded once.

Lady Sarah and Mammy Pleasant laughed like schoolgirls, clapping enthusiastically, and Carl followed suit, with polite, appreciative applause.

Master Harry acknowledged each of them, then turned to Ilse. "Ilse, dear, I believe that's some of my blood you have in your cup. If you could spare it, I'd appreciate it, because I'm a bit low."

Feeling like a prize idiot, Ilse got up and went to the far end of the table, handing Master Harry her tea, which changed back to blood the moment it touched his lips.

"Almost got you, Harry," Lady Sarah said, her voice echoing down the length of the hall. "Almost got you that time."

"You ain't got that many lives, you old cat!" Mammy Pleasant cackled and rubbed her hands. "We'll skin you yet."

Master Harry set down the teacup, white and shining and licked clean. "If there weren't any danger, there wouldn't be any challenge. But you ladies will have to try better next time." He took Ilse's hand and kissed it as she took a seat next to him. "Where did you crib that one from, Sarah? 'Hansel and Gretel?'"

"Is that what you want to call the trick, Harry?" Lady Sarah leaned forward and leered. "I thought 'Cut out his heart and feed it to the cat' might be better."

"Too long," Master Harry said. "An illusion's title is best short and poetic." Not letting go of Ilse's hand, Master Harry got up from his chair and pulled Ilse from hers, escorting her down the length of the table so where they wouldn't have to shout.

He slipped out her original chair for her, then extended his hand to Carl. "I don't believe we've been formally introduced. Harry Houdini, at your service, sir."

Carl laughed and stood up partway. "I'd rather guessed that. Carl Magnuson," He extended his own hand. "A pleasure to meet you. You've always been one of my idols."

The mortal mage and Ilse's master shook warmly. "I'd thought the world thought me dead," Master Harry remarked, releasing Carl's hand with a nod and a smile.

Carl smiled back. "Can you think of a better thing for idols to be?"

Master Harry nodded in agreement, then turned to Lady Sarah, who was still looking at the empty cake plate and the overturned teapot. "'The Lebküchen Heart,'" he supplied. "That's the name for the trick you're looking for."

Lady Sarah looked up, prim. "That's redundant," she said. "*Lebküchen* already means *beloved cake*. That translates as 'The Beloved Cake Heart.'"

Master Harry shrugged and reached over to Mammy

Pleasant's cup, picking it up and draining the last of the tea, which changed to blood on contact with his lips. "Since when does reality have anything to do with illusion?"

"Oh, why don't you call it 'Feed the Cat' an' have done with it? Lan' sakes, but you two go on." Mammy Pleasant smiled and turned to Carl. "So, Carl boy, are you plannin' on stayin' a spell? I've got a nice bedroom on the top floor I could fix up a treat for you."

Carl smiled, one finger stroking his signet ring. "I'd say I could stay for a night, but as I understand from Ilse, that's a good deal of time here."

"Ooh, he's a sharp one, he is!" Mammy said and shoved Ilse with her fingertips, laughing. "Jing Wei's gonna be just furious when she finds you snatched him out from under her nose."

Carl looked around the table. "I wasn't aware that I was a prize to be snatched." He paused. "And I thought my relationship with Jing Wei was private."

Master Harry smiled back. "You'll find that few things are private among the Tremere, relationships most especially. And Ilse and Jing Wei have a certain…rivalry, as you might expect among blood-sisters."

Carl gave Ilse a sharp look, and it wounded her to the heart. "Hmph. well, I suppose you can't choose your relatives."

Master Harry smiled. "But don't you see? That's the point — we can." His eyes scanned Carl. "With a certain notable exception. It's a rare thing to be hosting the first mortal mage in Clan Tremere in almost two hundred years."

Carl laughed, though it sounded strained. "Pardon me if I don't raise a glass to celebrate. The past couple weeks have been difficult for me."

"Yes, cast out of the Order, as I understand?"

"Well, yes. All I did was say that you blokes might not be all bad, then someone found the skeleton in my closet, or should I say the bloodstain on the family tree, and hey-ho, I was out on my ear, even if I wasn't the first to say it." He shrugged. "So I decided, well, if I was going to get kicked out for associating with you, I might as well do it and see what it was like, so I talked to this person and that person, an' next thing I know, I'm off to L.A., and I hit it off with Jing Wei, but she doesn't tell me much, then next night I'm set for another date with her, and Ilse shows up instead, followed by the Undead Chowderhead, and we nip out the back and end up here." He nodded towards Ilse and winked his green left eye, and Ilse felt her blood turn to water. "Works fast, she does."

"We're not so very bad," Master Harry said, producing a pack of cards from nowhere and fanning them with both hands.

"Hey, those are my" — Mammy started, interrupted by Lady Sarah. "No, remember, they're my"—

"Girls, please." Master Harry folded the fans back up, shuffling the cards back together, then dividing them and flipping them from hand to hand in two arcs. "We drink blood, and we can't stand sunlight, but that's about the sum of our vices. As I understand, if you go to some of the newer clubs, they've becoming rather fashionable among the mortal set as well." His hands moved faster than the eye could see, cutting the cards, stacking them, and cutting them again. "Care to pick a card?"

Carl laughed, "What, we're going to play 'Find the Lady'?"

"'Find the Lady?'" Master Harry echoed. "Let's see… 'Queen, Queen, Kissing Machine, Let the Ladies all be seen.'" He flipped over the cards, fast as his magician's patter, revealing the Queen of Cups, the Queen of Wands, the Three of Cups, then in rapid succession the Queens of Swords and Pentacles, the Two of Swords, the Eight and Nine of Swords, the Nine of Pentacles, Strength, Justice, the Star, the Empress and lastly the High Priestess.

Master Harry smiled as Mammy Pleasant clapped her

hands, and even Carl conceded a grin. "That isn't how I play 'Find the Lady,' but I still wouldn't want to play it with you."

"Play? Why play?" Master Harry inquired. "Magic is serious business, and now that we have all these ladies, let's see if we can find them some men. 'Found the Ladies, then again, They all need their Gentlemen.'" The cards flashed down, Kings with Queens, Emperor with Empress, and the Hierophant with the High Priestess. He tapped the last pair, clucking his tongue. "Definitely not Catholics, these two. Protestants of some sort. See?" He flipped over the top card of the deck, revealing the Lovers, and deftly cast it down to cross the Hierophant and the High Priestess.

"There's something in the background on that one," Carl said, then reached out towards the deck, looking for permission from Master Harry. Ilse's master nodded, and the mortal mage turned over the next card of the deck. "The Devil. The Lovers always have someone pulling their strings."

He set it down atop the three other cards, the Devil sitting resplendent on his throne, with the Lovers happily chained before him.

Master Harry gathered up the cards and presented them to Lady Sarah, looking pleased "You may not be able to pick your relatives, but you're a fine addition to the clan nonetheless."

Carl nodded back and smiled. "As I was saying to Ilse, so long as this isn't like the Hotel California, I don't really much care. I rather like my sunlit hours."

Master Harry rested his chin atop his hands and studied Carl, eyes dark and intense. "Well, yes. I can tell by your accent you're from England, and you haven't seen enough of them for them to lose their novelty." He raised his eyebrows in amusement. "But let me put a stake through the heart of your worries. Even if you wanted to become a full member of the bloodline, we wouldn't take you. Not because you're not qualified, Carl, but because you're too useful to House Tremere as you are. You see, we think it's about time for our House to rejoin the Order, and umpteen centuries is long enough for the shock to wear off over what we've done and what we've become. And the plain fact of the matter is that we have more in common than we have at odds. We love magic and want to see it return to the world. At least, that's why I joined the Tremere, and I suspect that's why you joined the Order."

Carl nodded. "Some of your old tricks led me there. Funny, eh? Though so far as the history goes, most of the Hermetics seem to paint all of House Tremere with the same brush, saying you're a bunch of power-mad wackos who sold their souls for immortality."

Master Harry waved one hand, grumbling, "You're part of House Tremere. Are you a power-mad wacko? Did you sell your soul?"

"No," Carl said, "but then I'm not immortal either."

"Point taken," Master Harry said and clutched his chest, then looked at it with surprise. "Though not in the heart, strangely enough. Oh, yes," he said, coming back to himself, "the cat ate that. Wait a second, I'm the cat, aren't I? Or did I swallow the cat? Come here, you." He reached into his sleeve and pulled out a white dove, looking at it for a moment, then threw it in the air to flutter up to the antlers of one of the deer. "That's not it."

He reached into his other sleeve and produced another dove, tossing it in the air. "Not it either. Where did it get to?" He reached into his jacket, pulling out one dove after another, followed by a murder of crows and an unkindness of ravens, flapping up one after the other to perch on the antlers and heads mounted about the room.

"Ah, here we go," he said, putting his hands on top of his head and pulling on his scalp. "I always forget what's on my mind."

His scalp separated from the rest of his head, becoming a sleepy, fluffy black Persian cat which he held by the scruff of the neck, his real hair still on top of his head, unharmed. Master Harry set the cat down on the table before him, and it sat there, purring smugly.

Ilse's master looked up at them. "You know what we have here, don't you? This is the proverbial cat. Oh, not the one in the bag, that's that one there."

He pointed to Mammy Pleasant, and a white Persian cat popped out the top of her dashiki and jumped to the floor, running to the servants' door at the far end of the hall and disappearing through the crack.

"No, this is a very different one," Master Harry said, petting the black cat, which was still purring smugly. "A very different proverbial cat. Now spit it out," he ordered and grabbed the black cat by the back of the head and pulled until its mouth came open.

He held up a finger before its mouth. A tiny yellow bird crawled out onto the digit, looking frightened, and the black cat stopped purring. "Enough of you," Master Harry said, and he took the cat by the scruff of the neck and set it on the empty trophy base.

The black cat did not look at all pleased with losing the canary and growled low in its throat, springing with a furious, "Rowrrr!"

Master Harry snapped his fingers, and the cat froze in place, again the taxidermized wildcat that had been there at the beginning of the tea party.

The canary sat there on his other hand, shivering in terror, and Master Harry petted it with its free hand, smoothing down its ruffled feathers and cooing to it softly. "Poor thing, it's terrified. See, it's so frightened it laid an egg, everyone looking at it." He showed the tiny egg in his palm, then took the little yellow bird onto the index finger of his other hand and held it before his face, looking it in the eyes. "You realize you'll never make it in vaudeville if you keep doing things like that."

The canary cheeped apologetically, and Master Harry set

in on his shoulder, then closed his other hand over the egg and squeezed. He opened it, the contents expanding to become a mummified human heart covered with dark blood.

Master Harry shivered, a melodramatic look of disgust coming over his handsome features. "That will never do."

He closed his hand over the heart again, compressing it down to nothing, poking in the last few bits with the index finger of his opposite hand, then held the hand with the heart out to Mammy Pleasant and Lady Sarah. "If my lovely assistants could pass their hands over it and say the appropriate magic words?"

Mammy and Lady Sarah both giggled, then waved their hands over Master Harry's. "Shango!" said Mammy Pleasant with a great voodoo roar, while Lady Sarah wiggled her fingers and gave a prim, "Hey-presto!"

Master Harry took his hand back, opening it to reveal a small heart-shaped chocolate cookie, a miniature of the *lebküchen* Lady Sarah had had earlier. "There," he said, prestidigitating the cookie until it was between his thumb and forefinger, then bringing it up to his mouth.

"Now would I do something like that if I were power-mad?" He took a bite of the cookie, chewing appreciatively. "Good cookie," he said through a mouthful of crumbs, glancing to Lady Sarah.

The canary on his shoulder chirped hopefully, and Master Harry replied. "No, sorry. I'm the only one who's going to eat the rest of my heart. Now take your friends, and get out of here."

The canary flitted off his shoulder, flying up the chimney, followed by the doves, then the crows, and finally the ravens. Master Harry popped the last of his cookie in his mouth, then sucked the crumbs from his fingers.

"The Order would have a fit if they saw you do that," Carl remarked.

"What? My trick?"

Carl shook his head. "No, licking your fingers. Fussy bastards."

Master Harry leaned back and laughed, deep and long. "There's probably a number of things we'll have to get used to. But I'm sure we can get things together, if we just have someone to go speak for us. Where is it exactly you're from? London?"

"Lately, at least."

"Good. We've got a chantry there already, Malmsey House on Curson Street. Once you have a chance to talk to Dr. Dee, the local Proctor, you can see what you can do about arranging talks between your old Order and our House."

Carl paused. "Dr. Dee? Dr. *John* Dee. Queen Elizabeth's Dr. Dee, an' I mean the first one, not the one we got now, Miss red-hair-and-syphilis, the 'Virgin' Queen Elizabeth, and her court astrologer, Dr. 'You show me your shew-stones, I'll show you mine' John Dee? That one?"

Master Harry smiled. "I believe so, though I don't know whether he'd be amused or offended your summary of his mortal life."

"Offended," Mammy Pleasant said. "Definitely offended. That boy lost his sense of humor a long time ago."

"Probably used it up dealing with Queen Liz," Carl remarked and whistled. "My, you Tremere sure get around. You didn't take Queen Liz while you were at it, did you?"

Master Harry shrugged. "We didn't. I can't speak for the Ventrue, though I wouldn't put it past them."

"Ventrue?"

"The Blue Bloods. Another clan of the Kindred."

"Politicos," Ilse supplied. "They like to be in control of things. Always plotting and politicking."

Carl rolled his eyes. "Sounds like some other people I could mention."

"Everyone needs a hobby." Master Harry produced his multiplying balls, juggling and fanning them between his fingers for practice. "And as for plotting and politicking, much of it's just human nature. Everyone wants to be the best, to be appreciated, to have someone watch them."

The balls between his fingers multiplied and diminished, going from three to five to two, red to blue to black and gold. "But while competition is all well and good—" He passed half of the balls from his right hand to his left, four in each hand, red, blue, gold and black, silver, orange, violet and green. "You sometimes find that the sum is greater than the parts," — he put his hands together over his head — "and if you just get it all together " he cupped his hands together, letting the balls disappear inside, " maybe there'll be something magic."

He took his hands apart, and a thousand balls cascaded down over his head, like Bunny Rabbit's trick with the ping-pong balls and Mr. Moose, bouncing and rolling across the table, and Master Harry, now the magician and the entertainer, laughed,

He leaned back then, brushing the colored spheres from his vest. "After all, Carl, you may be an outcast right now, but with the appropriate ceremonies and laurels, an outcast can become a peace child." He picked up a handful of balls at random and began juggling them. "And in any case, you'll always be welcome here. We haven't had a mortal mage in a very long time."

"No," Carl said, "not from what I've heard of Tremere history."

Master Harry tossed a ball into the mouth of the stuffed wildcat, where it stuck. "A stupid oversight. When the elders consolidated the House as vampires, they were too drunk on power to realize that there were some things vampires couldn't do." He tossed another ball in the cat's mouth. "Easily at least. The Giovanni were much more clever about it, or maybe I should say that they profited by our mistake. They've got both mortal mages and vampires in their family, though since you probably haven't heard of them, that shows they're no great shakes as either."

Master Harry finished stuffing the mouth and began pitching the balls so that they stuck on the wildcat's outstretched claws. "But I'm very glad to see that the elders were not quite so thorough as they first thought in co-opting our human heirs. And that—," he said, juggling another handful, "— is the main reason no one in Clan Tremere is going to give you the Kiss, even if you wanted it. We need you to bear an olive branch to the Order and to restart our mortal line."

Carl leaned back in his chair, blue eye and green eye both twinkling with wry humor. "You're saying you want to put me out to stud." He chuckled, "I don't know how well that will sit with the Order. Cult of Ecstasy would be all for it, and even some of the witches might be keen on the idea, but the Order of Hermes?" He snorted, blushing furiously, and smothered a laugh with one hand. "I'm sorry," he managed at last, "but I'm afraid the Order has become a very different body in the years since House Tremere left it, at least if you think they'd give their blessing to *that* sort of magic. The Grand Lodge of London, anyway."

He chuckled again, stifling a guffaw, and turned very red in the face. "Can't say I'm not flattered, though, at your estimation of my capabilities."

Master Harry laughed and juggled two balls. "Well, you're welcome to father as many children as you like, Carl, but honestly, we were thinking of something a little more immediate. I've always prided myself on great escapes, and what greater escape could there be than from death itself? And not only from death, but from Death and Damnation?"

Carl blinked and brushed the tears from his eyes, looking at the magician.

Master Harry smiled, having center stage. "Of course, if you want to do any escape, the easiest trick is to have your man on the outside. That would be you, Carl. The blood is the soul and the soul is the life. House Tremere is not truly dead, or damned, until its last member is. You're neither.

You're our man on the outside. And with your help — and the Order to provide support — we can pull this trick out of the hat and do the greatest escape of all time."

Carl brought up one hand, mouth open, then paused, brows furrowed. "Let me get this straight. You want me to play anchor while you Tremere blokes do some big vampiric blood-magic ritual and undo the spell that made you vampires in the first place?"

"From the top on down," Master Harry said, nodding. "The entire Pyramid."

Carl's mismatched eyes blinked. "Well," he said at last, "that's some trick if you can pull it off, but what's in it for you? More than that, what's in it for the Order of Hermes if they help you, because from what I guess, it's going to take a lot more mages than me to pull all of you out, even if I'm the linchpin for the whole trick."

"What's in it for us is mortality as mages. What's in it for the Order of Hermes is the biggest membership drive in the history of magecraft, because while the Order's star has been falling, House Tremere's has been rising, and we've got nearly the whole Pyramid filled, seven by seven down to the thirteenth generation. And if all of those were to become mortal again, that would be a rather impressive number of mages."

"And then?" Carl asked, eyes wide.

"And then…," Master Harry finished. "House Tremere will go after what it's always been after — power. We'll rejoin the Order of Hermes, swelling its ranks until we're the biggest magic gorilla on the block. And where does a magic gorilla sit? Well, for starters, the head seat of the Council of Nine, consolidating all the wonderworkers into something properly organized, making for an even bigger gorilla. And then what happens?" Master Harry grinned, challenging Carl to complete the thought.

The mage blinked. "We kick the Technocracy's bloody butt, that's wot! Right into the next dimension."

Master Harry stopped juggling. "Think the Order of Hermes will go for it?"

Carl exhaled, looking stunned by it all. "Can't exactly say, but it's worth a shot. What you're offering the Hermetics is what they've always wanted — the chance to sit at the top of the Council and the top of the world. It's just a matter of whether they hate the Technocracy more than they hate House Tremere and whether they'd want to share the Council seat with a bunch of former vampires. But I've run into the Technocracy, and I think it's a pretty safe bet that the Order of Hermes hates them more than they don't care for you. Or I should say us, since I'm a Tremere too, when you come right down to it."

He stood up. "I'd best be getting back to L.A. My plane leaves for London tomorrow morning, and I'd like to get packing if I'm going to go back to the Order and sell them on your scheme. It's convoluted and power-mad, and they just love that sort of thing." He looked at Master Harry and grinned. "I think we really are related."

Master Harry stood up, fangs extended in a wildcat's smile, and leaned on the table. "We really must be."

"Don't worry about catching your plane, Carl, dear," Lady Sarah added. "Malmsey House is one of the few places that has a permanent door to my own dear House of Mystery. All you and Ilse need do is wait for the sun to set in London, and we can just go and open the door in the Ching Parlor. And you'll be there."

Mammy Pleasant rubbed her hands and giggled. "Jing Wei will be just furious!"

Saturday, April 24, London — The Masters of Magic

Kurt had only just arrived in Los Angeles a night earlier, when, while waiting to meet with Jing Wei, the target of his search threw chowder over his clothes and scalded the hell out of his face in the process. He was rapidly growing to dislike his adversary, attractive or not. When he'd regained his senses enough to stand again, he was ready to find Ilse Decameron and rend her flesh from her bones, to say nothing of her little friend.

He stormed past the waiter who was busily stamping out a small fire caused by the mage's spell and set off in search of his prey. With every step he grew calmer, remembering his years of etiquette schooling and his position within the Camarilla. He'd have to make certain that no one who'd taken his picture saw anything unusual, but that was easy enough to accomplish. He'd handle the matter as soon as he'd finished with the important business of gaining a little revenge.

Ten minutes later, he gave up in disgust. The wench was nowhere to be found, and wherever she'd gone, she'd apparently taken her little friend along for the ride. His irritation must have been obvious, because Jing Wei was on her best behavior when she approached him. "Perhaps you'd like a place to clean yourself, Kurt?"

"Yes, I'd appreciate that very much. Thank you."

"It is always my pleasure to be of assistance to you." Her voice was as saccharine as he'd remembered, and her accent was just as phony. He knew very well that Jing Wei was fluent in seven languages and could speak with perfect native inflection in each. When she opted to speak with less-than-perfect diction, it was only to suit her own purposes. Still, with her athletic frame and small breasts, she was always a pleasure to look at. Jing Wei was diminutive, almost classically so for a Chinese woman, and her lustrous black hair flowed freely down to her shoulders, rather than pinned up as she normally kept it. Despite her dubious honesty and even more dubious claims of wanting to help, Kurt had to admit that she was a very attractive woman. And very distracting.

The Chinese Kindred moved gracefully over to where a man in a waiter's outfit was waiting patiently and whispered in his ear. He smiled thinly while looking at Kurt, whispering in Jing Wei's ear in return. The smile faded when Kurt glared back at him. The man spoke with Jing Wei a moment longer, and then she gestured for Kurt to follow her. She led him to a private room in the back of the restaurant, spartan in the extreme, but with a sink and a shower stall where he could wash. He chose the sink, but would have preferred the luxury of a shower. The woman waited patiently until he was finished with his work scrubbing and the touch-ups on his khaki shorts and shirt. The red marks on his face's reflection almost made him look alive.

"You were not expected by me. What brings this honor to your humble servant?"

"I'm looking for one of your clan, a woman named Ilse Decameron. I found her when she showed up here." He paused for a moment, forcing his lips to fall away from the sneer he felt creasing his features. He looked at her reflection behind his own and clenched the chipped porcelain edges of the wet sink. "She and her pet sorcerer left after making a rather rude introduction."

"Pet sorcerer?" The warmth left Jing Wei's voice as she spoke, her tones barely above a whisper and bordering on a hiss. Then she caught herself and brought her emotions under control. Whoever Ilse Decameron was, Kurt was willing to bet she'd just offended another member of her own clan. "I fear Ilse has always lacked in the social skills. She would never have been accepted into your own clan."

"No doubt." Again he forced himself to relax. The proximity of the fireball earlier had set him on edge and his system refused to calm down. "Do you know where she would have gone?"

Jing Wei frowned prettily and shook her head. "I am afraid I cannot be of assistance in this matter." Then she suddenly smiled, a radiant image of Eastern perfection. "But I have an associate who could possibly help you."

"An associate?"

"Yes. He is a mage, and he has an interesting familiar who is skilled in hunting down troublemakers." She stepped close behind him, her breath warm from a recent feeding and the smell of fresh blood still redolent on her lips. Kurt felt the need to feed himself and had to remember that the woman behind him was a member of a warring clan in order to stop himself from taking liberties. Jing Wei always had that effect on him. "He is only a short distance away. He could be here within the hour."

Kurt paused long enough to swallow the lump that was forming in his throat before he answered. "Yes, I would greatly appreciate the help, my dear." He turned to face her as she slipped her arms around his waist. "And while we wait, perhaps you could tell me where a hungry Kindred could find a willing blood doll?"

Jing Wei threw a sultry and not entirely false pout his way and lightly pushed her body against him. "You want only a human tonight?"

"I think that would be for the best. I am particularly thirsty."

She slid away from him, her eyes seeming to promise a great deal of pleasure. "I shall make the necessary arrangements. Perhaps later, after you meet with my friend, you would like dessert?" She moved away before he could answer.

When he was alone in the room, he straightened his collar and combed his damp hair back into place. "Perhaps I would at that."

>€

Almost exactly an hour later, Kurt was standing at the edge of the ocean, staring into the late night sky and recalling the last sunset he'd ever seen, when the roar of a powerful motorcycle's engine thundered across the sand. He waited until the bike stopped a few feet from him and the engine shuddered to a halt. For a moment there was no sound at all, save the rushing sigh of the tide running along the shoreline. Kurt let the silence stretch out, allowing the man behind him to make the first move.

"Excuse me? Would your name be Kurt Westphal?" The voice was almost too casual, with a lack of inflection that Kurt had come to think of as a "universal accent," with no emphasis on this or that syllable. In two sentences, the man had established himself as a traveler who had likely spent lifetimes in a dozen different countries. Jing Wei had interesting friends.

"It would indeed. You are the friend Jing Wei spoke of?"

"That'd be me. Thadius Zho at your service."

Kurt turned and faced the man for the first time. He sat leaning against a large black motorcycle, his arms crossed and an arrogant smile pasted across his face. Thadius Zho was, without a doubt, one of the most interesting mortals he'd ever met. He had an air about him, a presence that demanded attention. The man was dark and brooding, dressed all in black from his motorcycle boots all the way to the old fashioned tunic that covered his lean, muscular torso. The mane of dark brown hair that surrounded his face crested in a widow's peak and was accented by the black eyepatch that covered his left eyebrow and ran down to his cheek. The eye that could be seen was an icy blue. It took an unusual man to carry off the green pentagram on the patch and come out not looking foolish. Zho was undoubtedly an unusual man.

Kurt stepped forward and extended his hand. "It is a pleasure to meet you, Mr. Zho. I wish to thank you for coming to my aid."

Zho took the offered hand and shook it with a strong grip. Kurt returned the grip, squeezing briefly and assessing the physical strength of the man he faced. Strong for a human, but still only mortal. Had Kurt been merely human, the strength the mage used would have probably broken bones. "I wouldn't say thank you just yet, I'm not certain how much help I can be in tracking down the woman you're searching for."

"Just the same, even taking the time to see me is appreciated."

"In that case, you're welcome."

Kurt withdrew his hand from the man's own. He studied his counterpart and was studied in return. When the careful assessments were done, he was certain neither quite knew what to make of the other.

"So, what can you tell me about Ilse Decameron?" After showing a photograph of his prey and describing the man she'd fled with, Kurt waited for the mage's response.

Zho seemed lost in thought for a few seconds, his right eye slightly glazed. Then he became alert again, and Kurt wondered if he hadn't imagined the episode. "Did you happen to hear the man's name?"

"She called him 'Paul.' I believe he responded by saying his name was 'Carl, Carl Magnuson.'" In truth, Kurt had heard none of their exchange, but the patrons around them had, and it had taken little to control their minds and make them forget about the incident while walking around and apologizing for any disturbances he might have caused. He'd spent most of his waiting time convincing the weak-willed patrons of the restaurant to remove the film from their cameras and destroying any evidence of his near-frenzy. Several rolls of exposed film were sitting in the inside pocket of his still-damp jacket. The remainder of his time had been spent gathering information and clouding the memories of the other patrons in Gladstone's.

Zho smiled, a thin razor-line that curved slightly upward. "I believe I might be able to help you, Mr. Westphal."

He returned the smile. "Please, call me Kurt. What form of compensation would you like for this assistance?"

"Kurt it is. Please, call me Thadius. I think we can work out the details later, but I have to warn you, my services do not come cheaply. Now then, there are certain...limitations to your traveling abilities." Kurt forced himself not to make any facial changes, though the task was far from easy. He hadn't confided his vampiric nature to the man. "I imagine you have ways of handling travel on your own. Perhaps it would be best if we joined together in London."

"London?"

Zho smiled again, and Kurt decided he preferred the man's face without that particular expression. Something about the mage made him uneasy. "That's where we'll find your Ms. Decameron." His expression must have changed, because the man facing him leaned back against his motorcycle again and continued his answer without any prodding. "She and Carl Magnuson have business there, or at least they will two days from now."

Kurt decided he didn't want to know how the man knew about the couple's future plans. Sometimes ignorance was truly bliss. They made their final arrangements and went their separate ways.

➷➻

The following night, Kurt awoke with a distinct feeling of claustrophobia and a severe case of jet-lag. The nine hour difference in time zones had been merciless on his system, and his hunger was worse than it normally was. He'd had little time to rest before the sun rose in Britain and felt the lack of sleep. Perhaps his body was trying to tell him that traveling so heavily was a bad idea. Only minutes after he'd come awake, the lid to his coffin was removed and he was greeted by Jackie's smiling face. "Welcome to London, boss. Or more accurately, Stanstead Airport."

Jackie attempted to help him out of the coffin, but he brushed her hand aside and sat up on his own. The air was damp and cold, just like the last time he'd been to the British Isles. "Must you always be so damnably cheerful, Jackie?"

"Would you rather I pour hot water on you to wake you up?"

"No, but you could at least suffer from sleep deprivation once in a while."

"Oh, that'd go well. You locked in your suitcase and me sound asleep and too tired to care about you pounding on the old exit ramp. Yeah, I think that'd be a really swift move on my part." She faked a yawn and playfully started shoving him back into the casket. "Back in you go, I need my beauty sleep."

Kurt waved her back, grinning in spite of his foul mood. "I'm hungry."

"What else is new?"

"Upstart."

"Old coot."

"What did I schedule for tonight?'

"You've got about two hours to spare before you meet with the witch-man, and before then you have to meet with Lady Anne and feed your face."

"You're vulgar."

"Only 'cause you like me that way."

"Nonsense, I've never said anything of the kind."

"You've never stopped feeding me, either."

"We'll have to see about that."

"Careful what you say, Kurt, or the next time you climb in that traveling case of yours, I'll ship you to the North Pole."

"Ingrate."

"Power-happy neck-biter."

"Mind your manners, and get the car."

"It's got, boss."

Ten minutes later, they were stuck in London's nighttime traffic, with Jackie driving the rented limousine and grumbling about being on the wrong side of the road. Kurt sat back and stared out the window, watching the landscape go past and thinking about the woman who'd nearly blinded him while taking his picture. "How much longer until we reach Lady Anne's haven?"

"Four miles and thirty minutes with the way these morons drive." Jackie rolled down the window, mumbling to herself about which parts of the driver in the next lane she would like to remove with a dull knife. She opened her mouth, taking in a deep breath to scream, her vocal cords tightening in a way Kurt was familiar with. She paused, looked in the rearview mirror, and apparently decided against it. "Why'd she have to have her haven in the middle of nowhere anyway. And worse, the middle of nowhere on the other side of London?"

"I imagine most of her visitors arrive from Heathrow, not Stanstead."

"Don't blame me, blame the travel agent."

"Mmm. And who chose the travel agent, my dear?"

Jackie made a bitter face and swerved the car through three other lanes of heavy traffic as she located her exit point. "Your problem is that you're too busy worrying about minor details like who picked the travel agent."

"Your problem is that you are too impetuous and too rude for anybody's good."

"I tend to think of it as 'aggressive,' not rude."

"When you bother to think." He smiled at her reflection, noting the scowl she tossed his way. "Don't try it too often, Jackie. I rather like your vacuous nature."

"Bite me."

"Only for pleasure, dear, never for food."

"Flatterer."

A few moments later, the limousine pulled up in front of a monumental house resting on more land than seemed possible for any place in Europe. A man dressed in evening finery came briskly forward, while Jackie donned her chauffeur's cap and all but ran around the vehicle to open the door for Kurt. All attempts at humor and friendliness were gone, and she was once again only a servant doing her work. Kurt climbed out of the car and stated his name for the man who'd come to greet him. The effect was immediate, and he was led promptly into the mansion in front of him.

The building was all but a museum, with suits of armor in every other corner and a long line of family coats of arms adorning the walls. After fifty years as a member of the Ventrue clan, he still never quite got used to the vast opulence most of his clan members took for granted. The majority of his waking hours were spent in an endless procession of hotel suites, nice enough, but not on par with what the more established members of the Ventrue were used to. He noted the seemingly endless paintings, sculptures and antiques in the rooms he passed through with an appraiser's eye and mentally calculated the wealth of Lady Anne Bowesley at slightly less than what he'd originally expected. Either she was doing poorly in the financial gains department, or she kept the most obvious valuables elsewhere.

Finally, after roaming what seemed like a hundred halls of expensive carpets and oak-paneled walls, he was led into the library, where the self-proclaimed Queen of London waited for him. She was an attractive woman, seemingly frail to those who were unaware of her powers, with dark hair carefully coifed and electrifying blue eyes. Her delicate features seemed unable to hold the sheer force of her personality, and Kurt could see why she ruled over all of London during the troubling times of the last half-century.

She stood and he bowed formally before her. "Good evening, Milady. It is a pleasure to make your acquaintance at last."

"Welcome, Mr. Westphal. I hope your journey was uneventful."

"If anything, it was boring." He smiled, pouring on the charm as he walked forward. "Democritus send his regards, Milady, and asks that you extend your hospitality to me, his lowly servant."

"In light of all that you have done for Clan Ventrue, how could I possibly say no?"

"You are too kind, Milady."

"Make yourself comfortable, Mr. Westphal."

"Please, call me Kurt."

"You may call me Lady Anne."

"Thank you, Lady Anne."

"Has Democritus sent you to assist me against the damnable Tremere?"

"In a manner of speaking, Lady Anne. I am in pursuit of one particular agent of that foul clan, one Ilse Decameron. She may have already presented herself to you."

"No," she sniffed. "She has not as yet presented herself."

"She may well avoid doing so, as she apparently has no regard whatsoever for the Ventrue."

"Should she forget her manners, I will be forced to remind her of the laws governing the Camarilla."

"One would hope she hasn't gone so far away from tradition, Milady. Still, I do understand she has information of great importance to the Ventrue and that she should be observed in action rather than punished." He flashed a bitter smile as the thought of hot fish chowder running through his hair crossed his mind. "Unfortunate though that may be."

"Naturally, I shall abide by Democritus' wishes in this matter."

"I thank you, as does my sire."

"How can you be certain that this Ilse Decameron will show herself in my fiefdom?"

"I have an associate who assures me that she will be here no later than tomorrow night, Milady." He paused a moment, continuing when she indicated that he should. "The man is a mage of some notoriety and assures me that tracking her is going to be child's play."

"And your friend's name?"

"Thadius Zho, Milady."

Lady Anne actually grimaced for a full three seconds before returning to a more sober version of her usual pleasant expression. "Thadius Zho? Well, I haven't seen him in over a hundred years." Once again, Kurt did his best to hide his surprise. He'd have never guessed the man's age at over forty on the outside. "I should be careful around that one, Kurt. He consorts with demons."

"I shall take that advice as gospel, Milady."

A few minutes were spent discussing pleasantries and the present troubles in London. Not surprisingly, the Tremere seemed to be a nuisance in London as well as in the States. At present, the elder of the Tremere in London, Dr. John Dee, was sharing a very fragile truce with Lady Anne. The truce was being tested almost nightly, as Dee and his associates reacted with vulgar verbal assaults and constant insinuations that the Ventrue would likely break the pact as soon as look at their faces in the mirror.

In short, Lady Anne had her hands full.

A short time later, after feeding on an amazingly well-endowed chambermaid, a sated and much more relaxed Kurt Westphal bid his farewells with a promise to return later in the evening, and went off to meet with Zho.

᠁

The place Zho had chosen was easily found, and even the guards at the Tower of London were willing to let a stranger through the gates after closing...provided the stranger in question could literally force them to forget he'd ever come past. In the courtyard of the ancient building, amid flawlessly manicured lawns and places where the air was unnaturally chill, Zho sat Indian-style on the grass, his face buried in the shadows. He was dressed in a black suit and matching greatcoat. Kurt literally overlooked him twice before he finally spoke up. In the darkness, the pentacle on the mage's eyepatch actually glowed with a faint, chilling light.

"You're late, Kurt. I expected you to be more punctual."

"I was here on time, but had a little difficulty with the locked fence."

"They tend to slow things down." The sarcasm was heavy in the man's voice, but Kurt decided to ignore the barb and continue on with his reason for meeting the mage in the first place.

"So, have you had any luck in locating Decameron?"

"I trust your trip was uneventful as well..."

Kurt calmed himself with an effort. He needed the mage's help and could not allow himself to fall into a rage over a few petty slights. "My sincerest apologies for my rude behavior, Thadius. I'm afraid I do not take well to long journeys. They wreak havoc on my sleep cycle. I had assumed by your presence and fast wit that your journey was uneventful."

"I just know that hurt your delicate ego." Zho was apparently in the mood for an argument, but Kurt simply refused to be baited.

"Yes, well, I'm terribly sorry to have inconvenienced you, Mr. Zho. Rest assured I do appreciate all of your efforts on my behalf. If I can ever return the favor, please do not hesitate to call."

The mage fairly doubled over laughing, his fists pounding the ground and his whole body shaking with mirth. Kurt contemplated ripping his throat out for the sheer pleasure it would bring, but decided against it at the last minute.

From behind him came the voice of the man sitting before him. "My apologies, Kurt. It seems Charnas is in a mood again." He turned to find Zho glaring over to where his doppelganger was going into convulsive fits on the lawn. Behind the sober version of the mage, Jing Wei stood looking on with mild amusement. Kurt turned back again, staring at the still giggling man on the ground. The likeness between both mages was absolutely flawless. Zho stepped forward and planted one boot-clad foot on his impostor's stomach, applying just enough pressure to make the man laugh all the harder. "Enough, Charnas! If you continue with these antics I'll be forced to lose my patience!"

The man on the ground sobered immediately, and Kurt was astonished to see the transformation that occurred before his eyes. Where seconds before the pinned figure had resembled Zho, it now twisted and warped, reshaping itself and becoming a different entity entirely. Charnas sat up, wiping tears of laughter from his eyes and switching his perspective from the mage to Kurt himself. "Oh…my…I like him, master, I do. He's so stiff, his sweat could starch shirts." The creature fell on the ground and started laughing a second time, literally kicking his legs in the air. After a few moments he finally stopped, still prone and looked at Kurt with a dangerous grin on his face. Kurt was not amused.

The creature stood up and bowed low before Kurt, his eyes alight with mockery and mischief. "Your Majesty, I am Charnas the Imp, servant to Thadius Zho and all-around naughty boy. Please forgive my jest, I simply could not resist." Despite himself, Kurt found he rather liked the obnoxious homunculus that stood before him. The creature was dressed abominably in black leather attire better suited to a member of a biker gang, but his saturnine features were alight with pleasure, and his humor was almost infectious. Charnas had slightly fanged teeth that almost seemed to glow against the dusky purple of his skin. His body was long and lanky, but paradoxically short. If he was an inch over five feet in height, Kurt would be surprised. A thick head of curly black hair was framed by long, pointed ears, and he was reminded of an elf from one of Tolkien's novels. The imp lifted one hand and held it before Kurt, ready for a handshake. "Friends?" he asked hopefully.

Kurt looked at the hand skeptically for a second and then reached out and gave a firm handshake. The creature was surprisingly strong. "Apology accepted, Charnas."

Zho leaned forward and slapped the demon's hand away from Kurt with a look of fierce rage on his face. "Never, never again! Do you understand me, Charnas? Never again. If I ever see you impersonating me again, I'll boil you in holy water."

"You have my services, 'master.' You need not threaten my life." The creature's eyes narrowed with anger, and its voice was filled with contempt. "Not that such drivel coming from the likes of you could do me any harm."

"Watch yourself, wretch. Or I'll have you cast back down."

"Waste of a good investment." He looked at Kurt, then to Jing Wei and pulled back in mock surprise. "Oh, my! I think we've kept your friends waiting long enough. Why don't I just vamoose, and then you three can talk." With a fiery belch of smoke, the imp disappeared, his voice echoing faintly as the cloud of blackness and sulfur engulfed him. "Toodleoo, kiddies!"

"My," Kurt started with a slightly shaken grin, "you do have strange friends, Thadius."

The mage shook his head, his face warring between a smile and a scowl. "Don't let his attitude fool you. Beneath that obnoxious exterior beats a heart of pure evil." Zho slapped Kurt lightly on the shoulder, a gesture that he found almost too intimate from a man he'd only met once before. "On the bright side, he does obey me when he's so inclined, and he is almost flawless as a watchdog. Let's be on our way, shall we? This place is a little too public for what we need to discuss. I didn't realize there'd be so many guards."

Zho led Kurt and Jing Wei into the depths of the Tower of London, down several flights of stairs and along four separate corridors that seemed virtually endless, to where the ground was slightly damp and the air smelled stale. After a few minutes of fumbling around in the faint light, he opened a door and led them into a large chamber filled with rusting torture devices. Kurt was almost positive that somewhere along the way they'd traveled beyond the confines of the actual tower, but decided against asking the mage exactly where they were.

Beyond the mildewed dungeon antiquities, a warped wooden door led into another room almost as large as the one they'd just left. The walls of the room were lined with books on magickal theory and various subjects that could only be of interest to a mage or a Tremere. An oak desk and a coffee table complete with several plush Victorian chairs filled the center of the room, and Kurt felt a moment of confusion when he saw the computer sitting on the desk. At a guess, everything else in the entire chamber dated back to sometime before his human birth.

"Have a seat, folks. Let's get on with business." When they were all seated, Zho continued, "You want to know where Ilse Decameron is. At the present time she in nowhere on earth. Don't look that way, Kurt — I have no reason to lie to you. I won't bore you with details, suffice it to say she is beyond your ability to reach her. However, all it took was a modicum of divination, and I discovered that she will soon be in London and will even be in your presence in less than twenty-four hours. That's about all I can tell you at this point."

"How could you possibly know—?"

"I'm a mage, Kurt. I dabble in dark arts. Seeing the possible futures is child's play. The only hard part is guessing which of them will be right. Most of them say you'll be in the same room with Ilse Decameron in less than twenty-four hours and that both of you will walk away from the meeting under your own power."

Jing Wei smiled enigmatically and added a comment of her own. "Will you not tell him what you told me?"

"I'm getting to it, woman. Be patient."

"As you see fit, Thadius Zho."

The man rubbed one finger under his eye-patch and winced. He then shrugged and looked at Kurt again, a mildly distressed expression darkening his features. "There's a good chance that either you or the one you seek will die later the same night." He paused, apparently at a loss for words.

Kurt reeled under the information, a cold pit of worry blooming in his chest. "How good a chance are we talking about?"

"Fifty-fifty, at a guess. All I can tell you for certain is that you need to meet with Decameron tomorrow night and you need to find a man named Ozmo before you make that meeting. He knows what the source of your possible death is."

"Can you describe him?"

"Tall, muscular, long white hair and very pale skin, either a vampire or an albino, possibly both. I gather that he's insane."

"Well, if he is a vampire, that should make all of this a little easier."

"I have personal matters to attend to now and possibly I can learn a little more about this predicament of yours later. If I learn anything, you can expect a message from me personally, from Jing Wei or from Charnas."

"I thank you for that. I am in your debt."

"We can discuss that later. For now, you can do me two favors."

"Name them."

"Don't let anyone know that Jing Wei is here, and try not to get yourself killed."

"You may consider both favors done."

⇒←

After giving brief consideration to the size of London as a whole and his own unfamiliarity with the territory, Kurt decided that Lady Anne had a much better chance of tracking down Ozmo than he did. He waved Jackie over from where she'd parked the limo and watched as she expertly maneuvered the vehicle off of the main road and into the loop in front of the Tower of London. She was sneering slightly, and he braced himself for the inevitable question.

Jackie slipped from the driver's seat and walked around to open the door for him. "So, the Hong Kong Hooker came along for the ride, eh?" There was an edge to her attempt at a joke, which Kurt recognized as the closest she normally allowed herself to come to actual jealousy. She did not like for Kurt to see other women, and she especially did not like that Jing Wei was around. The past history between Kurt and Jing Wei was not something he had kept a secret from Jackie, though from time to time he wished he had.

"Yes, Jackie. Jing Wei opted to join us in London, though I honestly couldn't tell you why." Kurt climbed into the back of the limo as he spoke.

"Jeez, Kurt, you don't have to sound so defensive. I was just making an observation." The door slammed harder than normal, but at least Jackie had the decency to let him put both legs all the way in the car before she threw her weight against the door. Running around to the driver's side door, she slipped back in behind the wheel and started pulling back into traffic. Her eyes narrowed in the rearview mirror as she looked back at him. "I mean, I just like to stay informed of who's around you and who I should maybe keep an eye on, because I don't really like the idea of you getting double teamed by a mage and a vampire that thinks she's a mage. You might trust those two, but both of 'em give me the creeps."

"It's not a matter of trust, and you know it. They are my allies for the present time and the only real source of information I have available to me in this town." He tried to sound as calm and polite as he could, knowing that any other attitude from him might send Jackie off on a tirade. Kurt could easily admit to himself that he loved his chauffeur, but she had a tendency to get too possessive and that always annoyed him. "You should worry less about the company I keep while on business and worry more about the traffic."

Jackie swerved around a slow-moving bus, almost colliding with a boxy little car the likes of which Kurt had never seen outside of Britain. The offended driver honked vigorously on his asthmatic horn, and Jackie promptly raised her right hand in a one-fingered salute. "Fuck you too!"

"Jackie, calm down. Now."

Jackie's face was a study in innocence as she responded. "Hey, can I help it if the people in London can't drive worth shit?"

"Of course not, dear. Just try to get us to the prince's haven in one piece. I've grown rather fond of this body. And of yours for that matter."

"Hey, you're the boss." The sting had faded a little in her words, but to prove her point, she floored the gas-pedal, launching the limo into high speed as she wove through the partially-snarled traffic. Kurt gave up. When Jackie had a mood, it was simply best to let her do her own thing. He reached for the cellular phone and dialed the number for Lady Anne's office. A few moments later, the phone was answered by Courtland Leighton, her right-hand man.

"Hello, Courtland. This is Kurt Westphal. Seeing as I'm new to your fine town I was wondering if you might be willing to do me a favor."

"Certainly, Kurt. You've only to tell me what you need."

"I'm looking for a Kindred named Ozmo. Do you know of him?"

Leighton chuckled in a don't-be-foolish-of-course-I-know-him manner, and Kurt felt his teeth start to grind together. "Certainly I do. Nasty little bit of work hanging with Crowley and his crew."

"I was hoping perhaps you could have a few of your men pick him up for me. I'd like to ask him a few questions."

"Consider the situation handled, Kurt. What shall I tell the little man you want from him?"

"Don't tell him anything. I rather like to see them squirm."

"I imagine the boys can have him for you within a few hours. Is that satisfactory, then?"

"Delightful. Thanks for your help."

"Anytime."

Jackie was still in a mood, so Kurt just hung up the phone and held onto the side of seat in front of him as she went through her list of combat maneuvers in the process of finding her way back to Bexborough Manor. The night air seemed chillier now, perhaps as a direct result of her attitude. That, or just possibly the heavy fog rolling across the land.

"Jackie?"

"Yes, Kurt?"

"Why don't you find a nice, secluded stretch of land and pull over?"

She looked puzzled, but nodded and found a long field of grass on the way down a secondary road that would, at least in theory, allow them to avoid the worst of the traffic on their way to the manor-haven of the prince. "How's this?"

"Ideal."

When the limousine had come to a complete stop, he opened the door and waited. Jackie opened her own door and came back to look at him, curiosity etching her features. The overhead light illuminated her face, accenting her full lips and highlighting her cheekbones. Kurt patted the seat next to him as he slid over, giving her room to climb in beside him. When she was situated, he reached past her and pulled the door closed.

"What—?"

"You're looking a little peaked, my dear." He smiled and pulled her close, feeling the warmth of her skin even through the jacket, vest and blouse that covered her. "I thought a little vitæ might help you feel a little more lively." Jackie smiled warmly, her lips parting slightly in anticipation. Kurt ran one fang lightly across his wrist and held the wound up for her to see. Dark blood welled slightly from the cut, and Jackie actually licked her lips. "Take what you need from me."

She leaned over his wrist, and Kurt immediately felt the warmth of her breath as she opened her mouth and played her tongue across the wound. She was shivering with need, and he scolded himself for making her wait so long between feedings. He closed his eyes as she started sucking, first lightly and then with more passion. He raised his free hand to her dark red hair and tossed her cap aside, then grabbed a handful of her tresses. Her lips moved against him, a dozen little gasps of suction with a dozen pauses to increase the effect. Finally he pulled his wrist away, noting the disappointment in her eyes.

"Did you like that, Jackie?"

"Oh, yes."

"Would you like more?"

"Please. Oh, please." Her pulse was loud enough for him to hear, and he placed one hand over her heart, feeling the vitality that rushed through her. He stared into her eyes, studying their depth and loving her as much as he ever had.

"Then kiss me." He opened his mouth and ran his tongue over both of his extended canines. Once again the blood started to flow. Jackie leaned forward and pressed her lips against his, opening her mouth wide. Kurt thrust forward with his tongue and felt her begin to suck again. With both hands freed, he started caressing her warm flesh through the fabric of her uniform, pulling her closer until she was laying atop him. She moved her legs and straddled him as his fingers pulled at the jacket on her back. They separated briefly, Jackie having to pause a moment and catch her breath. "I love you, Jackie. You know that, don't you?"

Jackie smiled down at him with crimson lips, leaning forward to kiss him again. "Of course I do, silly. I love you too." Again they locked themselves together, lost in passion for a time.

>€

The sun was close to rising when they finally reached Bexborough Manor. Even so, they returned to the temporary haven before the brutes working for Courtland Leighton finally managed to bring Ozmo in. The vampire was tall, with hair that jumped wildly from the top of his head and ran down to his shoulders in uneven spikes the same color as snow. His skin was equally pale, as if he hadn't consumed blood in some time. Despite a body all but designed for breaking other people's bones, Ozmo grinned nervously as he stared Kurt in the face. Kurt did not return the smile.

"Your name is Ozmo?"

"Yeah, well, I'm not Little Mary Sunshine, now am I? Cor, mate, what'd ya want wif me? I ain't done ya no 'arm now 'ave I?"

"Not that I'm aware of."

"Then let me go. Sun's up in anover 'arf an hour, an I'd just as soon not be 'angin' 'round ta greet it, if'n ya sees my point."

Kurt smiled then, a broad grin that made his acquaintance uneasy, at least if the mild dew of blood-sweat on his brow was any indication. "Oh, no, I'm afraid not. No, you'll be staying the night here."

Ozmo looked ready to bolt, but the men holding him were too strong. "The only question is whether to give you a room in here, or leave you in the trunk of my car. Which will it be, Ozmo?"

Ozmo opted to remain inside. Kurt let him.

⊰⊱

It was from darkness into darkness that the door in the Ching Parlor opened out, and Ilse led Carl through, fumbling about for a light switch and hoping that Malmsey House was modern enough to have one.

Her fingers only scrabbled along cold stone, but then a voice said, "Here now, I knew that door would open up sometime. Come, let's have a look at you."

Without a sound, six flames sprang up in the darkness, flickering brighter, the pools of radiance expanding to reveal six candles, then six skulls, then a woman sitting in the middle of them, her legs folded in the lotus position and her hands twisted into sacred muhdras. She crossed her arms once before her face, elbow over elbow, then threw them wide, muhdras coming undone in a grand flourish. All about the room candles flared into brilliance.

The glare was dazzling, but Ilse knew enough of the gestures to recognize a master of the Lure of Flame when she saw one, and so only had to shade her eyes with one hand. Carl sucked his teeth and murmured, "Hermetics would have a bloody fit if they saw me do something like that."

The woman unfolded her legs and came to her feet in a fluid motion, her long fuchsia hair almost brushing the candle flame as she bowed. "Welcome to London, blood of my blood and kin of my kin." She came back up, sweeping her hair back with one black-nailed hand, and took them in as they looked at her in turn.

The woman was Kindred, obviously, her aura pale with the

gray of pain and the blue of intellect, though to judge from her face, she had been taken only in her late twenties. She had a number of gold rings in one ear, and around her neck, sharply contrasting with the black of her sweater, was a magical monad, an elaborate sigil formed with gold wire, held by a silken cord the same color as her hair.

She reached to her belt, taking out a fencing foil with a sharpened tip, and made a quick salute, the blade hissing as it cut the air. She then lowered the point and, with two quick slashes, cut a door in the Hermetic circle in which she had been meditating. Swiftly she stepped through the gap, turning then, and with an even quicker stroke restored the sanctity of the circle, so that it once more lay unbroken on the earth of the floor. She saluted again, then sheathed the blade. "Pardon me, but I was not expecting you this evening."

"Expect the unexpected," said Carl, glancing about the room.

Ilse did as well, seeing the candles were set on shelves made of slate. Black and white wax pooled onto black stone, and the ceiling was low above them, only inches from Carl's head, while behind them was a smooth slate wall, like an old-fashioned blackboard, a door sketched in faded chalk, bleeding from the slight moisture in the air.

The woman with the fluorescent hair inclined her head. "This used to be the cold room, back when there was a need for one." She didn't explain any further, but then didn't need to. "I am the Guardian of the Gate, though you may know me as Sarah Cobbler. Welcome to Malmsey House and the Tremere of London. How may I know you?"

"You can know me as Carl Magnuson," the mage said. "That's the name in the phone book, and if I wanted to keep people from knowing it, it would take a whole load of bother, so I might as well tell you straight off."

Sarah Cobbler nodded, seeming to accept this, then looked to Ilse.

"You may know me as Ilse Decameron," Ilse said. "That is the name I have taken for myself since I became a member of this House. I am the childe of the Seven above me, though my direct sire is Houdini."

"Your fame proceeds you. I have seen your photographs and would be interested to learn your techniques."

Ilse placed one hand possessively about her camera. "It is a difficult Path to learn."

"Few things of value are easy to gain."

Sarah then seemed to relax, though her violet eyes still held the same somber expression, and it was clear that the time for formalities and pleasantries was over. "Listen, ducks, I'll tell it to you straight. London is in a bad way for the Tremere right now, though you probably knew that already." She looked directly at Carl.

He looked back at her blandly. "Sorry, love. I just joined up."

She paused. "Who is your sponsor?"

"Don't got one," Carl said, grinning. "I'm mortal."

It was to Sarah's credit, or perhaps a testimony to her willpower, that her only reaction was to raise an eyebrow. "A mortal of House Tremere?"

Carl nodded.

Sarah lowered her eyebrow. "I'll have to inform the Doctor of this. He'll be wanting to know." She paused. "I was going to say that the war's still on with the Ventrue, but it's gone cold for a spell, and we've officially got a truce. But if this doesn't throw a conker, I don't know what will. Come along." She took hold of an old green brass doorknob set in one of the more battered slate walls, opening the door out into what appeared to be an undercellar. "I'd best make you comfortable and ring the Doctor up."

Sarah took one of the white candles and held it aloft, leading the way through the cellar and up the stairs, going past a well-cared for and obviously well-used wrought-iron gate that Ilse could only assume led to the crypt. Their path led them through the wine cellar, the brewing room and chambers with bare shelves which had to have once been the greater and lesser pantries, until they went up another flight of stairs and emerged into the kitchen.

It was ancient, with huge butcher blocks and cooks' tables which had to go back centuries, but also with a few modern amenities, including a new stove, a microwave and three sparkling white refrigerators. Looking into the last of these was the most proper British butler Ilse had ever seen.

"Mr. Winthrop!" Sarah exclaimed, then quickly blew out the candle. "Thank the gods! Here, you see about getting these two set up in the drawing room. The lady's kin and so's the man, but he's mortal. And if you can figure that out, you've got one on me 'cause, love a duck, I'm going to have a time of it explaining *that* to the master." Sarah paused, then looked back at them, her expression once again serious and somber. "Pardon me, but I do leave you in capable hands. Mr. Winthrop will attend to your every need."

So saying, Sarah tossed the candle on a sideboard, then turned on her heel and rushed out of the room, her fencing foil clanking against the door on her way out.

Mr. Winthrop did not even raise an eyebrow at this, only quietly shut the refrigerator with one white-gloved hand and nodded to them. "It will be a pleasure serving you. How may I be of assistance?"

His voice was cultured, and more British than the Queen's — Elizabeth's, at least — and he looked quite a bit older as well, steel gray hair receding at the temples from a much lined face.

Carl didn't seem to appreciate any of this, though from his next comment, Ilse could see why. "You can tell me where the loo is. I've been hanging out with these Tremere blokes for half a day, and I think it's a safe bet that they don't use them."

Mr. Winthrop smiled, but only with sympathy. "You may use mine, sir. That green door at the far end of the kitchen." He gestured elegantly, and Carl dashed off towards it.

Well, at least that explained why the mage had been so testy of late. Ilse looked to Mr. Winthrop who gazed placidly back, giving her his full attention. "I'm just a bit thirsty. Would you..."

Mr. Winthrop put up a hand, signaling her to speak no more. "I must apologize, good lady, that we have no mortal vessels on hand to suit your needs. It is on the master's orders, due to recent unpleasantness in the city." He gave no additional explanation, but his tone turned even more regretful, apologizing yet further. "I am also sorry to say that my services do not extend so far as to serve in that capacity. However, we do have libations on hand to suit your need, delivered but hours ago from London General. Would that be sufficient?"

Ilse was bewildered by the elaborate courtesy and took a moment to figure out what he was saying. "Yes, of course."

Mr. Winthrop nodded, evidently pleased. "Excellent. Would Madame prefer her libations in a glass or the package from the hospital? Cool or warmed, and if so, to any particular temperature? And if I may be so bold, does Madame have any preference as to type?"

Ilse was almost as bewildered as before, but was becoming used to Mr. Winthrop's manner of speaking. "Warmed, in a glass, whatever else you think best."

"Excellent, Madame. Allow me to escort you to the drawing room, and I will return with your libations shortly. They will take a few minutes to warm in the *bain marie*, but I find that a much better way to heat the precious fluid than these new microwaves. I've been told they affect the flavor, but if Madame feels it necessary, I will use ours, though I do recommend against it."

"No, no trouble," Ilse said, then heard the flush from the green door at the end of the kitchen.

Mr. Winthrop remained expressionless, but said, "Perhaps we might wait a moment for the gentleman."

Carl came out a few seconds later, and Mr. Winthrop nodded to him, saying, "I was just about to escort the lady to the drawing room. If you would care to join us?"

Carl gave a longing glance to the refrigerator, and the corner of Mr. Winthrop's mouth quivered just a twitch. "I will be serving libations to the lady in the drawing room. If there is anything you might care for, you have but to ask. I was just about to prepare my own evening meal, but I could easily make enough for two. Would the gentleman be partial to medallions of pork sautéed with green peppercorns and marsala wine?"

"Sounds wonderful," Carl breathed. "I'm famished."

Mr. Winthrop bowed. "Then if you would be so good as to follow me."

He led the way out into the hall, holding the door open for them, then escorted them along the way, past a gallery with portraits of elegant lords and ladies, up a spiral staircase covered with red wool carpet woven with interlacing gold threads in the form of the monad Sarah wore around her neck, and through an archway into the drawing room.

The wallpaper was flocked with the same pattern, gold on gold, and the motif was picked up in the carved marble of the fireplace and the hand-done interlace around the edges of the ceiling, in the center of which was a fresco of the summer sky, the sun and its rays picked out in gold leaf in the middle. The furnishings were just as elegant and continued the theme, brocaded fabrics upholstering each chaise lounge and love seat and settee, cushions with the magical sigil embroidered in gold thread thrown in the corner of each. The tables were painted with idyllic springtime scenes, shepherds and shepherdesses, lords and ladies, all of them frolicking in the gold leaf sun.

Carl and Ilse took seats on the settee Mr. Winthrop indicated, and Ilse watched as the older man went silently to a black lacquer cabinet, retrieving a brandy snifter and a crystal decanter filled with pale gold liquid. He unstopped the flask, pouring enough into the glass to cover the bottom, then lifted it with his palm, swirling it once to release the fumes.

With an elaborate bow, he presented it to Carl. "Very special old pale, sir. There are a few casks in the undercellar which the master put by when he did more entertaining than he does now, and they have aged considerably. You should find the flavor exquisite."

Carl took the snifter, breathing deeply of the fumes, and Mr. Winthrop turned to Ilse. "If Madame finds the scent of cognac pleasing, I could fetch her a glass as well."

"No," Ilse said quickly, "we can share." She put her hand on Carl's, her fingertips resting on the glass.

"Very good," Mr. Winthrop said. "If the gentleman will allow me to take his coat, I will go see about preparing the rest of the refreshments."

Wordless, Carl let Mr. Winthrop take his overcoat, still folded across his arm, then once the butler had left the room, turned to Ilse and said, "My, you work fast."

Ilse felt a blush rising of its own accord, perhaps bidden by the fumes of the cognac. "I'm sorry. You remind me very much of someone I once knew." She paused, looking away. "He's dead now."

"Well, yes, so you said," Carl remarked, "but the question is, is he still around?"

She looked at him sharply, and he suddenly went a shade paler than normal. "I'm sorry, I didn't mean to be so flip about it. Here now, stop that," he said, brushing at her eyes. His fingers came away, stained with blood. He looked at them, mouth open, then handed her the cognac and took out his handkerchief, wiping them and handing it to her.

Ilse dabbed at her eyes, passing back the brandy snifter, and sat up straight, moving away from him. "I'm sorry."

"No need. That was very rude of me." He looked at her,

his odd eyes holding the same sad look Paul's had when he knew he'd hurt her. "This person I remind you of — the one with the eyes like mine — was he rude like that too?"

Ilse nodded. "Sometimes. He — Oh, I don't know." She wiped her eyes again, more of the blood coming. She realized she must look like Smudge, then laughed once nervously, and continued to cry.

Carl set his brandy snifter down on the table with a chime like a temple bell. "Here now, I'm sure it's not all that bad."

"Have you ever lost someone?"

"Well, not a lover, not like that, but yes, I can see what you mean." He looked at her seriously, mouth creased in a grimace of worry. "Here, if you'd like my drink, you can have it. It's rather good, but I'm not in the mood for it now."

He lifted the glass towards her, cupped in the palm of his hand, and she caught both, pulling them towards her. "Please, I need you to hold it. My hands can't warm the cognac."

"Well, love, you're not the first woman who's said that to me. Quite a few women with cold hands, so don't think it a problem."

Ilse just breathed deeply, savoring the rich, heady warmth of the cognac and the feel of his hand, warm beneath her own, both of which she could enjoy, so much so that she was quite giddy by the time Mr. Winthrop brought her vitæ and Carl's dinner.

"Here, love," Carl said, taking the brandy snifter away as she inhaled one last noseful, then in answer to her hands clutching after it, handed her the vitæ in a glass cup set in a lacy silver holder and handle.

Ilse giggled and took a sip, realizing but not caring that she'd become completely drunk on the cognac fumes.

"If there will be nothing else?" Mr. Winthrop asked.

"Nah, everything's just fine," Carl said, and Mr. Winthrop left as Carl began to attack his pork and peppercorns and whatever else composed the vile stew he'd ordered.

They were thus engaged when a man appeared in the doorway. He was of medium height and elegant build, with tousled brown hair and a beatnik's mustache and goatee, and dressed in an eighteenth century black velvet coat with matching knee-breeches, heavy lace cuffs and collar attached to the former, robin's egg blue silk stockings and black shoes with diamond buckles below the latter. He was just in the act of removing a voluminous, gold-lined black wraparound cloak and handing it to Mr. Winthrop.

"That will be all. We will ring if needed." His voice was old, very old, and colder than the grave.

Mr. Winthrop made a sharp, nodding bow and left. The gentleman in the Goth ensemble entered the room, followed by Sarah Cobbler, her prismacolor hair looking somewhat disheveled, as if she had just stood out in the rain for a moment and had not yet had a chance to fix it.

"Please, remain seated," the gentleman said, coming over by the settee and studying Carl intently, who gazed back at him. "Hmm, yes, definitely the look," the gentleman murmured, then reached out and placed a black velvet-gloved finger under Carl's chin, tilting the mage's head up to face him and turning it from side to side so as to gaze upon both eyes. "Definitely of the line...but mortal." He released Carl's chin and brought his hand up to his mouth, sniffing the fingertips, then putting out his tongue and tasting them, "And of the sub-line. Hmm, this complicates things badly."

"Are you going to check my teeth next?" Carl inquired, voice heavy with sarcasm.

The gentleman in black velvet paused, seeming to seriously consider the question, then shook his head. "No, I don't believe that will be necessary." He looked off into the air abstractedly. "Problematic. I'll have to revise my calculations. Most disturbing."

"What's disturbing?" Carl asked, at the same moment as Sarah rushed up to the gentleman in black and said, "Doctor, oughtn't you be introducing yourself?"

He looked at her blandly. "Why, Sarah? The man already knows who I am, and the woman will as soon as she recovers from Mr. Winthrop's cognac." He shrugged, sitting down on corner of the chaise lounge opposite them. "Why else would I have allowed you to accompany me to this audience?"

Sarah Cobbler seemed to realize that introductions were hers, whether she wanted them or not. "Doctor, these are Carl Magnuson and Ilse Decameron. Carl, Ilse, this the Doctor."

Carl snorted, "Huh, in that get-up he looks more like the Master." Sarah looked scandalized, but the Doctor ignored the remark entirely.

Sarah laughed nervously then, her accent going pure Cockney. "Well, Doctor, Master, h'it doesn't really matter which. This is the illustrious Dr. John Dee, who you've probably heard so much about."

"So where's the TARDIS?" Carl murmured.

Dr. Dee smiled slightly, which Ilse guessed was the closest he ever came to outright laughter, "'Time and Relative Dimensions in Space.' Amusing you should mention that," but explained himself no further.

"Do you 'ave h'any question for the Doctor?" Sarah asked.

Carl shrugged. "Did Queen Liz really have syphilis?"

"Of course not," Dr. Dee said. "Diseases are a modern invention. A toad made a nest of her hair while a demon lover ate away at her soul. She died of complications of both."

"Oh," Carl said.

Sarah beamed and leaned on the arm of the wingback chair next to her, and Ilse thought, *Score one for the Doctor*.

Dr. Dee gazed impassively at the two of them. "We haven't time for pleasantries or irrelevant questions. Great forces are at work, and we must prepare. I am aware of your mission, Carl Magnuson, and it is imperative that you return to the Order. We will assist you in every way possible. Sarah will work out the details." He looked directly at Carl as he said this last, and Sarah smiled, fingering her amulet.

The Doctor's eyes then turned to Ilse. "Directly after sunset tomorrow evening, you will take a cab to Bexborough Manor, where you will introduce yourself to Lady Anne and warn her that if you do not return to us safely before the end of the night, we will blow up Parliament. You will then return by magical means, as we do not wish this location compromised. Before and after that time, we will leave you to your own recognizance and judgment, deciding how best to assist the mage here and thereby House Tremere. Are there any questions?"

"Well, yes," Carl said. "What was that you meant earlier by me having 'the look'? And things being complicated by a sub-line? So far as I know, the only other bloke who's got eyes like mine is David Bowie, and I don't think we're related."

"Not in any significant manner, leastways," Dr. Dee replied. "We already investigated the Bowie possibility, but his eye came from an accident in childhood. Hardly the same thing. Your eyes, however, indicate something far deeper. The rites we must enact require a direct descendent of one of the Circle of Eight. Precisely who should become clear relatively soon, and the troublesome aspects of your ancestry will become inconsequential provided we take the right steps."

"What?" Carl asked.

Dr. Dee gazed upon him blandly. "You are better off not knowing, Carl Magnuson. Walls have ears, and you may better present our case to the Order of Hermes without being troubled by inconsequential details."

"Inconsequential? I like that! Here you go, dropping hints about bloodlines and family secrets, like something out of an Agatha Christie book, then add cryptic remarks about time and space. Next thing you know, I'm going to find I'm caught in some sort of remake of 'The Five Doctors'!"

Dr. Dee stood, murmuring to Sarah, "Ring for Winthrop," then to Carl said, "There are seven Doctors. Not counting myself."

Mr. Winthrop appeared in the door, Dr. Dee's black and gold cloak over his arm. The Doctor took it from him and threw it over his shoulders with a flourish. "Arrange for a cab to pick up the woman at a distance no less than five blocks away just after sunset tomorrow evening, assuming she's sober. Leave the man to his own devices. Sarah, come. We have much to discuss."

Sarah released the brocaded bell pull and followed, her Day-Glo hair, fencing foil and rumpled leather boots making a sharp contrast to the Doctor's elegant attire.

Mr. Winthrop nodded to Ilse and Carl, "You have but to ring if you have need of anything," then followed the master and lady of the house.

"My," Carl remarked, "the Doctor goes through companions quickly, but I'd never thought he'd take up with a punk vampire." He picked up his knife and fork and proceeded to cut another piece of pork medallion. "Especially after that silly episode with the giant space bat and the rocket ship."

He chewed for a moment, his odd eyes contemplative, then at last he swallowed. "Ah, well," Carl sighed. "I suppose it's part and parcel of being the seventh son of a seventh son. I should probably be thankful for not leading a boring life."

Ilse reached down and retrieved the brandy snifter, bringing it up to her nose and inhaling deeply. She suddenly felt a need to get very, very drunk.

Sunday, April 25, London — To Visit The Queen

Bexborough Manor was on the outskirts of London, but beyond that Ilse hadn't the faintest idea where she was going. That was probably all for the better; Ilse hadn't ever thought she'd be quite so glad to have the Iron Key as now.

The cab dropped her off, and Ilse gave the driver a handful of pound notes Sarah had given her, tipping heavily. Some Ventrue would no doubt intercept the cabbie and Dominate him into telling where he'd picked her up (at a club blocks from Malmsey House) but the last thing she wanted them to get was the impression that the Tremere were cheap. And anyone who had to deal with the Ventrue deserved something extra for his trouble. Fair was fair.

The manor house was one of those stately homes they kept renting out for BBC costume dramas, and it looked like the sort of place they'd give school tours during the day. For all Ilse knew, they did — it wasn't as if Lady Anne had any use for it then — and who knew, maybe one of her staff had a predilection for schoolboys or tourists. The Ventrue were like that, with their petty foibles about which blood they'd drink and which they wouldn't.

Ilse paused to adjust her gray silk dress and check her

earrings before starting up the steps, evening bag clutched in one hand. Mr. Winthrop had located them all in one of the numerous closets of Malmsey House, and after a touch of the iron and a spritz of Chanel, they were ready to wear, for all that they dated to the Thirties. Everything fit perfectly, except the shoes, and Ilse felt the tissue paper she'd stuffed in for padding scrunch annoyingly against the toes of her stockings.

She was positive someone was watching, despite the fact that the lights were turned out, but it was just like the Ventrue to keep someone waiting just for the pleasure of hearing the sound of their own door knocker. The knocker of Bexborough Manor was in the shape of a harpy, and with what Ilse had heard of Lady Anne, she wasn't sure if this was a conscious choice or just unintentional humor.

She toyed with her quizzing glass while she waited for the door to be opened. It might be an unusual necklace for a lady, more appropriate to a man's costume of the Regency period, but first and foremost it was a lens, the crystal a perfect mate in size and shape to the Monocle of Clarity attached to the camera in her purse. By crossing the Eye Spy charm with the discipline of Eagle's Sight, they were now linked by sympathetic resonance, and she could take pictures of whatever thirty-six items she pleased without having to change film or doing anything aside from fidgeting with her jewelry.

The door finally opened, and Ilse got to see the silhouette of a tall man, the light of the manor blinding behind him. The voice was so impeccably upper-crust British that she wouldn't have been able to understand it if she hadn't been expecting some words to the effect: "You must be the woman from the Tremere."

He said the clan's name as though it were some filthy social disease, and Ilse thought, *And you must be the obligatory snobbish Ventrue pig*, but only extended her hand in a ladylike fashion and said, "Why, yes. Ilse Decameron, at your service."

She half-expected him to say something like, "The servants' entrance is around the back," but he only avoided taking her hand and kissing it (for which Ilse was grateful) by opening the door wider and gesturing for her to come inside. "Please, come in. Lady Anne is expecting you. Courtland Leighton, Lady Anne's personal secretary."

Ilse slipped in, feeling the tissue paper shift inside the toe of her right shoe, and turned to take in Lady Anne's personal secretary as he shut the door.

Courtland Leighton appeared to be in his early thirties, dressed in an impeccably tailored blue suit, with skin pale as skim milk and hair gone shock white. His eyes were as gray as slate and just about as charming. She didn't even have to look at his aura to tell that he was Kindred, and he definitely didn't look the type to prey on tourists, so Ilse decided it was probably the schoolboys who were his preference. She twiddled her quizzing glass flirtatiously, snapping his picture, and felt the camera in her purse vibrate as it advanced a frame.

The Ventrue gave an expression of abject disdain and shuddered. "Let us not keep Lady Anne waiting," he said and proceeded down the hall. Ilse nearly had to jog to keep up. She felt the tissue paper trying to work its way out her shoes. Bastard.

The hall was long and grand, with suits of armor and pole arms and interesting curios in cases and a great many things that Ilse would rather have looked at than rush off to her appointment with Lady Anne. Then again, there were a great many things she'd have rather done than meet with the self-styled Queen of London. Visit the Nosferatu, for one. They might be ugly and smell bad, but at least they weren't condescending for no good reason, and besides that, they had information she actually wanted to know. For example, the identity of the Kindred in L.A. who'd been so intent on getting her camera before she'd flashed him and dumped a bowl of chowder on his head. She had a couple eight by ten color glossies of him in her purse, both with and without the chowder, and they were going to the first Nosferatu she found. If that didn't work, she'd just have to stick pins in them and have done with it.

Courtland Leighton unlocked an elaborate great door with more gold leaf on it than the entirety of Dr. Dee's drawing room. He stepped inside, barring her entrance with one arm, and announced, "Lady Anne, if it would please you, I have Miss Ilse Decameron of Clan Tremere. Shall I send her in?"

He still said the clan's name as if it were a social disease, and he'd badly mangled her own name too, but then with his thick accent it was probably impossible for him to pronounce anything apart from "Darjeeling" and "crumpet."

A pleasant female voice responded, "By all means, Courtland. Send her in."

Lady Anne's secretary put down his arm, and Ilse was able to enter the room and see the Queen of London herself.

The Queen was a slightly built woman, with curly, mouse-brown hair immaculately coifed and held in place with a diamond pin, matched by the brooch on her azure wool jacket. She sat in a grand throne at the end of the reception hall, the type of thing that probably had a tour guide during the day telling how it had been constructed by Duke something-or-other for Henry the VIII, for those times when the king wanted to take a relaxing day in the country, but still finish it off by kicking back in a throne and eating turkey drumsticks. King Henry had probably never made it out here, and the throne had never been used by any ruler of England, at least any mortal one.

Lady Anne sat back in it as if it had been made for her, but aside from her almost palpable regality, the most immediately apparent thing about the Queen of London was her eyes, which were blue as sapphires and piercing in their intensity.

Ilse lowered her own eyes and picked up the sides of her

skirt, dropping a low curtsy. The Red Queen's advice from *Through the Looking-Glass* came back to her: "Curtsy while you're thinking what to say. It saves time." Unfortunately, not much, for a moment later she was back up and locking eyes with the Queen of London.

Lady Anne smiled graciously. "Please, come closer, my dear. Let us see you. And allow us to offer you refreshments. After your long flight, you must be famished."

Ilse looked over to where Courtland stood by a high table with a full carafe of blood warming in a chafing dish. She took the Red Queen's advice again and curtsied a second time. "Thank you, Your Majesty, but I've just eaten."

Lady Anne raised her eyebrows. "You've already hunted in our fair city?"

Ilse curtsied a third time. "No, Your Majesty. I was greeted by Dr. Dee upon my arrival, and he offered me refreshments from his own supplies, preparatory to sending me here to meet with you."

Lady Anne nodded, running her fingers across the arm of her throne. "I see. Did the learned Doctor entrust you with any greetings for us?"

"After a fashion."

"Yes?" said Lady Anne, her blue eyes burning like sapphire flames.

Ilse dropped yet another curtsy. "Beg — Begging your pardon, Lady Anne, but there is no way to put this delicately."

Lady Anne smiled. "The good Doctor's sentiments are seldom delicate. You may convey them nonetheless."

"Yes, Your Majesty," Ilse said. "The Doctor told me to inform you that if I do not return unharmed this evening, he will consider it a declaration of war. And he will respond by blowing up Parliament."

Ilse heard Courtland Leighton gasp, but Lady Anne only continued to gaze at her mildly, then inquired, "In session or out of session?"

Ilse stared at the floor. "I'm sorry, he didn't specify."

"How very like the Doctor." Ilse heard the sound of the great lady rising from her throne, then the tap of her heels down the marble steps. "You may look up, dear. There's no need to scrutinize the masonry, and I seldom kill the messenger, at least not when that is the message."

"Thank you, Your Majesty."

"Think nothing of it." Lady Anne paced across the floor, her steps echoing in the great reception hall. "I do, however, have some other questions. Or, perhaps I should say, a representative of Clan Ventrue has some questions. Courtland, if you would be so kind as to bring in Mr. Westphal?"

Lady Anne's secretary nodded and went to the side door of the reception hall, opening it and ushering in a tall, handsome man with brush-cut brown hair and an impeccable black suit. Ilse blinked in amazement. When last she saw him, he'd been wearing a Polo shirt and a bowl of chowder, but there was no mistaking — it was the same Kindred from Malibu.

He smiled like a shark with porcelain-white teeth.

Lady Anne smiled as well. "I believe you two already know each other?"

The European Kindred by way of Malibu replied, "We've never been formally introduced."

Lady Anne continued to smile pleasantly. "Then give us the pleasure of introductions. Herr Westphal, this is Ilse Decameron, of Clan Tremere. Ilse, this is Kurt Westphal, Archon of Clan Ventrue, and childe of our Justicar, Democritus."

Ilse tried her best to smile and was surprised her teeth didn't break with the effort. "What an unexpected surprise."

"I'm certain it is." Kurt Westphal snapped. "Lady Anne, upon our last meeting, this Kindred violently attacked my person, causing me grievous bodily harm and loss of dignity. I demand satisfaction."

The Queen of London inclined her head. "This we may be able to grant, within reason."

"I'm certain I don't know what you're talking about," Ilse said and clutched her purse closer.

"You most certainly do, you witch!" Westphal's blue eyes blazed. "Only two nights ago in Malibu you seared my eyes and boiled my skin!"

"Oh, that," Ilse said, then turned to Lady Anne. "Your Majesty, the incident to which he refers occurred in Baron Fortier's demesne, both outside of your realm and the bounds of the Camarilla. But even so, I acted with regard to the laws of both, for the spot where this took place is one contested by the Lupines, and therefore most perilous for any breach of the Masquerade, and it was there I encountered Mr. Westphal. I must confess that I am shocked to find that he is a member of your clan, for I presumed he was some Malkavian or perhaps some foolish Kindred who had decided to let his hair down, as it were, heedless of the danger. But now that I am aware of his clan, I must assume that he was unaware of the peril of his location, and the fact that it is *de facto* Elysium, and had then partook of the wrong vessel and succumbed to a drug-induced frenzy. See, here is a picture taken while he was under the influence of whatever drugs were in his system."

Ilse undid the catch of her evening bag and took out the topmost of the two eight by ten color glossies. It was a lovely photograph showing Kurt Westphal with a crazed expression, arms raised and fangs bared, while in the background were a couple of shocked-looking women holding margaritas, part of a Cinzano umbrella and the neon fish from the end of the Gladstone's sign.

Ilse handed the photograph to Lady Anne and let the picture do the talking. The Queen of London surveyed it for a good minute, then passed it on to her clan's Archon. "Herr Westphal?"

He took it, and Ilse played her trump card. "After

witnessing that shocking spectacle, I wished of course to immediately preserve the Masquerade and so used the first thing that came to hand and a bit of magic. Unfortunately, while it worked to trip the waiter, the easiest thing with which to cover up Mr. Westphal's fangs was a loaf of bread which, as it turned out, was filled with hot chowder, in which case I must apologize for the burns he suffered, but I'm sure he will agree that any sacrifice is necessary when it comes to preserving the Masquerade."

Ilse took out the second photograph, showing him lying amid the spilled drinks and salads, the bread bowl and chowder obscuring his face.

Lady Anne surveyed it, then handed it on to the German. "Herr Westphal, do you agree with Miss Decameron's appraisal of the situation?"

"I do not!" he snarled, crushing the photographs with one hand. "The truth is that she flashed her camera at close range, causing me to frenzy momentarily from the light, and then she poured a bowl of hot soup over my face, causing me yet further pain and indignity."

Ilse did her best to look shocked. "But, sir, I'd never met you before. What reason could I have to so baselessly attack a fellow Kindred, and in such a perilous spot?"

Westphal seemed to realize she had him stymied. "You photographed me. I told you I objected."

"Yes," Ilse said, allowing the truth to finally come out, "and I offered to send you a copy of the picture and the frame from the negative."

Westphal grimaced, fangs showing. "You then represented yourself as a member of Clan Toreador."

Ilse smiled demurely. "I did nothing of the sort. I asked you what possible objection you might have to your picture being shown by Clan Toreador."

He continued to grimace, saying nothing, causing Lady Anne to look to him and prompt, "And then?"

"And then," Westphal ground out past his fangs, "I told her I objected to my photo being held by Clan Tremere, and when I attempted to take her camera, she flashed me in the eyes, causing my momentary lapse of reason."

Lady Anne glanced to Ilse, eyebrows raised. Ilse spoke in her own defense, "He attempted to steal my camera, and he so much as admitted to spying on me. I consider my reaction mild under the circumstances." She paused, still meeting Lady Anne's sapphire eyes. "As for the soup, I did do that to preserve the Masquerade, and Mr. Westphal's unlife. If I hadn't, he might have enjoyed sunrise in Malibu."

Westphal stared at her with murder in his eyes, then turned to Lady Anne. "Your judgment, Queen of our clan?"

Lady Anne looked very put out. "Our judgment is that we don't care to waste our time any further over petty bickering. You can take it up yourselves outside our chambers, and we've no doubt you will, but we consider the matter at a close. The Masquerade has been preserved, and that's all that matters. And you, Archon Westphal, we will caution to keep a tighter rein on your emotions, and you, Miss Decameron, we will advise to be less possessive of your toys and more forthright when dealing with the rulers of those cities you visit."

"What of the photographs?" Westphal asked. "I take exception to the Tremere having anything of mine."

"And well you should," said Lady Anne. "However, we're certain Miss Decameron has secreted the negatives in the Tremere's damnable chantry, so you shan't be getting them unless you negotiate." She looked to Ilse. "Is there anything you might do to assuage Mr. Westphal's worries?"

Ilse smiled as graciously as she could. "I will promise to take no actions against Mr. Westphal so long as he takes no actions against me." She turned to the German. "Why were you spying on me?"

He glanced about the room, apparently not wanting to meet her gaze, but then finally did. "You are under suspicion by Clan Ventrue, and I have been assigned to ascertain your actions as regards the well-being of my clan."

Lady Anne turned to Ilse. "And you, Miss Decameron? What business brings you to our fair city? Because, truth to tell, while we must respect Dr. Dee's vile threats, we have not yet decided whether we will allow you to remain in our fief. We have quite enough Tremere as it is." She grinned like a tigress. "So, what business do you have in London?"

Ilse tried to look as demure as possible. "Respectfully, Your Majesty, I cannot say, except insomuch that it concerns no clan but my own, and does not violate the Masquerade in any way."

Lady Anne pursed her lips. "We would like to believe that, but we must let Herr Westphal be the judge. You may remain in London, but so long as you do, Herr Westphal has our permission to observe you." She smiled and inclined her head. "And, Miss Decameron, you may convey this back to Dr. Dee: If, while you are staying here, anything untoward happens to Herr Westphal, *we* will consider that an act of war… and we will decide the appropriate response at our leisure."

The Ventrue bestowed picture-perfect smiles on her. Ilse closed her purse and tugged on her quizzing glass, snapping their picture. She was going to need all the ammo she could get.

"Thank you, Your Majesty, for your gracious audience. If you have nothing further to say, then I must beg my leave of you."

Lady Anne continued to smile. "Courtland will show you to the door."

❧

Unholy rage fairly described Kurt Westphal's attitude as he watched Ilse Decameron leaving the room, escorted by Courtland Leighton. Once again, he forced himself to remain calm; the woman was absolutely infuriating! He turned back to Lady Anne with a smile on his face that felt false even to him. "I really could learn to hate her."

Lady Anne returned the smile. "Now, Kurt, that is no way to talk about one of the clans of the Camarilla." Her wit was dry, typically British, but appreciated just the same.

"At least this time she is wearing civilized clothes."

"I should say so. That dress is as elegant today as it was when I last saw it on one of the Tremere back in the Thirties," she said. A devilish little grin turned up the corner of her mouth, making her look a decade younger that she normally appeared.

Kurt smiled in response and bowed gracefully from the waist. "Touché, Lady Anne. I'm afraid I must excuse myself. I have some unfinished business with the wretch brought into my custody last night."

"Be careful of Ozmo," she warned. "He can be very useful for gathering information, but he can also be a nuisance if you offend him too heavily."

"Rest assured, dear lady, he hasn't the least chance of causing me trouble."

He turned sharply on one heel and left the room, heading down to where his guest had spent the night. Long before he reached the reinforced steel door that barred the Malkavian's exit, he could hear the madman screaming.

"You bloody, fucking bastards better let me out of 'ere soon, dammit! I've got places to go and people to see! I'm a bloody important man in this city!"

Jackie was standing outside of the room, along with one of Lady Anne's bodyguards. They both looked amused by the raving on the other side of the door. "Hello, Mr. Westphal. I'm afraid your visitor is getting a touch upset about his accommodations. One might think he was suffering from P.M.S. the way he's going on."

"I 'eard that you snotty little tart! I'll bleed you like a damned juicin' machine if you don't let me out o' 'ere! I'll…"

"Oh, do shut up, Ozmo," Kurt called. I want to ask you some questions. Afterwards, you're free to go."

"'Oo the fuck do you think you are, you soddin' bastard! Oi've got friends, y'know! I can make your life shit if you don't ease this 'ere door open and leave me t' my business!"

Kurt gestured for the guard to open the door. The guard nodded and flipped the dead-bolt, stepping aside as Ozmo threw the door wide. The Malkavian stepped out of the cell, his pale face breaking into a vicious grin, and started rooster-strutting out into the hallway. Jackie and her new acquaintance both leveled automatic weapons in his direction. Ozmo's smile grew even more savage. "Well, look a' that. You've got yourself some little friends to help wif keepin' me stowed away."

Kurt increased the wattage on his own smile by a few thousand volts and stepped forward, one hand blocking the Malkavian's attempts at slipping past. "Calm yourself."

Ozmo spit in Kurt's face from less than a foot distant. The guard looked ready to step forward, but Jackie placed a hand on his arm and shook her head. Her face was set like stone as she took a step back.

Kurt calmly removed the silk handkerchief from his breast pocket and wiped the bloody phlegm from his cheek. "That was stupid of you." He took a long step forward at the same time that he lifted Ozmo off the ground and hurled him back into the room he'd just vacated. Ozmo slammed hard against the far wall, and the sound of something breaking inside of him was like a pistol shot in the sudden silence.

"Christ! 'Ave you lost your bloody mind?" Ozmo started standing again, and Kurt walked into the cell.

"Not at all. But we are going to have a discussion now, and you are going to answer my questions."

"An' wot if I don't feel like it, mate? Wot then?"

"This can end one of two ways, Ozmo. You can tell me what I want to know and leave here a wealthier man, or you can continue acting like a damned Brujah and I can leave you staked for the morning's light."

Ozmo never missed a beat. "Just 'ow wealthy a man would I be if I cooperated then?"

"That depends on how well you answer my questions. If you are a good boy, I could arrange ten thousand pounds for you."

"Cor, mate! Why din't ya just say so from the beginning?"

"You never gave me the opportunity to say much of anything."

Ozmo frowned. "Yeah, there is that, I s'pose." Then he grinned again, a much more cordial smile. "What is it you want to know about?"

"Who in this town wants to hurt me?"

"Well, I did, until about three seconds ago. But other than me, I don't know of anyone." The Malkavian sat back on the hard bed that was the only furniture in the small room. "Nope. That's it, mate. Cept maybe for the little bimbo coming in to see the Tremere."

"Ilse Decameron?"

"Yeah. That's 'er. Nice little number from wot I've 'eard."

"How did you know she was coming into town?"

"Oi've got me ways."

"Is there someone after her?"

"After the witchy-girl? I dunno. Maybe." The lunatic wasn't very good at hiding his feelings, and Kurt stared at him for a second longer before he started growing impatient.

"Who's after her?"

"'Old on, old boy. Incoming fax, as it were." With that, the man slumped back in his seat, a grin on his face and his eyes closed as if in deep contemplation.

"What are you—?"

"Shut up a minute then! I told you I was receiving somefing now didn't I?" Ozmo waved frantically for him to be silent and then leaned back on the bed for a moment. Kurt resisted the urge to jump up and land on the man's chest only through a serious effort. "Yeah, I got your information, ifn you really want it."

"I want it. Talk to me."

"Well, I just had a nice little conversation wif me sire. 'Ee's got a lot on the ball, our Mistah Crowley does. 'Ee says the bully boys want to have a little party wif the little tight-ass."

"Why? What's she done to them?" Kurt leaned forward, hoping for the news that the chowder-throwing little miscreant was about to be revealed for crimes against the Camarilla. Petty, yes, but he wanted to watch her squirm after the last two times they'd met.

Ozmo started laughing at him as if he'd overlooked the obvious. "'Ss'not what she's done, boo-bah-lah. It's what Dr. Dee said earlier, ennit?"

Kurt reached forward and grabbed the man by his collar, lifting him half off the bed and lowering his voice. The Malkavian seemed to be rethinking his strategy in consideration of Kurt's new impatience. "Talk. Now. Or die."

"'S'all right now. Calm yerself down, mate." Ozmo's voice was shaking, but otherwise there wasn't much to show that he was afraid. Kurt was grateful for his ability to inspire fear or friendship in others. "Lady Annie said it a while ago, and I just now 'eard of it. If the bimbo don't show up intact, Parliament goes up in a beautiful ball o' fire." Kurt knew enough of Dr. Dee's history to believe the man would do it too, if only to save face. Whatever truce existed at the present time would be over, and the Ventrue and Tremere would be at war on a grand scale. Kurt didn't think the fiefdom could remain in Lady Anne's hands in such a situation; her grip on the city was too shaky for that.

Kurt grew cold, the implications of such an act reaching deep and freezing him solid. "The Brujah would do that?"

"'Ell, yes! They don't like neither of your clans, and Appolonius ain't liked Lady Anne since the first time they met. Calls 'er a 'frigid little trollop,' 'ee does."

"Where is she?"

"'Ow the bloody 'ell should I know? I don't go consortin' wif witchy trash."

"All right. One more question and you're free to go."

"'Bout bloody damn time, too. I've got a date wif the Wilkershire triplets, don't I? You can bloody bet I do."

"Where does Appolonius hang out?"

"Where else are you going ta find a whole bloody 'erd of arseholes wif bad attitudes in this town? Aside from Parliament, I mean. Soho. That's the place you'll be wanting ta scope out. Appolonius is quite fond o' that little section o' the city. 'Ee likes to 'ang wif the real serious punkers. Besides, I 'eard she'd be headin' that way."

"How could you have heard about any such thing?"

"Oi've got me ways, mate. Oi've got me ways."

Kurt stormed away from the room, pausing only long enough to throw a large wad of cash at the maniac on the bed. He ignored Ozmo's last comments as he and Jackie ran for the staircase. "Pleasure doing business wif the likes of you and all that shit. But next time call first, you arsehole!"

Minutes later, the limousine pulled away from Bexborough Manor just as the Bentley Ilse Decameron had left in was returning. Jackie waved the vehicle over, pausing long enough to learn where the driver had dropped Ilse Decameron, and the fastest way to get there. Kurt looked at his watch and hoped they wouldn't be too late.

Thirty minutes later, they finally reached the Soho district. Kurt had thought he understood just how seedy a town could get, but Soho made even the worst parts of Berlin seem tranquil. Here, the people walked through the center of the streets, crossing over to other locations with a total disregard for the traffic trying to move along. Worse yet, the stripped remains of several other vehicles blocked access to most of the parking spaces and even entered into the roads proper. Kurt had no doubt that Uriah Winter would feel completely at home in this stretch of London.

Jackie was constantly edging the too wide limo down the narrow street, often bumping the pedestrians who moved along the road in the process. Despite constant insults and hand-gestures thrown at them, no one ever took offense from her actions. Most of the people on the streets were too wasted on drugs, booze or lack of sleep to really care.

Jackie slammed her hand onto the horn for the twelfth time in five minutes and finally looked over at Kurt through the rear-view mirror. "We'll never find her in time if we don't just walk, Kurt. And we probably won't be able to see her from the road anyway. Not if she's in one of the clubs." She had the tone of voice that made it clear she was expecting an argument from him. He decided to listen to her, because she'd grown up in areas just like this one and he knew better than to think she'd lead him astray.

"Well, then, let's start walking." He opened his own door, standing up quickly and slamming it shut even as Jackie was climbing from the driver's seat. "May as well lock the car, for all the good it will do us."

"Hey, it's a rental. We can afford the loss. I always buy insurance on these things."

"True. Just the same, it was a comfortable ride."

Kurt stood and stared at the Soho's barrage of bizarre denizens before Jackie tapped him on the arm to get him moving. He followed her, too stunned by the strange and often gender-confused people of Soho to worry about appearance. One look at his clothes had half the scavengers of the area wanting to try their luck, but again his ability to invoke emotions kept them away, and Kurt enjoyed watching predator and prey alike scurry away like an army of rats. He finally managed to catch up with Jackie just as she turned the corner at the end of the block. He knew in his heart that he'd never see the limousine intact again.

Half a block down the way, a line of humans waited to get into a trashy dive playing music so loud that it carried all the way to where he was standing. Jackie had come to a complete stop and was gesturing for him to do the same. "What is it?"

"You said Decameron was wearing a gray dress?"

"Yes."

"I think she just got herself in trouble." She pointed down to an alley entrance just past the long lines of humans waiting to enter the club and indicated a large group of very angry-looking people. They were following a woman who moved too swiftly to be anything but a Kindred, rushing down the mouth of the alley with unnatural speed and grace. "There, she just went around the side of the building."

Kurt smiled. "I would guess that you are right. I do not like the odds, however."

"Should I get the heavy artillery?"

"Just the close-range specialty items."

"You get the ring, I get the knife?"

"Of course, dear. You know I hate knives."

Jackie handed him a silvery ring from one of her jacket pockets and two extra clips of bullets for his .44 magnum as well. "All set?"

"Yes, but I think we should try to head them off at the pass, as your Westerns like to say." Kurt pointed to a rusty and treacherous-looking fire escape that ran up the side of the club. The ladder was up a good ten feet, but he wasn't exactly worried about so minor a detail. On a bad night he could clear twenty feet from a standing jump, and he knew Jackie could do the same. "There, the fire escape. Let's go for the high ground."

➤◆

Courtland insisted on her taking the Bentley, which had smoked windows, leather seats, and, thoughtfully, a cellular phone and a chilled bag of blood. These last two items, Ilse was certain, were bugged and drugged, respectively. The chauffeur had of course asked her where she would like to go, and Ilse had told him to take her to the club district, Soho in particular, where she planned to be meeting someone.

Once the car stopped, she wished she'd known more about London and had picked somewhere a little more upscale to meet with her mythical contact. So far as she knew, Soho was just a place you could get lost, which was what she required for the Rite of the Iron Key. Now that she could see Soho firsthand, she knew it was a *bad* place to get lost and an easy place to disappear. Not that she hadn't been in places like it before, but if she'd known, she'd have worn the uniform and had leather and chains and more zippers than she knew what to do with. Looking out the window of the Bentley, Ilse knew she'd come to the birthplace of punk, and judging by the sneers on the young faces looking at the Ventrue's ever so aristocratic, hoity-toity classic car, the residents were as uptight as only the orthodox heirs to the punk movement could be.

Gray silk tea dresses were right out.

About the only thing Ilse had that fit the mood of the place were her cigarettes, so when she got out of the car, she struck a pose, lighting one up and trying to look like an eccentric *film noire* groupie, instead of just a frightened vampire from out of town.

"Well lah-di-dah," said a voice as Ilse lit her cigarette, closing her eyes against the glare. "Look 'oos dropped in to pay us a visit. I think h'it's Lady Di."

"Will there be anything else, Madame?" asked the chauffeur, who, in spite of being a hulking Blood Bound Ventrue ghoul, still showed a trace of anxiety at being in the middle of Soho after midnight on a Sunday night.

Yeah, I wish you'd get the hell out of here. You're making me stick out like a sore thumb, Ilse thought, but only blew cigarette smoke in his direction and said, "No, thank you. That will be all."

and the next six from a red-haired girl standing in the shadows only inches behind Ilse. The five notes that began the next phrase came from a punk in a blue military beret, surrounded by a similarly clad gang of young men in berets and steel-toed Docs, two more notes from a girl with a hot pink mohawk coming from her place at the end of the bar, two more from a young woman in whiteface with an inverted anarchy symbol on her forehead just leaving her place at the center table, one from the redhead in the shadows, and the final six from Appolonius himself, looking directly at her with his smoked glasses and jauntily bobbing his head from side to side.

*...whatever you got to fear...*Ilse filled in the final words of the verse, Appolonius' notes.

"These are my mates," Appolonius said, and Ilse realized that under the Cockney punk, she could hear a faint French accent. "Bianca." He gestured to the girl in whiteface, "Angel" — the pink mohawk — "and Dre."

The man in the military beret snarled, showing a quick flash of fangs, and Appolonius smiled. "And his mates, the Cold Dawn."

Dre subsided, his crew acknowledged, and then the red-haired woman slipped out the shadows, trading them for the one behind Appolonius. She placed a hand on his arm, peering demurely out at Ilse from behind it, In the next second there was a *snick!* sound, and a blade appeared in her hand, the cutting edge just over Appolonius' mail patch.

He moved his head slightly. "And Black Cat." Her switchblade disappeared as fast as a cat would sheath her claws, and Ilse saw the tattoo on the woman's arm, a witch's cat in silhouette, back arched and hissing. The woman smiled faintly, the rings in her nose and her eyebrow twitching like feline whiskers.

Angel, the pink mohawk, came forward, a Celtic cross swinging from her right ear. "Pretty," she said with an Irish lilt. "Always wanted a dress like this." She reached out and lifted one of the folds of Ilse's gown, feeling the material between thumb and forefinger.

"Don't be seduced by material wealth," said Dre, and the pack of young men around him mimicked his expression.

"Don't fault others for having it," said Bianca. Beneath the whiteface and the anarchist symbol, her voice and bearing were cultured and aristocratic.

Black Cat said nothing, only watching from Appolonius' shadow, but had somehow switched to the other side.

"Now I like this," Angel said, and quick as thought, she snatched Ilse's quizzing glass and had the chain over her head before Ilse could even blink. Celerity — the girl had used the Brujah gift of vampiric speed. "Look at me," she said, twirling about, her black skirts flying in an arc. "I'm a lady."

Angel held the quizzing glass to her eye and peered at Ilse, then Appolonius, Cat, Bianca, and finally Dre and his gang. Ilse felt her purse vibrate under her arm, the camera advancing frame after frame.

The punk girl leaned over comically, one leg coming up over her back in a dancer's arch, and examined Dre like a Sherlock Holmes ballerina until he snarled, "Get that thing out of my face, or I'll make you eat it!" The camera whirred in Ilse's purse, taking a lovely portrait of Dre and his enraged aura.

Angel spun back to earth, laughing, and Bianca looked at her, hands on hips. "You realize that glass is a man's toy, don't you?"

Angel smiled. "If it's a man's toy, then I like it all the more." She put the chain around her neck, letting the quizzing glass tangle with the two pendants and beads she already had in place.

"Ladies," Appolonius said, "don't steal the moment from Cat. She found it all out."

"She disappears," Dre said, looking to Ilse, "and the witches kill the riches."

"Like the Kilkenny cats," Angel said.

Bianca leaned back, resting her arms on a chair, letting her silk jacket fall open to reveal a black lace bra and nothing else. "More for us."

Black Cat said nothing, only giving her ghost of a smile from Appolonius' shadow.

Ilse knew that whatever move she made, they could make faster. Angel had proven it already, and Ilse suspected the mohawked girl was the youngest of them. She knew they could have killed her already, but the Brujah had a perverse sense of honor, and, as Appolonius had said, it was Black Cat's moment. And she wanted to toy with Ilse.

If the woman wanted toys, she could have them. Slowly, with the faintest of the Movements of the Mind, Ilse unclasped her purse, then reached inside with her thoughts, searching for her flash cubes. Glass and plastic and bits of tungsten and magnesium, soaked in blood and left to dry in the sun of midsummer high atop an office tower in Phoenix, built on the ruins of an ancient Hohoken holy spot.

It was the timing that was crucial. Carefully, Ilse let them nudge open the flap of the evening bag. A moment later, they streaked out to hang suspended in the midst of the group, winking and twinkling in the dim light of the bar like three crystal eyes.

Ilse dove for the floor behind Appolonius and Cat as she willed the cubes to give up their flash. All summer in an instant, each cube twirled, exploding in a brilliant burst of sunlight.

The Brujah screamed, their skin searing in agony, far worse than what her mundane flash had done to that annoying Blue Blood, and she cried out herself as she felt her left leg catch fire through her stocking.

Ilse dashed for the door, one shoe flying free with its tissue paper, only to find her way blocked by Black Cat, the woman untouched, having hidden safely in the shadows. "Run, little mouse," said the Brujah in a voice both purring and husky. "We will hunt!"

Ilse was willing to take what gifts were given her and dashed out the door as Black Cat stepped aside, rushing into the street and looking all about. If she could only find a lost place and elude her pursuers for but an instant, she would be safe.

The Iron Key flew out of her purse at a touch of her mind, and Ilse dashed down the street, turning right into an alley, the way lit by the dying flames on her leg. She grasped the talisman in her right hand and gouged her thumb onto the rusty spur, glancing back once.

Black Cat stood at the mouth of the alley, smiling her suggestion of a smile, but moving no further. Behind her, the Cold Dawn arrived, and Ilse realized they were all mortal, all with matching jackets, Doc Martens and chains. Black Cat pointed, her switchblade flashing out like a single claw. "We hunt!"

Ilse dashed down the alley and rounded into a side alley, dodging a dumpster as the sound of a gang of steel-toed Doc Marten's pounded down the cobblestones after her, along with a far more deadly, silent tread she knew she'd never hear.

It was a dead-end alley, but off to one side was a doorway in shadow, heavily recessed. If she could just get to it and use her Key, the Rite would take her safely away to the House of Shadows. She prayed that Cat would want to play just another moment, hoping to find Ilse boxed in, hiding and cowering in the alcove.

The key slicked with blood, Ilse tried to fit it into the rusted iron padlock that chained the doors together. It wouldn't go she wasn't lost by lost ways. Someone, somewhere, knew where she was.

"Thank goodness we found you," said a voice, and the next thing she knew, Kurt Westphal rushed out of the shadows on the other side of the alleyway, along with a tall woman with a chauffeur's cap and a gun.

The Ventrue leapt into the doorway next to her, a classic James Bond stance, readying an elegant chromed pistol, then glanced around the corner of the brickwork. "Another moment and you would have been lost, Fräulein *Ilse*."

"Cut the heroics and get ready to shoot!" snapped the woman, leveling her Saturday night special down the alleyway.

If she'd have been lost another moment, she'd have been saved. Ilse felt the bloody key slip from her fingers, the charm broken, and she fumbled for it, cursing them both.

As she did so, she looked out of the archway and saw Black Cat, staring at her round the corner of the dumpster, her green eyes glowing in the moonlight. At end of the alleyway, the Cold Dawn were crouched with military precision, their assault rifles ready, Westphal and his chauffeur hopelessly outgunned.

Black Cat flashed Ilse her enigmatic smile. "Both mice in the trap," she said. "Fun."

➤◄

"My Fräulein, I see that you manage to make interesting friends wherever you go, don't you?" Kurt watched the hoodlums getting closer and felt a desperate need to vacate the premises as soon as possible. Just the same, all points of access seemed properly blocked.

The gang members dropped themselves into every nook and cranny of the alley, blocking all but small portions of their bodies from attack. Simultaneously, they blocked the only easy way out of the alley. Taking one look at the automatic rifles they'd produced since when he and Jackie had seen them entering the alley, Kurt started having second thoughts about helping the Tremere standing slightly behind him.

The woman (Kindred most likely) who was apparently in charge of the group of ruffians slid forward and grinned. "Would the mice like to play or just beg for mercy?"

"Would the tattooed hooker like to kiss my ass?" Jackie was, if nothing else, eloquent in her own way.

The cat-like woman, however, didn't seem to like Jackie's attitude and rushed towards her with blinding speed. That cemented it — she was either Kindred or a ghoul, and as Kurt preferred to over-estimate an opponents flaws, he was willing to bet on Kindred. Jackie and the feline vampire both fell into the shadows, propelled by the force of the wild woman's impact. The street gang turned to look, and Kurt saw his chance to move. Ilse Decameron apparently had the same idea. He had no idea what she did, save murmur a few words under her breath, but even as he was firing his .44 magnum, one of the thugs started screaming, his skin turning a hideous shade of red and steam rising from his body as blood boiled from his mouth and nose.

Kurt fired five times, hitting one of the paramilitary punkers before they remembered to turn and face their enemies. The fourth bullet he fired struck a gang-banger looking right at him, tearing through his kneecap. The man screamed, but managed to turn his rifle towards Kurt and fire, even as he was falling.

Bullets slammed into Kurt with hideous force, tearing through his jacket and clothes as if they weren't even there and pounding into his torso and ribcage. The lead slugs crashed against his skin, folding and spreading themselves in the impact, but not breaking through to his insides. The bullets stopped abruptly as the woman beside him pointed her finger at the man firing and chanted softly, "Bubble, bubble, toil and trouble. Fire burn and cauldron bubble." For the second time, one of their enemies started roasting from the inside, thrashing on the ground and screeching in agony.

Jackie was hurled from the shadows, her lovely face bloodied, her uniform ripped half away from her body. She was conscious and fuming. She carried the Sengir Dagger, a large, ornately carved artifact, the bloodstained blade a good foot long. Speeding out of the shadows after her came the Brujah woman, her left side sliced open by the ancient weapon in Jackie's hand. Both had apparently had easier battles in the past. "Come on, bitch! I'll tear your fucking heart out!" Jackie's inner-city accent had crept back into her voice as she spoke, a sure sign that she was royally pissed-off.

The Brujah did not speak, only hissed like a scalded cat. Kurt fired three times at the woman, but she literally weaned and bobbed around the bullets' paths, intent only on her target. Once again the two met in combat, but Jackie's injuries were obviously slowing her more than the wounds her opponent had received. The creature slashed out with her hands, and the dagger flipped away, landing in the litter-strewn shadows.

Kurt wanted to go to her aid a second time — for all the difference his first attempt had made — but there were still too many of the bullies left with weapons in their hands, and he didn't know how long he could last against the constant barrage of firepower. Even with his supernaturally tough skin, the bullets hurt when they hit him, and he was certain a few ribs had been broken. He fired again as the remaining punks got into position and cut loose with their rifles. One of them was lifted from the ground and smashed into the alley wall as another lost a portion of his head to Kurt's shot. The front of his jacket literally shredded into cloth confetti as more bullets pounded into him, and beside him the Tremere cried out. Kurt cried out too, pain and rage driving him forward as the firing pin in his pistol clicked repeatedly against the empty chamber inside.

A few of the thugs, seeing him stride forward through a hail of bullets, lost their resolve and formation, running from his infernal pursuit as if he were the Devil himself. Those of stronger will continued firing, and Kurt felt the constant agonies of more lead slugs pounding into him. He distantly heard the sound of Jackie crying out, and the woman she was fighting screaming in pain at the same time. He was beyond caring as the pain he endured drove him into frenzy. Every remaining weapon was focused on him, and he felt more bones crack, felt his skin splitting in a few places, even as the vampiric healing factor started reknitting bone and sealing the wounds. One of the men before him screamed as his flesh caught fire, and Kurt in his frenzy lashed out, snapping the man's neck and scalding himself in the process.

Down the alley, a group of shadows ran forward, moving as quickly as the cat-woman doing battle with Jackie. Faster by far than could be humanly possible. Brujah. A wall of flame erupted between the incoming Kindred and Kurt, cutting of the offending gang's cavalry before they could intervene. The remaining hoodlums broke rank, trying to get past Kurt without being struck. Most succeeded, but one man managed only to end his life, screaming as Kurt tore out his throat and started drinking, the blood refreshing him and allowing him to heal still more of the substantial wounds he'd suffered. The sweet red vitæ became all that he knew for a few seconds, until finally he could see and hear again. See the lifeless corpse he held in his arms and hear the sound of applause from behind him.

Kurt whirled around, dropping the husk of his enemy, and stared at the people in the alley, confused by the increase in numbers. Five pale men stood in the litter-strewn area, aside from himself, the Brujah and Ilse Decameron. Ilse lay staked in the arms of one of them, a brute of a man with wild hair and a torn straightjacket as his only clothing. The wooden stake driven through her chest explained very eloquently that she would no longer be of assistance in the battle. The female Brujah lay motionless on the ground next to Jackie, whose wounds looked grievous indeed. Jackie held the dagger in her hand again and was licking the blade, obviously in need of life-sustaining blood. The other four Kindred stood applauding Kurt, grinning with bared fangs and different degrees of enthusiasm. Kurt recognized Ozmo immediately.

"Ozmo—"

"'Ello, Mistah Ventrue." Ozmo's voice was filled with glee as he pointed to the stocky man beside him. "This is me mate, Aleister Crowley." He looked at the others around him. "Bugger the rest, they're just along for the ride." The vampires with Ozmo all laughed at his little joke, but Kurt found nothing amusing about the situation. "Can you guess who gets to play the horsie?"

Kurt knew right away, but just to make certain he understood, Ozmo and two of the others ran forward, waving the wooden stakes in their hands and grinning evilly. Kurt felt the stake punch into his heart at the same time another was driven through his left kidney, and a third tore through his leg. His efforts to fight back were useless. As the vision started leaving his eyes, he thought he saw a purplish face peering down from the top of one of the buildings.

Charnas. The imp had been watching the whole thing.

Monday, April 26, London — Mad Dogs and Englishmen

Ilse awoke to darkness, a smell like old cinnamon and cloves...and the chill touch of manacles around her wrists, holding them flat to the wall on either side of her head. She tried to move, but then felt a third metal band digging into her waist, separated only by the thin silk of the tea dress and forcing her into a seated position on the cold, stone floor. She heard a bolt rattle as she tried to twist her way out, but it was no use, and cold metal cut into her ankles as well, pinning them down, her legs numb with the chill. At least she was no longer staked. She might be clapped in irons, but it was better than being paralyzed.

Ilse peered about. Nothing but blackness, and echoing silence. Then, from beside her, she heard a sharp grunt and a rattle of chain. "*Verdammt...*"

She recognized the snarl — Kurt Westphal, the Ventrue Archon.

Ilse froze, remembering how much he hated her, then paused. She was lost, forgotten in darkness, and the man who'd spoiled her last invocation of the Iron Key sat beside her, but as far as she could tell, hadn't noticed her yet.

It would be a stretch for the charm, but chains had locks,

and locks had keyholes, and keyholes took keys. She cast about with her mind, searching for her talisman, then felt pain lance through her left wrist. Cold, colder than the grave, cold as ice in midwinter, it knifed into her lifeblood and sent a chill dagger shooting into her heart, paralyzing her with the pain of its touch.

A moment later, it melted, and Ilse was left with only the memory of pain and the knowledge that it had stabbed at her through the thread of her magic. She didn't know what ritual had created the manacle, but the ward blocked her Thaumaturgy even more effectively than had the stake through her heart or the hours of daylight.

Ilse leaned her head back, trying to let her eyes adjust. It was dark as a tomb and just as silent except for the dead man next to her straining against his chains and cursing softly in German. But Westphal was not truly dead, for he still had a soul, as did she, and even though the light of the souls of the Damned was weak and sickly, their faded glow was still more than nothing.

Ilse turned to the lesser powers, hoping the discipline of Auspex might work where the greater magics of Thaumaturgy did not. She steeled herself for the knife of pain and ice, but it never came, and Ilse was able to extend her perceptions, the wan light of their souls to expanding to light the room.

The chamber snapped into focus at once, and it was as if she were seeing the world through high-resolution infrared goggles. Everything was washed in blood on blood, painted in shades of crimson and brown like an illuminated manuscript from the Burning Times, a cavernous room filled with slabs and boxes and huge hanging chains and metal hooks. And there, in the center of her field of vision, was the source of the red light, the egg-shaped sphere of another soul's aura, painted crimson with lust, spotted brown with old hatred, streaked black with the marks of sin, and sparkling with the power of magic. And all these tints swirled in the hypnotic spiral of psychosis, the colors marbling the walls of the chamber with the ever-changing patterns of a magic lantern.

Ilse closed her eyes, allowing her Auspex to dim, then opened them again, peering closely. Within the monstrous aura was a man, tall and heavy-set, his face bloated and dissolute but his eyes regal as an emperor's. He was dressed in long robes which might have once been white, but were now stained with blood or by his aura, Ilse wasn't sure which. It probably didn't matter. Beneath the bloodstains, the vestments were embroidered in gold with the paths of the Qlippoth — the dark reflection of the Kabbala — and the base Chakras of Hindu mysticism, while atop his head, he wore a mitered cap, edged in gold and worked with Hebrew letters trimmed in precious jewels. In one hand he held a crosier, a bishop's staff, though where the cross or crook would usually be at the top, there was instead a Shiva lingam, overflowing with the energy of the Kundalini. The man locked eyes with Ilse and smiled. "Ah, Miss Decameron. You're awake." His voice was cultured, distinguished as an Oxford don's. "It is always pleasant to be gazed on appreciatively by an attractive young woman."

"Where are you, Crowley?" Kurt Westphal snarled beside her. "Show yourself!"

"You will address me as Master Therion, Mr. Westphal." Crowley stood there and continued to smile, absently caressing the shaft of his wand of power. "And please, don't distress yourself. You will see me soon enough."

Westphal growled, but seemed to gain control of himself, and Ilse looked over at him by the light of the madman's aura. He was less securely bound than she was, manacled to four chains secured to a ring at the base of the wall, instead of having shackles pinning him directly to the stone. But he also looked much worse for the wear than she felt, with that slightly glazed expression that Kindred got when they were starved for blood after succumbing to frenzy. Ilse mentally measured the length of his chain and was not sure whether she was grateful that it was just beyond the reach of where she sat.

Crowley paced forward, tapping out his stride with the base of his staff, the iron foot striking sparks from the granite floor, then stopped just inches shy of Westphal's forward reach. "Please, Mr. Westphal. You are in my temple of Aiwass — 'Do What Thou Wilt Shall Be the Whole of the Law.' Your aura is positively sick with worry, and yet you cannot bring yourself to ask about your woman or her state of health. Whatever might the trouble be?"

The German said nothing, and Crowley continued to smile. "It's not as if you didn't see her, Mr. Westphal, or perhaps I should say, gaze upon her, for I believe your eyes were open the entire time, and you were unstaked as well. Yet conscious? Well, I'm afraid you fell prey to the infirmities the immortal blood is heir to, as it was day at the time."

"Is she alive?" Westphal croaked at last, staring blindly in a direction not quite towards Crowley's face.

"Ah, a reasonable question. Very reasonable, given the circumstances. Well, she most likely would have died unless I had intervened, and by ancient law, that makes her life mine. If, of course, you wish to go by anything so proscriptive as ancient law." Crowley chuckled, fingering his staff. "Yet since she belonged to me, both by ancient law and my own, I chose to give her to my Beast. He desired her, and her red hair is a mark of great power and passion."

"*Schweinhund!*" Westphal screamed, lunging for the madman. But Crowley just stood there and watched with vague amusement as the Ventrue thrashed against the length of his chains, fangs gnashing, face contorted into a mask of rage, until at last the German fell prostrate at his feet.

"Actually," Crowley remarked with dry humor, "it's not a *Schweinhund* at all. At least, I do not believe so. As for precisely what my Beast is, now *that* is a good question." He glanced towards Ilse. "I assume you're familiar with the process of Gangrel de-evolution?" Ilse said nothing, and neither did Westphal, so Crowley continued. "The Gangrel Clan is unique in that the immortal blood warps their outward form to reflect their inner Beast. Or, in this case, the Beast of another.

"Now this is rather complicated, so please, follow and bear with me. On the isle to the west of here, there are a number of werewolves, what most Kindred prefer to term Lupines and who they themselves term Garou. Eire also possesses a great history of Fair Folk, properly referred to as the Sidhe, or in vulgar terms as faeries. I located a man I believed to have the blood of both running in his veins, for my divinations indicated him to be a direct male-line descendant Cuchulainn, or Cullen's Hound, that hero so beloved of Yeats and Lady Gregory, the warrior Setanta," He glanced to Westphal. "A redhead like your own Miss Jacqueline, marked for lust, passion and witchcraft, kin to wolves, faeries and witches, yet still latent in his power."

Crowley gestured with his crosier. "I took this man and fed his lusts in manners both mundane and magical, giving him the means that all men crave to sate their passions while also allowing him to drink from a cup mixed with the blood of a Gangrel elder and the blood of one of the ancient giants who walked the earth in days of yore. Which giant, I cannot say for certain — the provenance on the cask I acquired is somewhat fanciful, alleging the blood of the Merovingian Kings, of Bran the Blessed, or Finn the Fair, or Bres the Beautiful, the Fomor King, or even that it contained a measure of the blood of the first giant, Ymir, from whose corpse the dark and light elves purportedly sprang as black and white maggots. It really doesn't matter. The histories are endlessly muddled, and for every legend that speaks of Finn MacCool as a clever giant, there's another that speaks of Fionne MacCumhail, the greatest of the Fenian warriors, and genealogies that prove him to be an ancestor to Cuchulainn.

I leave that sort of petty dickering to Yeats and Lady Gregory, as it makes so much little nevermind.

"Suffice it to say, whoever or whatever the blood originally belonged to, my regimen worked. My subject grew in stature and strength, the giant's blood lending him potence, the vitæ from the Gangrel elder drawing out the Beast and increasing his fortitude, and the changes of the Gangrel line began to come upon him as well, aided, I believe, by his kinship to the wolves, and by the fact that I had been conditioning him to accept my will as his own. I then used a petty discipline to unleash my own Beast into his body, and my greater lust united with his own, beginning to craft a suitable vessel for my own passions."

Crowley paused, leaving the only sounds in the room the low, animal growl in Westphal's throat, then the madman continued, "I then began to experiment with rituals. The Sabbat have a rite known as the Shadow of the Wolf, where you take a skin cloak and use it to change shape in the manner of the Lapp shamans, which, while amusing, proved insufficient for my purposes. Then there was another ritual along similar lines which I'd discovered during my travels in India, the Rite of the Sacred Rebirth, involving both ingredients you would expect and that you might not expect: blood and sugar, asafetida and saffron, various rare pigments and herbs, and a cloak sewn from the skins of not one, but five, Lupines.

"With the aid of my Gangrel minions, I procured the requisite number of shapeshifters, a pack of renegade Garou, lust-filled degenerate half-breeds who belonged to some peculiar Scottish cult that worshipped a corrupt interpretation of the World Serpent, *Jormungandr*. I then added my own flairs to the ritual, skinning each of them at the full of the moon, the time of their birth, then locked them in pens, still alive. This done, I proceeded to loose my own Beast into the body of my Gangrel-ghoul-changeling-childe, persuading a number of Gangrel to do likewise, while I whipped and tormented the skinless Lupines." Crowley paused, a beatific expression on his face, and he fingered the lingam staff in his hand. "The metamorphosis was astonishing. Though only Kin, my subject transformed into the monstrous war-form of the Lupines, a great, red-furred Beast, driven wild with lust and hunger, taking for his own form even more that of the Great Beast than any of the pathetic half-breeds I tormented and much larger. A wolf from the Dawntime, and a creature that begins to approach a worthy vessel for my lust."

Crowley looked down and smiled. "I was not certain what I should do next to increase the power of my Beast, but then Providence supplied me with a beautiful, debauched redheaded woman…"

With a snarl, Westphal launched himself at Crowley, screaming in frenzy. Crowley gazed on, faintly amused, still an inch shy of the extent of Westphal's chains. "Please, do not alarm yourself, Mr. Westphal. Your paramour displayed unusual fortitude for my impromptu rite of Shiva and Kali. Truly, she played her part quite well."

Westphal thrashed against his chains, cutting his wrists on the shackles. Dark blood sprayed in an arc, staining the hem of Crowley's vestments. The madman idly stroked the wood of his crosier, not seeming to notice. "I believe she may even still be alive, though I would have to check to make certain."

Westphal screamed again, cutting himself deeper as he thrashed, gnashing his teeth as he tried to reach Crowley. But the cuts were dry, and a moment later he fell to the floor, all his blood burned in frenzy.

Crowley took the foot of his staff and poked Westphal, then flipped him over, tilting his head up so Ilse could see Westphal's eyes, now glassy with torpor, and the film of dried blood on his fangs. "A pity this one wasn't taken as a Gangrel, don't you think? He would have made a splendid Beast. So many passions locked so deeply inside. He lusts for his woman, and even though he has never seen its true splendor, he envies my Beast from mere implication, and that leads to wrath and vanity, and of course, pride. With the Ventrue, one can never forget pride. Five of the Seven Passions. If he were only trained in the proper arts, what a potent spell he might craft." Crowley sighed elaborately. "Truly a pity."

Ilse looked at Crowley, his face lit only by the psychotic swirl of his aura. "I suppose it's redundant to say you're mad."

He removed his staff, and Westphal's head fell back to hit the floor with a sickening crack. "Oh, please, Miss Decameron. I think thoughts most mortals shall never think, dream dreams that others cannot dream, see sights that few will ever see, walk boldly where angels fear to tread, and where for that matter even the devils dare not venture. And I am mad?" He looked at her, smiling slightly, the sepia tones of his aura swirling around him. "Go out into the streets and tell the people what you see every night, what you know to be true, the unthinkable secrets you've discovered — they'll lock you up! Vampires — Stuff and nonsense! Only the mad believe in vampires! Witchcraft — Balderdash! Only little children believe in witches! Ghouls and demons — Oh, please! No one in their right mind believes such silly stuff!"

He sneered, shaking his head. "And you inquire if I am mad?"

Ilse felt her blood turn chill, and she sank back against the wall. "Why are you telling me this?"

"Because I enjoy shocking people's sensibilities," Crowley replied matter-of-factly, "and because I hate the Ventrue and the Tremere equally, although the Ventrue are so much easier to shock." He kicked Kurt Westphal, then stuck the base of his staff in the German's open mouth, admiring the juxtaposition for a moment before removing it.

"You Tremere, however, are somewhat more aware of the world's possibilities and are therefore a bit more sport than the poor, hidebound Ventrue." His expression was the patient look like a father might give a favorite child, still fingering his crosier. "You are nevertheless blind in peculiar ways, and you inquire if I am mad."

Crowley's expression became a bit kinder, though his aura still showed the cancerous brown of hatred. "I suppose I shouldn't fault you if you dare not think as grandly as I might. The Tremere line is tainted with cowardice twice over, and it's a fault all of your blood are heir to." He leered. "Don't you wish to know why?"

"No," Ilse said, cold rage helping to move her blood.

"There, you see, more of what I mentioned," Crowley said. "There are questions you dare not ask. You clothe it as pride and loyalty and respect, almost as bad the damnable Ventrue, but it all boils down to one thing — cowardice."

"Oh, save me your spite!" Ilse snapped, unable to take it anymore. "I know why you hate us. it's a standard lesson. The Ventrue had a Malkavian embrace you and tell you you were of our line, so you'd run amuck and embarrass our clan. Well, it worked for what little it was worth, but the cat's out of the bag, and the most I can do is say I'm sorry that we didn't invite you in before the Ventrue played their little trick. The charm on the manacle does you credit, and you might have made a place among the Tremere, but what's done is done and it can't be changed. You'd have to be crazy to think otherwise."

The cold rage that had filled Ilse had spent itself just as quickly, and she suddenly wondered what she'd done, for she saw the scarlet of anger swirl for a moment amid the crimson of Crowley's lust.

Then Crowley smiled. "What a good girl! She's learned her lessons. Yet, we wonder, has she been brave enough to question them? Has she learned how to read between the lines of the approved histories and make a guess as to the actual truth?" He patted her on the cheek, but withdrew his hand quickly before she could bite him. "Silly girl. You would truly be a fool if you thought even for a second that I would allow anything to happen to myself that I did not already want."

He turned, pacing a step away, tapping the stone floor with his crosier. "The truth of the matter is, my good child, that I am what I always have been — a magus, what you might call a mage. You really thought I was just some foolish cultist and charlatan who the Ventrue used as their dupe?" He laughed long and loud, his voice echoing through the chamber. "The reverse is far closer to the truth."

"You see, though I was a mage, I had discovered for myself the unpleasant truth that your own founder had already learned — magic was slipping from the earth. Credit where credit is due, Miss Decameron, I must admit Tremere beat me to it. Then again, he was born centuries before me, and the truth of it is something that any fool can see, so there's no great honor in the discovery. But never mind. I had discerned this truth as well and became concerned with my own mortality. Oh, not with dying, mind you — I'd done that many times before and remembered every one of them. No, it was rather the tedious business of birth and childhood and remembering what I'd been doing before so I could pick up where I left off."

Crowley turned about, pacing back the other way. "I then did research, as did your own Tremere, and ascertained the immortality of the Damned, then learned of Tremere's gambit before me and of his cowardly mistake.

"Do you hear me, Miss Decameron? Tremere was a fool, a cowardly fool. Climb down any sewer and bring a rat and you'll find an ugly vampire willing to tell you the story in exchange for a nip of its neck. Really a very common story; not even worth a rat unless well-told. I'm sure you already know the whole sordid affair — Tremere lusting after the power of the Antediluvians, the third generation from Caine, finally tracking one down and committing diablerie, that most unthinkable of acts, drinking the elder's heart-blood and devouring his soul. And for what? Power. Pure, sweet, power."

Crowley leered, leaning on his staff and clutching it with both hands. "And Tremere did it, make no mistake. He gave the Dark Kiss to one of the oldest beings to walk this earth. Yet, of all of Caine's grandchilder, whom did he chose? Ennoia, the Queen of Beasts? Nosferatu, Master of the Hidden Places? Perhaps Arikel, the Sculptress, the Subtle One, who shaped the arts down through the ages and thereby shaped the lives of men? No, none of these. He chose Saulot, Caine's favorite. Saulot, the Holy Martyr and Healer."

He chuckled conspiratorially. "I've always wondered, once Tremere rises from torpor, what does he plan to do for an encore? Kill Mother Teresa? Phaugh!" He swung the staff, dismissing the thought, then leaned down and stared Ilse in the face, eyes blazing. "Let me ask you this — when one has set one's sights on power, which you Tremere so proudly state that you worship, what sort of fool would chose the Holy Martyr when the only thing he has to recommend him is that he's the most lightly guarded and the least likely to put up a fight?"

Ilse chose her words carefully and told Crowley what she thought he wanted to hear, "A cowardly fool."

"Bright girl," Crowley said. "Go to the head of the class." He patted her twice on the cheek and straightened up. "A cowardly fool indeed. He took the straight and simple course, settling for what seemed good enough, when any fool could see that if one desired magical power, the proper choice was not Saulot the Blessed Healer, but Malkav the Magician."

Crowley sat down on the floor before her, taking the posture of a patient teacher, his crosier across his lap. "Tremere took the easy choice, not the proper one, and your line has been tainted forevermore with cowardice, both Saulot's holy cowardice and Tremere's unholy cowardice. For this, your magic has suffered. So you can see why I arranged to be taken by the line of Malkav."

"Then why do you hate us so much?" Ilse asked. "If you didn't want to join us, why do you resent us?"

"I don't resent you," Crowley said, leaning forward. "I just hate you for the same reason I hate the Ventrue. I see no reason to suffer fools gladly, and both clans are composed of fools, arrogant fools and cowardly fools. I must hate you because it is either that or pity, and hate is so much more satisfying." He smiled, running his fingers up and down the length of his staff. "There's also the matter of a personal grudge between me and Dr. John Dee. You see, among other things, I am also the reincarnation of Edward Kelly, the mage who first deigned to teach Dee anything of spirits or the ways of Enochian magic. We were quite fond of each other once — there was even an open marriage between ourselves and our wives — yet he betrayed me, and while he continued on as a learned doctor and then vampire, I was cast into prison and died during my escape. It was a very painful death, let me remind you, and one that I shall never forget. I have had four hundred years to plot my revenge, and it is just about ready."

Crowley leaned back, smiling. "You're holding up well. You're made of much sterner stuff than most of your line. So, what uncomfortable truth should I tell you next? I know. Look at my aura, my dear, and tell me what you see. Look closely. I know you've been glancing at it the whole time, but like most creatures, you've blinded yourself to the shocking and the obvious. So look now and *see*."

Ilse did not want to look, but she did, the madman's aura holding that same sort of horrid fascination as did accidents or freaks or shocking acts of perversion. The outer shell of his soul swirled with psychosis, the colors as she had seen them, brown and black and a full palette of reds, mostly crimson and scarlet. Yet the aura was bright with magic, Ilse realized, bright as that of a mortal mage, and in the expectant silence, she could hear the madman's heart beating."

"You're..." Ilse could not finish.

"Say it, my dear. Say it. What word are you searching for? Alive?"

"No, a ghoul. You're just some puppet. Where's Master Therion?"

The man laughed, stroking the wood of his wand of power. "Right before you, my dear, or have you refused to see the riddle I've set you? My soul is stained by the Black Kiss, and how could a mere ghoul have come by that?"

Ilse looked at his aura and shrank back, blood turning to ice in her veins. "It's impossible..."

"Please, that's a vulgar word. Why, sometimes I drink six impossible things for breakfast. You're impossible, after all. Ask anyone on the street." He smiled broadly, showing too many fangs, his mouth like the maw of a manticore. "Can you guess how I did it? Or why? It's very simple, all just part of my plan. I never intended to remain a vampire, only to bide my time and learn and steal a bit of their immortality, as it was one of the few simple ways left in this modern world. So, once I was taken by the line of Malkav and slew my sire, I procured a catamite, a young man related to me by blood, and with him performed the rites of Zeus and Hermes, thereby bonding him to myself. He drank my blood and soul, diablerizing me, my spirit flowing into his young, living body and my immortal blood coursing through the marrow of the wand into his living veins. I had my immortality and my mortality. Once I have finished learning the rest of what I require, I shall do what Tremere never had the courage to do — track down Malkav and take his power for myself. After that, I believe I shall proceed to Caine, then God. Lilith I'm not certain of, though I believe I'd like to enjoy her company for a time before deciding whether I should do without her."

"You're insane."

"No," said Crowley, getting back to his feet, "I'm just not a coward like those of your line. Why, looking to your clan as example, less than a thousand years ago, a mortal usurped the power of one of the grandchildren of the third mortal to walk this earth. Or fourth or fifth mortal, actually, if you count

Lilith and the nameless virgin. Second man, anyway, and that's what counts for power." He fingered the lingam. "Given that as a precedent, why shouldn't I be able to kill Malkav or Caine or God, if I have a mind to? I am the Beast, and what I do shall be the whole of the law. It is my desire to kill God and take his place, and my destiny that this will come to pass. Read the Bible if you don't believe me, then read between the lines. They leave so much out of the official histories, but those who are clever can still discern the truth."

"What do you want with us?" Ilse asked.

Crowley gestured and shrugged. "I have a desire to rule London, and a certain measure of malice for your clans. Both have sworn vengeance on the other if anything untoward happens to either of you. It being a night past these oaths, and neither of you returned safely home, they should now be going about their shortsighted war, Dr. Dee blowing up Parliament, Lady Anne responding with whatever takes her fancy. It hardly matters. They will be trapped by their enmity, and, on the off-chance that Dr. Dee does not make good on his threat, the Brujah will make certain that any possible hint of diplomacy is negated by the actual destruction of the House of Lords and the House of Commons.

"This act of vandalism will be attributed to the Tremere, whether or not they actually did it, and this will be matched from some equally appalling atrocity by the Ventrue. After the struggle is begun in earnest, I will release you and Mr. Westphal to run back to your own clans — jointly or separately — it hardly matters, and allow you to tell them of the perfidy of the Brujah. They will of course unite against the common enemy, but poorly, as they hate each other more and will have both just indulged in the most spiteful and heinous crimes against one another. Regardless, the victory of whatever clan shall come to the top of the heap shall be short-lived, for I will then step in myself and seize it.

"The only thing you and Mr. Westphal might do to thwart

me would be to remain here and do nothing, allowing the Brujah to consolidate their power and making them that much harder for me to dislodge, but I find that unlikely. The Ventrue is far too arrogant, and you are far too cowardly to do what would be most sensible and spiteful, so you will do what I said, loyal not so much to your clans as to your own pride and cowardice and thereby bringing about your clans' downfall."

Crowley crouched down, reaching into the sleeve of his vestments. "But before I leave you to your amusement, one last thing…." Like a conjurer, he produced an old pair of silver pliers with an elaborate loop-and-pincer arrangement at the end.

With the ease born of long practice, Crowley slipped the instrument over Kurt Westphal's left fang. "So good he already has them extended. Less chance of damaging the tooth." With a wiggle and twist, Aleister Crowley extracted the fang, dropping it with a flick into his empty hand. He pulled the other fang just as neatly, then turned to Ilse.

Crowley smiled, showing his own teeth, rows and rows of them like a shark. "Now, Miss Decameron, if you would be so obliging? I really hate to damage the tooth; it spoils it for my purposes."

Ilse bit back on her anger, trying to force herself to remain calm, to keep from extending her fangs as both Crowley and her instincts wanted.

Crowley looked at her, smiling. "Good, very good, Miss Decameron. Not so weak-willed as you might be. But observe—" He grabbed her by the throat, forcing her to meet his gaze. "Bitch! Shrew! Whore! Mewling coward!"

His will pressed against hers. Ilse felt her growing fury, and her fangs extended on reflex. Quick as thought, Crowley forced her mouth open and grabbed one, then the other with his forceps, yanking them out and dropping them into the palm of his hand with Westphal's.

"Thank you, Miss Decameron," Crowley said. "That did

very nicely." He released her chin and stood back up. Ilse's head fell forward as cold rage flowed through her, blood pouring into her mouth in place of her missing fangs. She held her lips tightly closed, not wanting to lose a precious drop.

"I think you might find this interesting, Miss Decameron. Watch carefully." Crowley lifted his upper lip with the thumb of one hand, using the nail of the other to stab the gum in a space between two pointed teeth. Carefully he inserted one of the pulled fangs, where it took root, then proceeded to the other side of his mouth where he placed its mate.

He smiled at her like a barracuda. "It is a standard belief that the parts of one's enemies hold a share of their power, and if you consume them, you gain a portion of that strength. The quintessential part of a vampire is, of course, the fangs, and these, thankfully, are fresh."

He then proceeded to his lower jaw, putting the other two fangs in place, and Ilse felt the blood flow in her mouth in sympathy as he snapped his jaws and smacked his lips. "There is, of course, another belief, that so long as one holds a portion of one's enemies, they can never act against him. Otherwise, they destroy themselves." Crowley pointed the iron tip of the crosier over her heart. "I have your fangs, Miss Decameron, the core of your vampiric magic, and you would do well to remember it."

Crowley sucked his teeth, seeming to savor the taste. "I was right," he said at last. "Mr. Westphal has much stifled passion, and you, Miss Decameron, also have a measure of ...unrequited love?" He looked askance at her, then nodded, as if he'd already answered his own question. "My, what a rare passion to find among one of your clan. I was given to understand that tragic love affairs were solely the province of the Toreadors. Never mind. Unrequited love makes lust all the more urgent, and you're linked to mine now, you know. Taste and you will feel the passion."

Crowley stroked his staff, and Ilse felt a wave of hot animal lust sweep through her as the blood poured through the holes where her fangs had been. "You see? Delicious, isn't it? Now, perhaps we should do something just as nice for Mr. Westphal. Ozmo! Dana!" He rapped his staff twice on the floor, striking sparks, and Ilse felt ecstasy surge through her. "Bring Miss Jacqueline in!"

"But I've hardly finished her make-up, Aleister, darling!" came the distant call of a husky falsetto with an ever so proper British accent. "She'd be terribly embarrassed to be seen like this. I know I would!"

There was the sound of a large door slamming open somewhere beyond Ilse's range of vision, and light spilled in, almost blinding her before she could dim her heightened senses. "'Oo gives a rat's arse wot you think, Davie?" came another voice, much louder, male, speaking in an almost incomprehensible Cockney dialect. "Mistah Crowley wants 'er, 'ee gets 'er, wit' or wit'out 'er make-up."

"My name is Dana, Ozmo! Dana! How many times do I have to tell you?"

"Yer name's Dave Wilkins, mate, and yer nuttier than a fruitcake from 'Arrods, that's wot you is. Now get yer arse out o' me way, or I knock you right down the bleedin' stairs!"

There was a ladylike gasp, then tripping down the steps with nimble feet came a woman in a beautiful silver fox stole and a long purple evening gown, her matching panorama hat piled high with scarlet ostrich plumes, the same shade as her lipstick and gold-framed cabochon earrings. Or *his* lipstick, Ilse suddenly realized, for it was a very large woman and moved with that exaggerated femininity you only saw in transvestites and transsexuals.

Dana/Dave stepped back as another man came down the steps after her. This one was a huge bruiser with snow white hair and skin, an albino and a vampire at that, wearing a denim jacket sewn with hundreds of pearly buttons and the legend "P.K.B. — Pearly King of Battersea." His pants and cap had more of the buttons, and the only part of him that had any color were the glittering multicolored plastic rings on his fingers. In his arms he bore Westphal's chauffeur, Jackie. "Where d'you want 'er, Mistah Crowley?"

Crowley smiled at Ozmo and gestured to Westphal. "In his lap, if you would be so kind. I'd like her to be waiting for him when he wakes up."

"I really must fix her make-up," Dana protested.

"You need to fix yer bleedin' 'ead, that's wot needs fixin'!" sneered Ozmo, carrying Jackie across the grey stone floor of the chamber. "Yer a fuckin' loony, Davie, that's wot you is."

"Please, Ozmo," said Crowley. "If you would be so kind…"

"That's me, Mistah C, soul o' kindness. Promised this 'ere little tart I'd get even wit' 'er, an' wot am I doin'? Why, nuttin' more than lettin' 'er take a loverly restful nap in 'er boyfriend's lap. A nice long 'un…"

He set Jackie gently across Westphal's legs, the chauffeur now dressed in a long, peacock-blue beaded gown and a gigantic feathered hat like something from the Ascot Races scene of My Fair Lady, her long Titian-red hair done into a fall of tightly sprung curls down one side of her face. There was a bruise on her cheek, visible even under the heavy make-up, and a bandage on her arm partially covered by one of the long silk gloves. Her head lolled back, eyes blind with shock. From the pale persimmon color of her aura, Ilse could see the woman was near to death, or at least would be if she suffered even the slightest additional injury.

Westphal just lay there and stared up, eyes also frozen wide, mouth open and empty except for the dried film of blood across his remaining teeth.

"He'll kill her," Ilse breathed. "When he wakes, he'll kill her…"

"That's the gen'ral idea." Ozmo grinned, fangs extended. "H'ain't Mistah Crowley got a wonderful mind? Provides fer alluvus, 'ee does."

Crowley smiled fondly and patted Ozmo on the shoulder, making the buttons rattle. "I would not be overly alarmed,

Miss Decameron. As I've taken the precaution of removing Mr. Westphal's fangs, any damage he does to his woman will not be a crime of passion, but of careful consideration. He shall not salve his conscience with the pleasant lie that he had no choice. His choice is clear and simple — once he wakes, he may either savage his woman, drinking her blood and extinguishing her life, or refrain by an act of will, allowing himself to slide into that night from which there is no return."

"I really hope he decides not to bite her," Dana remarked. "Do you have any idea how difficult it is to get blood out of silk?"

Aleister Crowley leaned upon his staff, the Shiva lingam at the tip throbbing with power. "One last thing, Miss Decameron. On the off-chance that I cannot be here when you are released, please convey the following message to Dr. Dee: First, that I am not the only one he has displeased, and that the Comte expresses his disapproval of your current scheme in the strongest manner possible; and second, and more simply, just inform him that my revenge has begun."

He straightened up then, still smiling. "Thank you for your time, Miss Decameron, but I must now be off. I have other matters to attend to. Ozmo! Dana!" Crowley turned sharply and swaggered out of the room with his bright, mad aura, as Ozmo and Dana followed him out of Ilse's field of vision.

A moment later, the door slammed, and the room was once again plunged into darkness.

Ilse allowed her enhanced senses to return, the persimmon shade of Jackie's aura fading, but still brighter than either hers or Westphal's. She then turned and studied the cuff, the manacle that prevented her from using her magic. It was heavy and incised with old Etruscan charms, iron twisted with silver and gold for power and strength, snug about her wrist. The lock was at the far side on the base, impossible to reach with her mouth, even if she could get to her pick. It was a trap worthy of Master Harry. Feet were right out too, since Crowley had bolted the ankle shackles so tightly to the floor Ilse couldn't even feel them.

However, Ilse's hands were fine and slim, and she tried to see if she could slip free directly, pulling straight through the cuff. The metal was sharp and jagged, a saw-toothed edge formed by the crudely incised charms, but Ilse began to work at it, slowly dislocating the bones and letting the muscles slide one over the other. The skin of the back of her hand caught on a metal spur. It was nothing, just a scratch, barely a wound, but a drop of her vitæ oozed from it and rolled down around her wrist and down the side of the cuff.

Ilse heard the sound of a chain clank beside her and froze, but the drop of blood continued on its course, and Westphal began to rise from his torpor, his nostrils flaring like a stallion's that scents a mare on the wind. "Fräulein," he breathed, coming upright, eyes still glazed, like some vampire from a B-movie.

Unfortunately, the B-movie producers had captured the expression of a rousing Kindred all too well, but then Westphal's expression changed, going from a look of dazed, undead Hunger to a human expression of shock and horror as he somehow recognized the woman he loved lying prone in his lap, possibly scenting the blood from her bandaged wounds.

He leaned forward to her, whether to kiss her or to Kiss her or to sob, Ilse could not be sure. "Don't," she said quickly. "Her lifeforce is almost gone. If she suffers even the slightest injury, she'll die."

Westphal turned to Ilse, staring at the trickle of blood running down the back of her hand, the pupils of his eyes dilated into sightless black voids. He leaned towards her, but then his expression became stricken. He realized that she was just beyond his reach, and he would never gain the life-giving drops of vitæ before he fell into a torpor from which he would never return.

He had a minute, tops, and Ilse tried to work more at the

cuff, twisting and sliding her bones, but she'd never make it. With an act of will, Ilse pulled her hand straight down. The pain was intense, bones dislocating, wrist slashing itself on the sharp edge, but Ilse had felt pain already, and she ripped her hand through the manacle, the skin of the back catching and peeling up in a raw flap.

Ilse thrust her bloody hand out towards Westphal. "Here! Take it!"

She need not even have spoken. At once he grabbed it, nearly stuffing it in his mouth, drinking desperately of the precious blood. Ilse felt the joy of the Kiss and the wave of his pleasure cresting over her, almost overpowering in its intensity. She was unsure whether this came from his Hunger or that she was possibly just the thing to suit his peculiar Ventrue tastes.

"Enough," she said at last, attempting to pull her hand back. He clung, continuing to nurse, then suddenly seemed to realize she was struggling against him and let go.

"*Danke schön*, Fräulein," he gasped out.

"*De nada*," Ilse responded, the Spanish expressing the thought best: *It's nothing*. She felt weak and drained and knew that Westphal could hardly feel any stronger than she did.

He sobbed once then, a sharp sound of loss, and cradled Jackie's unconscious body, showing a face so stricken with grief that Ilse felt her own dead heart contract in sympathy. "Jackie…"

"Hush," Ilse said. "She's still alive."

Westphal took his wrist to his mouth, but then discovered he'd somehow lost his fangs while he was unconscious. He looked towards Ilse. "Give her some of your blood. Please."

Ilse sighed. "I can't spare any more, and neither can you. What she needs is a hospital, but first we have to get free ourselves." She turned her mind to the shackle on her other wrist and the one about her waist, but they didn't respond, some lesser charm of Crowley's preventing her from rotating the mechanisms. "Can you pick locks?"

The Ventrue looked about, as if afraid that someone would hear him admitting to such a *de clasé* skill, then whispered, "Yes, if I have the proper tools."

"I have them." Ilse reached out with her mind and took her camera out of her purse. "Guard your eyes." With a flick of her mind, she turned on the high intensity lamp, slipping the heaviest of the lock picks out of the camera strap.

The manacles on Westphal were old and primitive, with large, rusty keyholes and locking mechanisms. But they were painted with charms in blood, and the lock pick dropped from the air once it got within an inch of the manacle. He retrieved the twist of wire without comment and went about picking the lock by hand in a businesslike, if amateurish, fashion as she continued to hold the lamp. One by one he removed the shackles, then gently placed Jackie on the floor beside him and stood up, rubbing his wrists.

Silently, Westphal then knelt down beside Ilse, taking the lock pick and camera and working on the manacle on the other side of her. He removed a bit of red sealing wax stamped with an intricate sigil, then remarked, "This lock appears to be more complicated than mine." He poked about a bit more with the wire. "Do you have anything finer?"

Ilse removed the entire set from the strap and let him choose among them. "Crowley considered me more of a threat."

The Ventrue only grunted, choosing not to dispute this, but he was good to his word and far quicker than Ilse would have expected. The right manacle popped away from her wrist, and Westphal pushed it back against the wall, allowing her to take down her arm. He then proceeded about picking the lock that held the larger iron band around her waist and the twin shackles around her ankles.

"Bravo!" cheered a voice. "What an amazing escape! I'm sure Houdini would be greatly impressed. Only one hand mangled, but then, I guess it would have been difficult for you to chew it off at the wrist."

Ilse looked wildly about, shuddering with fear-frozen blood as she searched for the source of the mocking voice. Then a shadow slipped out of the deeper shadows, a small, elfin shape, fulgent against the darkness, lightless black, but the blackness that composed it was the dark of sin, a silhouette cut from pure evil.

It capered about, striking attitudes and clapping its shadowy hands in delight. "My goodness, Master Therion has the whole vaudeville show. Beautiful women, escape artists, transvestites — Why, he even has performing beasts upstairs! I *must* recommend this to my friends."

"Charnas!" Westphal snarled. "Where are you, you damned gadfly?"

"Oh," said the silhouette. "A riddle he's set me, but in reverse. Let's see, where's Charnas?" The shadow ran about, avoiding the spot of Ilse's camera which Westphal shone everywhere, trying to catch the demon. "Can you find Charnas in this picture? We can make it a children's book — *Where's Charnas?*"

The shadow raced around, bouncing and capering over bales and boxes, swinging from hooks and chains without a sound, light as a soap bubble. It was a long time before it came to rest where Westphal could get the spot on it.

When revealed in the light of reality, the demon had violet skin, pointed elfin ears, puckish features and a mop of curly black hair offset by biker leathers and the lack of a shirt. Any portions outside of the light were pure black evil. It was also kneeling next to Jackie's unconscious form, chest puffed out, head thrown back in a heroic pose, one hand twined in her hair. "So, whatcha think?" the creature asked. "Do I look like Fabio or what?"

"Unhand her, fiend!" Westphal snarled.

"Unhand her?" Charnas repeated. "Well, okay, since you asked. I'm sure Crowley has a butcher knife around here somewhere...."

The demon began to look about as Westphal snarled and lunged, and Ilse somehow managed to save her camera and trip him all at once, but then, telekinesis was often useful.

Charnas squealed with laughter, bouncing out of the way. "And funny clowns! Oh, my! Mr. Crowley's show has it all!"

Westphal got to his knees, teeth grinding, and spoke after a long moment. "Do not be alarmed, Fräulein Ilse. I know this…creature. Charnas!" the German snarled then. "Where are we?"

"Somewhere where they don't know how to put on make-up." Charnas struck an attitude of shock, one hand on his cheek, the other pointing to Jackie. "Would you just look at that! All that foundation, and that heavy eye shadow… My goodness, if you didn't know better, you'd think she'd been made-up by a transvestite!"

Westphal growled, "I meant here, in London."

"Oh, that," the imp said, coming out of his pose and striking an attitude of nonchalance. "Well…assuming you're in London, you're in the basement of Masters Kensington, Pope and Kelly, spice merchants. The smell is from the spice that's been stored here for decades, and Master Therion has done a wonderful job of converting it into a secret temple. No need to drench everything with rare oils and precious spice around here — it's already been done."

It seemed the creature couldn't keep still for long, for the next moment it spun about, bobbing in a low bow towards Ilse. "Charnas the Imp, at your service." He came up like a jumping-jack, striking another off-hand pose. "Well, really, I'm in Thadius Zho's service, but he asked me to keep an eye on you, so here I am."

Ilse naturally distrusted all demons, but the Ventrue seemed to know this one, so she ventured to speak to it. "You're here to rescue us?"

Charnas made a face. "Oh, Heavens, no! and Hell, no! and all the layers in between! Rescue you? You must be crazier than Crowley!" He giggled wildly. "My service only extends to being a spy and a gadfly, and that only for Thadius Zho. If you want me to do anything different, you'll have to negotiate with my greater half, Charnas, the Lord of Misrule." He held up a sheaf of papers in one hand and a handful of pens in the other, fanning both. "Deals with the Devil?"

"We don't want a contract," Ilse said. "All we want is to get out of here. If you won't help us, you can leave."

"Ooh…" Charnas said, squinting his eyes and pursing his lips. "Icy…I think the temperature just dropped a good fifty degrees in here." He exhaled, his breath condensing like frost, and he rubbed his hands for warmth, then turned and looked at her over the top of the black Ray Bans which had suddenly taken the place of the contracts and pens. "I can see why you're not gettin' any, sister. What they say about Tremere girls is true — colder than a witch's tit. Or was that witches with cold tits? I get confused, but I think both work." He grinned. "You know, if you wore the brass bra that's supposed to go with those, you wouldn't get staked and it would give you the bonus of extra support. Not that you need it with those little things."

"Don't let him bait you," Westphal cautioned her. "Now, Charnas, where are we? Besides the planet Earth and the basement of a spice company."

"*Former* spice company," Charnas corrected. "It's the Undead Vampire Temple of the Damned now, remember? Or the Temple of Aiwass — call him 'Eyewash' and you'll really piss off Crowley, not to mention Aiwass himself. But anyway, if you find your way up and out, and avoid the guards, and the cultists, and Crowley's little vampire cronies — not to mention his big, *big*, beastie boy, since that's who you'll run into first — why, then, I think you'll find you're at the Canary Docks, on the Thames, on the East End of London. I wouldn't usually answer riddles so easily, but Thadius wanted me to help, so here I am. And I *have* helped you — never forget that."

He grinned and bowed then, coming back up with an Elizabethan mask of Comedy, a long-nosed goblin-face with ivy and ribbons down the sides. "But please, if this shadow has offended, think but this and all is mended: You may have had a nasty surprise, but I know someone who's *gonna get a worse one!*" He sing-songed the last, laughing like a malicious child, then roared like a Baptist preacher, "Can't escape your sins — they *always* come back to haunt ya!"

The imp leered at Ilse as he said the last, and she knew that he knew something she didn't. He winked conspiratorially and went up in a gout of violet flame, like a piece of magician's flashpaper, leaving behind the stench of brimstone and lavender.

Ilse actually took a deep breath, not for the air, but to calm her nerves, then shone the spotlamp about, hoping the Pentax's batteries would last. "Get Jackie, then let's get up the stairs."

"Do you have a plan, Fräulein?"

Ilse picked up her purse, checking through it. It appeared that Crowley had left her everything, including the Razor and the Key. "Do you have a gun?"

He search his jacket. "No, but they did leave me this." He held up his right hand, displaying a silver ring, apparently Art Nouveau. "It is the Rowan Ring. It can form a wooden stake for but a drop of blood."

Well, that sounded vaguely useful. Ilse rested her finger on the Iron Key, considering, but unfortunately, the imp had told them precisely where they were, and there were other complications. "I don't suppose you'd accept a Blood Bond to Clan Tremere?"

The German did not even deign to answer, and Ilse scratched the thought. No point in even explaining the rites and rituals by which it might be done, even if it would allow him access to the House of Secrets.

"Let's go," she said, starting up the stairs. "We'll deal with things as we come to them. It's better than waiting here and letting Crowley have his way."

"We're in perfect agreement on that, Fräulein Decameron."

Ilse paused at the door at the top of the stairs, switching the lamp off once she was certain that Westphal was not too close to the edge of the stone steps. She then placed her hands against the door and listened, straining her senses, and heard the sound of low panting. Focusing upon a mantra of calming: *Om Mani Padme Hum*, she stilled even the slightest flow of her blood, disciplining herself until her soul slipped free of her body in a psychic projection.

She passed through the door, ready for any horror Crowley might have devised, and was not disappointed. Amid the psychic wreckage, she saw a soul, a white one, mixed with gold, green and red, the colors of purity, kindness, compassion and rage. Wrapped around that soul, shackling it, were chains of crimson and black, Crowley's unclean lust, dark rites and the power of the Blood Bond. There was power here, magical power aplenty, but fettered and subservient to Crowley's crazed will. She looked with the eyes of her soul and was met by the bound soul in turn, unquestionably male, his aura flushing pale yellow for a moment, a plea for help.

Ilse slipped back into her body. Gathering from what Charnas and Crowley had said. She had seen the soul of Crowley's Beast, the victim of the madman's unclean experiments.

Before even trying the lock, Ilse merely took hold of the doorknob. It turned, Crowley so mad and cocksure that no further obstacles had been set in their way...

Except, of course, what lay beyond the door. Ilse opened it and saw a room illuminated in red, the light coming from the eyes of the Beast chained by a silver collar to an iron staple set in the floor. And it was a great beast indeed, a gigantic, monstrous, red-furred Lupine thing that towered over them, and that was standing on all fours. The teeth were long as daggers, and the claws were sickled hooks that rasped across the stonework as it padded towards them.

"*Ach, liebe Gott…,*" Westphal whispered in horror behind her.

Ilse reached into her purse for the enchanted razor. It was a desperate gamble, but she knew they'd never survive unless she tried it…and she'd never be able to forgive herself if she didn't. Ilse unfolded the razor and cut herself down the vein so that vitæ flowed down onto the pulpy mass of her hand. "I do not know your name, but I can break the bond that binds you, replacing it with one of my own. You must wish for this change, and all I can give you in exchange is my solemn promise that I will be a kinder master than he who currently holds you in thrall. If I am not, then my hold over you is broken, and either way you shall go free." Ilse held up her bloody hand towards the Beast. "I offer you the Kiss of Fealty. By this Kiss you pass three nights in one and take the Bond now, becoming my Thrall as I become your Regnant."

She looked into the glowing red eyes of the Beast. "I cannot force this upon you, for it is a grave thing, and by charm and —"

The Beast lunged forward, biting down, crushing her hand between his teeth and sucking hard. Ilse screamed and pulled away, the bones of her wrist parting. Westphal caught her, before she could step back too far and fall from the stairs. He pulled her against himself and Jackie, grabbing her severed wrist and pressing his thumb against the pulse to stop the spurting blood. The evening bag dropped to the floor, and the razor slipped from her hand, chiming once as it hit the steps before it plummeted into darkness.

Wrestling against Westphal's strength then, Ilse straightened her arm, pointing the gory stump at the red-eyed Beast at the end of his chain. "By this blood and this flesh, I bind you to myself! You are now vassal to Clan Tremere, and I am your liege. You now have no will but my own, or what I allow you, and all allegiances and loyalties you held before are hereby severed!"

She signaled for Westphal to let her go, and he did. Ilse held the pulse of her own stump and moved forward to the Beast. This was the test of the Bond, and if she'd failed, or Crowley's magic proved too much, it would all be over. "And yet, my vassal, I promise to be a kinder master, and as the first act of that, allow me to free you from your chains."

The Beast lay down on all fours, his long, red tongue lolling out like a friendly dog's. Relieved, Ilse willed the ragged stump of her wrist to seal over, leaving only bare skin and scars. She was nearly drained and weak with Hunger. It would take a great deal of blood before she could regenerate the hand, but the deed was done. Ilse looked into the glowing eyes of Crowley's Beast — her Beast now — then examined the collar.

"Is — Is it safe now?" Westphal asked.

"It will be." Ilse rested her head against the side of the Beast, too drained even to frenzy. "Get my bag and my razor, then help me pick this lock."

Ilse examined the lock. It was a simple thing, and aura reading did not even reveal any additional charms or bindings. Exhausted, she slipped a mental skeleton key into the mechanism, and the huge silver hoop fell from the Beast's neck.

Westphal returned a moment later, Aaron's Feeding Razor in his hand, the blade quivering slightly. He stood over Jackie, where Ilse supposed he'd laid her down on the threshold, and the blade continued to vibrate. "Fräulein, this blade is magic? It seems to be telling me where I can find blood."

Ilse nodded. "It has that power."

The feeding razor seemed to be responding remarkably well to the Ventrue. It dipped slightly as he stepped over Jackie's body, jerked towards Ilse, then led him straight across the room. There was a cabinet in an alcove, just out of the range of the Beast's former chain, inscribed with pentacles and other signs. Westphal pulled it open, pushing aside ritual paraphernalia, then using his undead strength to rip open a false back, not even searching for a hidden mechanism.

He came back a moment later, a wooden cask like a small wine barrel in his hands, the whole of it carved and gilded. Westphal held it in one arm, the razor quivering. "It seems to think…" He allowed the feeding razor to have its will, whereupon it buried itself in the waxen seal at the end of the cask. Convinced, he pried off the seal, and the scent of rich vitæ wafted up, strong as that of elder blood. Westphal raised the cask to his lips, tasting once before he drank, tilting it back one-handed.

He stopped a moment later, blood running down his chin, and laughed. "This is rare blood, Fräulein Decameron! Drink and be well!"

He dropped the cask into her lap and spun around, singing, "*Frau Rauscher auf die Klappergass, die hatte Beul am Ei…*"

Ilse had seen Ventrue drunk on power before, but never quite so literally. Then she took a sip of the blood and understood why. It was giant's blood, the ancient vitæ Crowley had spoken of, and it rushed through her veins, invigorating her, filling her with power and strength until she positively laughed aloud.

"Fräulein, hush," Westphal warned, but Ilse could only giggle at his serious expression. It was half a moment more until the buzz wore off and she remembered the danger they were in.

Westphal slit his wrist with the razor and had Jackie's head propped up, holding the cut to her lips and allowing her to drink of his vitæ. Life still flowed within her, but weakly, so he did not give her the Embrace, only healed her as she nursed from his arm. As she watched, Ilse felt a new hand bud forth from her stump and new fangs slide into her mouth as well. She raised the cask and took another sip of the giant's blood, which was indeed a mighty and magical thing, then set it aside, the stuff too potent to be partaken lightly.

The Beast's tongue lolled out and licked the top of the cask. Then he took it from her and broke it open in his huge jaws, cracking it like a marrow bone and lapping up the spilled blood from the floor.

The air was pierced by a scream. Jackie stared at the Beast, her face a mask of dread. "Keep it away from me! Keep it away!"

"Jackie, *Liebchen*, hush," Westphal attempted to soothe her, but the woman was having none of it. She grabbed up the razor and leveled it at him. "And *you*. You corpse! You just lay there and watched, while that thing—"

She broke off in another scream of abject terror. Westphal looked at her desperately, then stared into her eyes, fangs bared. "Jackie — *Hush!*"

The cry died on her lips, and her eyes went glassy. Dressed in Dana's dress and hat, she looked as posed and lifeless as a china doll.

Bloody tears ran down Westphal's face as he took the razor from her hand. "Jackie, *mein Schatz...*"

The Beast put his head up then and turned towards the door on the far side of the chamber. Ilse knew what that meant — Company.

The door opened, and Ozmo stood there, a lantern in his hand. He took in the whole scene in a second. "Bleedin' 'ell!" he exclaimed. "If this doesn't send Mistah C. 'round the twist, I don't know wot will!"

The Beast lunged forward, and Ozmo threw the lantern down to shatter, then suddenly vanished from the mind's eye as if he'd never been. The Beast only stood there, whining, a pool of flames lying in the open doorway.

Ilse grabbed her purse and gestured to Westphal. "Quickly, we need to get out of here." She tugged on the fur of the Beast's flank, getting him to lie down, then climbed atop him with strength she hadn't realized she had. Westphal mounted up behind, Jackie propped between them. Ilse stroked the

Beast's mane, twining her fingers in it, then leaned down and whispered in his ear, "Take us out of here. You remember the way out. I know you do."

The Beast bounded through the flames, ducking low even for the huge double doors, and loped along through the cavernous underground halls of the spice company, going up a flight of stairs and coming to another gigantic portal, ripping the doors away from their hinges.

They entered a larger chamber. A group of young boys in blue choir robes ran screaming or stared in terror at the appearance of the Beast. He snarled in reply, then loped across the room, pulling on a long, looped chain and opening the paneled door at the side of the warehouse, the lock snapping with the force. The Beast then bounded out into the night air, his red eyes illuminating the docks and the mud flats of the Thames at low tide, and loped down the pier, past a nightclub in a fashionably converted warehouse. Patrons on the upper balcony pointed and stared, some screaming, others making speculative comments.

"We need to get to Parliament," Ilse said. "Dee and the Brujah both are going to be blowing it up, if they haven't already."

"We can't ride this thing all the way there!" Westphal hissed. "What of the Masquerade?"

Obviously the Ventrue fell back on tried and true points of order when things got overly confused. "Oh, please," Ilse retorted. "Do you see any vampires here? Let the Lupines deal with it if there's a problem."

They dashed down the street, past cars and taxis, Gypsies reading tarot cards, gangs of Goths in black leather and lace, and second-generation Punks selling pictures of their mohawks to tourists. Chaos, confusion, and outright wonder flowed in their wake, the Beast loping along until they came to an open area with trees and grass.

"This isn't Parliament!" Westphal snarled, his arms tightening around Ilse's waist, fingers locked in the Beast's fur.

Ilse gritted her teeth. "Pardon me, but this is my first time in the city."

"Evidently so," said a voice from the shadows, then one of the shadows separated itself from the rest and bounced out onto the path, taking the form of Charnas the Imp.

"See, Daddy? See, I found them. I've been a good boy. Do I get an ice cream cone?" There was no answer from the other shadows he looked back towards. The demon jigged up and down on the balls of his feet. "Look what we found in the park, in the dark. We'll take him home. We'll call him Clark." Charnas yammered gleefully. "Will our mother like —"

"Charnas!" snapped the first voice. "Stop your infernal chatter!"

"But, massa, infernal chatter is the only type of chatter I can make!" Charnas protested

"I know," said the voice, and then the owner stepped out from under the trees.

He was tall, with long, gray-streaked dark brown hair falling in fine waves from sun and wind, the same elements that had etched his face with deep lines. He looked to be just over forty, in a dark, nondescript green trenchcoat, a patch over his left eye stitched with an inverted pentacle. The right eye, however, was blue, the same blue as Carl and Paul, and the man's aura was mage-bright, blue and gold, but streaked with black and sullied by darkness, and painfully familiar.

Ilse caught her breath for the third time since she'd died, having seen the second ghost in as many days. The ghost of the man she loved...

Charnas flashed her an unsettling fanged grin and winked, and Ilse knew that *he* knew. "*Master,*" the imp then said to the mage, "you know the man, and you've seen the dress-up doll, but may I have the pleasure of introducing Miss Ilse Decameron?" The creature smirked. "Of course, her *real* name is Leslie Dicks, but that isn't very poetic, is it? A rose is a rose is a rose, by any other name, and it still has the same old thorns." Charnas leered. "No matter what the name."

The mage looked stricken, gazing at her with his one, Paul-blue eye, then shook his head, regaining his composure. "Thadius Zho, at your service." He nodded.

"Zho!" Westphal barked. "We'll have time for pleasantries later. For now, where's Parliament?"

"Where it always has been," Zho (Paul? Carl?) said, taking out a cigarette and lighting it, fingers trembling slightly. "If you want my help getting there, though, you'd best keep a civil tongue in your head, or I'll cut it out. There are uses for vampire tongues, you know."

The imp started to open its mouth, but Zho interrupted the unspoken comment. "Go to Hell, Charnas. *Now*." He added, more softly, "I'll call you again if I have need of you."

Charnas pouted like a child who's been sent to his room and disappeared in a gout of violet flame, leaving behind the stench of brimstone and lavender. "My apologies for my familiar," said Zho.

Westphal clutched the fur of the Beast tighter. "Thadius, you will have my gratitude if you help us and my enmity if you don't, but we can't afford to waste any more time. We need to get to Parliament."

"Agreed," said Zho. "It's not far, but allow me to work a Seeming if you intend…Clark…to accompany you." and Ilse was struck by how much (and how little) he sounded like Paul. As if he were Paul, but without the wit or soul. Still he had a shred, just a shred of Paul's wit and humor, a soul that was similar yet different. But when she looked with her sight, she again saw the dark stain of evil, different from the diablerie marks of Smudge or Crowley, but no less tainted, overlying faded colors like those of the soul of the man she loved.

>=<

Conversation was kept to a minimum as they approached the building. Too much had happened to all of them, excepting only Zho, and he was not one for idle chit-chat. Jackie came back to herself, or at least to consciousness, as they traveled. She remained quiet and withdrawn, and Kurt could not blame her. She tore the feathered hat away from her hair, tossing the hat-pin in one direction and the preposterous headpiece in the other. The dress she left alone, except for ripping away most of the skirts, thus freeing her legs for any actions she might need to take.

The only topic discussed was whether or not to let the Brujah survive the night. Despite an almost universal wish that it could be otherwise, the final decision was to try capturing the group. Let Lady Anne decide the Brujah's fates if they were successful. What they needed more than the satisfaction of obliterating at least one enemy was evidence of the plot that Appolonius and his clan members were attempting to unleash on the unsuspecting Kindred of London.

Kurt's patience was at an all-time low. After what seemed like a hundred hours, they finally reached the Houses of Parliament, a massive, hulking building that stood as a testament to Britain's golden era, both proud and heart-wrenchingly pathetic as it brooded in the light fog coming ashore from the Thames. Kurt knew the sort of building all too well, another reminder of times when the world seemed simpler. Even a few decades ago, before the Second World War and his Embrace, the world had still retained some shreds of its innocence.

Kurt stared at the building, his heart aching for simpler times and peace such as he'd not known since the days of his youth. Beside him, Jackie still held her arms around herself, chilled by the torments she'd suffered at the paws of the mindless brute the Tremere woman now petted and crooned to. Twice he'd tried to offer comfort in his own awkward fashion. Twice he'd been rejected with a look or gesture. He knew in the cold, lifeless thing that passed for his heart that she would never be the same again. Damn Crowley and his Malkavian hordes! Kurt swore to himself that vengeance and justice would be served. If not tonight, then in the very near future.

Zho walked over to him, an odd look of concern on his haggard face. Kurt suspected the man was unused to feeling the least worry for anyone save himself. "Are you all right, Kurt?"

"Yes, Thadius, I'm well enough, but I must apologize for my earlier threats against you. I'm afraid this night has taken its toll on both my manners and my emotional state."

Zho smiled briefly, an honest smile that was entirely different from every look Kurt had seen in the past. "Nothing to apologize for. Between Crowley, his creature and Charnas, you've every reason to be in a foul mood."

Jackie looked over from where she was standing, away from Kurt and the mage and well away from Decameron and her Beast. "Let's get this done. I need rest."

"Of course, my dear. Apologies for...for my lack of consideration." Kurt's words caught in his throat at her chilly tone.

Zho stepped forward and gazed at the Parliament building, his eyes seemingly unfocused, but his posture indicating that he was concentrating closely on something that Kurt could not see. "They're around the other side of the building; I can sense them. I believe they've come here by way of the river. There's no feeling that they've been on this side of the building."

Jackie strode ahead, anger and frustration apparent in every move she made. Kurt could feel a measure of her pain through the bond they shared, the bond almost broken by the damnable monster that now walked next to Ilse Decameron, sheathed in a wall of illusion created by Zho. Looking at the young man beside the Tremere, Kurt could almost believe that vile thing was truly human. The mage did his magicks well.

Jackie increased her pace, and the rest of them were obligated to run in order to match her. Kurt tried to catch up with her, but her anger gave her extra strength, despite her injuries.

Zho whispered as he jogged along, and Kurt heard the words from Wagner's "Call to the Mists" carried away from the mage by the wind. The fog on the Thames grew denser, spreading out across the shore and reaching with heavy tendrils towards the Houses of Parliament. In a matter of seconds, the mist had enshrouded the massive building.

Jackie finally slowed, unable to see even the structure ahead as the vapor continued to thicken. She came to a complete stop, and Kurt moved towards her, only to be stopped by the mage. "Kurt, allow me to speak with her a moment, won't you?"

"I—" Kurt almost said no, fully prepared to handle his woman in his own fashion, but reconsidered when he took a second to think of his own state of mind. In all the time he'd known Jackie, he'd done his best to avoid forcing a conflict between them. Now was not the time to make her do his bidding as a pawn; pawns could be stolen away. Besides which, his fondness for Jackie was one of the few things left that helped him remain stable. She was, for him, a humanizing factor. "Very well, Thadius."

Ilse Decameron stopped beside him, her face a blend of impatience, worry and other less recognizable emotions. The Beast of Crowley's torture chambers started moving forward as well, but stopped when its new master made a gesture. He suspected that something far beyond what had occurred was troubling the woman. She had not been the same since seeing Zho. Manners won over his curiosity, and Kurt left the matter alone.

"Is she going to be all right?" asked the witch, indicating Jackie with a tilt of her head.

Kurt stared at the Tremere through the continually thickening blanket created by Zho's spell and shook his head. "I don't know. I've never been…violated in the ways that she has just experienced. Jackie is a strong woman, set in her ways and often volatile, but the tortures she has been through…" He shook his head, looking at the pale silhouettes of his woman and the mage as they argued. No sound came through the fog to his ears. He had no way of knowing what was said. Only the jerky, almost violent motions of Jackie as she responded gave any indication that the two argued at all. "I just don't know. I hope so. She means so much to me—" He cut himself off, remembering that the woman he was speaking to was only an ally for the next few minutes. There was still much that had not been resolved between the two of them, and she was still his mission, though he'd begun to wonder why.

Ilse looked back at the pseudo-man lagging just behind her, her face now a clean slate. More than anything, Kurt wanted the creature dead.

"I hope so too, Herr Westphal."

"Call me Kurt."

"Call me Ilse."

Kurt smiled, noticing that his face seemed unfamiliar with just how to make the expression that normally came easily. "Then it is done, Ilse."

A moment later, Zho and Jackie came back over to where the two of them stood. Jackie seemed better in control of herself than before. Kurt shot a questioning look at the mage, but Zho simply shook his head in response.

"Let's get this matter settled then, shall we? I don't mind aiding you in this matter, but I've pressing business elsewhere that will not wait much longer."

"Thank you again, Thadius."

The mage nodded in response, leading the way through the clouded air, apparently unhindered by the product of his own spell. Semi-shapes surrounded the troupe as they moved forward: a tree still leafy and full but barely recognizable in the dense fog, a well-manicured hedge that led to a wrought-iron gate which in turn led to a stairwell and the vague shape of a door beyond the final step. After several moments of silence, the mage held up one hand and gestured. Where he pointed, down in the depths of the stairwell, a figure could be seen, just barely visible in the deep, endless white that sheathed them all. He pointed again, and twice more, each time locating a figure that could be seen only after Zho had indicated their locations. When the mage spoke again, his words called out in their minds alone: *There are your enemies. I will take the fog away and you will have your chance to attack.* There was a pause and then the single spoken word: "Now."

In an instant the fog was gone, burned away as if it had never been. Four people stood, dressed in dark clothes. The cat-woman with the red hair was down at the bottom of the stairwell, crouched before a large, open suitcase. Inside the luggage, several bundles of gray clay-like putty could be seen — plastique. The Brujah was in the act of inserting primers in the explosives, a faint blood-sweat painting her flesh a healthy pink. Kurt was stunned by how close they came to being far too late.

Surrounding the stairwell were three others, but none he could recognize as easily. No, he amended, the man was familiar enough; the Ventrue Clan's dossier on him indicated that he was a serious threat and not to be taken lightly — Appolonius. The other three seemed surprised by the sudden appearance of interlopers; Appolonius simply snarled.

Jackie moved forward with her usual grace, reaching into the jacket Kurt had given her and pulling out a shaft of wood almost as long as her forearm. She glanced sidelong at her opponent from the previous night. The angle was wrong, and aiming from the top of the stairs to where the feline Kindred crouched, her best attempts would almost surely end in failure. Her decision was immediate. Jackie's skill with melee weapons was phenomenal, and Kurt hardly had time to register her change in target before she heaved the stake directly at the left breast of the other woman present, a mere girl with flamboyant pink hair and an assortment of costume jewelry. Still surprised by the appearance of Kurt and his companions, the girl tried to dodge — too late — and could only cry out as the sharpened wooden blade rammed through her chest. She toppled over, as stiff and unyielding as a store mannequin. Jackie had managed to pierce her heart, and once it was penetrated, the vampire was immobilized.

Appolonius moved then, a blur, and grabbed Ilse Decameron by her wrist before she could do more than tense in preparation of some movement or another. "No more hocus-pocus, witch-bitch!" he hissed.

Kurt moved as well, reaching for the Brujah elder, prepared to return Ilse's earlier favor, but the Lupine beat him to it. Even as the Beast attacked, the illusion that surrounded it started to fragment, an odd juxtaposition of nine-foot tall monster and 5'10" human. With equally terrifying speed and a deafening roar, the Beast raked its front claws down Appolonius' back, even as the pressure he applied to Ilse's hand made her cry out. The Brujah's stained denim vest shredded with the blow, each of the werewolf's claws leaving red furrows from shoulder to hip. Appolonius' voice roared out to mingle with the fading echoes of Ilse's scream and the Beast's battle cry.

Appolonius faced the monstrous brute before him, his eyes goggling slightly as he stared at the distorted illusion around the Lupine. With a savage efficiency, he swung at the snarling face of his opponent, striking the Beast a glancing blow off its bristling hide.

Kurt reached behind him for the heavy, iron gate as he turned to the other two terrorists. He pulled until the rusty hinges of the gate shrieked in protest and snapped. A man in a black beret produced a small, lethal-looking Uzi from within his trench coat and aimed at Kurt, a feral sneer peeling back his upper lip and exposing his fangs as he pulled the trigger. The sneer mutated into a grimace of pain as the weapon kicked violently in his hand, once, twice, and then exploded, sending smoking metal fragments slicing through his skin. Kurt changed his target without conscious thought, noting Zho's humorless chuckle as the screams from the gunman spiraled out of the audible range.

The woman who had battled Jackie the night before started weaving her way up the dew-slicked stone steps with the confidence of a natural predator. Before she could reach the edge of the stairwell's entrance, Kurt heaved the wrought-iron gate at her. The points of the ornamental spear tips atop the thrown gate slammed into her, skinning her right ear and piercing her throat, her left breast and left elbow. The force was not enough to stop her, but certainly enough to hurt. She staggered backwards, hissing like a scalded cat, and toppled down the stairs towards the explosives. The fence that stuck awkwardly from her body was ripped free as she bounced off the stairwell's brick wall, the spear-tips on the gate taking with them a large piece of her neck and a sizable fragment of bone from her punctured elbow.

In seconds she regained her feet and fairly flew up the stairs, her frenzied face a mask of unspeakable rage. He braced himself and let her come forward, punching the small burr on the inside edge of his silver ring into the flesh of his finger and feeling the talisman's magic activate as it fed on his blood. The Brujah rushed in for the kill, fangs bared and hands outstretched, lunging for Kurt's throat. Heat flashed through his hand as the Rowan Ring changed, the ornate seed-shape at its front sprouting and growing into a massive barb, a razored tip adorning the end of the nine inch spike that bloomed from the delicately woven silver strands. The woman's hands clenched at his neck and collar, her canines gleamed in the pale moonlight, and the silver spike on Kurt's hand rammed straight into her chest, piercing her heart. A sigh of cold, rancid air erupted from the woman's mouth and wheezed from her punctured throat as well. She fell to the ground, paralyzed, the disguised weapon and its barbs slipping free from Kurt's bloody hand.

Kurt turned to the man with the ruined arm, just in time to see Jackie hold him by his hair with his pulped limb forced behind his back, and Ilse used her sorcerous skills to impale him with the gate that had earlier failed to stop Kurt's target. Three had been downed in a matter of seconds, leaving only the most dangerous of the Brujah still standing.

Kurt pivoted to see the battle continue between the Lupine and the ancient vampire, Appolonius. Both were in a rage, swinging wildly, gnashing their fangs and screaming incoherently. Kurt wondered idly why no guards had shown before remembering that the humans who worked as guards at the Houses of Parliament were long since Blood Bound to the Queen of London. He suspected half the Ventrue of London would be on the scene before much more time had passed.

Crowley's great Beast, the illusions now completely destroyed, lashed out with a bloodied paw and slammed Appolonius into the ground. Kurt was certain he heard bones break in the assault. Just the same, the Brujah came forward from a crouch, sinking his teeth into the monster's shoulder, even as his fists pistoned into the gargantua's stomach. The creature roared, and Kurt shivered with revulsion. Whatever tortures Crowley had put the monster through had twisted its already damaged psyche beyond repair. It enjoyed the pain Appolonius inflicted, was excited by the carnage it administered in return.

Despite Appolonius' reputation and prowess, the end result of the conflict was never really in question. The wolf-thing wrapped its powerful arms around the Brujah elder and squeezed with all its might. Appolonius screamed as his back was broken, and the scream in turn was cut short by the powerful jaws that tore into his throat. The Lupine apparently was poorly kept by Crowley. In a maddened state of rage, it chose the closest target to feed from — the very vampire it held, broken and shattered, within its arms.

Ilse called out, trying to regain control of Crowley's Beast, but to no avail. The need to feed was too strong, its wounds too serious for it to ignore. The raw anguish in her voice almost moved Kurt to intervene on her behalf, but common sense and a well-developed instinct for self-preservation prevailed over his need to treat Ilse as a maiden fair in need of a champion. While it was true that Kurt Westphal was of royal Prussian stock, he had long since set aside any desire to charge mindlessly into battle for the honor of the weaker sex. Or at least he liked to believe he had.

When the creature had drunk its fill, it dropped its victim to the ground and rained blow after blow on his body, breaking more bones and driving him deeper into the death-like trance caused by massive trauma. When the Lupine was finished with Appolonius, sated at least temporarily, it looked around and sniffed the air, as if searching for more interesting sources of amusement.

Perhaps old habits died hard in the Beast. It turned towards Jackie and even managed a few steps forward, before Zho intervened. The mage stepped to Jackie's side, a slight smile again of his face, and stared at the creature. "Say the word, my lady, and the deed is done. I am a man of honor despite my numerous flaws."

Jackie too stared at the Beast as it lumbered forward, her face pale and drawn. "Do it! Do it now!"

"So let it be done." Zho gestured, speaking in a foul tongue repugnant to Kurt's ears. Jackie cried out, and Kurt's attention was drawn to her, his stomach tightening in a spiraling knot of fear. Where he had dreaded a look of terror across her lovely face, he saw instead a feral grin. Her cries were not of anguish, but rather of triumph, and the reason was immediately obvious: where seconds before she had been weaponless, she now held a .357 magnum. She aimed carefully at the creature coming her way and fired.

Nearly mindless or not, the Lupine moved to avoid the bullets, but slightly too late. A blossom of meat and bone exploded away from its right shoulder, and the creature stopped in its tracks. For one instant the world seemed silent, and then the Beast cut loose with a thunderous howl.

Jackie prepared to fire again, mumbling to herself about removing the monster's manhood. Ilse moved first, grappling with Jackie for the pistol. "Leave him alone!" she screamed, her voice strained by anger and shock. "He's just a poor animal! He can't control himself!"

"Get away from me, or I swear I'll kill you too!" Jackie's voice cracked too, though for all their intimacy, Kurt could not tell if it was anger, fear or anguish that made her sound the way she did.

Ilse sputtered for a moment, her face a study in shock, before turning to rage. "Why? He was harming no one! Crowley's hold on him was destroyed!"

Zho pointed to Appolonius on the ground. "No one? Then I should hate to see the mongrel outraged."

"Because that thing *raped* me! You find yourself a new pet!" Jackie spat, shrill with rage. "That one's dead in about three seconds!"

Ilse turned away from Jackie's screams, looking toward the brute behind her. Crowley's Beast clutched at its shoulder, alternately glaring at Jackie and looking anxiously at Ilse. Ilse decided quickly. "Run, damn you! Run away from them! They'll kill you!"

Hearing her cries, the creature turned and started across the darkened path leading from Parliament. Jackie flexed and shoved her weight against the Tremere, knocking the woman sprawling. She took aim and fired again and again, pulling the trigger even after the gun's chambers were all empty. Tears ran down her face, leaving thick black streaks trailing across her heavily painted cheeks. Kurt longed to reach for her, to give her some form of comfort, and more than anything, he wanted to wipe the dirty streaks away and soothe her anguish.

But he had been rejected twice already and a third time would be more than he could handle. He remained where he was instead.

Ilse looked from where the Beast had been and then to Jackie above her. Her expression was blank in helpless confusion. Kurt knew that something had happened between her and the Beast, but he did not know just what that magic had done save to make the Lupine listen to Ilse's commands. Whatever the case, she apparently felt some connection to the monster, a heavy emotional connection. Kurt stood ready to attack the woman if she even considered hurting Jackie, but his fears were unwarranted. Her anger was apparently for Zho alone, and she appeared incapable of blaming the woman Kurt loved.

She turned to the mage with a look of hideous, wrenching betrayal on her face. "How could you? Of all the people here, how could you do this to me?"

"I made a bargain, and I kept it — silver bullets and the gun to fire them in exchange for patience and rational thought." Zho spoke softly, his words barely audible to Kurt's ears. His voice was distorted by anger or sorrow, Kurt could not tell which. "I am not Paul Carroll, Ilse. Nor am I Carl Magnuson. I am only Thadius Zho. Either of them would have handled the situation more humanely. Don't hold your anger at me against your memories of one or the budding affection you hold for the other."

Kurt thought back on the first time he met Ilse, back to the shocked face of the man who stood with her as he came to demand satisfaction for the burns he'd suffered and the humiliation he'd endured after the fish *chowder* incident. Until Zho had spoken, he'd never noticed the now obvious similarities between the man, Carl Magnuson, and the mage who stood in the shadows. The eye-patch had distracted his attention.

Ilse cast her head down, studying the dew-damp grass with

a sudden, passionate intensity. "I—," She paused a moment, her face hidden by shadows, but her body language reflecting a painful conflict within. "I must visit Dr. Dee. He must be made aware of all that has transpired tonight."

Kurt spoke at last. "Of course, Ilse. Your clan and the Ventrue as well. There is the potential war to consider, after all. I am glad you thought of this — I have been too distracted."

Ilse smiled, a weak faded expression, and nodded her gratitude. Then she turned and walked quickly around the edge of the building. Jackie finally came back from wherever her mind had taken her and dropped the empty pistol on the ground. She looked around for a moment before finally focusing on her attention on her hands.

After an awkward silence had reigned for several seconds, Zho called out, "Charnas, come forth." With a flash of black smoke and purplish flame, the creature was there, his mouth already opened and doubtless ready to start making comments about the entire situation that would have them all ready to destroy him. "Silence, foul demon. Do not even start with me. You will follow Ilse Decameron for me, and you will do so discreetly, or I will inflict upon you every torture that could possibly cause harm to you. Do you understand me?"

Charnas lifted one finger, fully prepared to make his point anyway, then looked deep into his master's single cold, blue eye and lowered his finger. His face was filled with obvious displeasure. "Very well, 'master,' but don't think for a second that I won't remember this." The creature faded from view, a sulking violet shadow that slowly dissipated.

Zho turned back to Kurt, his face tense and his gestures abrupt and angry. "We'll meet again tomorrow night. For now, I need to rest, and I need to study what the Fates say of the future. Good night." The mage walked away, leaving Kurt and Jackie alone with each other in a cold, bitter silence that stretched on until Jackie looked over to him and explained that she needed to disarm the explosives. Kurt nodded, leaving her to that task and the task of sorting out her feelings, while he gathered together the defeated Brujah and waited for the Queen of London to arrive.

Ten minutes later, Lady Anne, Courtland Leighton and a small army of retainers appeared from around the side of the building. Kurt moved away from Jackie and the remains of the Brujah bomb, expertly guiding them to a distant spot. Lady Anne only glanced in the direction of Jackie Therman, but upon hearing the anguished sounds coming from Kurt's lover, she made certain that no one went too close to the woman. Occasionally, everyone needed time to suffer in peace.

➤◄

Ilse cut around the House of Lords towards the Thames. She'd never seen Parliament before, and the remaining mist from Zho's spell (or the natural fog of the area, Ilse wasn't sure which) would also aid the rite.

To her left, she happened upon a darkened stairwell with a shadowy door at the end, almost passing it by, but then turned and started down. Stray pebbles on the old stone steps cut painfully into her bare feet, her other slipper lost during the Beast's ride.

She hoped...She didn't know what she hoped. So many things had happened, all so confusing, and it was hard to tell the victims from the villains, if there'd ever been such clear distinctions.

Brushing at a bloody tear, Ilse took out the Iron Key and cut her thumb until the iron was stained red and dripping. "House of Shadows, House of Mystery, open your door to me, open your door to one of the blood..." The invocation was different each time, because, by its very nature, the charm had to be forgotten, or at least badly remembered. There was nothing so antithetical to the House of Secrets as common knowledge.

The Iron Key, and its bloody teeth, slipped into the new lock of the ancient door, fitting perfectly, but the Key did not turn.

Ilse glanced to either side. She wasn't quite sure where she was, and no one was looking at her, but…

The hair stood up on the back of her neck, one of the few human reflexes she had left, and she looked over her shoulder…

Atop the wall at the head of the shadowy stairwell was Charnas the Imp, perched like a sinister Harlequin doll, one leg crossed over the other.

The second after she caught sight of him, he clapped his hands to his face with a Macauley Culkin expression of amazement and tipped backwards over the wall.

A moment later, his head peeked back over the edge, the imp pulling himself up on his fingertips. "No fair, you saw me." He raised himself back up and swung his legs over, flipping them into their former position. "No one's supposed to see me, unless…" He grinned. "You've given me a riddle. I like that. I suppose the answer is one of those Heisenberg Uncertainty Principle things: By the very act of observing, I've changed what's being observed. If I hadn't been looking, everything would have been fine, but since I did look, it didn't go the way it would if I hadn't, and the end result isn't what you wanted." He held up one finger like a professor making a point. "You needed secrecy for your charm to work."

Ilse pursed her lips, and the imp giggled. "I'm right. I like that too."

"What are you doing here, Charnas?"

The imp uncrossed his legs and started rocking back and forth, kicking his heels like a little boy. "Are you really going to trade the riddle I owe you for something you already know the answer to? Fair's fair."

Ilse relaxed her face. "You're spying on me."

"And the lady says the secret word!" Charnas exclaimed, then reached behind the wall and pulled out a large raven.

Quoth the raven, "Spy."

He tossed the bird in the air, and it disappeared in a flutter of black wings. "I think that works much better than a duck with a cigar and glasses, don't you? A lot more demonic."

"Why are you spying on me, Charnas?"

"Why do you think?"

Ilse sighed. "Because Thadius Zho asked you to."

The imp clapped his hands, but didn't produce any ravens this time. "Good answer! Good answer! But fair's fair, like I said, and I owe you the answer to a question. Don't throw it away, Ilse. It's not often you get something from the Devil that you don't have to pay for afterwards." His brow puckered. "Isn't there *any* question you'd like me to answer, truthfully, without any attempt at deception?"

Ilse considered. She knew that demons worked from their own dark purposes, but could also be trusted to hold to the letter of their word, especially if it suited their designs. If Charnas truly owed her a straight answer, there was one question she wanted to know, and that the imp should be able to tell her. "Thadius Zho seems very familiar to me. Why is this, exactly?"

Charnas applauded, the very picture of sardonic delight. "Excellent question! I was afraid you weren't going to pick up on my hints and I'd have to go through some other elaborate ruse to get around my oaths of secrecy to Zho." He lounged out on the top of the wall, propping his head up on one arm. "For your one question, you actually get quite a bit, including the answer to many other secrets and mysteries. One is that reincarnation is, in fact, a fact, or at least in your case. You are the reincarnation of a woman named Gwyneth la Salle, *née* de la Courte, wife to Tiberius la Salle, who is, in fact, one and the same with Thadius Zho — no reincarnation involved." The imp grinned, apparently relishing the tale. "Tiberius made a bargain with my greater half, the particulars of which I'm not at liberty to divulge, except in that the price of the bargain was that Tiberius sell his firstborn child and sacrifice the child's mother, to, as you might expect, Charnas, the Lord of Misrule. It was only necessary that he love the woman — not that she love him — but hey, it made the betrayal all the more painful, and who's gonna complain about a bonus?"

Charnas sat up and kicked his feet against the wall. "*You* were that woman, Ilse, the one he murdered and whose baby he gave to a demon. *That* is why he seems so familiar. That, and the fact that your soul has had a long series of affairs and involvements with the souls of the men of his bloodline. You're the Dulcinea to their Don Quixote, the Pocahontas to their John Smith, or, in the case of Thadius, the Margaret to his Dr. Faustus. And *that*, Ilse, is why he was so disturbed by your appearance. Thadius knows there's nothing sweeter than revenge, except maybe a guilty conscience, and all debts come due eventually."

The imp gestured, the image of convivial mirth. "And *now* I've answered the riddle I owed you." He leaned forward then, his features sly and conspiratorial, and he pointed one finger directly at her heart. "And if you'd like to play Nimue to his Merlin, I can help. After all, we both have a score to settle with Zho."

Ilse felt her blood turn to water, phantom memories surfacing in the back of her mind, recollections of a life — and death — she hadn't known that she had. "Go away, Charnas," she whispered, trying to push them away.

He grinned impishly. "No."

Her blood began to boil with rage, and tears started in her eyes. "Go to Hell!"

"Ah-ah-ah, no can do," Charnas said, tsking his fingers at her. "Only Thadius has that power over me, by the compact. Unless you want to set up your own contract with my greater half, Charnas, the Lord of Misrule?"

"*No*," Ilse said and attempted to banish the horrible memories that had sprung up at the imp's words.

"Well…," said Charnas, shrugging and throwing his hands

up and looking heavenward, as if for divine guidance. He tipped sideways off the wall until he caught himself at the last moment with one leg, swinging back and forth until he came to rest, suspended like the Hanged Man, though instead of looking complacent, he had the same devout expression as before, this time pointing downwards.

"Well," Charnas repeated, now in the proper position, "if you're ever in the mood to sell your soul, here's hoping you remember *us*. We're the fun side of evil, and we offer much more innovative torments and tortures than the other demons and devils. Just ask Thadius." The imp looked pensive. "Not that we've got his soul. Yet."

Ilse shivered. "I wasn't aware that evil could be fun."

"Of course it is," said Charnas, "or, I should say, *our* brand of evil is — or at least we'd like to think so." He smiled mock-beatifically, holding his hands together in reverence. "Other demons and dark lords try to disguise what they are, appear as angels of light, all the rest of that shtick, or else show up with great roaring voices and flames and the 'Why have you summoned me, pitiful mortal?' routine. I ask you — Would *you* sell your soul to someone like that? Angels don't buy souls, so if a guy with wings and a halo asks for yours, you know he isn't on the up-and-up. And why would you want to sell your soul to some loud-mouthed pompous windbag, unless you're seriously into B&D? Which, if you are, we can accommodate, but it's not our main stock-in-trade — unless you *really* enjoy it.

"We're the fun evil," Charnas said, continuing. "Charnas and me, me and Charnas — really, it's the same thing. He's the Lord, I'm the Knave, or the Fool, of Misrule, and we thought, 'Hey, let's make evil fun! Then everyone will want to sell their souls!' Or at least that was the general idea." The imp shrugged, penduluming slightly. "At least we're honest about it, unlike *some* demons I could mention. Different strokes for different folks, I suppose, and if it weren't for that, everyone would just be selling their souls to 'Evil' with a capital *E*, and we'd be out of a job."

"Go to Hell," Ilse repeated.

Charnas smirked. "Eat my shorts."

"I don't think you wear any."

The imp seemed so tickled by this that he kicked his heels with glee, losing his grip on the wall and falling on his head. Ilse was pleased, but unfortunately Charnas didn't seem any worse for the wear, clutching his stomach and rolling on his back, snickering.

But he did seem off guard. Ilse slipped her key back in her purse and quickly unloaded the camera, readying another roll of film. If she could just get the proper rite prepared...

At the last moment, Charnas hopped up. "Ah-ah-ah," he said, "you didn't say, 'Mother, may I?' You know you can steal people's souls with those things."

"I knew," Ilse said and lifted the camera into position, hitting the button.

Charnas disappeared in a gout of violet flame the moment before the flash, his trademark sulfur and lavender wafting down the stairwell, then there was a second burst of purple fire right in front of Ilse, and Charnas reappeared midair, dressed in black and magenta tennis gear.

He grabbed the camera from behind — "Image is everything!" — and vanished in another flash of fire.

Then he appeared back on the original wall in his original motorcycle leathers. "You're nasty," he said. "I like that in a woman."

"Where's my camera?"

"It's in Hell. I bet you didn't know there was a separate Hell for cameras."

"I'm sure you'll tell me all about it, whether I want to hear it or not." Ilse hugged her evening bag to herself, trying to cover up the hole in her dress. "Listen, I've got a war to prevent, and I don't have time to chat with demons."

"Well, don't let me be keeping you. Run along, run along!" He made a shooing gesture with his long fingers, then grinned. "Though I don't know what Dr. Dee is doing in the maintenance room. That's where that stairway leads."

Well, so much for the Iron Key. It seemed there was less chance of being able to use it than there was of using her camera.

Charnas snapped his fingers. "Let me guess — Dr. Dee did his 'Oh, let's be so secret and mystical' shtick and you're not allowed to go back to the chantry by any usual way, like the front door, the chantry, of course, being either the house on Pudding Lane, Garter-Cross near the Tower, or Malmsey House on Curson Street." The imp began ticking them off on his fingers. "Now the house on Pudding Lane is right by the solicitors, which means Ventrue, so —"

"Is this all common knowledge?"

"What?" said the imp, looking up. "Oh, no. It's worth quite a few petty souls to the right people. I wouldn't know, except I know Zho, and Zho knows Tremere, and what Zho knows, I know, y'know?" He put a finger to his chin and studied her. "I'd be guessing you need to get to Malmsey House."

"If you tell Lady Anne…"

The imp grinned, and Ilse knew she'd confirmed his suspicion. "What, you'll make me wish I was in Hell? You'll visit me with unspeakable torments? You'll visit me, period? You know, I might just like that. Lady A's just around the corner; I could tell her right now."

Ilse didn't say anything.

Charnas chuckled and held up one finger. "Listen, sugar, don't threaten a demon. We wrote the book on it. So, why don't you do your job, and I'll do my job, and everyone'll be as happy as pigs in a brothel." His look dared her to think of all the possible interpretations. "Now you just run along to Malmsey House, and pretend that you never saw me, and I'll sneak along after you, and I won't tell anyone that we talked. It'll be our little secret."

Ilse bit her lip, not wanting to admit how helpless she felt. "The fact of the matter is, I don't know where Malmsey House is."

"Didn't I tell you?" Charnas asked. "It's on Curson Street."

"I don't know where Curson Street is either."

Charnas whistled. "Boy, you're really hating unlife, aren't you, lady? If you lost that bag of tricks, you'd be up the River Styx without a paddle, to badly mix a few metaphors, but what the hey, if a dead Englishman can get away with it, so can I." He jumped down from the wall but remained in a crouch, beckoning with one finger. "C'mon, follow me, and I'll get you there." He grinned evilly. "You don't have any choice but to trust me. Isn't this great?"

Ilse knew when to give up. "Just get us there quickly."

"Follow me."

Charnas led the way up and around Parliament, moving with a ludicrously exaggerated sneaking gait that Ilse suspected would have been impossible for anything other than a spirit. She just followed as quietly as she could, the grass of the lawn cool beneath her feet and wet with dew.

Near the fountains and reflecting pool, they came upon a stretch of road where a chauffeur waited by a Rolls Royce Silver Ghost. Charnas rubbed his hands as they crouched behind the bushes. "Oh, this is going to be fun, but quick," he promised. "Wait here."

Charnas then strolled around the hedge and down towards the chauffeur, metamorphosing into the very image of Lady Anne, down to the jeweled pins in her hair.

"My Queen," the chauffeur said, standing at attention, only moving his lips and the one arm necessary to open the door.

"Oh, Clarence!" Charnas cried, rushing up in a very ladylike manner. "Oh, I do not know how I can take it any longer! Oh, kiss me!"

The imp, in the guise of the Queen of London, draped herself around the hapless chauffeur, still standing at attention, and planted a large, passionate kiss on his mouth. The chauffeur swayed at attention, one hand still holding the door of the Rolls, and Charnas finally came off him. "My — My lady…" he stammered.

Charnas quickly looked flustered, primping her hair, then turned to Clarence and clutched his arm. "Oh, Clarence, do forgive us. That was most unbecoming."

"Think — Think nothing of — "

"Oh hush, Clarence," Charnas said. "Let me just look at you for a moment. Oh, I must apologize. You know I took you as my ghoul for I was attracted to you, but these pressures — Oh, Clarence, please, hold me for a moment! the attempts on my life by these horrid Brujah and those damnable Tremere…Oh, the others must not see my moment of weakness, but I don't care! Do you hear me, Clarence? I don't care!"

Charnas held her wrist to her forehead, the hapless chauffeur merely standing there and attempting to keep a stiff upper lip. Charnas tore the pins from her hair, screaming, "Look at me, Clarence! I don't care if I'm dead! I don't care if I'm a Queen! I don't care if you're gay! I am a woman, you are a man, and I must have you!"

She shook out her hair, embraced him once, sobbing, then pushed him away and pointed to the bushes a short distance from the ones Ilse was behind. "Go behind those bushes and take off your clothes, Clarence. Once I compose myself, I will join you. But I wish for you to feign that your passion for me is as strong as my passion for you. Make me feel like a woman!"

"I — I will try my best, My Queen."

Charnas stood there, gesturing imperiously, and Clarence left, with only a glance or two backwards, the water of the fountain sparkling with the lights of Parliament.

Once he was behind the bushes, Ilse took that as her cue and ran down to the car. Charnas grinned, and his semblance of Lady Anne dissolved into his regular black-leather bad-boy appearance as he held up the keys he'd lifted from the chauffeur.

Ilse climbed in the back of the Rolls and slammed the door as Charnas hopped into the driver's seat, bouncing up and down happily. "A motorcar...," he said in a completely different voice from his own, as if he were quoting something. "A lovely red motorcar..."

He was definitely quoting something, because the Rolls was silver, not red, but he started it up anyway. "Put-put!" he said, and it purred to life, almost silent. Charnas piloted it away from the curb. "Put-put and off we go!"

Ilse ignored the imp's comments, looking back at the fountain and the bushes sparkling in the moonlight. "She's going to kill him."

"Hopefully," Charnas responded, back to his usual mischievous tone. "Really sucks to be a Ventrue chauffeur tonight, doesn't it? What do you think they pay them? Blood?" He grinned in the rearview mirror.

"One would suppose so."

"They'd have to," Charnas said, whipping into the main flow of traffic and flipping off the cars behind them in response to the angry honking. "You know how many souls it takes to get that kind of loyalty from a demon?"

Ilse decided to take it as a rhetorical question and so made no comment. Charnas only responded by driving over the divider onto the right-hand side of the road, threading the needle between two oncoming cars. "Look at me!" he cried. "I'm an American tourist!" He floored it then, still in the lane of oncoming traffic. "Now I'm a German tourist! *Ja! Die Autobahn!*"

Ilse was plastered back into the soft gray upholstery, hearing the squealing brakes and smashing fenders around them. "Get to the other side!"

"What's the third type of awful tourist?" Charnas asked, giggling.

"I don't know, I give up!" she babbled, praying that the crazy demon wouldn't drive her straight to Hell.

"A Japanese tourist!" he answered, then swerved back onto the left-hand side, causing three more accidents in the process. "Here, take some pictures! You can't be a proper Japanese tourist without pictures!" Charnas held up one hand, and a ball of purple flame appeared in it, flickering out and leaving behind her camera.

"Whoops," he said, snatching it back and taking his other hand from the wheel. "Can't let you be having this. Not that I object to the idea of stealing souls with a camera, mind you, but I'd rather not be captured on film myself. Ruins the image." He detached the Monocle of Clarity and tried to hand her the camera.

Ilse only had eyes for the railing of the bridge. "For God's sake, steer!" she cried out, then reached out telekinetically, grabbing the wheel and preventing them from crashing into the Thames.

"For God's sake...no," Charnas mused. "For your sake ... maybe. But you're doing a pretty good job of it, so maybe I should take the pictures." He leaned over across the passenger's seat and snapped a shot of a car plowing into one of the lampposts. "Thadius said for me to follow you, not drive you, anyway."

"I don't know where we're going."

"To Malmsey House, wasn't it? What, you mean it really *is* the house on Puddin' Lane?" Charnas grinned, facing her and holding her camera offhandedly.

Ilse grabbed it. "You drive. I'll take the pictures."

He laughed, Ilse supposed, because she'd finally given in to his game. "Okay," he said, tossing the Monocle of Clarity back into her lap as well and putting his hands back on the wheel. "But you can't snap my picture, 'cause if you do, you're lost, and if you're lost, you aren't gonna have anyone to show you the way to Dr. Dee."

Ilse fitted the Monocle back on and raised the camera, taking a direct shot of Charnas. The flash went off bright in the interior of the car.

"Think again," Ilse said and lowered the camera.

Charnas was still there.

He held up the yellow roll of film in one hand. "Psych."

Ilse felt her fangs press against her lower lip, and she tightened her grip on the camera. "Just get us there," she ground out, biting back the incipient frenzy.

"Okay," said the imp, taking a corner too hard, then wrenching the wheel. The Ventrue Rolls spun out, slamming Ilse into the left door tires squealing like pigs at the slaughter, until with a bump and a jump and another bump, they fetched up against the curb.

"We're here!" the imp laughed and disappeared. The next second, the door behind her popped open and Ilse tumbled out onto the street.

She looked up at Charnas, grinning gleefully at her. "Okay, I've kept my part of the bargain. Now you go on in, and I'll tag along."

"In your dreams, imp!" Ilse spat, but Charnas only snickered and vanished, not in a gout of flames this time, but in a puff of lavender smoke.

Ilse waved it away, then picked up her evening bag and the camera. The Monocle was still attached, but the lens cover had come off its string. She snapped it on the end, hearing the echo of Charnas' annoying laughter, and got to her feet.

She wished there were a worse place than Hell for creatures like Charnas.

><

Staggering slightly, but not much more bruised than before, Ilse made her way up the steps of the mansion, resting her feet on the plush gold carpet remnant below the front step, monogrammed with Sarah Cobbler's sigil. The door opened before she could even reach for the knocker.

"Miss Decameron, please, do come in." Mr. Winthrop ushered her in before she could say a word, shutting the door behind her. "Though I'm doubtlessly certain that you wish to freshen up, I am also certain that the master will wish to see you immediately. If you would be so good as to come with me?"

Anticipating her every need, Mr. Winthrop conducted her down the hall, lifting a long, crushed royal velvet cloak from a peg and draping it about her. "I'm certain that Miss Cobbler will not mind me taking the liberty, given the circumstances and the state of your dress."

"Thank you, Mr. Winthrop."

"Tut, think nothing of it. I live to serve." He opened a door, ushering her into another suite of rooms and down a grand staircase. "Shall I also take the liberty of bringing you refreshments, Miss Decameron? I judge that yours has not been a pleasant evening."

"No," Ilse said, hearing Charnas chuckle in the back of her mind. "It has not. And yes, please, as to the vitæ."

"I will see to it at once."

They stopped outside a pair of tall, black doors, marked in gold with magical monads, Sarah's on the left and another, equally complicated one on the right.

"The Doctor's conjuring room," Mr. Winthrop explained. "I am not permitted inside except in absolute emergencies, but I'm certain the Doctor will excuse you, given the circumstances." He bowed with a click of his heels, gesturing to an antique Chinese lacquerware table. "Your refreshments should be awaiting you here when you emerge."

Mr. Winthrop took the handle of the right-hand door and twisted, pulling open the massive portal and letting out the smell of incense and smoke and the sound of chanting.

"By Adonai and Elohim, I bind you!" cried Dr. Dee as Ilse

slipped inside. Mr. Winthrop shut the door behind her with a muffled boom. As she stepped over a sigil on the floor in front of the door, Ilse heard a *snap* from her camera, the lens cap popping off and rolling across the floor through the drapes that screened the chamber from the door.

"By El and Eloha and He who is known as Tetragrammaton, I bind you! By Elohim Sabaoth and Sadai and Adonai Melech in the High, I bind you to do that task for which you were summoned and no more, returning thereafter to the hell which is your prison, foul spirit, to trouble this earth no more."

"Bugger all that, you old Anglican lackey!" said a voice, hissing and whispering with the crackle of flames. "Are you going to let me blow up Parliament this time or not?"

Ilse edged round and slipped through the black draperies, looking in to see Dee in the center of one conjuring circle, Sarah and her sword in another, and in the middle of a third, a hideous Spectre, sparkling and crackling with flames. The thing was dressed like a scarecrow, flaming rags and tatters bound together with firecrackers and bits of twine, the fuses hissing but not burning down. The creature's head was a huge rotten turnip, carved into a jack-o'-lantern with coals of hellfire behind the eyes and open mouth. A crown of sparklers hissed in an infernal halo over its head.

The Spectre was the first to notice her. "Eh wot?" it said, then held up a string of firecrackers and a handful of sparklers. "Sparklies, girly, pretty crackers. Let us out, and we'll have some fun, eh? You helped to make me. You burnt me and hated me with all the little ones. We taught you how to play with matches, love, and all we ever gave you was fun. C'mon, let old Guy Fawkes out and we'll have a lovely time of it, just like old days. First Parliament, then the rest. The Great Fire will seem like nothing. It'll be a jolly holiday for everyone."

Dr. Dee's head snapped around sharply as if he had heard something, then gave a quick glance to his apprentice. "Sarah! See to Fawkes."

"Yes, Doctor." Sarah raised her sword and held it before her. "By Michael in the East, I bind you, unclean spirit. By Raphael in the West, I bind you, damned one." She turned to each quarter, invoking the archangels and binding Fawkes.

Ilse spotted her lens cap on the floor near Dr. Dee's circle. She started to reach for it, but he held his hand up in warning, staring at it intensely. He gestured with his ebony wand and ordered, "By the sight of God focused upon this room, I conjure you, whatever you may seem to be, to appear in your true form, with no deceits or trickeries. By my will and the will of God, let it be done!"

The lens cap twitched and disappeared in a puff of smoke to be replaced by Charnas the Imp.

"Rats!" pouted the demon, snapping his fingers. "That was one of my best tricks too." He stuck out his tongue at the Doctor.

"Charnas," breathed Dr. Dee.

"The Imp, not the Lord — otherwise, *you'd be in trouble*," Charnas sang mockingly, skipping around the room and looking at the circles. "Wow, nice wards. You copy 'em out of a book or something?"

"Let me out!" crackled the Spectre. "Let me out, little imp, and we'll turn this city into an inferno!"

"Good idea if you ask me, but these wards are tighter than a Tory's purse strings. For social programs, that is." Charnas poked a nail at the one around the flaming scarecrow, and the air sparkled with divine light, the tip of the nail disappearing in violet smoke. "Ow!" Charnas yelped and stuck his finger in his mouth, sucking on it. "Sorry, guy. You're stuck in the can — though you don't look a thing like Prince Albert."

"I'll blow him up too!" hissed the Spectre. "I'll blow up all the wicked Anglican kings!"

Charnas pointed one thumb at Guy Fawkes and with the index finger of his other hand made the crazy sign to Ilse.

Dr. Dee had his attention divided between the bound Spectre and the unbound imp. "Out with it, Miss Decameron. Quickly."

"Out with it?" Charnas fell to the floor in a fit of giggles.

"Kurt Westphal, the Ventrue Archon, and I were both captured by Crowley. We just escaped." Ilse paused, collecting her thoughts. "We just stopped the Brujah from blowing up Parliament."

"Yes, let's blow up Parliament!" cried the Spectre. "Let's blow it all up!"

"Unnecessary," Dee said, responding to Ilse, not Fawkes, "I already suspected the Ventrue would. The Brujah were merely a distraction and alibi. However, they did set explosives?"

"Yes," Ilse said, "but the police and Ventrue will have already dismantled them."

"Immaterial." The Doctor glanced to Charnas. "Yet the imp means that Zho has made his presence known, as I feared he might, and Crowley is always a random factor in any equation. Did the madman mention anything of import?"

"Yes, he said his revenge had begun, and that the Comte was displeased, whoever that is."

A dark look came over Dee's face. "That would be St. Germain. A fig for Crowley's revenge, but the Comte is another matter altogether. We can't risk it. Sarah, begin the banishment."

Sarah began calling out names of angels as Fawkes screamed, "What?! You were finally going to let me blow up Parliament, you wicked old negromancer! I always knew you were an Anglican! We died for you, you old fraud! Once a black magician, always a black magician!" The fuses strung throughout his clothing sizzled brighter and his fingers shot flames like Roman candles, the sparks disappearing at the borders of the ward.

"By Adonai and Elohim, I banish you!" Dee cried. "By El and Eloha and He who is known as Tetragrammaton!"

"Back to Hell!" Sarah cried, getting into the spirit of things. "Back to Hell, you flamin' wanker! Back with the other conspirators! By Gabriel, Michael, Uriel and Raphael! By Matthew, Mark, Luke and John! By Tahaoelog, Thahebyobeaatanun, Thahaaothe and Ohooohaatan, the Kings of the Elements and the Four Quarters they each preside over! By all these and more, we banish you and we bind you!"

"By Elohim Sabaoth and Sadai and Adonai Melech the Most High, get you to Hell!" boomed Dr. Dee.

The Spectre went up like a fireworks fountain, hellfire shooting up between his rags and bits of string. A hole opened in the floor at his feet, skeletal hands wreathed in flame reaching up and dragging him down, screaming. Like flames winking out on spilled alcohol, the hellhole then irised closed, vanishing with a final shimmer and wail.

"Yeah!" cried Charnas, shaking his fist. "And don't you come back! We like the Anglicans where they are!"

The imp then grinned at everyone and vanished in a puff of lavender smoke.

A second later, a black teacup poodle ran past Ilse's ankles and out through the crack in the drapes, yipping happily. Ilse couldn't be sure, but she would have sworn that the dog had a tiny purple mohawk.

Sarah made a move to go after it, but then Dee held up his hand. "No, Sarah. Do not be distracted by what occurs outside the circle. Demons and black spirits are ever drawn to these invocations, even ones which do not concern them. Now give your thanks to God and dismiss the quadrants."

Sarah nodded, and she and Dee went about the end of the ritual, giving thanks each of the angels and archangels and acknowledging God by each of his permitted names. At last Sarah cut her circle with her sword and Dr. Dee his with his wand.

"Thadius Zho," Dee murmured as he came up alongside Ilse, gesturing for her to follow as Sarah held aside the curtains. "This means trouble, though I should have expected as much after meeting Carl Magnuson."

"How... ?" Ilse began, but he put up a hand for silence.

"No more," he said. "Our conversations are not secure until we banish that imp from this house. But I know the Imp of Charnas, and where it goes, Zho soon follows. It's part of their bargain."

They passed out of the black-draped room and through the door, which was open a crack. "Charnas is far too clever to be sealed in a locked room," Dee said, shutting the door and turning the handle downwards. "However, he will most likely hide in plain sight, disguised as some object the color of his soul, such as your lens cap."

"Oh, lordy!" Sarah exclaimed. "We've got to play 'Button, button, who's got the button?'"

"Quite." Dr. Dee looked about, but between the black lacquer table, the black enameled vase, the ebony frames to the pictures and the black doors, there were a great number of places for the imp to hide.

Mr. Winthrop was good to his word, however, and on the table were a teapot and cosy, along with three cups, Royal Doulton china stamped with Dee's personal sigil on one side and the seal of House Tremere on the other. Nothing apart from the table, however, was black, and Ilse took a cup, Sarah assisting her with the British vampire tea ceremony.

"I take it," Dee said, rather distractedly, "that the imp witnessed all of your dealings with Crowley and this Archon, Westphal?"

Ilse nodded. "In detail."

"Then relate them."

Ilse did so, with only the occasional question from Dee or exclamation from Sarah.

"Mr. Crowley's really gone crackers this time, that's all I can say," Sarah remarked finally, pouring herself another cup of blood and trying to get the Doctor to take his, which remained on the tray, untouched.

Dee continued to ignore it. "Crowley is the least of our problems, Sarah. When I first met him, Edward Kelly was an overconfident charlatan who'd had his ears cropped for counterfeiting, and if Crowley is truly his reincarnation, then all I can say is that the man has changed very little." Dr. Dee scanned the hallway. "Thadius Zho and the Comte de St. Germain, however, are both troubles worth countenancing."

He turned around, taking stock of everything in the hall, then paused at Ilse, his eyes coming to rest on her camera. "Miss Decameron, that is a Monocle of Clarity?"

Ilse nodded.

Coldly Dr. Dee put his hand out, accepting the talisman without a word, then raised it to his eye and scrutinized the passage. An instant later, the left pupil of a duchess in one of the portraits shed a single inky tear which ran down her cheek, landing on her finger and blossoming into a painted black bird. "'One for sorrow!'" cried the crow, then flew out of the painting and down the hall, laughing raucously.

"Bother," said Dr. Dee, with all the emotion he seemed capable of. "We will have to ward each room in turn — or negotiate with Zho." Dee tilted his head slightly then. "Or negotiate directly with Charnas. The fiend hates Zho and will try to swindle him as wickedly as Zho swindled it. Or, I should say, its Lord."

"Doctor," Sarah said, pouring Ilse the last cup, "shouldn't we be worrying more about Mr. Crowley? I know you don't like to talk about him, but Master Loony Toons is a lot more trouble than just some old demon worshipper."

Dee started down the hall with Ilse's Monocle, gesturing for them to follow. "Zho is no demon worshipper. He's a demon swindler, and that's something far more dangerous." They rounded the corner of the hall, into another of Malmsey House's endless ornate passageways. "As the imp told Miss Decameron, he made a pact with Charnas, the Lord of Misrule, for various favors in exchange for his firstborn child.

I was not aware that the murder of his wife was part of the deal, but as this is the case, I suppose the fiend did get a consolation prize of sorts."

Ilse felt a chill finger down her spine at Dee's cold and clinical analysis of the horrible memories that still fluttered at the back of her mind, but the Doctor only continued, "Unfortunately for the Dark Lord, there are peculiarities to the magical laws regarding the sale of children, or at least there were in the contract he signed with Zho. Either way, the Lord of Misrule could not take Zho's child, or its soul, until such time as there were no members of the bloodline with a superior claim." The Doctor inspected a black candlestick with the Monocle, then moved on. "That has not happened as yet, as Zho is not the first immortal mage of the line."

"Who?" Ilse began.

The Doctor waved for silence. "Not now, Miss Decameron. Walls have ears, and while the demon no doubt already knows, there's no sense in confirming any suspicions he might have. Likewise with the Comte, so consider the matter at a close."

Ilse was already familiar with the imp's ability to ferret out information, though she suspected that Dee did not want to keep the information so much from Charnas as from her. But you couldn't be a Tremere without knowing how to bide your time in silence. Ilse followed.

Sarah was the first to broach the last permissible subject. "Doctor, what are we going to do about the Ventrue?" Her fencing sword scraped the wainscoting as she hurried down the hall after him.

"Absolutely nothing," Dee said, "and the imp may tell its master that, if it so chooses. We've taken no direct action against the Queen of London, and we'll deny all knowledge of the Brujah's pathetic attempt to carry out our threat. If Lady Anne wishes to take hearsay by way of a demonist and his familiar to the Camarilla, she's quite welcome to do so."

He investigated the tail spots of an ermine mantle in a coronation portrait. "At very worst, she'll discover we control the restless soul of Fawkes and have him ready to do our bidding, though that knowledge should prove as disquieting as it is useful. We'd suspect she already knows, for we sponsored Fawkes and the first Gunpowder Plot, and we have fostered the bonfires and rituals for the four centuries since to grant his spirit the dark Memoriam necessary to create a Spectre of unparalleled might. The revilement of four centuries' children is a font of destructive power even Lady Anne should be able to appreciate."

He continued down the hall, pausing to examine a black marble Cupid. "It's time that she knew we have this weapon at our disposal, and to convey this information, I can think of no better means than a small fiend, especially one as malicious as Charnas."

Dee smiled faintly then and dandled the Monocle, as if relishing the expression Lady Anne would have when Charnas told her of the Spectre of Guy Fawkes. "I shall hope for Lady Anne's sake that she has taken no reprisals on behalf of her missing Archon. Otherwise we may truly have to give Fawkes the holiday he so much desires."

"And Mr. Crowley?" Sarah asked.

"Crowley, by his very nature, is unpredictable," Dee said as they entered another room, this one as dark as Charnas' spirit. "The best one can do is try to expect the unexpected. But as for the imp, its psychic traces lead here. Sarah, shut the door."

"Yes, Doctor."

The room was black, but then Sarah flipped the switch, and the chandeliers lit one by one with a sparkle and hum of electric lights. It was a theater, with balconies and a stage and an endless number of props and costumes stacked and stored about, looking as if it hadn't been used in at least a hundred years.

"Hmm," said Dee. "The Theater, the Devil's rightful playground, and doubly so for one such as Charnas." He perused the room, scanning with the Monocle.

"Very well, imp," he said at last. "We haven't the time for this, and in that you've won. Now reveal yourself, and perhaps we can strike a bargain."

The only sound that greeted Dee's words were faint echoes from the corners of the hall.

Dee handed the Monocle back to Ilse and stood, regarding the room. "By Adonai and Elohim, we conjure you to appear before us, Imp of Charnas," he intoned, voice heavy and solemn, "and by the name of your own Lord, Charnas, and the titles by which he is known, do we charge you to reveal yourself: Charnas, Lord of Misrule, Margrave of Mockery, Master of Foul Merriment, Duke of Dark Mirth, Fiend of Frivolity, Baron of Black Comedy, Mountebank of Mischief, Clown of Carnality, Harlequin of Horror..." Dee's gaze traveled across the room as he said this and paused as he came to an old Punch and Judy theatre in one corner, a knowing look coming over his face. "...and Prince of Puppets."

In the rack of old puppets to one side, the black Devil twitched to life, wiggling as if a long-fingered hand were inside it. "That's Professor of Puppets!" the Devil cried out in Charnas' voice. "Prince goes with Pernicious Puns!"

The puppet then tumbled out of the rack, growing in size and unfolding its legs until at last Charnas landed on the floor in his usual form, a red Devil puppet on his left hand. "Hello!" he said, waving the puppet's arms, not breaking his sly grin. "I've come to take you to Hell, Dr. Dee!"

Dr. Dee's face was impassive. "If I am to take the part of Mr. Punch, Charnas, the script says that I will destroy you."

"Yes!" said the Devil puppet on Charnas' hand. "But have you made the necessary sacrifices? Have you killed your own child, your wife, your mistress, a servant of Order, a minion of Chaos, a creature of Balance, a murderer, a scholar, a beast, a ghost and Death itself?"

"I have!" said the Punch doll to Charnas' right, and fresh blood gleamed on the end of his slapper as he began to bludgeon the Judy puppet.

"We are not children," said Dr. Dee. "We are not so easily amused. What price would you take to leave this house?"

"Your soul!" cried the Devil puppet.

Dr. Dee gazed on impassively.

"Their souls?" the Devil inquired, glancing

"You cannot sell that which you do not hold claim to, Charnas," Dr. Dee said with faint malice. "Surely you, of all demons, know that." He regarded the imp for a long while, eroding the fiend's grin with an icy stare. "What exact task did Zho set you?"

Charnas took up the Beadle puppet, adding a black eyepatch. "Silence, foul demon! Do not even start with me." The Beadle puppet waved its arms at the Devil, and the voice that floated through the air was Zho's. "You will follow Ilse Decameron for me, and you will do so discreetly, or I will inflict upon you every torture that could possibly cause harm to you. Do you understand me?"

The Devil puppet looked ready to respond, then quivered and lowered its arms. "Very well, 'master,' but don't think for a second that I won't remember this."

Dr. Dee regarded this for a long moment, then at last said, "I'm sure you find your psychotherapy very amusing, Charnas, but the plain fact is that you've already disobeyed your master's order to be discreet."

"I was discreet as I could be!" the Devil said defensively. "I was the very picture of discreetness until Pretty Polly there caught me looking at her knickers!" The puppet pointed to another, this one a pretty blonde doll that bore a strong resemblance to Ilse. "Mangy little witch! It was all downhill from there."

The Devil pretended to cry, but then when the Beadle turned his back, he produced a slapper and gave him a whack upside the head, hiding it as the Zho puppet turned around. Charnas smiled with malicious glee.

"Very well, Charnas," Dr. Dee said. "You were charged to follow Miss Decameron discreetly. If you were now to leave the house, you could follow her when she leaves on the morrow. Discreetly."

"Yes," said the Devil, "but how do I know she won't just nip out the back? She's a witch! I've seen her try it before!"

"I'm not a witch!" cried Pretty Polly.

"Yes you are, you little tart!" cried the Devil and began to bludgeon the Polly puppet as it screamed with Ilse's voice. Charnas grinned all the while, and Ilse began to feel sick as she saw herself being brutalized in effigy, the Devil holding the slapper before him and thrusting it against Pretty Polly's raggedy cloth form.

Dr. Dee let this go on for a full minute before he spoke. "If you've had enough of your psychotherapy, Charnas, I will offer you fair trade and assurances in exchange for your vacating these premises. I will give you Miss Decameron's location on the morrow, if you swear to leave and not return this night."

The Devil paused in its rape of Pretty Polly. "I can come back after that?"

"You will never be welcome here, Charnas. But I've no doubt you could insinuate yourself by trickery again. All I ask is your vow that you will leave and not return this night. In exchange, I offer Miss Decameron's location on the morrow. It is a generous offer. You will have the rest of the evening to yourself, and the rest of the day as well, unless your master chooses to summon you, which he dare not lest you lose the scent."

The Devil puppet came away from Pretty Polly, the slapper left imbedded in her limp form, staking her. "Okay!" cried the Devil, arms waving.

"Swear it," said Dr. Dee. "Swear it on your name."

"I swear," said the Devil puppet, then Charnas tossed it and the Beadle aside. "I swear it on my name, Charnas the Imp, lesser half of Charnas, Lord of Misrule, that I will abide by this pact."

"And I shall swear by mine, Dr. John Dee, that I will abide by it also." Dr. Dee reached into his doublet and withdrew a square of vellum, creased and folded to form an envelope, with a large seal of red wax in the center incised with the seal of House Tremere, red ribbons bound round the letter and through the wax.

He held up the packet. "This letter is from the Tremere chantry in Vienna, from the Council, addressed to Miss Decameron, care of myself. Though I have not opened it, there is but one meaning I know for such a missive: The recipient is to proceed to Vienna at once."

"Do not pass Go, do not collect two hundred?" Charnas inquired.

"Possibly," Dr. Dee replied. "Now I have seen to my portion of the bargain. See to yours, fiend."

"Gone is gone!" Charnas exclaimed and vanished in a gout of purple flame, leaving the puppets back where they began, neatly stacked in their racks and coated with dust.

Silently, Dr. Dee handed the letter to Ilse. "Sarah, see that the puppet theater is burned. Once dolls have been inhabited by a demon, it is best not to keep them around."

"Yes, Doctor," Sarah said, and Ilse thought she heard a note of sorrow in the woman's voice.

❧❦

Ilse broke the seal, cutting the ribbons with a pair of stork-handled gold scissors Sarah lent her, and unfolded the letter, the vellum smooth beneath her fingers.

A second, smaller packet, sealed with green ribbons and green wax, fell forward into her hand. Ilse slipped the enclosure behind the larger sheet, looking at the beautiful, flowing script, red on cream.

> *Our Most Esteemed Childe,*
>
> *We have monitored your progress in recent weeks and laud your efforts to further the interests of House Tremere. We now wish to express our gratitude in person, and we also wish to interview our descendant, the mortal mage of our House whom you have located. We desire that you bring him with you to Vienna, where he shall also be made welcome. Do this at your earliest possible convenience, no later than the night of April the 30th, for it is paramount that the House attempt the great work on Walpurgis Night, before the forces opposed to our designs may consolidate their forces.*
>
> *More than this, our dearest Ilse, we cannot say, but this is a momentous occasion in the history of House Tremere, and we are grateful for the part you have played and will continue to play. Please come with all haste.*
>
> *With deepest affection,*
>
> (signed)
> *Councilor Etrius*

The signature was done in the same lovely, flowing hand as the rest of the letter, with gold leaf sprinkled across the ink while it was still wet. Ilse smelled the heady scent of elder vitæ; the Councilor had signed in his own blood.

Ilse felt very lightheaded all of a sudden, and Sarah placed a hand on her shoulder. "Are you all right, Ilse? You look a mite peaked."

"No, no, I'm just fine." Ilse brushed her away, folding the letter before the punk girl could steal a glance at it.

"So wot's it say?" Sarah asked, curiosity shading her usually solemn expression.

"Nothing," Ilse said. "Nothing you wouldn't expect, I mean. I need to go to Vienna, and I should take Carl Magnuson with me."

Sarah nodded. "Good thing he's got the blood of the House in his veins. That'll make travel a lot easier. You want I should track him down? Sun up's in less than an hour, and besides being lights out for the likes of us, it'll also put the mickey on the door to the House of Secrets. Not that I've ever been awake enough to try it during the day, mind."

"Yes, please," Ilse said, wanting to take another look at the letter. "That would be good, assuming he's already made the arrangements with the Order of Hermes."

"Oh, yes," Sarah said. "Things have gone swimmingly, or at least so I gather. The Doctor hasn't had any complaints on that end, though I suppose Carl could tell you best." She glanced once around the room. "I'd best be getting you to the downstairs anyway. All the skylights in Malmsey have been blacked, but the theater hasn't been used for a spell, and what with the pigeons we've got on the roof, I can't vouch for its safety."

She led the way out into the hall, shutting off the lights behind them. "There's a parlor downstairs where you can receive the living gentleman once I hunt him up, then I'll go see about kicking open the gate in the ice house. May not be able to get to Vienna tonight — unless the Cobweb Castle's in a peculiar mood — but at least you'll be able to get out of London, and that's worth something with Master Crackerbox on the warpath."

Sarah glanced back at her, rounding the corner. "Come along. It looks like this is going to be a dawn operation as it is, and I don't want to meddle with a day operation while we're at it. Like I said, I've been told that daylight and the Midnight Palace don't mix, and I can't vouch for my wakefulness if I had to test it."

Sarah led the way down the grand stairway and through

an arch, bringing Ilse to a sitting-room just off the kitchen. Thick, heavy velvet draperies covered what windows there were, and Ilse assumed there were heavy shutters behind them. Otherwise, it was as grand as the rest of the house, with Regency furnishings in green and gold brocade. The old gas brackets flickered to life at a simple gesture from Sarah as she left the archway.

Ilse sat down in one of the voluminous wing chairs by the dead hearth, reopening the letter. The smell of Councilor Etrius' blood wafted out, sweet as woodbine, and Ilse looked at gold leaf and the elegant script in the amber glow of the gaslight. It somehow seemed very familiar.

She reread it twice. *Dearest Ilse...deepest affection...*It somehow read more like a love letter than one of the fabled "Letters from Vienna." Too touching, too personal, but then Etrius, leader of the Council of Seven, was also rumored to also be the head of the secretive *Humanus League*, and was said to regret his loss of humanity more than any of the vampires of Clan Tremere.

The ancient ones, at least.

Ilse refolded the vellum square and tucked the edges back into the broken seal, looking to the smaller packet that had been enclosed. The ribbons were as green as springtime, and gold had been used on the seal as well, a leaf of it laid down before the ring had been pressed into the wax. Across the back, in one of the four squares formed by the ribbon, were the words, *To That Most Beloved and Rediscovered Son-of-Our-Heart, Carl Magnuson*, while in the square opposite, *To Be Delivered, as Always, by Our Faithful Ilse*. The ink was green and beautifully lettered in Councilor Etrius' hand. Ilse wasn't sure if it was just the residue that had rubbed off from her own letter, but she thought she smelled his blood from it as well.

There was a creak of the floor behind her, and Ilse looked up to see Carl Magnuson slipping into the room, spruce and tidy in his dark suit and white collar, but his eyes looking for all the world like Paul's. "There you are, love," said the mage, his aura tinged golden with concern. "We were worried about you and, my, it looks like you've had a devil of a night."

"It was an imp, but same difference."

He came over, sitting down on the footstool before the hearth and taking one of her hands in his own. "Go ahead, and tell me about it." His hands were warm, and Ilse could feel the beat of his heart through them.

It all came out at once — the terror, the capture, Crowley and his Beast, Westphal and Jackie, Zho and Charnas, the horrible memory the imp had prompted. By the time she finished, Ilse was in tears, blood dripping down onto her arm and the dirty gray silk of her dress.

"There's a girl," Carl said, sounding like a British version of Paul. "Chin up. You made it through, and much less worse for the wear than the rest of them." He tried to put a finger under her chin and raise her head up.

Ilse didn't want to look him in the eyes. "Crowley's right. I'm nothing but a coward."

"Crowley's a nasty piece of work, that's what he is." Carl gave up on trying to lift her chin and instead just stroked her hair with the back of his fingers. "I hate to say it, but I've had my run-ins with him too, but not as badly as your lot. And here I was just thinking he was just a dark mage. The Order will be heartily surprised when they discover the Tremere hate him just as much as they do. Generally, they just lump everyone together, which is always a mistake." Carl stroked her hair again. "What you'd call cowardice I'd call just a good bit of self-control and common sense. From what you said, that Westphal chap just went into hysterics till he fainted, and that didn't do his girlfriend a bit of good. If it hadn't been for you, the whole mess could have turned out a great deal nastier than it did."

Ilse felt the tears trickle down her cheeks and the growing heaviness in her eyes that always preceded sunrise. "Wha—"

"Hush, love. The night's been interesting for me too, but hardly as exciting as yours has been. All I can say is that what your Dr. Dee lacks in manners, he makes up for in connections, because before you could say, 'Bob's your uncle,' I had my mates in the Order welcoming me back or at least willing to listen to what I had to say about the Tremere, especially Houdini's greatest escape." He grimaced. "Of course, there's always a few firebrands who'll listen to anything that will give the Technocracy a bad day, and since it's no skin off our nose if it fails, they're all for it. Brave lot, the Order, aren't they?"

The deep and dreamless sleep that accompanied daybreak began to come over her, and Ilse struggled to retain consciousness, clasping Carl's warm hands in hers. "We—"

"Everything is in readiness," came Mr. Winthrop's voice. "If we could make haste to the undercellar, Mr. Magnuson, Ms. Cobbler would appreciate it."

"Quite right," Carl said, and Ilse nodded weakly, murmuring vague acceptance, then felt Carl's arms lifting her as if she weighed no more than a doll. The letters fluttered down beside her.

"Wait," Ilse murmured, trying to reach for them.

"I have them," Mr. Winthrop said, finishing her thoughts, as always. "If you could…"

"Of course." She heard Carl's heartbeat and felt the warmth of his life through his suit, the mage carrying her down the stairs as darkness tried to claim her.

She heard Sarah's voice chanting an invocation in Enochian, the magical language Dr. Dee had first set down, the swishing of the woman's sword, then Carl ducked forward with her, and she heard a slam and a shudder of glass.

Ilse began to rouse, the sleep of day giving her a sudden reprieve, and she looked up to see the door of the curio case in the Ching Parlor that formed the gateway to Malmsey House, the ivory figures on the other side jumbled about by the slamming of the door.

Carl set her on her feet. "Just in the nick of time, I'd say." He yawned. "And now, I think, we get to turn the tables. You may be feeling bright and chipper after having gotten away from daylight, but I've been up a deucedly long time, and I'm going to have to sleep." He smiled at her, mismatched eyes sparkling like Paul's…and like Zho's in her horrible memory of that past life the imp had made her recall. "I think I'll take Mammy up on that offer of a room, because after what you've told me, I've got an awful lot to sleep on, and I'm certain you want a chance to get cleaned up as well."

Ilse nodded. She was in fact very tired. Not in body, but in soul, and she wondered if she'd ever feel clean again.

➣❮

Kurt and Jackie joined the Ventrue of London, prepared to head back to the safety of Bexborough Manor. Lady Anne was speaking about something — for the life of him, Kurt couldn't quite understand, his exhaustion destroying his attention span — when the Queen of London's chauffeur, sans clothes or limousine, flung himself at her. "My Lady! I am ready for you at last!"

Kurt stepped back, suddenly very wide awake, and watched as the Queen's entourage surrounded the hapless man. "Pray tell, Clarence, whatever is it you're supposed to be ready for?" Lady Anne had, doubtless, seen much in her time. Despite a moment of surprise, she recovered quickly, her stunned grimace replaced with the dryly amused expression that only the upper-class British ever seemed capable of carrying off properly.

With a shriek of abject horror, Clarence managed to all but fly backwards into the shrubs he'd just emerged from, eyes wide and hair literally standing on end. Kurt noticed with some amusement the shock and then raw anger that danced across Courtland Leighton's face before the man regained his composure; he suspected the anger came from a sense of betrayal. "Milady? I did not expect you'd have company…"

"Obviously not, Clarence. Would you care to explain yourself?"

"Begging your pardon, Milady, you—" The man's face had almost mystically transformed from the color of human flesh to the same shade as cooked beets.

"Yes?"

"You only moments ago said you wanted me. In a carnal way."

"Really?" Now she seemed surprised. "One would think I'd remember making such a proclamation." Clarence groaned, his face red enough to make Kurt fear he'd have a stroke from the pressure.

Courtland Leighton stepped forward, all but placing himself completely between the humiliated man and Lady Anne. "Shall I handle this matter for you, Lady Anne?"

"Oh, please do, Courtland." Despite herself, the Queen of London seemed on the verge of hysterical laughter.

"With pleasure." Leighton stepped forward, his paces measured and restrained, but his body showing the rage he was surely feeling.

"But Courtland—"

"Yes, Milady?"

"Do leave him alive. I believe we shall have to discuss his activities and find the source of so unusual a delusion."

"Yes, Milady."

The Queen of London called to one of her other aides, and in a matter of less than forty minutes, a rented limousine approached and they were soon on their way. The group was most of the way to Bexborough Manor before Kurt realized that Jackie was smiling for the first time all night.

>€

By the time Kurt finally managed to break free of his fellow Ventrue, a Blood Hunt had been called against Aleister Crowley. Lady Anne had been very interested in hearing about the Malkavian's plans, and with his haven uncovered at last, she sent her minions to the Canary Docks as soon as they arrived back at Bexborough Manor. All that remained of his unholy church was evidence that he'd been there; the humans and vampires had vacated the underground haven beneath Kensington, Pope and Kelly Spice Merchants. No one was surprised that he'd escaped again. The old bastard had more lives than a pride of kittens.

Appolonius and his crew were being held until a meeting of the primogen could be arranged, and that in turn was being held until Courtland Leighton and John Dee could once again work out a new agreement and possibly even work out a longer peace this time around. No one expected the peace to come easily as a result of the previous night, nor did they expect it to last.

Despite her protests that she was fine, Kurt insisted that Jackie take the night to rest and recover from the ordeals of the previous forty-eight hours. Jackie did not complain overly much.

Enjoying the gentle breeze and pleasant weather, Kurt had one of Lady Anne's servants give him directions to a pond on the Bexborough estate, and there he waited for Zho. He did not have to wait long before the mage showed himself. The mage's face was haggard, and Kurt suspected that lack of sleep was not the only thing taking a toll on the man who'd been so helpful in his quest to keep track of Ilse Decameron. Zho sat down on one of the stone benches that surrounded the pond at sporadic intervals and nodded his greeting before closing his eyes for a moment.

When he looked up again, he seemed far more in control of himself and his surroundings. "Hello, Kurt. You must forgive me if I am late, please. I've been very busy."

argument we'll say that Heaven and all that it implies is indeed an actual location or state of being. Eternal life, no war or pain or suffering, just happiness everywhere. If one were to assume that good deeds and good thoughts were responsible for reaching such a paradise, there is the possibility that I was not of a mind to believe I would go there. Perhaps I'd already committed several sins before considering placing my soul on the auction block. Perhaps there was a chance of redemption, but a small one, not much of an opportunity at all. In consideration of this, the certainty of power and an expanded life cycle would almost be worth eternal damnation." He stopped speaking, his face gone dreamy and a little sad. Kurt suspected that Zho had indeed committed a few sins in his time, but opted to listen for a while, saving any speeches or questions for later.

"Just the same, what good is a little power, when the price is eternal suffering? Mind you, this assumes that Hell is as real as Heaven and filled with suffering and strife. What could provoke a man to surrender his eternal soul in exchange for something as fleeting as power and a few centuries of borrowed time? Let's think about this." He held up his right hand in a loose fist and with his left started bending the fingers back, marking each potential reason with one lifted finger. "The love of a good woman? Would that be enough? Yes, there are several mages I know who have sold themselves to the darker forces for just that reason. But that was not my reason. Money? Not in my case. I could have had as much as I wanted and was already very wealthy, even by today's standards. More power? No, not enough would be offered to make it worth my while. Immortality? I knew vampires even then, Kurt. I could have become one at any given point. No, immortality was simply not enough. So what does that leave? Security. Yes, I think that would be a good enough reason. I sold my soul to Charnas, the Lord of Misrule, for security."

"I don't understand."

"Be patient, and I will explain." He paused again, staring out at the waters and tossing another stone. The flat rock skipped twice before flipping sideways and cutting into the water with nary a splash to mark its passage. "I sold my soul because I had no soul of my own to sell. Don't ask — I'll explain in my own way.

"I was born to a long line of mages, a family where at least one person from every generation learned magick at an early age. That was the way it had always been in my family for centuries and centuries. Sometimes from father to son, sometimes from distant uncle to nephew. But I was not quite as easily satisfied as most of my ancestors. I could not accept that good breeding and a solid education could be the only reasons for so many mages in one long family line. So I decided to research the matter. Forgive me if this is convoluted; I've never actually told anyone of my research, and it's been a few decades since I even really gave the matter any thought."

Zho stood up, walking aimlessly for a few minutes, pausing from time to time only to gather more stones. There were actually quite a few rocks left, and Kurt accepted that the man needed to gather his thoughts. He sat patiently, throwing a few more projectiles at the water and relearning a childhood talent. Eventually, the mage came back and sat down again, dropping a large collection of new missiles in the process.

"The entire situation apparently started with a young man named Aldiis Etriuson. Aldiis, son of Etrius." Kurt sat up a little straighter, all of his attention forced back to Zho. "Yes, the same Etrius who is one of the founding members of the Tremere clan of vampires. Aldiis was a bastard, his existence unknown to most of the Tremere chantry. I am a descendant of Etrius."

"But what have the Tremere to do with you selling your soul?"

"I was getting to that. Still more research, and a great deal of time delving into records that few even knew existed — letters from Etrius to the mother of Aldiis, a woman named Lisle Zho and a Gypsy at that. Her last name is only my last name only because I chose to use it, by the way, not because of any actual continuous use of the name. And my first name was not Thadius until I decided a change of name could be conducive to my continued existence. Actually tracing my lineage would be an exercise in futility anymore, as I destroyed the records.

"But I digress. Etrius explained in his letters what is now common knowledge among the Awakened: The world was changing, and magick was changing as well. Sorcerous spells were being replaced by a different magick, replaced by technology. The laws that governed the world were going to change, and the Tremere chantry feared that they would die out with the end of the Mythic Age. Tremere believed he could save them from that fate, but there was likely going to be a price to pay.

"Lisle was very much in love with her man, Etrius, and she wanted to be with him forever. However, Etrius had told her of Tremere's schemes, plans to gain immortality through a powerful ritual that would convert Tremere and his chosen associates into creatures that were as long-lived as vampires without the natural flaws that vampires suffer: no feeding on blood, no severe reaction to sunlight, et cetera, et cetera. But Etrius was afraid. He suspected the ritual might fail, or possibly change all of the mages into Kindred — time proved him right — and so he decided to ensure that he would have a way to return to life as a mage, rather than being trapped as a vampire for all time. He spoke with Lisle at length, and the two of them devised a method for protecting his soul from the worst corruptions, allowing him to maintain his humanity no matter how much time he spent as a vampire.

"At the time of the great change, Etrius' worst fears were realized — he did indeed become a vampire. Lisle was devastated, as was Etrius. Despite their best efforts, he would suffer from all the flaws of vampiric life."

Zho looked at Kurt, his eye blazing with an inner light. "Tell me what you know of how Tremere came to reach the lofty powers of an Antediluvian." It was not a question, but a demand.

"Everyone knows the answer to that." Kurt tossed another stone, disappointed when it sank after only one bounce off the water's surface. "It's fairly common knowledge that he diablerized Saulot of the Salubri Clan. Normally he'd be punished for his actions, but there are few who could hope to harm one of the Kindred only twice-removed from Caine. His power is that of a demi-god."

"Yes, that is just so. Saulot died, his soul consumed by Tremere. And the seven followers of Tremere were there to see it happen. But there is more to the story, Kurt. More than most of the Kindred know. Tremere did indeed commit diablerie, but Etrius committed grave robbery only seconds later. Etrius plucked the third eye from Saulot's head, the eye of wisdom and judgment. He preserved the eye by keeping it surrounded by his own blood, and later he cast powerful rituals upon the orb that keep it safe from harm."

"What would he want with such a thing? What possible use could anyone have for an eyeball, even the eyeball of an Antediluvian?"

Zho smiled, shaking his head. "That part took a lot of learning. Years and years of research. With the Eye of Saulot, Etrius preserved some of the powers of Saulot. The Eye permits — and mind you, this is partially guesswork and certainly unconfirmed — Etrius to keep his soul from growing dark with the taint of his actions. That is why he wears the Eye of Saulot."

"Surely someone would have noticed something that powerful long before now..." Kurt was willing to go along with most things. He easily granted that the world had many secrets beyond his knowledge and many possibilities that he could not comprehend. He was the first to admit that he was not knowledgeable in the ways of magic, but this was going too far.

Zho chuckled, "The best magicians use misdirection to protect themselves from being caught. Everyone that sees Etrius sees the Eye of Saulot. The Eye is better known to most people as the Soul Gem of Etrius."

"You are mad." Kurt shook his head, refusing to believe what the mage told him.

"No, Kurt Westphal, I am a mage. I can see what is easily missed by most Kindred. Those that could see what Etrius has done would hardly care one way or the other. Besides, the Soul Gem is a crystal — it hardly looks like an eye. That is how Etrius manages to keep his soul clean, how after almost one thousand years, he is still as kind as when he was mortal. His soul is one of the few that has not been corrupted by the nature of Caine's curse. Oh, don't look so surprised — I did a great deal of research into the Kindred as well.

"All that I'd learned of my distant forefather was interesting, but hardly important to me, until I realized what he intended to do with his Soul Gem. When the time came around, Etrius intended to escape his vampirism by literally forcing his soul into a mage's body, but not just any body. The ritual he and Lisle Zho had crafted required a specific set of conditions be met.

"The mage taken by Etrius had to be a blood descendant and, more importantly, had to be the seventh son of a seventh son, just as Etrius was the seventh of his own father, who in turn was the seventh of his father. The requirements made Etrius' chances of locating a suitable host fairly rare, but not impossible. I myself knew of one who would be ideal for his plans — Me. He could potentially seize my body. I would no longer be who I thought I was. I would be a portion of another being, one that was stronger and more experienced than me, one that could, in all likelihood, consume everything that made me what I was and rule the body through sheer force of will. Thadius Zho would cease to be, making room for Etrius the mage when he returned to the mortal world from his time in the realm of vampires.

"Had I known then what I know now, I probably wouldn't have made a deal with the Devil. But back then I feared that I would be destroyed by Etrius' return to the mortal world. I never had a reason to worry, because the great escape Etrius had spoken of wasn't even going to occur for another couple of hundred years. Again, I'm getting ahead of myself.

"Etrius planned to cure himself of the curse of Caine, but he didn't plan to cure only himself. By maintaining connections with certain members of the Order of Hermes, he hoped to transform the entire Tremere clan. For almost a thousand years, Etrius has been biding his time and waiting for a chance to bring back the Mythic Age, with himself as one of the rulers of the Order of Hermes. Just how he plans this I cannot tell you, but I can tell you he plans on doing it soon."

The two sat in near-perfect silence for a long time, listening to the faint murmurs of nocturnal insects and the occasional splash as one or the other skipped a stone over the water. Finally, Kurt could bear the silence no longer. "Have you any proof of this?"

"Only the words from manuscripts long destroyed, and the words of one Tremere who is uncertain if this is the right move for her clan to make."

"Ilse Decameron?"

"No. Ilse has her role to play, but she is not the one who I've spoken with on this matter. Jing Wei is the Tremere in question." Zho looked away, studying something in the distance that Kurt could not see.

"What part does Ilse have to play in this?"

"Ilse is to deliver the mage to Etrius."

"The mage?

"Carl Magnuson."

"Magnuson? The man I saw in Los Angeles, talking with Ilse Decameron?"

"Yes. None other."

"Well, then, all we have to do is warn this Magnuson to stay away from the Tremere, especially Ilse Decameron."

"Far too late, Kurt. They have been together since you met in Los Angeles. He is at Malmsey House, Dr. Dee's haven. And he is likely with Ilse Decameron even as we speak."

"Then how do we stop this insanity?" Kurt's mind was reeling with the implications of what Zho had explained. As it stood, assuming that Zho was telling the truth (a daring assumption when Kurt considered the man's associates), the very Camarilla could be in danger from the shock waves that would ripple through the Kindred society. His voice was edged with the anger and helplessness he felt.

"Simply put, we do not. You do. You must meet with Ilse Decameron and make her understand that if she takes Carl Magnuson to Vienna, he is as good as dead. He will be destroyed only a few days from now, and his mortal body will be possessed by Etrius."

"There is simply no way that I can gain entrance to Malmsey House. The tensions between our clans are too strong."

"You have to find a way, Kurt. Because if you do not, you and your entire clan will find yourselves surrounded by mages that hold a long grudge against you, mages that can walk in the sunlight and can easily arrange for a one-way ticket to the sun for you and anyone else who gets in their way." Zho stood then and started walking away. "Think on that, Kurt. I'm only one mage, but there must be hundreds of the Tremere. Think what they could do to all vampires if they decided to. And remember which clan has given them the most grief over the centuries."

Kurt thought for a long time, growing more and more

chilled before finally fleeing into Bexborough Manor in time to escape the rising sun.

Tuesday, April 27, Vienna— *Die Fledermaus*

Kurt was awakened the following night by Mary, a very attractive chambermaid who was also his source of food while visiting with the Queen of London. She left him as soon as he was awake, but not before passing on the message that a Mr. Thadius Zho requested his presence at the same location as the night before.

After taking a very short shower and changing quickly into a fresh suit, he slipped from his apartment in the manor without encountering anyone else, and he was glad for the short time alone. Despite his full day's sleep, he felt tired and restless. He vaguely remembered unsettling images from the day's dreams, but they slipped away from him whenever he tried focusing on what had occurred during his slumber. Kurt had seldom been able to remember his dreams since his Embrace, one of the apparent side-effects of his new life that he still regretted. Germany. Something about Germany. Even the thought of Berlin made him homesick. *Soon enough*, he thought. *This nightmare will be over soon enough, and I can go home.*

A short time later, he was back at the stone bench where he had last seen Zho. The mage was waiting for him, a sour look on his face. He nodded to Kurt, gesturing for him to sit.

"I'd have seen you at the manor, but I'm afraid Lady Anne still holds a grudge for what Charnas did to her when last we were welcomed. I fear she took the pig's blood a little personally."

"She does tend to remember past slights." Kurt felt it best not to ask for the gory details. He hunted up a few stones and started skipping them across the pond's surface, still tickled by how much pleasure the relived childhood memory held for him. "What was so urgent, Thadius?"

"The Tremere woman, Ilse Decameron, will be in Vienna tomorrow night. She's taking Carl Maguson with her. I believe they're to meet with Etrius himself." The sorcerer stared intently at the moonlight reflected off the pond's waters. "We've already discussed the implications, Kurt. This cannot be allowed to happen, for my personal sake and for yours as well."

"How can you be certain that Etrius can even achieve such a magnificent feat?" Kurt looked at Zho, wanting a straight answer to a question he had trouble formulating. "Surely if mages were this powerful, they would have destroyed the Kindred and Lupines of the world by now."

Zho stared at Kurt for a long moment before answering. Whatever he was thinking he kept well-hidden. "Magick is not as easy as it once was. That's true enough, but there are still ways around the problem. All that is really required is enough belief."

"I don't —"

"If you'd let me finish, please." Kurt was rapidly learning not to like Zho's impatience. "The matter of belief gets complicated, so please bear with me. Mages do no not perform magick without a certain element of risk. Whenever a mage attempts to create a storm or change a person's appearance, the very fabric of reality has to be altered. Reality does not like to be tampered with.

"That wasn't always the case. Before the Inquisition, during the times most people call the Dark Ages, magick worked with a fair amount of ease. But history has been rewritten by people who refuse to accept that the sort of magick I perform ever existed. And people all over the world have been 'educated' to believe that science is the only law that works. In truth, magick and science are pretty much the same thing, just applied differently. If you'd tried running an internal combustion engine five hundred years ago, you'd have been wasting your time. The world's perception of what was possible would have denied the possibility that steel cylinders, a little fuel and a dash of electricity could make anything happen.

"Be patient. I know it's complicated. What it all boils down to is that a group of mages literally changed the ways in which magick works, so that technology became the dominant rules of the world, and magick, in the truer sense, became a lie. The biggest change came as a result of the Inquisition, when many of magick's practitioners were burned at the stake or worse. Think about this: The very laws of physics were transformed by history books and by teaching the masses how to look at the world; if the books had all said that magick was viable and technology was a lie, you would likely do your transcontinental traveling via flying carpets or perched on a broom handle."

"You're saying that the perceptions of the people on the planet changed the way the earth is allowed to operate?"

"Something like that. Simply put, any endeavors to pull off what Etrius is attempting have a decent chance of ending in failure. Reality would sense what he was trying and slap him into the next century for his audacity."

"Then why do the Tremere manage their magic so easily?"

"They don't attempt to work the same sort of magick. With the Tremere, everything they do is ritualized, performed the same way by all the Tremere who know how to do a certain spell. With magicians like myself, there is no need for a ritual. I could call down lighting right now, simply by thinking about it and willing it to happen, but reality would be rather touchy about me casting lightning out of a clear sky. Either the magick would fail, or the laws of the world would make me suffer in some way for breaking the rules. That's the difference. The Tremere have to follow the rules of nature, but I can make nature bend to my will. My magick is more powerful and more limited at the same time. I can do things the Tremere can only dream of, but there is always a price to pay."

"So if the laws of nature say Etrius cannot perform his great spell, we have nothing to worry about." Kurt smiled, certain he'd discovered the answer to all of their dilemmas.

"Not true. The laws of nature say that he cannot perform a feat like he desires by himself, but the spells he used to create his Soul Gem are not the same as those he can use today. So long as he has the Soul Gem and a body to inhabit, he can pull off his ritual. Or at least have a reasonable chance."

"How?"

"Old magick, combined with rituals he has likely been studying and perfecting for years." Zho stared into the distance, his cold blue eye taking on that glazed look again. "If he works his spell properly, he'll be able to make himself into a mortal mage again. He'll have the power to destroy you and all of your clan. If he does it the right way, with publicity and deliberate breaches of the Masquerade, he'll be able to make the world believe that magick is still possible. Magick could become the dominant force again, and science could be pushed back. He could create a new Mythic Age, all the while bringing about the downfall of all his vampiric enemies."

"He would not! No one would dream of bringing back the Inquisition." The very thought chilled Kurt's soul. "The Kindred could not survive against today's technologies."

"What would Etrius care? He'd no longer be a vampire. He'd be a mortal man with the power to change the world with only a thought."

"Dear God in Heaven. If he could accomplish such a feat…he could destroy us all." Kurt took his turn staring out at the darkness. "But what makes you think he'd commit such an atrocity?"

"I believe he'll attempt something along those lines, because it's what I'd do in the same situation. And he will, if that's the only hope he has to become a human mage again. Mind you, you don't need to take my word for it, you could just wait a few days…"

"Why are you being so helpful, Thadius?" Kurt did not believe all that Zho had told him, but even the *possibility* that Etrius could manage such a feat had to be investigated. This, then, was the reason for his being assigned to keep an eye on Ilse Decameron. At last he understood. He would call Democritus when he arrived at a pay phone, but he already knew what the man would say — No matter what the cost, Etrius had to be stopped.

"Because we have a mutual foe in this situation — Etrius. It's nothing personal against the old vampire, but he's unaware of all the ramifications. He needs to be made to see what he could possibly do the balance of the world."

"Then there is no time to waste. I have a few phone calls to make, Thadius, but I believe I might be able to reach Vienna in time." He looked at the mage, thoughts whirling. "Will you come with me?"

Thadius Zho smiled, that nasty smile of his that always made Kurt think of a predatory animal ready at last to pounce. "My dear Mr. Westphal, I wouldn't miss it for the world."

➤❤

Kurt loaded his suitcases as quickly as he could while Jackie handled the travel arrangements. He made a mental note to allow her a few days or weeks of rest when this was all done, assuming, as he always did, that they would both survive the trials ahead of them. Breaking into the literal stronghold of the Tremere definitely ranked at the top of his list of dangerous assignments. She'd been working far too hard, and the stress was showing both physically and mentally.

Jackie finished her phone calls. The good news was that they'd be able to arrive in Austria before sunset the next day. The bad news was that no planes were leaving for Vienna from London or Paris until after nightfall the next night, too late for the trip to be a good idea. They'd have to take the trains, and that meant a few extra stops along the way, some during the daylight hours. While a vampire could stay awake during the day, the sun's rays would still cause massive damage at the briefest contact with flesh, and the effects were unpleasant at best. If Kurt was lucky, most of the trip could be handled in the tunnels.

The first stretch of travel would be the easiest; all they had to do was take the Channel Tunnel from Dover to Calais, then on to Paris. Paris would be relatively easy, save for the actual exit from the train tunnels into a waiting limousine. There would be a few uncomfortable minutes of waiting for Jackie to locate the limo and for him to get situated. After that, Kurt suspected the majority of the trip would be far harder. He snapped his suitcases shut, checking the locks twice before he was satisfied that they were properly secured. Before he left, he had to pay a final visit to Lady Anne. Circumstances as significant as these meant that not all of the communications could be taken care of before they had to leave for Calais.

Lady Anne was occupied in a rather heated argument with Dr. Dee, at least if Courtland could be believed, and Kurt saw no reason not to trust the man. He scribbled a message on a piece of stationary the Queen's assistant offered and bid his farewells. There was no time to stand on formality.

In another ten minutes, Jackie was steering a rental car onto the main road and heading for the south of London on the way to Dover. Their usual banter was gone, replaced by a strained silence that Kurt could not find a way to breach.

Jackie performed her duties as flawlessly as ever, but she could have been anyone at all, just a servant instead of his friend and lover. Everything she'd endured in the past had been overcome with ease, but the incident with Crowley's degenerate Lupine had changed something inside her, a fragile ethereal element that was somehow integral to what made her the woman Kurt loved.

Much as he wanted to cross the distance that was growing between them, Kurt could find no words to make his sorrow known. Everything he considered fell short of saying what he wanted. Perhaps it was fear that kept him from speaking out, or maybe it was only embarrassment. Kurt could not say. He kept his best professional face in place, all the while feeling his heart fragment into splinters of ice.

For Jackie's part, her face too was expressionless. Even her normal muttered curses for the other drivers were gone. The silence was deafening. Honor demanded that he go to Vienna and stop the Tremere's schemes. Duty to his clan and his sire had been his everything for the last few decades. But Kurt felt he was simply going through the motions. Everything that seemed important only two nights ago now seemed like a pathetic waste of time. He wanted to reach out to Jackie, to touch her and tell her that everything would be all right. Somehow the distance of a few feet seemed more like a thousand miles. He looked to the rearview mirror from his seat in the back of the car, hoping to catch a look at Jackie without her seeing him. Their eyes met in the shiny silver surface. Kurt looked away first.

The remaining time spent traveling to the Channel Tunnel in Dover was an eternity for Kurt. Learning that he was somehow unworthy of the woman he loved made the time stretch on for what felt like centuries.

The silence continued as they unloaded the rented sedan. The area was almost completely deserted, the only signs of life being an unconscious bum, a woman dressed in punker regalia talking on the pay phone and the lights from the terminal building where they would enter the Channel Tunnel. Kurt looked around, noting that even the bar, a quaint little place called The Slaughtered Dove, was closed for the night. Their train would leave in less than an hour at four a.m. Kurt wished for sounds, distractions to keep his mind from returning to the silence that separated him from Jackie. Sometimes wishes come true.

The quiet ended in a thunderous roar when the car exploded. Both of them were far enough away that the initial fireball did nothing more than singe their hair, but the shock wave threw Jackie across the street and slammed Kurt into the wall of the Slaughtered Dove hard enough to stun him. He was dimly aware of his arm shattering on impact with the ancient bricks and automatically started forcing his blood to the area, speeding the healing process.

On the other side of the street, Jackie stood shakily and stared at the remains of the rental car. A secondary explosion lifted the back half of the sedan off the ground and sent streamers of fire racing through the air and across the cobblestone pavement. A flaming shard of metal found the now-conscious bum and tore through the upper half of his skull, ending his life instantly. Jackie pointed past the car while calling out to Kurt, but her words were lost to the ringing noise that wailed in his skull, and he realized that his eardrums had ruptured as well.

He turned to where she was pointing and saw the punk girl walking towards him. Beside her walked a man who at first glance was terribly close to the description of Dr. Dee. The man's gray-shot black hair was slicked back and framed an angular face with eyes only a few shades darker than his off-white skin. The dark gray London Fog suit and overcoat, as fine as any of Kurt's, spoke of money and breeding, but his expression of raw arrogance detracted from what should have been a look of sophistication. Fear spiked through Kurt as he searched his memory for more details about Dee and lessened only when he decided that the man approaching could not be the Tremere elder unless he were disguised. Not likely; everything he'd read about the man said that Dee was too arrogant to hide behind another's face. This man was clean-shaven; Dee sported a beard and mustache. The overly pale skin and the fact that he actually floated a bit off the ground made Kurt certain that he was a vampire, more likely than not a Tremere, but not Dr. Dee.

Next to him, a woman dressed more like a Brujah than a Tremere stepped forward. The only signs that she was indeed of the Tremere were the occult icons she wore on her person. In truth, Kurt had limited knowledge of what any of the symbols meant, but he felt safe in assuming that it would be the Tremere out to stop him on his quest. Black clothes and fingernails, along with fuchsia hair and too much makeup, finished her outfit, but could not hide the attractive woman underneath for all the attempts. Unlike her counterpart, she seemed to worry about a counter-attack from him.

Kurt had no doubt they were present for the express purpose of killing him. He tried to rise, but the damage to his ears sent the world spinning away when he tried to move. He once again shifted the blood in his body, forcing the vitæ to regenerate the damage done to his ears. It took him a moment to realize that the woman had spoken. Kurt heard nothing and indicated as much with a gesture to his ears. She spoke again, this time in his mind: *I've notified the police department about a car-bombing. If we'd wanted you dead, you would be a cinder inside the remains of your car. This is a warning: Do not attempt to follow Ilse Decameron. You are safe enough in England — the peace treaty between our clan and yours still stands, and we will do nothing to harm you. But if you proceed to the continent, our forces will destroy you.*

With an effort, he forced himself to stand, cursing the vertigo that seized him. The pain caused by his knitting bones was almost enough to drive him over the edge. The man before him sneered and shoved him back. While the damage was less than it had been moments before, Kurt's inner-ears were still out of order, and his balance was tenuous at best. He fell to the ground, growing angrier by the second. Punk girl said something that was only a mumble to Kurt's ears, but her expression told him she was unhappy with what the man had done. Jackie stepped forward, limping, and pulled out an Ingram Mac-10 — and where the hell had she hidden that was a mystery to him — as she approached. From only ten feet away, she fired on the male vampire, smiling as his left shoulder exploded into pale red jelly and splinters of white bone.

The Dr. Dee doppelganger turned from Kurt and hissed at Jackie, and Kurt heard the garbled sound of her screams through his ruined ears. He turned to where Jackie stood, watching her face drain of color and grow ugly, twisted by mixed expressions of pain and terror. She fell backwards, striking her head on the cobblestones, and Kurt heard a muffled yet sickening crack as she landed. Her body spasmed, arms thrown above her head and legs spread wide. She thrashed and twitched, and Kurt growled as realization struck him. Somehow the warlock was making her relive the tortures she'd endured in Crowley's dungeon. Jackie cried out, a thin anguished sound that wrenched Kurt's heart, as her body moved in twisted parody of lust.

Kurt acted to end the battle before it could begin in earnest. He turned to face the Tremere again and grabbed the man's arm to gain his attention. The warlock looked, and Kurt seized his mind in a last attempt to end the conflict quickly. *Leave her alone! Leave here immediately!* Kurt focused his will as he spoke with his mind and mouth simultaneously, forcing his thoughts and desires upon the mind of the man before him.

The man hesitated, fighting back against Kurt's efforts to control him. The punk girl chose that moment to let Kurt know he'd made a mistake in picking the man as his target. She spoke as she pointed one hand at him. Though the ringing had lessened substantially, Kurt still could not hear the words she said. Fire tore through his entire body, running rivers of lava that boiled from his chest through to the rest of his person and caused him to scream in agony. His skin blistered and scalding-hot blood ran from his mouth. His vision wavered and danced as the heat continued to increase and his mind gave in to the pain.

For just an instant, the bar, the people and the buildings around him faded to black. When next he could see, the world was painted in a thousand shades of crimson, and the Beast inside reared its ugly head, demanding retribution for the pain it suffered. Kurt felt the vibrations of a growl and only dimly realized the sound came from within him. Rational thought was gone, and in its place a killing machine came forward.

The man was first in his line of sight, still frozen by his battle with Kurt for dominance of his own mind. He was dimly aware that the Tremere warlock would have left if he could have pressed his advantage. The primitive, demanding force that ruled did not care. Blood-lust drove him past the pain to seek retribution. Kurt reached out with burned hands curled into claws and sank his fingers deep into the pale skin of the man's arrogant face. Skin ruptured like the flesh of a rotten orange, and rich red vitæ spilled across his fingers as the bones of his enemy's skull began to crumble under his assault. Kurt liked the way the man thrashed in pain.

The witch-woman tried her magic again, but Kurt was better prepared this time, more expecting of attack, and whatever she had attempted washed over him with no ill effects. He growled again, glaring at the woman as he squeezed even harder on the cheekbones beneath his grip, feeling the skull fracture and then shatter. The man stopped thrashing, and Kurt lost all interest in him.

It was the woman he wanted to kill. She was the one who'd

hurt him, caused his mind to stick on things he did not want to think about — like his sweet Jackie being brutalized by a red-furred demon or the purple man who taunted and teased...

The thought of Jackie was enough. The frenzy ended as abruptly as it had begun. The rage that had consumed him faded away, leaving him weak and confused. In the distance, he dimly heard the rapid clatter of heels over cobblestones and saw the woman who'd burned the very blood in his body running as quickly as she could. His hearing was coming back, the very curse that drove him insane also healing the wounds he'd suffered.

Jackie sat on the ground not far away, her body pulled into a fetal position, and her face covered with warm, salty tears. Kurt looked down at the man before him, his face warped by sheer strength, and then stared at the bloody smears across his blistered hands. In a week's time he had lost control of himself on four separate occasions. Worse still, he had every reason to believe he'd used his vampiric powers without realizing what he was doing. Minutes before, Jackie had been forced to relive what Crowley's Beast had done to her, but her reaction now was far worse than it had been on the actual night of her rape. Surely just reliving the past could not have so powerful an effect on her. The female Tremere had run fleeing into night as if the forces of Hell were in infernal pursuit, yet she must have seen worse than what he'd just done to her counterpart in her time. Was he using his own powers to inspire fear without realizing what he had done? Kurt suspected he was, and the thought filled him with dread. His own actions seemed less his own and more the maneuvers of the primal self that all vampires sought to control — the Beast.

Already disgusted with his lack of control, he bent and lifted the warlock he'd ruined, and, after looking around to ensure privacy, sank his fangs into the man's neck. The blood was cold, but potent, vital. Energy surged into his body, giving back what the man's companion had stolen from him. He stopped himself from finishing the man with a concentrated effort. The desires of the Beast wanted him to finish the task, but he denied it this last thing.

He dropped to his knees before Jackie, softly crooning to her and trying to evoke a reaction aside from the shivering, feverish fear she suffered through. Eventually he was able to rouse her and coerce her into moving again. He did what he had always tried to avoid — he forced his will on her and made her forget what she had seen and experienced. He desperately needed to remove the memory of what he had done to help her recover from the shock he believed he'd accidentally inflicted, to cure the damage he himself had made her endure. Somehow, that didn't make him feel any better about doing it.

When they stepped aboard the tunnel's train, it was Jackie who led, while Kurt pulled within himself, staring at nothing and seeing more than he wanted.

❧

The next few hours were an agony for Kurt. Despite being under the English Channel when the sun came up, Kurt could sense the fiery orb rising and feel his body demanding rest that he could not permit. From time to time, his entire body grew stiff and hot, and he would fade from consciousness, graying out and becoming almost entirely unaware of his surroundings. Beside him, Jackie held him in a position that seemed natural — leaning against her body, his head propped against her shoulder and supported by a pillow, a blanket draped over his entire body — forcing him to retain some semblance of consciousness with sharp nudges and the occasional whispered words in his ear.

The spans when he was quasi-conscious increased as the day grew older. In Paris, in the Metro underground — the last he could remember was boarding the train in Calais — he remembered awakening to the sound of combat, guns firing and people screaming, Jackie, sweet Jackie crying out in pain and the sound of a man pleading for mercy before a much closer source fired several times...brilliant flashes of white-hot pain hitting his own body...his eyes opening and his hunger growing ferocious, all-encompassing...soothing warm washes of vitæ coming into his ravenous system... drifting softly into the void, a pleasant emptiness that bathed him in peace at last...and finally gaining back his full consciousness as the sun set, and he found himself lying in the back of another plush limousine, Jackie in the seat beside him, cold and seemingly lifeless, save for the sound of her heart beating against him.

He sat up abruptly, looking to the driver's seat where Charnas sat, wearing Jackie's chauffeur's cap and talking animatedly with Thadius Zho in the seat beside him. "What in the name of God—"

"Well, would you look at that? Sleeping Beauty is finally among the living again. Well, as close as he'll ever get, at any rate." Charnas' voice was irritating, but better than the images he'd seen again in his dreams, images that refused to allow him a closer look before they shifted away again.

"Good evening, Kurt." Zho spoke with a serenity that Kurt found enviable. "I'm afraid you left a bit of a mess behind in England, but I managed to take care of the worst of it."

"The vampire I attacked —"

"Ignatius? Oh, nothing to worry about, he's alive. He has Charnas to thank for that, though I doubt he'll be thankful when he realizes all that he agreed to."

"None of that," Charnas scolded. "He knew the deal when he signed the contract. I probably would have helped him anyway. He's a deviant and a scoundrel — things I can respect in a member of the Damned — but I couldn't resist at least trying to make him pay a price. What can I say? Now and then you get lucky."

"Shut up, Charnas. I'm talking here."

"Yassuh, massah! I be a good slave fo' sho'!"

"Count yourself lucky, Kurt. We came across you and Jackie at just the right time. It seems the Tremere would rather you not make it to Vienna. Ms. Therman did an admirable job of fighting off their cronies, but no one is an army unto herself."

"Is Jackie all right? She feels cold."

"The poor little ducky!" Charnas laughed as he spoke. "She's suffering from physical exhaustion. It seems she hasn't slept since the Big Bad Wolf—"

"Shut up!" The words came from Zho and Kurt simultaneously.

"Huffed and puffed?" Charnas sounded shocked.

Zho continued on his own. "You have the manners of a rutting pig!" Zho stopped, glaring at his servant. When he started speaking again, Charnas spoke with him, mimicking every sound he made. "*You* serve *me*, Charnas, and you should try to remember that! I have grown tired of your constant interruptions and your vulgar attitudes! And will you quit that? Stop imitating me! Damn you to hell, Charnas! Must you constantly mock me?"

Charnas continued the tirade by himself when the mage stopped speaking. "'I've been a fair master to you, I've never forced you to do anything you were opposed to, and I've never demanded anything unreasonable from you!' Do you have any idea how whiny you sound when you start your tirades, 'master?' Could you possibly come up with something new? A different threat? At least a unique torture? Two hundred years of this nonsense! Get a life!"

"That's precisely what I'm working on."

"Oh, I forgot. Never mind then." The imp spoke with saccharine cheer, and Kurt opted to ignore him again.

"Where are we, Thadius?"

"We're in Austria, Kurt. We should be in Vienna within the hour. Early enough that most of the night can be spent in pursuit of Ilse Decameron and her mortal lover."

"Mmmm. Then all will be well." Kurt stared out the window, one hand caressing Jackie's hair. He doubted anything would ever be well again.

➣€

It had been a short day or long night, depending on how you counted time in the House of Secrets. Ilse had had time to talk it all over with Carl, attempting to puzzle out the many things left unsaid by Dr. Dee, and time to sit and reflect by herself. In the end, there were more questions than there were answers. If the word of a demon was to be trusted (and the phantom memories it conjured up), then Ilse, or at least her soul, had had an extended romance with the men of a magical bloodline. Seventh sons of seventh sons, men with mismatched eyes marked for power.

One of her lovers had been good, and had died young — Paul. She had still not gotten over his loss.

One had murdered her, and was still alive — Zho. His betrayal was like an ancient wound reopened, explaining pains and fears she'd never understood, while at the same time causing new ones.

Then there was the third son of the bloodline who she was aware of, Carl, and he was not yet her lover, though the attraction was there. Ilse looked at his soul, seeing the differences from Paul's and the great divergence from Zho's... at least the Zho she had seen, not the one she remembered.

She still wasn't sure how she felt. There had been such joy when she found Carl, for she'd thought he was Paul, returned to her as he'd promised. Then there was such fear with the memory of Zho, mixed with anger and pain, and, yes, still a measure of love, which made it all the more terrible.

Ilse squeezed her eyes tight, not wanting to be blinded by memories or fantasies. What she had to remember was that Carl Magnuson was his own person. A seventh son of a seventh son, yes, and a man with magical eyes, but his own person all the same. Paul, Carl, Thadius and whoever else was linked into the chain of sevenths, were not the same person or even the same soul, only brothers or relations who shared some of the same characteristics and same magic.

Carl was more a cousin to one, multi-great-grandson to another, or at least so they gathered from Dee's talk of "sublines" and "problems." To be descended not only from a dark mage, but one who had promised his child to a demon, and to then be descended from that child in turn, was something that could cause troubles with any magical ritual, and, as Carl had said, was even more excellent grounds than being related to House Tremere for being kicked out of the Order, if it hadn't been the actual reason to begin with. There was really no way to tell without confronting the Preceptors of the Order of Hermes, and that, of course, was inadvisable.

Then there was the eldest of the magical line, the immortal mage who by his mere existence had allowed Zho to swindle Charnas. That mage had to be one and the same with the member of the Council of Seven who would form the other link at the top of the great chain of resurrection that would spell the end of Clan Tremere and the rebirth of House Tremere, a house of mortal mages. They had only supposition to go on, but it was strong, and that man had to be none other than Councilor Etrius. Etrius, the youngest of Tremere's Circle, and the seventh of his magical children. The seventh of seven. All the signs pointed to him, including the letters, and the chantry of Vienna was Etrius' stronghold.

They couldn't be certain, of course, but they'd have their doubts dispelled soon enough.

"C'mon, Ilse," Master Harry said. "It's hardly good to keep a member of the Council waiting, even if it's just an old sweetheart like Etrius."

Sweetheart, Ilse thought. Had she been Etrius' lover as well, in a previous life?

Her thoughts were quickly brought back to her present life, such as it was. "Jesus Christ!" Carl swore. "This bag weighs a bloody ton!"

Master Harry paused and smiled, his brown eyes twinkling. "Lady Sarah's idea of light packing dates back a century or so." He shrugged. "You're a mage — why don't you just make it sprout legs and follow you down the hall?"

Carl set the heavy suitcase back down and squared his shoulders, stooping to look Master Harry in the eye. "Listen, mate, I know you Tremere want to put me through my paces and see what I can do, but there are limits and there's always a price. And having my suitcase wander down the hall like something out of a fantasy novel isn't something I fancy trying unless I want to get tattoos all over my body proclaiming that I've been shipped everywhere from Cairo to Bombay, 'cause that's what would happen, like as not."

Master Harry gestured to the air around them. "You may still be mortal, Carl, but you're not in the mortal world anymore. Physics don't necessarily apply in the Labyrinthine Hall." He took a step from floor to wall, leaning back then and standing at a right angle to the passageway. "The only thing you might need to worry about is Lady Sarah getting mad about you tracking mud on her nice clean wallpaper."

Carl looked like he was attempting to appear unimpressed, but not quite succeeding. "Master Harry, that may be okay for you, but one of the first things they taught us in the Order is that even if you're in the innermost isolated secretest *sanctum sanctorum*, you don't do magic unless there's a serious need for it."

"More's the pity." Master Harry stamped his foot, and a shiny red apple fell horizontally out of the wallpaper on the opposite side of the passageway, landing in his outstretched palm. "If that's the way of mortal magic, then I'm very glad I became a vampire, and I'm even more glad that we Tremere are going to change things once we become mortal again.

After all, where's the joy in anything if you rule out impulse and wonder?" He took a bite of the apple, blood running down his chin as the peel became gray and withered. "Not to mention sheer delight and amusement?" he added around a mouthful of bloody fruit.

He chewed and swallowed, licking his lips. "Our tricks may be rehearsed, but at least we can do them on a whim." The mummified fruit turned to powder and drifted down to merge with the wallpaper. Master Harry dusted off his fingers, wiping the last of the blood from his chin with one and licking it clean, then jumped lightly in the air, turning two-hundred and seventy degrees, and landed upright before them, hands out in a showman's bow. "Just because something's deadly doesn't mean it has to be serious."

Ilse shuddered. "You sound like Charnas."

Master Harry blinked, coming upright. "The Imp? I'd heard he'd gotten into this game. Can't say I'm surprised, though. His greater half's the demon in charge of the flesh and all that implies: carnage, carnal pleasures, carnal knowledge, charnel houses and, of course, carnivals." He reached down and picked up Carl's suitcase as if it weighed no more that a feather. "Alley-oop! Here we go!" He juggled Ilse's on top of it, holding them both stacked atop his fingertips like a waiter would a tray, then looked to Ilse. "Too bad there isn't a third. Standard rule of juggling — always have at least three. But then I suppose it's my own fault for having a room set up at the Vienna chantry."

He turned and waltzed down the hall, humming something by Strauss.

"Bloody hell," Carl remarked to Ilse as they tried to catch up. "Flesh, death and pleasure — I can see why your lot might have dealings with a demon like that. The question is, if Zho *is* my ancestor, what was he doing dealing with Charnas?"

Ilse considered. She'd studied very little demonology, but what both Carl and Master Harry had said made chilling sense.

Of all the demons she knew of, Charnas the Bloody Jester would have the most direct interest in the Damned and their goings-on. Bloody hell indeed. But as for Zho's motivation for dealing with the Lord of Misrule, Ilse couldn't say. Apart from her horrible death, there was very little she could remember (or wanted to remember) from her life as Gwyneth, if it had even been her life at all, though she had a chilling certainty it had. After all, she'd always had an interest in both magic and spirits, even in her mortal life. A tragic, albeit magical, past life helped to explain it. Her spirit photography could be taken as an expression of that, and she wondered if there were any way to capture images of her past lives, or if, indeed, she would even want to. She had never seen Paul's ghost, with her own eyes or on film, and she hoped he'd done well in his next life and the one thereafter. Looking at Carl, she still couldn't be certain whether the English mage could not actually be the reincarnation of her dead lover, changed by a lifetime or two in between. There was no way she knew to tell other than instinct, and hers were very badly confused.

Ilse shook her head and followed as Master Harry led the way down to where the hallway ended in a five-sided atrium, doors on each of the four walls. He paused, gazing at each in turn.

"Let's see. One is too obvious. Two would be an insult, because whatever the Vienna chantry might be, it's second to none, which means that it's first, not second. Which means that door number two is eliminated."

Master Harry weighed the two suitcases, now balanced atop one finger, and stroked his chin, considering. "Three is the number of magic, and therefore would seem the most logical choice, though four, when you reflect a bit, is the number of death. At least in the East, and Lady Sarah is terribly fond of Eastern mysticism, so that might be a possibility. But, which is more important to House Tremere — death or magic? Which is the proper choice?"

He looked to Carl, smiling.

Carl made a quick decision. "Magic," he said and reached for the third door.

Quick as an eyeblink, Master Harry grabbed his wrist, stopping him. "No, no, no, don't be so impulsive. Sarah's a lady, the Palace is Night, should you count from the left or count from the right?

"Right," Master Harry said. "One, two—" He took Carl by the wrist and counted counterclockwise round the ring, "Three," he finished, ending at what Ilse had first numbered as door number two.

The elder vampire released the mage and smiled, gesturing to the door. Carl glanced back for a moment, as if afraid that Master Harry was going to pull another trick, then slowly reached for the old brass knob.

They emerged into a completely different chamber, decorated in gold and crystal, with cabinets filled with demitasse cups and goldsmithing of baroque splendor, drinking vessels made from nautilus shells in the shape of hippocampi, and ostrich shell chalices fashioned to look like ostriches with real plumes attached.

In an ornate leather folding chair, some noble's hunting throne from the Dark Ages, sat a young Spaniard dressed in wine velvet, his long hair clasped to one side with a gold band. He lounged back, languidly smoking a cigarette, but looked up as they entered the room.

"Merrill!" Ilse cried out, glad for a familiar face. "I didn't know you were here."

He stubbed out his cigarette in the gold-edged ashtray beside his empty coffee cup and stood up. "Nice to see you again, Ilse." He opened the gold cigarette case on the chain around his neck and slipped the remaining half inside. "Everyone comes to Vienna sooner or later. Now do you make the introductions or do I?"

"Weren't you told of our coming?"

"Well, yes, but there's always the sake of appearances. Merrill Molitor," he said, extending his hand to Carl beside her, "and I'd be guessing you'd be Carl Magnuson?"

"You'd guess right," Carl said, taking Merrill's hand and shaking it. "You two...?" He cocked his head in Ilse's direction.

Merrill smiled. "Long past, I'm afraid. But watch her, my friend — she has a wicked bite."

Carl took his hand back and rubbed his neck. "I've already found that out for myself."

Ilse looked away as Master Harry said, "No greetings for me, you blackguard?"

Ilse knew Merrill was smiling with that Andalusian charm that had first drawn her to him. "Hello, Master Harry," Merrill replied, laughing. "I haven't seen you since what? Last week? No matter. Councilor Etrius wants to see everyone, or really Ilse and Carl, but he won't care if you tag along." He paused. "I'm glad you're already in formal wear, even if I know it's just your conjurer's trappings. We now only need find you a top hat —"

There was a popping sound, and Ilse looked back to see Master Harry flourishing a high silk hat and putting it atop his head. "Done." He reached behind Carl's head and produced a second, popping it out as well.

Carl snatched it and put it on for himself, murmuring, "I'd always heard hatters were mad..."

Merrill laughed, turning to Ilse and studying at the deep crimson crushed-velvet gown Lady Sarah had chosen for her to wear to the audience. "Oh, come now, Ilse." He stood back, hands on hips, his gaze lingering on her neckline. "Pearls were never your style, and we know you're not that innocent. Allow me..."

He raised his hands to his mouth, nicking each of his thumbs with his fangs, then put his hands to either side of her head, touching the earrings Lady Sarah had made her and looking deep into her eyes. Slowly and sensually, he then let his hands slide down, tracing the line of her neck from both sides and the string of pearls, ending with his fingers atop her breasts, blood dripping down into her cleavage like a kiss.

Ilse glanced down, seeing where the pearls had been transmuted to a heavy scapular of garnets. In the hollow between her breasts, the blood pooled and formed a pigeon's blood star ruby.

She looked up at Merrill, and he smiled, taking his hands to her wrists and adding heavy bracelets in place of the pearl watch Lady Sarah had crafted for her. "A woman looks best in jewels, if she is to be dressed at all."

Carl took her arm, retrieving her hand from Merrill. "Let's just skip the tiara, shall we?"

Master Harry laughed, and Ilse forced herself to give one too, but she knew it didn't sound right.

Unflappable, Merrill turned to the door at the end of the chamber and opened it. "Let me get someone to take your bags to your rooms, then we'll get along to Councilor Etrius. He's already at the Opera, but if we move quickly, we should be able to make the second act." He leaned out into the hall. "Frick! Frack! They're here! See to the bags, then follow us."

Two huge white-haired men entered the room, one in a white tux, the other in a black tux, both twice as rich and twice as plain as either tail coat Carl or Master Harry was wearing. The chantry's ghoul retainers were otherwise perfect mirrors, silent as monoliths. They took the bags from Master Harry and ducked out of the room.

Merrill smiled and gestured to the door. "The Opera House is not far, if you don't mind the walk, and I can fill you in on the first act while we do."

"Yes, please," Ilse found herself saying. "That would be lovely."

Merrill led the way down the hall and up the stairs, to the mansion's fourteenth century foyer where Frick and Frack waited to either side of the grand doors like sentinels. *Frack* of course referred to the formal frock coat and white-tie ensemble that the second ghoul wore, though Ilse's German was rusty and she couldn't remember what *Frick* would mean. As far as she recalled, the black tie and tails worn by the left-hand ghoul (and by Master Harry and Carl, for that matter) was properly referred to as *esmoquin*, though she could probably call the two chessmen Max and Moritz and it would make as much difference.

They exited the Tremere High Chantry, just across from the University of Vienna, and uncomfortably equidistant between the spires of the *Votivkirche* and the Cathedral of St. Stefan. Merrill led them down the *Herrengasse* towards the Opera House, Frick and Frack walking silently to either side of them, a ghoul escort against any possible troubles.

Somehow, by unspoken consent, everyone had switched to German, Merrill's Andalusian accent almost undetectable underneath the aristocratic Viennese dialect he'd affected. Ilse was left with halting *Hochdeutsch*, as was Carl, though his was much better, while Master Harry started up the same dialect as Merrill, laughing in a magician's patter as they went through the various jokes and plot twists of the first act of *Die Fledermaus*.

Somehow, Ilse was having trouble paying attention, probably because meeting with Councilor Etrius, the leader of the Council of Seven and one of the most powerful Kindred in the world, seemed to overshadow whether or not Herr Doktor Professor Franke had woken up with a hangover at the base of a statue amid the morning commute while still dressed in a bat suit. If she were a Toreador, the intricacies of the first act of *Die Fledermaus* would have probably been fascinating, but she wasn't, and even though her stomach was as dead as her heart, the butterflies seemed to be defying death quite nicely.

"That Merrill's slicker than Blackheath Pond in midwinter, isn't he?" Carl remarked, patting her arm with one warm hand.

"He's not that bad." Ilse watched as the Spaniard laughed and waved his cigarette in the air, tracing patterns for Master Harry. She desperately wanted a smoke herself, but knew if she took one out, Merrill would be back offering her his lighter before she had a chance to blink. "I was very fond of him once."

Carl looked askance. "In love?"

"No, passion." She made herself sigh, but it wasn't hard. "He was young and alive, and he made me feel alive. But I don't think he's ever forgiven me."

"You mean...?" Carl tapped his neck with two fingers.

"Yes." Ilse felt Carl's skin grow colder. Some further explanation was needed. "I — I didn't want to, but the Council gave me my orders."

Carl looked at her wryly. "Do you do everything the Council tells you to do?"

Ilse didn't answer, and that, she knew, was answer in and of itself.

They continued in silence, except for Merrill and Master Harry joking about musical pocketwatches and high-voiced Russian princes, until at last they came to the Vienna Opera House.

It was prettier than she remembered it, with mounted riders on the cornices and robed gods or statesmen on the second level, but then the last time Ilse had seen it was 1940, and she knew it had been bombed during the war. The rebuilding had surpassed its former splendor, or at least her memory of it. She hardly had a moment to gaze up at the grand façade before they were up the steps and the footmen already in position opened the doors, Frick and Frack escorting them inside.

Merrill dropped his cigarette in one of the ashtrays, the sand in the top pressed into the shape of the Austrian eagle, then pointed to the grand stairway, green plush carpeting held down with brass rails over white marble, gilded lanterns and pediments with Grecian statuary to either side. "Our box is on the top floor."

Ilse followed, along with Master Harry and Carl, Frick and Frack keeping silent pace to either side of them. From behind the sealed doors, Ilse heard the strains of an aria and a woman's voice, beautiful and compelling in its power, with a strange, almost mystical quality to it.

Ushers opened doors for Merrill at a single glance from him, and they were at last at a door just to the left of one marked with the imperial arms of the House of Hapsburg. A lesser coat of arms decorated this portal, but worked into the detail was the seal of House Tremere. Merrill brought out a key and quietly unlocked the door, holding it open for them with a finger to his lips. First Frick, then Master Harry, then Carl went inside, followed by herself, with Merrill and Frack bringing up the rear.

The first thing that struck her was the sound, for what had been haunting and beautiful in the hall outside had taken on a supernatural quality when she stepped through the door. On the stage, far below, was a raven-haired woman dressed in a long, iridescent, peacock-colored gown, moving in the heavy skirts with a sensual grace that belied their weight and the distance. Her voice, a rich, pure soprano, trilled the aria like a nightingale.

Ilse picked up a snatch of the words after a long while and translated them for herself. She claimed to be a Hungarian countess, but was very, very mysterious. What she had done and who she was must remain a secret, but behind her peacock-feathered mask, it was intimated that she was a woman of great fame, even infamy, possibly even the celebrated Countess Bathory, the fabled beauty whom men both feared and lusted after and who had kept herself forever young and beautiful by bathing in the blood of virgins.

With her black hair, pale face and the aching beauty of her voice, Ilse did not need to look at her aura to tell that she was Kindred, let alone Toreador. Her voice had an enchanting quality that told the story by itself, and it wasn't until Merrill placed a hand on Ilse's shoulder that the spell was broken and she was able to find her seat and take in the rest of her surroundings.

Besides herself and the others she had come with, the first who caught her eye was a small, dark young man, leaning on the edge of the balcony and peering with a preternatural intensity through a pair of opera glasses at the woman below. Across his knees and the edge of the box he had a black sketchbook open, and as he watched, his fountain pen flew across the page, tracing the woman and writing down snatches of verse and poetry with a speed and precision that would have seemed inhuman if the drawings with which he covered the page were not so very beautiful.

Another Toreador, Ilse was certain, and at the bottom of the left-hand page was the caption:

Adrianne
als
Rosalinda von Eisenstein
als
Die Ungarische Gräfin

"Dieter Kleist," Merrill whispered in her ear, altogether too close. "Councilor Etrius' chronicler."

Kleist sketched an ornamented border around his poetry, not even glancing at it, then flipped the page and began a new drawing.

Merrill nodded to one side until Ilse followed him. "Councilor Etrius," he said, then, "and Astrid Thomas."

Ilse didn't even glance at the woman, her eyes only for Etrius. He was to the right of her, and she could only see his right eye, but it was the same blue as Paul's, or Carl's, or Zho's for that matter, with the same expression of intent curiosity. Otherwise, the ancient vampire appeared young and pleasant-faced, smooth and clean-shaven, scarcely over twenty to judge by physical age, with longish sandy-brown hair. He was neither short like Paul nor tall like Carl, only just above middling height, which, Ilse considered, would have been quite tall for the middle ages.

Etrius was dressed in white *Frack*, but very old-fashioned, something an imperial officer would have worn at the end of the Austrian Empire. In place of the usual ambassadorial sash or military medals, around his neck he had a great golden chain of office, the type of ornament only seen in portraits of medieval chancellors or burghers, square diamond studs framed in gold with a Burmese ruby of the first water set as the central pendant. Under the chain, on a simple black silk cord, was an ornate iron key, the key of a chamberlain or steward.

Ilse refocused her sight, and around the chain and gem, and cord and key, as she might have expected, she saw the blazing lights of much warding and spellcraft. Beneath that, Etrius' aura had the faded quality of the vampire, though otherwise displayed the same soft patterns of blue and gold as did the auras of Carl Magnuson and Thadius Zho, though without Carl's life or Zho's black sin. And Etrius' aura had shadings of color which she had only seen once before, on the soul of Paul Carroll.

At least in this life and deathtime.

She became dimly aware of heat on her cheek and at last turned and met the smoldering eyes of the woman who sat next to Etrius. She was as beautiful as the woman on stage, with lily white skin and long, softly curled, dark hair, but the look in her eyes was murderous, her face a mask of jealousy and hate.

Mine! The thought stabbed into Ilse's mind like a knife, and Ilse turned away, blinking back tears of pain. The blood dripped down onto her breasts, mixing with the ruby, garnets and crimson velvet.

Merrill offered her his red silk handkerchief. "Astrid is the Councilor's consort."

He didn't finish the thought; he didn't need to. The next look the woman shot her was eloquent enough, though Councilor Etrius only turned and smiled at Ilse, his left eye green, and squeezed Astrid's hand before looking back to the opera.

Merrill nudged Ilse and gestured to the far seats. "Cassandra and Ulugh Beg."

Ilse looked, dabbing at her eyes. Cassandra was a heavy-set woman, nearing middle age, but still beautiful, her purple silk gown low-cut and corseted up to display a generous bosom. Her black hair framed dark eyes and pink cheeks, the first intense but abstracted, the second still rosy with the colors of life. Around her neck she had two pendants, a silver crescent moon and a golden circle set with a square of green malachite. Matching neither, on her left wrist she wore a simple tennis bracelet of white gold and rubies, while on the middle finger of the same hand was a ring of ancient design set with a Chinese turquoise.

Some charm was woven between the stones, Ilse could see it in the etheric traces, but as to what, she couldn't tell for certain. Whatever it was, she had no doubt it was potent. Cassandra was Magus Prime of the Vienna chantry and thereby second only to Etrius himself in matter of magic.

To the woman's side was a dark-haired, swarthy Turkish gentleman, dressed in an impeccable black tuxedo and watching the Toreador diva with a dark intensity that marked him as Ulugh Beg, the Watcher, the new Justicar of House Tremere. His eyes noted every movement as thoroughly as Kleist did in his notebook.

It was not a time for speaking, and Ilse at last turned her attention back to the stage and took Carl's hand for comfort, hoping to escape the looks of old lust from Merrill and undisguised malice from Astrid Thomas.

On the stage, the action had changed along with the aria, and a red-haired ingenue had replaced the black-haired diva. The girl, singing with a lilting alto, played the part of Adele,

Frau von Eisenstein's maid, wearing her mistress' gown while she went to the ball, masquerading as an aspiring actress. Though still lovely, the girl's voice did not possess the same supernatural quality as had Adrianne's, but she had a sweet, almost disarming presence, and an air of innocence able to enchant Kindred and kine alike. Ilse saw the paleness of the girl's aura at the same time as she noted the name in Kleist's notebook: *Felicia Mostrom*. Kleist's fingers flew over the page, smearing it with his blood from his slashed fingertips, painting her hair and lips a vivid red, and Ilse could tell from his absolute entrancement that the young Toreador was smitten.

Ilse pressed Carl's hand for comfort, feeling his warmth and the close beat of his heart, watching the opera and taking note of the players. The Toreadors of Vienna had come out in force; besides Adrianne and Felicia, the part of Dr. Franke was wickedly and brilliantly sung by an elderly Toreador who Kleist noted as *Elliot Sinclair*, while the part of Herr von Eisenstein was played with a passionate intensity by another Kindred known as *Ramiel Dupré*.

The silly business with the chiming pocketwatch that Merrill and Master Harry had discussed earlier came to pass, but with such passion and intensity that Ilse felt herself gasping on reflex. Adrianne flirted dangerously with Ramiel, Herr von Eisenstein not recognizing his wife, despite the fact that all she wore different was a mask and a ballgown and a mysterious air. But the magic of midnight was enough, and Herr von Eisenstein was unable to guess that the enigmatic beauty was in fact his wife, blind but for his passion for the Hungarian Countess, even when she grabbed the pocketwatch and dropped it down her bosom. The audience laughed with great hilarity, the power of the vampires on stage a potent drug, but Ilse was chilled. To love another, but not be recognized...

The rest of the act passed by in a blur of dancing and arias, until another pale-auraed man came onstage, this one with a violin, taking the part of a visiting performer at Prince Orlofsky's New Year's Eve Ball. *Dorian Strack*, Kleist noted in his sketchbook, devoting two facing pages to the violinist.

Dorian announced that he had had a dream in which the Devil had appeared to him and challenged him to a fiddling contest. The prize would be his soul if he lost and his heart's desire if he won. First he played the tune which he had played for the Devil, a beautiful, joyous song that brought tears to Ilse's eyes and caused the air of the opera house to flush golden with the glow of joy from the auras of the audience.

Strack then bowed to thunderous applause and asked the partygoers on stage and the audience at large whether he should now play the Devil's offering. A hush fell over the stage, as well as the audience, the fiddler's presence a palpable thing, but at last came the nods. Yes, yes, the music had been heavenly, but all wished to hear the Devil's offering and judge for themselves.

Strack's features seemed to blaze alight, his eyes glowing, and Ilse thought for a second the Masquerade had been dropped entirely until she realized it was just the footlights and the red spot the lighting crew had put upon the violinist. Then Strack began the Devil's tune, and Ilse was not so certain, for he laughed as he played, showing his fangs. The music was beautiful and chilling all at once, reaching into her breast and gripping her dead heart with iron claws, refusing to let go. A collective gasp went up from the audience, and one by one the partygoers of Prince Orlofsky's New Year's ball began to dance on stage, possessed by the music, and it was all Ilse could do to keep from throwing herself over the balcony to join them. Evidently the Viennese kept strictly to the standards of society and decorum, for not a soul moved in the audience below, Strack's demonic performance going on and on until at last the air came to an end.

Every light in the house fell, plunging the theater into darkness. Then, slowly, the red spotlight returned, Strack standing like the Devil himself, fangs bared, holding his fiddle in one hand and his bow in the other. "*Sag's mir!*" he cried out. "*Wer hat gesiegt?*"

Tell me, Ilse translated. *Who has won?*

The vampire on stage stood frozen for a long moment, then put his head back and laughed and collapsed in a heap.

The red spot died in that instant, and the lights of the house went back up, the party guests on stage milling about in fright, afraid to go near the body, speculating whether or not the fiddler was dead. Then, as they were about to go up and check, Strack sprang to his feet and laughed, "*Wir haben beide gesiegt! Der Teufel hat meine Seele, aber ich hapt seine Musik!*"

We have both won! The Devil has my soul, but I have his music!

The party guests and the audience all laughed nervously, the fiddler at best just a brilliant musician, at worst, hopefully, just a muddled madman. He then launched into a spritely waltz tune, with none of the demonic overtones of the last, nor the heavenly voice of the first, which was the cue for some visiting ballet troupe to prance out, giving all a moment to pause and recover from what had gone before.

Kleist's notebook was spattered with blood. He stubbed his fingers dry on his blotting paper, changed the page and went back to mere ink to record the dance of the ballet troupe.

"Well that was something, eh?" Carl asked and squeezed her hand.

Ilse squeezed back, chilled to her very soul by the implications of the Toreador's performance. Looking in the calm light of the ballet, she could see that his soul had none of the black stains of Zho or Crowley, or even of Smudge, but the intensity was there and the swirl of divine or infernal madness, she couldn't tell which. Strack was a true artist, and in his performance, she had seen truth. After her meeting with Charnas, she knew that the fiddler's fancy was indeed within the realm of possibility.

The second act ended, and the spell was broken, the audience parting like duckweed on a pond. Carl let go of her hand and got to his feet next to her.

"You must be Councilor Etrius. Thank you for your letter."

Ilse stood as the ancient vampire came up beside her, appearing as young as Paul when they'd first met. "You would be Carl." Etrius smiled, his accent faint but unplaceable. "Thank you for coming so quickly."

Carl grinned. "The Master calls, you come. They taught us that back in the Order."

Etrius laughed, a very human sound, and a claw as cold as ice grasped Ilse by the arm. "Come," said Astrid, her words heavy with venom, "let us leave the men. They have much to talk on, and so do we."

She dragged Ilse from the box with a strength that belied her delicate bone structure and pushed open the door across the hall, leading into the powder room intended for the women of the nobility. "Leave us!" Astrid hissed at the matron.

The woman did so without a word. After the door shut behind her, Astrid spat blood on the floor and traced a hex sign in the direction of the doorknob. A webwork of lines glowed around the brass, then faded into the wood. She then turned to Ilse, releasing her arm and gazing at her for a long moment.

Ilse was not expecting the slap, nor the force of it. She was knocked sprawling to the floor by a shattering blow, her neck almost snapped. The left side of her face went numb with shock.

"*That*," said Astrid, "for looking at my man that way." She bared her teeth at Ilse, fangs fully extended. "And I will kill you if I ever see you look at him that way again."

Ilse felt the blood rush to her face, wanting to heal the crimson handprint that was no doubt outlined across her cheek, but she forced it to hold back. It was with cold certainty that she knew that this woman would take it as an affront to see her handiwork so quickly undone. Astrid was a tigress, her eyes blazing with an inner light, and even if Ilse could summon forth the force of will to oppose her, she knew it would be a foolish thing to do. So Ilse turned to the only defense she had left — she sat down and cried.

Astrid gave her a look she had last seen on Crowley, one of abject loathing and hate. "*Ängstlich!*" she spat.

Coward. The word was like poison in Ilse's ears. In the next moment, Astrid stormed from the room, the door slamming behind her.

Ilse wept for a long moment before the knob turned again. In horror at being discovered in such a state, she pushed against the door with all the force of her mind. The door shut, then pushed back against her, the knob twisting as if in inquiry. Then the door moved straight open, shattering her telekinetic force, and Cassandra came into the room, shutting the door behind her and renewing Astrid's spell with a casual flick of the wrist, but without the spitting of blood.

"I should have warned you," she said, her voice deep and matronly. "However, I see that Astrid has already done that in her own inimitable fashion."

Ilse willed herself to stop crying and for the blood to flow into her cheek and heal the crushed skin and cracked bone. Cassandra came and offered her a hand up, along with a large white handkerchief edged in lace, at the touch of which the blood on Ilse's hands transmuted to salty tears. The Magus did not explain, only helped Ilse to wipe the blood-tears from her cheeks. "Astrid is a dangerous one to cross, as you've already discovered."

"I have," Ilse snuffled around Cassandra's enchanted handkerchief, then blew her nose to find mucus instead of blood in her hands. She folded the white linen quickly, but Cassandra held up her hand, not wanting it back.

"I may have to do the same for Astrid before this affair is done," the Magus sighed. "This is a game of high stakes we enter into and a desperate business. Astrid fears she will suffer a reversal of fortunes, losing what she has gained — her power, her position, her magic — in exchange for the mere mortality she left behind." The older woman's mouth gave a bitter twist. "One might even question her loyalties."

Ilse thought she understood. "She fears losing Etrius."

"And more," the woman said. "None dare oppose Astrid in public and few in private, but even she cannot control the Councilor…at least, not in this one thing he wants so very much — life itself." She grimaced. "They call me Cassandra for good reason, but please, I would ask you to watch Astrid carefully, if just for your own sake."

She paused, going over to the mirror and checking her make-up, taking a moment to retouch her lipstick. "Tell me, Ilse, have you heard anything of the Comte de St. Germain?"

Ilse wiped at her tears with the handkerchief. "Yes," she managed. "Aleister Crowley told me to tell Dr. Dee that the Comte was opposed to his schemes."

Cassandra paused, then finished applying her pale coral lipstick. "And what did the Doctor say when you told him?"

Ilse thought back. "He said that the Comte was a trouble worth countenancing."

Cassandra twisted the gold tube shut and slipped it back in her evening bag, pressing her lips together once and then checking the effect in the mirror. "The Doctor is a master of understatement."

The sound of music filtered through the walls of the powder room. Cassandra shut her purse and put an arm about Ilse's shoulders, steering her towards the door. "Come. The third act is about to begin."

"Thank you," Ilse said softly.

"Think nothing of it. But if I were you, I wouldn't discuss this with anyone else."

Cassandra opened the door, shepherding Ilse back to the Tremere box, and Ilse realized she was not going to be told anything more.

⇥❦⇤

Die Fledermaus ended and with it the "Revenge of the Bat," as Elliot Sinclair put it, the maid hitting it off with the Governor of the jail, her sister with the boyfriend, the boyfriend released, the husband arrested, the musical pocketwatch returned, and Herr von Eisenstein and Frau von Eisenstein reconciled to their mutual infidelity. It was all very silly, and all Ilse wanted to do by the time everything was over was go back to the Chantry, sit down with a cup of blood, and quietly talk things over with Carl. But duty called. A group had been assembled from the Tremere box, other boxes and the stage, and Councilor Etrius wished to regale them all with the Viennese tradition of after-opera coffee. Ilse could only assume that Etrius' excursion to the coffeehouse was similar in effect to Lady Sarah's tea parties.

It was. The coffeehouse was revealed to be nothing less than the famous Sacher Hotel at the top of the *Kärntnerstrasse*, just in back of the opera house, and the coffee was just that, coffee, though when Ilse raised it to her lips, it changed to blood as it entered her mouth.

Carl seemed to have no similar experience, or else had somehow suddenly acquired a taste for blood, as had the one other mortal guest, the man opposite him, introduced as Aries Michaels.

Michaels appeared to be in his fifties, and, apart from the black tuxedo, he looked like a sobered-up version of Hemingway, with neatly trimmed gray beard and hair and a seal ring on his ring finger that matched Carl's. His aura was also mage-bright, but Ilse hardly had to look at it, for to her right sat Dieter Kleist, who was already sketching it in with a set of colored pencils, a swirl of the dark blues, Prussian to cornflower, the colors of intellect, sparked here and there with ruby asterisks denoting magical power. A mage of the Order of Hermes, and a powerful one at that.

"So," Michaels said, leaning forward and looking Carl in the eye. "How are the Tremere treating you?" His accent was American, but beyond being obviously well-educated, Ilse couldn't place it.

"Can't complain." Carl sat to her left and added a spoonful of sugar to his coffee, just like Paul used to do. "And you?"

"Things could be better. I had to make several sacrifices to arrange matters." He took a sip of coffee. "They'll all be worth it if we pull this off. Melsinde has listened to reason, and that's the important thing."

Carl raised his colorless eyebrows. "*The* Melsinde?"

Michaels nodded. "The very one," he said. He offered no further explanation.

Carl sat to the right of Etrius, Astrid thankfully on the far side of the Councilor, while opposite Ilse was Cassandra. Ulugh Beg sat to the Magus' left, and to his left was a distinguished, if slightly Mephistophelian, gentleman Ilse recognized as Lazarus, Proctor of the Miami chantry and the Tremere with the greatest influence throughout Florida and the Caribbean. What business he had in Vienna, Ilse was uncertain, but it undoubtedly had something to do with the Kindred sitting opposite Ulugh Beg, a handsome man with long brown hair, a heavy mustache, and a fierce expression only surpassed by his aura.

"Coffee?" he demanded in English, holding his cup as if it were a urine specimen. "You get me kicked out of Miami, and you offer me *coffee?*"

Lazarus inclined his head and stroked his devilishly pointed black beard. "There's Sachertorte as well, but I don't think you'd care for it."

The man snarled, and Ilse glanced down at Kleist's notebook, which continued to provide liner notes. *Anvil*, the legend read beneath the sketch, and she only had to note the red rage in his aura to tell that the man was Brujah.

"The coffee is actually pretty good, if you're in the mood." The speaker sat at the end of the table, leaning back in his chair with a cigarette held flippantly in one hand, much more comfortable in his black tuxedo than either Anvil or the pale, balding, white-haired man with the nose- and lip-rings who sat between them, opposite Lazarus, eyes invisible behind mirror shades. "*If* you're in the mood."

The man with the cigarette turned his head to Ilse and smiled, eyes narrowing appreciatively. "Hector Sosa," he introduced himself, switching back to German, Viennese accent plain, "Would you care for a cigarette? I couldn't help but notice." He gestured with his own, and Ilse realized she'd been staring.

He displayed great social charm for a Brujah — for that was what Ilse guessed he was from the angry aura, earring, lip-ring, and spade-shaped red goatee — but she was not about to refuse. "Yes, please." The only other ready source of cigarettes was Merrill — down with Astrid, Master Harry and all of the Toreador contingent save Kleist — and Ilse did not wish to ask the Andalusian.

Sosa extended a pack, and Ilse took one, along with his lighter, nodding. "Ilse Decameron." She lit the cigarette, closing her eyes against the glare, then handed the lighter back, taking a drag and trying not to choke. The Brujah's smokes were much stronger than what she was used to, but good, and what she needed right now.

"You're welcome, Frau Decameron," Sosa said, and the lighter and cigarettes vanished back into his jacket

"Goddammit, did I join a bunch of fucking Ventrue?" Anvil demanded, still in English. "This is worse bullshit than we had back in Miami."

"No, Herr Calloway," Sosa responded, switching to English with a heavy Viennese accent. "You've joined a bunch of Europeans. Things are done a bit differently here, that's all." He took a long drag, then blew the smoke in Anvil's direction. "And Yuri here speaks worse English than you speak German, so unless you wish to alienate your only other clan ally, I suggest you — what's the phrase? — get with the program.

You may be the new primogen, but I'm you're native guide, and I'm telling you that you won't last five minutes here unless you take my advice."

"All right," Anvil growled, switching to German — his accent even worse than Ilse's, "but at least can we get something better to drink than this *Scheiße?*"

He slammed the cup down in the saucer, and coffee — perfectly ordinary-looking coffee — sloshed out onto the white tablecloth, staining it brown.

"Is there a problem, Herr Anvil?" Ulugh Beg smiled, his teeth very white against his dark skin. He was having his coffee in the Turkish style, sweetened with cardamom and ambergris.

"Yes," Anvil said. "Is there anywhere you can hunt in this city?"

"No." Ulugh Beg continued to smile. "We consider all of Vienna to be Elysium and keep the Masquerade enforced. Strictly." He nodded, then picked up his cup and took a sip. "But as all the coffeehouses carry Herr Professor's Special Blend, it should hardly cause a problem unless you are a Ventrue." He paused, looking at Anvil over the rim. "Or Salubri. Do you belong to either of those clans, Herr Anvil?"

They gazed at one another, eyes locked. Soft waltz music played in the background, something by one of the Strausses, quiet enough not to intrude on conversation, but loud enough to cover up the sound of diners at other tables. It was with subtle horror that Ilse recognized the tune as the "Viennese Blood."

"Ulugh, please." Cassandra placed her hand atop the Turk's. "Allow the man at least a moment to be overwhelmed by the differences from his homeland." She looked to the new Brujah primogen. "Councilor Etrius' blend is very popular. Ulugh and I helped design it, and people drink it throughout Vienna night *and* day."

Ilse sipped her coffee, tasting the rich blood that, while fresh as it would come from the neck, seemed to come from many different sources at once. She didn't have a sophisticated Ventrue palate to tell from where, but the special emphasis the Magus had given her last two words allowed Ilse to form a supposition: The beans were drunk by Kindred and mortal alike, both sipping from the same cup as it were, and thereby linked by sympathy. The vampire would drink while the mortal bled, sip by sip and drop by drop. The Ventrue, with their finicky tastes, and the Salubri — the soul-suckers who could only drink from willing victims — would both be at a distinct loss in a city where all Kindred drank magically blended blood. It was an elegant and effective foil against the enemies of the Tremere.

Anvil still stared at Ulugh, on the brink of a Brujah frenzy, until Yuri put his hand on his arm and said, "The hunting is much better to the south, in Bruck and Graz. When we want some action, we go down there."

The Brujah primogen appeared slightly appeased by this, but still glared at Lazarus. "You promised me that we'd get a prince, a Brujah prince, for one of the world's major cities. Then you weaseled out at the voting."

Lazarus picked up his serpent-headed cane and regarded its eyes. "We were already outvoted, Anvil. The Nosferatu Justicar turned the tide, and if he hadn't, Natasha Volfchek would have switched from abstention to siding with her clan, who were backing the Malkavians — as was patently obvious from the presence of the German Archon." The Tremere elder lowered his cane and gave his regard to Anvil. "It was merely prudent to give up on a lost cause, thereby saving face and power. And Mr. Crusher was your choice, not mine. Next time check more carefully for skeletons in the closet before you chose to back someone."

"You think I didn't? How the hell was I to know he offed a couple Sewer Rats?"

Lazarus stroked the serpent-head of his cane, eloquent as a shrug. "Next time, pay them a visit — and bring cash. I'm certain that's what the Ventrue did, and if the Nosferatu can't sell you any dirt on someone, then at the very least they can't sell it to your enemies." He paused for a moment, gazing blandly at the Brujah primogen. "But the ledger still stands, and while Appolonius was unsuccessful in his bid for London, there's no reason that he — or anyone we both deem fit — couldn't take the throne from Lady Anne." He smiled pleasantly. "Even yourself, if that's what you want."

Ilse nearly dropped her coffee cup and did spill several drops. "We were backing the Brujah?" She paused, then glanced swiftly to Anvil, then back to Lazarus. "In London, I mean?"

Ulugh Beg was the first to speak, "Dr. Dee has various alliances. You were never in any real danger."

Anvil finished the statement, "At least not much. From us." He smiled, showing his teeth. "If we wanted you dead, you'd be dead."

Ilse clutched her coffee cup and drew strength from the stern gaze of Frau Anna Sacher in the gold-framed portrait on the opposite wall, painted lips reminding her that while Sacher's might look the other way for many things, vampires included, it was not a place for a lady to make a scene.

"Will the Fräulein be having more of Herr Professor's special blend?" asked the fresh-faced young waiter, coffee pot at the ready.

"Yes, please." Ilse pushed her cup forward, hand shaking.

"Very good," said the waiter, filling her cup, and then went on to Cassandra, then Carl and Michaels, then Etrius, Astrid and the rest of the party. Ilse noted that Michaels requested a different blend from "Herr Professor's *Sondermischung*" for himself and Carl, not wanting, she supposed, to be sipped from, no matter how slightly. A slice of Sachertorte, the other house specialty, was set before the old wizard, while Carl received a plate of elaborate cookies dipped in chocolate and studded with slivered almonds.

Ilse sipped her blood in silence, then looked to Cassandra. "And the Malkavians' role in everything?"

As if on cue, a shabby street person rushed in and prostrated himself at the feet of Councilor Etrius. "Emperor Franz Josef!" cried the raggedy young man. "You have returned! Austria is saved!"

Everyone bristled, Frick and Frack suddenly standing ready from their table to one side, and the Brujah reaching into their jackets or grabbing silverware. Etrius himself only smiled and gestured for the stranger to raise himself up. "And who might you be, loyal subject?"

The street person bounced to his feet, revealing an old green-gray loden coat studded with rusted military medals and a white frock shirt spattered with bloodstains. "*Graf* Bobby!"

The drama was centered on the two of them, and down the table the only sound that could be heard were the strains of "The Blue Danube" and the scritching of Kleist's pen.

"How kind of you to come, Count Bobby," said Councilor Etrius. "I have heard so very much of your exploits. Where is Baron Mucki?"

"He's pushing the cannon up the hill."

Either it was a complete *non sequitur* or it was the punchline to some local joke, and Ilse knew she would probably never know which.

"Then you'd better go help him," Councilor Etrius said. "Right, *Aleph?*"

The young man paused as if struck over the head and went glassy-eyed for a moment, then smiled and nodded.

Etrius returned a benevolent ruler's smile, then handed his own coffee cup to the Malkavian, who took a sip and wandered out of the Sacher Hotel past the befuddled waiter. At the threshold he was greeted by another raggedy young man, this one dark-haired, but, as was clear from his aura, also vampiric and equally crazy.

"See, Normal?" Ilse overheard Aleph say to his dark-haired companion. "I told you the Emperor would give us some coffee!"

"Don't call me Normal!" protested the other Malkavian. "My name is Baron Mucki! Give me the coffee, Bobby!"

Kleist finished sketching his representation of the encounter, adding notations about Aleph and Normal, alias *Graf Bobby und Baron Mucki*, and a fragment of poetry about the Malkavians.

Ilse set down her coffee cup and looked to Cassandra opposite her. "Were those spies or just Malkavians?"

"Yes," the Magus answered simply.

❧

Wednesday, April 28, Berlin — The House of Etrius

Eight-fifteen p.m., Kurt looked away from his watch and stared at the place where he would be able to put an end to Etrius' mad schemes if all went according to plan.

They had been waiting for almost two hours, and the situation did not allow for idle conversation to pass the time away. Kurt was rapidly reaching the end of his patience, but tried his best to continue in a pleasant manner just the same. Pleasant, but quiet. Finally, Zho hissed lightly to get his attention and pointed to the west side of the *Kunsthistorischesmuseum*, where Jing Wei walked hand-in-hand with Carl Magnuson.

As with virtually all of the museums in Europe and the majority in the United States, the *Kunsthistorisches* was a part of the Elysium. Any attempts to attack another vampire on the premises would be certain to cause an outrage. Mages, however, were not a part of Kindred society and thus were not off-limits. Just the same, the attack would take place outside. The guards within the building would likely be used to Kindred visitors, but they were also most likely Blood Bound to the Toreador of Vienna. The Toreador were just as likely Bound to Etrius or other Tremere. Kidnapping the Tremere clan's pet wizard from inside the museum was asking for trouble.

Zho stepped back into the shadows, merging into the

darkness with ease. Kurt slid into the blackness as well, stopping himself from breathing in an effort to reduce sound as much as possible. While Kurt and the mage hid themselves away, Charnas contorted his body in a sinuous dance. Colors blurred, running across his body like molten wax, solidifying and changing every aspect of his form. In less than a second, a perfect image of Ilse Decameron stood in place of the imp. A few subtle changes came over the pseudo-Ilse, as Charnas apparently decided on a new plan of attack. Where seconds before the imp had been dressed in a crimson evening gown, the dress faded, replaced by tattered remnants of the same color. Clear skin became smudged, and well-groomed hair grew disheveled. The illusion was almost terrifyingly real, and Kurt had to make himself remember that Charnas was a demon rather than a woman who'd been tortured in some way.

Charnas turned and looked directly at him in the shadows, grinned and winked. Then the demon moved forward slightly, waving his arms and calling out, "Carl! Help me! It's the Ventrue, Kurt Westphal!"

The mage turned sharply, his eyes grew wide as he stared at what looked so very much like Ilse, only battered and bruised. "Ilse? Ilse! My God, what happened to you? Are you all right?"

He ran to Ilse/Charnas, gently placing a protective arm around her shoulder. In the distance, Jing Wei simply looked on. "It's the Ventrue," she sobbed, folding herself against him and shaking. He pulled her closer, his handsome face growing stony and his eyes flashing.

"What has he done, Ilse? You must tell me, what has he done?"

The mage's back was to Kurt, and, feeling like a true wretch, he stepped forward from the darkness, his arm cocked back. Kurt pulled the blow enough to make certain that no bones were broken, but the impact of his fist striking the back of the man's head sent Magnuson sprawling across the lawn.

Ilse/Charnas chuckled. "Done? Why, he's given you the bum's rush, and I helped. And now he's taking you far away from all those nasty little Tremere."

Zho materialized from the shadows and dropped beside the downed man. His fingers probed along his descendant's hairline and neck for a minute before he looked up. "Nothing's broken, Kurt. But damn, I'd hate to be hit that hard. He's already got a goose-egg the size of Texas starting on the back of his head. He'll be out for hours."

"I did not enjoy that. I don't like attacking a man from behind." Kurt looked away from the mages, spotting Jing Wei as she approached.

"Trust me, it's the safest way to deal with a warlock. He could have turned you into ash with very little effort."

"Just the same…"

Charnas stepped over to where Magnuson lay on the museum's walkway. He stared down at the man and started warping again. Seconds later, Carl Magnuson stared down at himself, a sly grin on his face. "Well, kiddies, I'm off to the chantry. Wish me luck."

Kurt said nothing, Jing Wei wrinkled her nose in disgust, and Zho looked at the imp with a warning glance. "Do not disappoint me, Charnas. We need at least a day to be ready for them."

"No problem, boss. You'll have the time you need." Kurt looked to the imp, amazed by how perfectly he matched the image and mannerisms of Carl Magnuson.

"Do nothing that you shouldn't. Do you understand me?"

"Yeah, right. You do what you have to do, and I'll do what I have to do. We both know our roles, don't we, Zho?" With that, the demon walked away, heading toward what was presumably the stronghold of the Tremere.

Carrying the unconscious man was easy enough, and with Zho to assist him, they managed to imitate two friends carrying a drunkard with little difficulty. Down the block from where they encountered their prize, Jackie waited with another rented limousine. She spoke little, save to make certain that everyone was present and accounted for. Kurt noticed when Jing Wei and his lover locked eyes, but he said nothing. The Tremere turned away first. The tension in the car grew heavier as they started traveling, but finally, they were on their way to Germany.

>€

The High Chantry had its own Turkish baths, and Ilse thought this was the most wonderful thing in the world.

An ancient holy site, the hot springs lay beneath the chantry, prehistoric pools of sulfur water and healing magic, and the Turkish baths made every use of them, water pumped in to fill the pools, hot to cold, mineral to fresh, and even one wonderful chilled bath filled with natural carbonation that bubbled about her and tickled her skin over every inch.

Ilse had tried every one of them and at last emerged from the shower at the end, wet and happy, the last of the sulfur smell rinsed from her hair. Short of being fed, there was nothing that warmed her dead flesh half so well as a hot shower, unless it was the Turkish baths. Vampires were supposed to hate running water, but so long as it was hot and came out of a Shower Massage, Ilse could take it all night long.

A beautiful, silent Turkish woman toweled her dry, then bade her lie down on a padded table, setting a pan of water filled with different colored glass phials over a charcoal brazier, tossing a handful of woodchips and twigs onto the fire below. The sweet smoke of sandalwood and lavender wafted up, and the woman selected one of the phials, pouring a measure of oil out into the palm of her hand and holding her other palm over it so as to concentrate the warmth.

She then smoothed it over Ilse's back and began the massage. Ilse wanted to signal for her to be brief, for there was no way of telling when Etrius might call for an interview, but then succumbed to the pleasure and the woman's expert hands. The woman was an artist every bit as talented as the Toreadors, and with slow, sure, strength she massaged Ilse's flesh back to the feeling of life, applying one scented oil after the other into an intoxicating blend that masked the pungent scent of the sulfur from the baths. In the background, the water cascaded from pool to pool, a soothing susurration, and Ilse wished she could slide back into them, but knew she couldn't spare the time.

At last, Ulugh Beg's masseuse (concubine? ghoul?) finished her work, pulling a soft, thin cotton sheet over Ilse. Ilse heard the rattle of the charcoal braziers, then the crack and sizzle of more incense being tossed on, followed by the sweet smoke of lavender, sandalwood, amber and musk.

Ilse certainly could get used to this, and though it was an hour past daytime, she felt sleepy and happy and began to drowse off, dimly hearing the click of the door as the Turkish woman left the room.

It was sometime later that she heard the crack and spark from the braziers again, followed by the sweet scent of lavender mixed with the sulfur from the pools. Warm hands then appeared on her back, delicately massaging her.

"Hiya, love," said a voice, British accent warm and charming. "Guess who?"

It was a relief to hear a kind and familiar voice, and to feel the warm hands of the living. "Carl…"

He didn't respond, but when she tried to roll over, said, "Hush. You just relax. We've been through a lot, you and me, and you deserve to be taken care of." His hands moved up, massaging her neck above the cloth, then sliding it down and working his way along her back.

"Mmmmmmm," Ilse purred with pleasure. "You've had a lot of practice at this."

"Of course, love." He massaged with greater intensity, working his fingers into the deep tissue, then took a hand away, and Ilse heard the sound of one of the bottles being taken from the warming pan over the brazier. "You'd be surprised what they teach back at the Order."

Oil sprinkled across her back, hot enough to sting for a moment, but delicious in its warmth as it cooled, and his fingers worked it in, sure and steady as the scent of lavender washed over her.

"With your permission, good lady?" he asked. "I need to get on top if I want to do my best work."

"Go ahead," she said. "I don't mind."

"I'm glad you said that." Quickly he climbed atop her, with a nimbleness that surprised her for such a tall man. But then Paul had also been dexterous, and grace seemed as much a spiritual thing as it was a physical, so Ilse supposed it all went together.

His knees slipped in on either side of her, just above her hips, and he placed his hands on either side of her neck, massaging the muscles at the base of her skull. Then he went lower, and Ilse stiffened as she felt him touch the small of her back.

"You're naked." She giggled; she hadn't expected this so soon.

"Naked as sin, I'm afraid." He paused and chuckled. "What's the trouble, love? You're naked too, and you didn't hear me making a big fuss about it."

"I — I just didn't expect it, that's all. I'd just thought things would move a bit slower."

"Do you want them to move slower, love?"

Ilse paused. "No, not really. I just wasn't expecting it, that's all."

"Sometimes the nicest things are the ones we least expect." He moved against her, brushing the base of her spine with a teasing sensuality. "Do you know what a turn-on it is for a lad to find a woman who's been waiting some sixty-odd years to get him in the sack, and she's still something great to look at?"

Ilse stiffened a bit at that, then relaxed as he kissed the nape of her neck, nipping slightly, then kissed it again and licked the spot, running his tongue up until it touched her hairline.

"That tickles…"

"It's supposed to. You want me to tickle something else?"

"Sure."

He tickled her armpits until she squealed and squeezed her arms down to make him stop.

"I thought you wanted me to tickle you," he said in a hurt tone.

"That's not what I meant!"

"Then what do you mean?"

Ilse exhaled, the tickling having made her breathe in deeply like she hadn't in years. "Make love to me," she said. "Make me feel like I'm alive."

"I can only do what you ask me to, good lady." He rubbed against her tailbone and kissed the nape of her neck, then moved lower, kisses trailing down her spine. "I can't come in unless you invite me."

"I thought it was only Kindred who needed an invitation."

"Since when do you Tremere girls need an invitation for anything, love?" He kissed the base of her spine, right over her tailbone, then licked her sensually.

Ilse writhed in delight as he teased her. "I guess we don't," she admitted at last. "Who does?"

"Gentleman do," he said. "Some others. Please, invite me in."

"All right, big boy. Consider yourself invited. Make me feel like a woman."

"I'm glad you said that," he answered, then moved down, lifting her up by the buttocks and pressing her face into the soft Turkish towels.…

❧❦

Ilse awoke on the Turkish towels, curled in her lover's arm, and she opened her eyes to gaze on his beautiful face and soul.

It was black, black as sin. Carl's face, but black to the eyes of her soul. The fiend's eyes went wide, then crossed and fell backwards into his head like a broken doll's. She gagged in revulsion and tried to push him away.

The false Carl changed then, shrinking and turning purple. "Rats," Charnas said, his arms still around her, long as Carl's. "That black soul business ruins things every time."

Ilse shrank back in horror, and Charnas leered. "Oh c'mon, Ilse. You can admit it. It was fun, wasn't it? Just a little?"

"I — I —"

"You what? You were saving yourself for Brad?" Charnas grinned. "Or was that Paul? Carl? Etrius? Couldn't be Thadius, now could it? You won't believe how long it's been since he's been laid. By anyone but me, I mean. But then, it's hard to get a date after you murder your wife."

"You fiend!" Ilse spat, bloody tears blurring her vision.

"That's me all right," Charnas smirked.

Ilse had never felt so filthy in her life, Charnas' stench of lavender and sulfur everywhere. "You…"

"Oh, come off it, sister," Charnas let go of her and bounced back to sit on the edge of one of the Turkish baths, completely naked and with all the marks of the Devil, "I didn't force you to do anything you didn't want to do, and I never claimed to be Carl, or Paul, or Thad, or Brad, or whichever soul-brother you're dating this week. We were two consenting adults, and I didn't do anything you didn't ask me to. C'mon, we're alone here. You can admit it. You enjoyed it, didn't you? Just a little bit?" Charnas waggled his tongue, leering gleefully. "Let's do it again!"

"No," Ilse breathed.

"The lips say *No* but the eyes say *Yes! Yes!* Trust me, I'm a demon. I can spot a lie a mile away."

He danced around on the lip of the Turkish bath, singing

falsetto, "'Toucha-toucha-toucha-touch me! I wanna feel di-i-irty! Whip me, beat me, mistreat me — Creature of the Night!'"

Ilse snarled and lunged for the fiend, grappling him and carrying him over into the sulfur pool. And then she moaned in ecstasy as she touched him.

Charnas grinned, pulling her in close. "You told me to make you feel like a woman, to make you feel alive, and to take you to the heights of ecstasy. Any time I liked. A demon doesn't have any power over you that you don't give it."

Ilse then felt the surge of ecstasy course through her, paralyzing her with pleasure and pain as Charnas continued to touch her and leer...

⇒◄

Ilse awoke to the terror of drowning, water filling her lungs. She thrashed her way to the surface, coughing and gagging, sulfur burning her throat and eyes, and struggled to the lip of the bath, throwing herself over and letting the fetid water drain out of her.

"Ah, there you are. I was told I might find you here. But really, Ilse, while the sulfur is wonderfully warm, if you want to wash your lungs, you'll find the effervescent tub much better for that purpose. Indeed, if you've soaked your lungs in that pool for any length of time, your breath will be reeking like a demon's for a week at least."

Ilse gasped the last of the stinking water out onto the tiles, then looked up. Merrill stood there, poised and arrogant in his velvet jacket and smoking another of his trademark cigarettes.

The Andalusian gave her a condescending smirk and tapped his ash to drift down to the floor. "Honestly, Ilse. Councilor Etrius is very indulgent, but he will be wanting to see you soon. You'd best make yourself ready. But that's not why I'm here." He took another drag, then exhaled, glancing about the room before taking another puff. "The Councilor wishes to see Carl Magnuson, and last anyone saw of him, Ulugh's little Turkish chit said he went in here, wanting to spend some time with you."

Merrill blew out, watching the smoke drift, but apparently too bored to bother with smoke rings. "Far be it from me to interrupt an intimate moment, but we all must obey the wishes of the Council."

He said the last with a sharp flick of his cigarette that belied the malice underneath. "Do you know where he is? Because if he's in that pool with you, he'd best have learned how to breathe sulfur water, or else Councilor Etrius will be very displeased." He took another drag, inhaling deeply. "For a change, the Council wishes to see one of your lovers alive."

"He — He's not here." Ilse sobbed once and felt the tears of blood begin to course down her face. "Merrill, it wasn't him at all. It was a demon."

"What? What do you mean?"

Ilse coughed out a last bit of sulfur water, the stench mixed with the reek of blood and lavender. "An imp, Charnas. He — It impersonated Carl, and he…" She sobbed again, feeling chilled to the marrow despite the heat of the pool. "I trusted him."

Merrill stood, considering, then flicked his cigarette. "Well, don't expect any sympathy from me." He gazed coldly at her. "There was a beautiful woman who I loved once, and I trusted her as well. Unfortunately she was a fiend in human form, and she killed me and took me to Hell."

"Merrill, it wasn't like that…"

"Really? I suppose betrayal feels different from the other end of things, but then I wouldn't know. The Council hasn't given me that order yet." He took a drag from his cigarette, blowing it out through his nose in a short burst. "I should probably take a small measure of satisfaction in knowing that there's still justice in the world, and what goes around, comes around, but call me a cynic. The best I can think is that since this is Hell, eventually everyone gets a chance to suffer."

Ilse sobbed, and Merrill looked at her with contempt. At last his face softened a bit, and his eyes showed some small trace of compassion. "Oh, please, get up. I could never stand to see you cry, even that damned blood, and we've got to go tell Etrius. If your new boyfriend's gone missing, and there's a demon impersonating him, then we've all got some serious problems."

Merrill grabbed a towel and a robe from a rack by the door, then pulled her out of the bath, thrusting the soft bathsheet into her arms. Ilse wanted to hug to him for comfort, but he pushed her away coldly.

Red blood ran onto the white plush of the towel in her arms. "Why are you being so cruel?"

"Why do you think?" He glared at her, the cigarette forgotten in his hand, and a bead of red began to form at the corner of one eye. "You killed me, you brought me to this, and by way of apology, you said you were sorry and swore you would love me for all eternity. And now here you are with another man, another living man, and you won't even so much as look at me when all you have eyes for is his neck and his *fresh red blood*," he seethed, his fangs sliding out to their full length. His whisper was barely audible over the sound of water draining from pool to pool. "What am I supposed to think?"

They stood there in silence. The cigarette burned down in his fingers and began to singe his flesh. His only reaction was to turn his head and look at it in disgust before flicking it away to land in one of the baths with a hiss and a curl of smoke. He then thrust the robe into her arms and extinguished his flaming fingers in the nearest pool.

"Save your crocodile tears for someone who hasn't seen them, Ilse." Merrill reached into his gold cigarette case and took out a new cigarette. "I have to go warn Etrius. Duty to the Council calls."

With a cold elegance, he leaned down to the charcoal brazier and lit his cigarette directly from the flames. Though a hideous burn wound, his fingers were already healed, and after sampling the smoke to make sure it was to his taste, he nodded to Ilse and left the room.

Ilse collapsed onto the floor, weeping into the towel.

⇥⇤

Disheveled, blood-streaked and stinking of sulfur — it was in this state that Ilse finally got to meet with Councilor Etrius and to talk with him personally. Her tongue stuck in her mouth, and she was unable to speak, even had she known what to say.

Astrid stood in the door of the parlor, dressed in a violet gown of simple elegance, the dress she'd worn when she'd gone personally to fetch Ilse from the baths. In theory, it was an honor to be summoned by so powerful a member of the House; in truth, it was nothing of the sort. Astrid had marked her for her spite and had taken pains to show Ilse to her worst advantage.

Councilor Etrius only came in, his mismatched eyes looking so very like Paul's that Ilse wanted to weep and so very like Zho's that she wanted to scream in terror. She did neither, shocked beyond any reaction but tears, while Astrid and Merrill watched her from each doorway, twin sentinels of spite and malice.

"You poor child," said the Councilor, the first words he had spoken to her save simple remarks in passing over coffee the night before. "Merrill has told me everything, but I must ask you to tell me yourself." He went down on one knee before her, taking her hands in his own. Through her red film of tears, Ilse saw only his look of concern and behind him, the basilisk's glare from Astrid. "Carl cannot be found. Tell me, if you know, what demon was it that took his form?"

Ilse squeezed his hands in return, taking comfort from the familiar aura, even though she had never met the great man before. "Charnas, an imp."

Etrius stuck out his index and least fingers, making the Cornu, a sign against evil, and turned his head. "*Vándr val-dÿr wæi-mærr!*" Ilse couldn't understand his swearing, but it sounded like something in Swedish or Old Norse.

He looked back, taking a moment to compose his features. "I know this evil one. But your Carl is in danger, *Lisle, mein Liebchen*, and I must ask you to trust me, though I know you do not wish to do that after what you have just suffered at the mercies of the fiend. Please."

The request was made with his eyes, not his lips, but Ilse understood all the same. He wished access to her soul, and even though he could have easily taken it, he chose to ask.

Wordlessly she accepted, his soul as familiar as her own, even though he had called her not Ilse, but *Lisle, my darling*, knowing perhaps, somehow, that her true name was Leslie. The colors of his aura were familiar and comforting, and Ilse felt him come inside, touching her spirit like a kiss, and saw, clearly, that he loved her.

The colors spun about her like a dream, and as his soul moved past to look through her memories, she had access to his. Not all, but one was offered up to her like a present, wrapped in the dusky rose of nostalgia and the pale green of yearning, worn and treasured with a thousand lifetimes of recollection, as glittery and unreal in its beauty as a fairy tale picture book kept since childhood.

Ilse touched it, and its story unfolded around her.

Unlike other mages, who took the form of hawks and eagles, or ravens and owls, when they flew over the fields of the Middle Country, she, Etrius, had taken the shape of a ringdove, a form for a mission of love and a guise for an errand of secrecy. Enemies would watch for hawks and kestrels, but none would notice a plain little bird, a messenger for nothing but love or peace. Magic was fading from the world, and the greater forms were difficult to take, tied to old power and old legends. But of the birds, the dove still had power, its symbol kept alive by the Church and by lovers, the little gray bird still thriving in this frightening new age.

She flew down, searching for the *vardo* of her lover, Lisle, scanning for the compass rose and the hearts, crosses and charmed pentacles that marked the roof of her gypsy cart. There, on the edge of the field of wildflowers, in the shade of a linden tree, she saw it. Sitting on the stoop of the wagon, her *dirndl* embroidered with the flowers of springtime and her basket filled with the herbs of power, sat Lisle, the gypsy-witch. Lisle Zho, the fortuneteller. Lisle, his love.

She was beautiful, with raven hair and sun-browned skin and startling blue eyes, but when Etrius remembered the face of his love, Ilse recognized it as her own, only the colors of the skin and hair changed. The eyes were the same.

And when she looked into Lisle's eyes, Ilse looked into herself, Etrius' memory awakening something deep inside her, something she'd forgotten and repressed, but she didn't know how she could have ever forgotten. The scene shifted, the fairy tale pages of treasured past glittered with turning about, seeing it from her own perspective and remembering the old and painful memories.

Lisle shivered, and from more than the chill air of morning. The herbs were too fresh and too powerful, thorn apple, henbane, aconite, monkshood and the belladonna which spoke to her with the voice of a poisonous maiden. Powerful, deadly herbs, murderous things that should not be touched except in the most desperate of times. But these were those. The birds had ceased to speak to her, the unicorn no longer visited the pond, and a cold wind blew across the fields, refusing to listen even when she entreated it in the name of Old Man Winter to stay away from her flowers.

Desperate times called for desperate measures, though she wondered what price would be too much. Hell below still had its strength, though the roads to the infernal realms were closing (thankfully, oh so thankfully), and Heaven was still there, though fewer and fewer prayers were answered. Yet the natural world, from which a white witch drew her strength, was losing its power, withering away like a tree sapped at the root, or, she hoped, perhaps just like a tree in wintertime, husbanding its strength and drawing its magic and vigor deep inside itself until spring came again. Yet here she was, the lover of a man who was prepared to risk an endless wintertime for the slim hope of an eternal spring.

The ringdove fluttered down and landed in her lap, looking in her basket and cooing softly.

She picked up the little bird, cradling it to her cheek. "Oh, Etrius, Please, do not do this thing. Let us just grow old, as is natural, and wait for to world to be green once more."

The dove cooed, looking at her with its clever black eyes, and it was a mark of the winter of the magic of the world that she could not understand a word it said, even though she was a witch and she knew it to be an enchanted sorcerer.

She reached into her basket, taking out the largest of the pods of the deadly thorn apple and split the spiky fruit open with her thumbnail, letting the grains spill into her palm, and remembering Avicenna's charm: one for strength, two for visions, three for madness, and four for death. Lisle hoped the one would be sufficient and chose the largest of the seeds, holding it up for the ringdove. The bird gobbled it down greedily, as if starving, then pecked at its breast like the pelican, blood welling up.

The transformation came suddenly, her lover tumbling down the steps of her cart, the tiny cloak of feathers flying through the air to land in the dirt.

Etrius sat up and dusted himself off, his gray robe snagged with twigs and briars, his mismatched eyes, blue and green, laughing at himself in the way she loved. "Magic is getting messier," he said, retrieving the ringdove's skin and placing it inside his hood.

"Winter is coming." Lisle slipped the rest of the thorn apple back in the basket. "It's only natural. Everything is messy in the autumn time."

He sighed, smiling up at her. "I wish my fellow coven-mates had your philosophy."

Lisle arranged the bundles of honesty and woundwort. "Meerlinda is a clever woman. I'm certain she knows this truth."

He laughed, "She does, but Goratrix does not, and it is his experiment we must try."

Lisle set aside her basket, going down and helping her love to his feet. "Do not do this thing, Etrius. Let Goratrix damn himself with his own folly, but leave your own soul free." She stroked aside his dirty blond hair, dark with years spent in the cloister, and looked at his sweet boy's face. "There are things more valuable than power or even magic. Things far more precious."

He kissed her then, sweet as sweet, but then drew away. "I know, dearest, and that is why I must do this thing. I am young, but Tremere, my master, is old, and he fears death and will face it soon in this autumn time of magic as you call it. To reclaim his youth, he must travel to Erebus and back, but he needs young hands to guide him. There are good souls among the others in my coven, but I fear that only I truly love the man."

Lisle put her head against his chest, listening to his heartbeat and taking comfort from his strong arms. "Goratrix is a fool, and a wicked one at that. The Damned are forbidden by ancient law. God placed His Mark upon the forehead of Caine so that no man would harm him or else suffer His Wroth."

"Goratrix is as learned as yourself, my dear, and that is why he insisted that Meerlinda remain part of the circle. God forbade any man, but it was Meerlinda who wielded the knife and drew the blood for the elixir."

Lisle shuddered. "When will it be ready?"

"At the full of tomorrow's moon. I must be there to complete the circle."

Lisle hugged herself to him, not wanting to lose him. "Then if you will not listen to my counsel, then I must ask you to promise me one thing."

"What is it, my love?"

She pressed her head against his chest. "Leave me a child. Give me a child to remember you by if you do not return and to raise with you if you do."

He gazed at her, smiling. "We are not married, my love. It is not right."

Lisle smiled back. "You are a *gadjo*, dearest. I told you, my family would not approve either way."

"Well, then, I would be happy to do the rites."

Carefully, she and Etrius laid the circle and said the rites, making love amid the flowers of the summer field, drinking the brew from the chalice and eating the seedcakes from the dish, ensuring that she would grow heavy with child and give birth in the springtime.

Etrius touched her hair. "Thank you, my love. I must go now, but if I survive the experiment, I will return in a fortnight. And then I will make you my bride and we shall raise our child together." His eyes laughed. "No matter what our parents think."

Lisle smiled, his words a bittersweet thing. "I will not ask you to choose between your loves or to divide your loyalties. Go with the old man if you must, but return to me if you can."

Etrius smiled, the same bittersweet pain as she felt showing in the lines around his eyes, old before their time with scholarship. He leaned forward and kissed her again, longer and more passionate, then pulled away. "I must leave, my love. Duty calls, and the old man has need of me."

"Do not go!" Lisle cried, her heart making her a traitor to her former words, but the next moment, her lover was gone.

In his place, a gray ringdove flapped in the air, cooing, then flew off for the far mountains, and Lisle cried out at her loss.

Ilse then remembered the rest of Lisle's days, the bitter pain and few simple joys. Etrius did not return, but his son, Aldiis, was born, raised in the tradition of the Gypsies. Though his eyes were both green, he still had the look of his father. Lisle never saw Etrius again and at last died a cold and lonely death, poisoning herself with her own herbs, the plants now able to work no other magic.

The blackness then cleared, turning to red, the ruby on the chain about Etrius' neck. "You left me!" Ilse cried. "You abandoned me and our son! You never returned, and you never died!"

"Yes, I did." Etrius looked at her with great sadness. "Surely you now know that I did. I did not return for I did not wish to visit you with the curse that my folly had brought on myself, and now, lives later, that curse has still come upon you. I am sorry.

"But there is still time to set right the great wrong that was done. There is still time for the broken promises to be kept, for life to be reclaimed, and for springtime to come again." He touched her cheek. "Forgive me."

Ilse sobbed, unsure of what to say, so many feelings coursing through her.

Etrius stroked her hair. "I must go now and find what has happened to Carl. He must be kept safe, if all is to be set right."

With a sad smile, Etrius left her again, abandoning her to the mercies of Merrill and Astrid, each looking at her with their own brand of venom.

At last Astrid spoke, "You knew him before. I can respect that, even appreciate it." She bared her fangs. "But never forget that he is mine now."

Astrid left, leaving her only with Merrill. He took another cigarette out of his case, considered it, then flipped it towards her so it landed in her lap. "Enjoy, Ilse," he said, and she couldn't be sure whether it was with cruelty or kindness. "You look like you could use one."

He left then, and Ilse searched about, seeing if he'd bothered to leave her a match.

>€

Ilse had at last cleaned herself, using the servants' shower and the harshest soaps she could find. Her skin felt red and raw, but the pain helped, even if it did little to wash away the stench of sulfur and lavender.

Cassandra, kindly, briefed her on the rest of what had been discovered as she led her to the chantry's arcane library. Not only was Carl missing, but Jing Wei — who had arrived half an hour before them the previous night — was also unaccounted for. There were hopes that the mage and the Chinese girl had simply stepped out for an hour or so on the town, but in her heart, Ilse knew this to be untrue.

Once they stepped through the doors, candles about the room flickered to life, levitating to helpful heights and illuminating the pages of open books. The library was a shambles, the long research tables piled with tomes and scrolls, books laid open haphazardly and stacked on the floors, paperweights glittering as the candles hovered about them.

"Ulugh Beg!" Cassandra growled. "That man... I scarcely have the room in order before he has it all looking like a *Scheißhaus!* And bloodstains on the pages!"

She pointed at one ancient tome, red spots scabbing to brown at the bottom of the page, which then changed back to red, rolling off the book like beads of chromic mercury as the volume floated up and put itself back on the shelf.

Cassandra suddenly seemed not so much the Magus Prime of Vienna as she did the proper Austrian *Hausfrau*, ordering the books about like servants with a stern look here or a finger pointed there, each tome snapping shut with military precision and levitating swiftly to its appointed spot on the shelves. Scrolls furled themselves like war banners and placed themselves back in the racks, paperweights leapfrogged one over the other to be the first to sit on the ledge at the end of each stack, and books evened themselves up in all the bookcases until all that was left was a pool of blood in the middle of the central research table, quivering like jelly at Cassandra's approach. With a severe look, she pointed to the nearest candle, and the jelly formed into a stream, leaping up and immolating itself in the flame.

All the candles glowed a shade brighter, and Cassandra kindly pulled out a chair for Ilse. "We do not allow drinking in the library, but if there is any book you wish to see, I will fetch it for you."

"Please, I would like to know more about that demon, Charnas."

Cassandra made the same gesture against evil as had Etrius, but refrained from swearing. "Will there be anything else?"

"No, thank you."

Cassandra nodded. "I will send Kleist in to assist you if need be. I am certain you have questions about Etrius, and he...has the best source, at present. But as to the wicked one..."

The Magus reached into her belt for a large brass keyring she brought up before her. Muttering softly in a language Ilse didn't know, Cassandra sorted through her keys, turning then back and forth around the ring, as if she were doing a puzzle or combination.

At last she stopped, holding a large, white key that looked to be carved from ivory or bone or grown into that shape like some tropical seashell. It had not been there before among all the brass, iron, silver and gold keys Ilse had seen on the ring, and Cassandra held it carefully by the head, as if it were something poisonous that might harm her if she touched the end.

Still muttering in the same strange language, Cassandra went to the wall, where there was a bookcase Ilse had not noticed before, ebony and black lacquer, with charms and protective seals etched into the glass front. The Magus took the bone key and placed it in a crack in one of the ebony doors, turning, and the door came open. Her left hand made the Cornu again, then she reached in, counting volumes until she found the one she wanted. There was a sound like the cry of a newborn kitten as she slid it out from the others

Cassandra took it out through the half-open door, slamming the right side of the case shut, and Ilse would have sworn that the Magus pushed back some volumes that had not been pulled forward before, books on shelves that Cassandra had not even touched. She locked the door with the bone key, dropping it onto the ring and spinning its mates with a jangle and chime, coming around to a smaller key, this one of gold, the type you would use for a jewelry box, or a book.

Cassandra paused at the end of one of the stacks to select a paperweight, dropping it into the pocket of her purple dressing gown, then went to Ilse and placed the book on the table before her.

It was bound in human skin. Ilse could smell the scent of it and recognize the blood it had been boiled in, the whole tooled and tattooed in disturbing patterns with the corners fitted with tarnished silver. Two heavy, red-embroidered straps about it, joined in the center by a gold lock engraved with the names of God. Next to it, Cassandra placed the paperweight, which was not only a beautiful thing of glass, but also held a perfectly formed Star of David in the center, marked with the Hebrew characters that made it the Seal of Solomon.

"You may read the book, Ilse, but speak none of the words aloud, and do not let any of them be copied down, even by Kleist. Especially by Kleist, because he does not yet understand that there is some knowledge that should not be recorded, and he does not know our ways." She examined the golden key, as if considering whether she should allow this thing to occur, then at last leaned down and inserted it in the lock. The seal rotated, coming undone, and each of the straps fell away, taking with them one of the names of God. "When you have finished, close the book and place the weight atop it. I will come and see that it is properly put away."

Ilse nodded, and Cassandra left, the candles following after her like a swarm of fireflies.

Ilse was left in the dark, but for six candles which stationed themselves in the air about her, forming a ward. Carefully she set aside the lock, then moved the straps away, reverent of each of the names of God tooled in gold leaf into the leather of each.

She then opened the book, smelling the unholy scent of murder.

The book was written on vellum, but the skin of newborn lambs was not of the standard variety, and written across the page, in the brown ink of blood, were the words:

Liber

Verborum

Infandum

Literally, *The Book of Unspeakable Words*, or, more accurately, *nefarious, unholy words*.

Ilse turned the page, reading the first section. The text was in black here, with words of particular emphasis in faded brown, but the whole thing smelled of human flesh, charred bones and blood.

The Latin was something she had read before, a variant on the first section of Genesis: *In the beginning, the world was without form and void, and Darkness moved upon the face of the Deep. Then there came the Word, and the Word was God.*
It was not quite the same as the Bible, growing more divergent the further she read, though much of the story was familiar.

God had spoken the world into being, and each word he spoke was a new thing.

Then — and here was where it diverged from texts she had read before — God became displeased with words he had spoken, and they were cast out and forbidden, stricken from the book of creation. Yet each word was a thought, and each thought was a soul, and each of those forbidden words, those sounds which must not be spoken, was a separate angel, a fallen one cast into the reaches of darkness and obscurity. Each of these thoughts, these evil sounds, these wicked words, formed a dissonance around the symphony of creation, attempting to work their way back into the pages of the Book of Life. Mispronunciations and half notes, they were very close to the words which God had approved. So much so that one could guess their powers if one knew the words of the True Tongue, that language which God had used, which was very close to Latin.

Charnas. Ilse thought the word over in her head, but did not voice it, thinking on what Master Harry and Dr. Dee had said. *Charnas,* close to *Carnas* — Flesh, *Cearas* —Blood, and *Chara* — Delight. Then there was *Charon,* the ferryman of Death. Flesh, Blood, Delight, Death — it was a powerful charm that went between them, all things often forbidden in and of themselves, but for an unspoken word between the lines.

The book strained under her finger, the pages wanting to flip. Ilse could feel it, but she then chose to allow it and removed her hand, ready to slam the Solomon's Seal paperweight down atop it all if it did anything more.

The pages flew by, one after the other, the book opening more than two-thirds of the way, until at last it stopped at a set of pages held together by a band of human skin, etched with pentacles and other protective seals. Across the page was writ: *Beyond here lie Damned words which must not be spoken, or else Evil will be loosed upon the World.*

One hand on the paperweight, Ilse carefully slipped the band aside, freeing the last of the pages. The top five flipped past, then Ilse was looking straight at the grinning face of Charnas.

He was dressed in the clothes of a matador clown, a jester from a medieval bullfight, but there was no mistaking the dusky purple face or the delighted leer. Around him lay carnage and gore, bits and pieces of human bodies, some of them still recognizable and most of them sexual.

Ilse glanced down to what was written below. Beyond the standard seals and bindings and *Beware this evil one* was more information, confirming what she already knew and had experienced: ... *for he is sometimes known as Bloodlust, or Delight-in-Death, but he is all these things and more. He is one of the first Evils to work his way back onto the Page of Creation, for when Eve tasted the Apple, it was this one who took Pleasure in the Fruit. When Caine slew his brother, Abel, it was this one who Delighted in the Murderer's Heart. When the Sabine women were Raped and the city Burned, this one was there.*

Know him by these Signs: his scent is Lavender, the herb of Killers and Harlots; his color is the same, the shade of Perversity and Perversion; his voice is that of the Kitten, the Pup, and the Spoiled Child, the note of Gleeful Cruelty. See him in the Smile of the Predator. Hear him in the Murderer's Laugh. Know that he is inside you when you sate Forbidden Lusts, or take Pleasure in that which you know is Wrong. He is the Joy of Evil Flesh, the Delight in Wrongdoing, the Satisfaction of Wickedness. Innocence is scant protection, and Ignorance is none. Beware this Fiend and Listen Not to his Temptations, for young or old, all Fall Prey!

"It's not a very good likeness," said a voice, and Ilse jumped and looked around, her dead heart almost leaping from her mouth.

But instead of Charnas, whom she'd half-expected to appear, there stood Dieter Kleist — in aura as well as form.

Hastily, she shut the book, then she heard the pages mewling under her fingers. She reopened it and fit the protective band around the pages of the last section, slamming the cover shut and placing the weight on top. The book lay there without a sound, looking like any other ancient tome underneath the glass sphere.

Kleist set his own book on the table, the large, black journal which he held tight to his chest when he did not have it open to work on. Now he had it out for display, and Ilse realized she was being given a singular honor. With a banker's precision, the artist measured back a number of pages from his latest piece, flipping them back to reveal a composite portrait of Charnas.

Blue ink and Kleist's blood mixed to match the dusky purple of the fiend, the sketches showing the imp leaping, jumping, changing form and frolicking with delight in a chronicle of his nefarious deeds throughout the chantry. He slipped inside in a deliveryman's pocket in the form of a peepshow keychain, capering with joy at his own cleverness…then took the form of Carl and gave instructions to Ulugh Beg's mistress outside the door to the Turkish baths.

Ilse did not want to turn the next page, knowing what she would see there, and it was not something she wished to relive, especially through the artist's eye. She feared that the imp himself would leap off the page, yet at the corners of each sheet, Kleist had inscribed potent charms, the Seal of Solomon set over an evil-looking design, which she could only assume to be the sigil of the demon Charnas.

She touched the page hesitantly, studying the artist's work. "How did you come by these?"

"The Spirit's Touch," Kleist said, and she looked up to see him placing his fingers beside his eye. "With it, I can see anything that was. What I see, I can record. This house has many memories."

Ilse turned back to the page. "I — I meant the seals." She

flattened the page under her hand, the candles illuminating them plainly. "This is the sigil of Cha — of the imp, isn't it?"

"It is the sigil of the demon, but they are one and the same." Kleist sat down next to her, tracing the strange curves and circles of the mark with his finger. "With the discipline of Auspex, one can see the soul, and if one has an eye for beauty, as do those of my clan, then one also has an eye for ugliness — if the seer can stand to look. Good is light, and light is beauty, and beauty is truth. But where darkness is their absence, evil is their inverse." He paused, his hand stiffening, then relaxed and traced the form of the imp. "Evil too has colors, if you have the eyes to see."

Ilse remembered her first glimpse of Charnas, in Crowley's chamber of horrors, a silhouette of evil, fulgent against the darkness. She shivered and looked away from the page, turning to the strange artist.

Kleist gazed at her with his penetrating dark eyes until he seemed satisfied that she understood. "Each color has a note attached to it, a note of fragrance, a note of music, a mathematical number. If you can perceive and remember them, you can graph them and know all there is to know about these things."

"This is High Magic you're speaking."

He shrugged. "Etrius has taught me some. It is little different from what I already knew in my heart and what I had been taught by my clan. Art is art is Art. It is all just a matter of perception." He perused her aura, his eyes scanning the air around her. "I can see where this one has touched you, and his fragrance lingers. Sulfur and lavender. Sulfur is the scent of demons, while lavender is the herb of war and prostitutes." He nodded to the volume Cassandra had gotten for Ilse. "I do not know what it says in that book, but I would suspect it is little different than what I have told you."

The Toreador was the most strange and chilling young man that Ilse had ever met, and she felt like she was in front of a camera, Kleist's dark eyes tracking and recording her every nuance and secret. Not judging or theorizing, solely observing.

She nodded. "What it says is similar. How do you know this?"

"Art is art. What you have read in these books here, I have heard in poetry or seen in paintings. The symbols are the same." He smiled, a bare twitch of the lips. "I may not know art, but I know what I like, and what I like is magic. That is the touchstone of art. A equals B, B equals A." He closed his book and hugged it to his chest, as if possessive of its secrets. "The Lesser Etrius has confirmed much of what I already know."

"The Lesser...?"

Dieter smiled, his eyes taking on that strange and abstracted look that Toreadors sometimes got when they were seeing something which others could not appreciate. "Would you like to hear a story? I know one. It's a very pretty story, and few of your clan know it. It is said to be a fragment of the *Book of Nod*, the tales of Caine, though I cannot say for certain."

"Go — Go ahead," Ilse stammered, staring at the strange expression on Kleist's face, as if he were seeing something completely different than what was before him, using her sullied aura as a scrying globe.

The Toreador smiled. "My clan likes to tell this tale, though it's not much of a story. More of an anecdote. You see, God is an artist, as are we. Oh, everyone likes to say that God is like them. The Ventrue say that He is a king, your clan that He is a magician, the Malkavians that He is mad, and the Nosferatu that He is cruel and ugly. There is truth in all these, I suppose, for beauty is in the eye of the beholder, and in beauty, truth. Yet we, who have an eye for beauty, and thus truth, hold that God is an artist. One has only to look at the world to see the truth in this. The world is beautiful, even where it is ugly and grotesque, yet no work of art is ever finished, only abandoned, and this is what God has done with ours. He is not dead; He has merely gone on to his next creation, as any proper artist should, and as for whether our world is finished or just hopelessly flawed, it is a matter of opinion.

"But as I said, God is an artist and was an artist, and all artists, before they set out to create a masterwork, do at least one study. God's masterwork for this world was Man, with all his folly and beauty, a portrait of the artist as a young God. But before God began His masterwork, he did His study, creating a smaller version of His Man, not out of flesh and blood, but out of wood and sap — the Mandrake. This was God's study, and this is why the root has the form of Man."

The Toreador gazed into space as if seeing God in His studio, a wistful smile across the young man's lips. "Like all studies, it was cast aside, becoming a lesser work in the Gallery of the Garden of Eden, a curiosity for scholars and students, forgotten while the greater work went on to achieve fame and prominence. Yet the Mandrake, being made in God's image, and thus Man's, was prone to the same desires as Man, and it envied Man, for the poor, forgotten Mandrake had no soul. This was at a time when God was still not finished with His creation and was in every artist's stage of fussing over and admiring His work, making last-minute corrections and revisions, and at this point, the Mandrake asked God if it too could have a soul, so it could be as Man, to which God replied that if the Mandrake wished to have a Man's soul, it should find a Man who was done with his and ask him. If the Mandrake could get the Man to agree, then at Judgment Day, when God cast the world anew — *if* God ever cast the world anew — the Mandrake would be given the Man's soul and would receive his share of immortality for the next world.

"This was small comfort to the poor little Mandrake, for what could it ever have to offer Man? Yet time passed, and the Mandrake grew in power. For unlike Adam and Eve, it never tasted the fruit of the Tree and therefore was not cast out of the Garden, and so did not suffer from the Fall of Man, and was not cursed with mortality, though its children may have been. Did I mention the Mandrake's children or his wife? No, I don't believe I did. There are variants on the tale, of course — that is why they call the stories fragments, for none are complete, and it is never certain which are true — but there is also a tale of the Mandragora, the Mandrake's wife, who may have been created at the same time as the Mandrake as a study for Lilith, or, with a cutting taken from the Mandrake by God, allowed to grow into a female as Eve was made from Adam's rib.

"However it happened, the next fragment of the tale tells of a great number of little Mandrakes. And, at the spot where Caine killed Abel, the little Mandrakes sprouted up in the spilt blood, though the legend does not say whether Abel agreed to let any one of them have his soul now that he was finished with it. But the Mandrake has grown around gallows' trees ever since, especially in the spots where the ground has been watered with the blood of an innocent.

"Never cast out of the Garden, the Mandrake thus had no need to reach God and thus did not impiously build the Tower of Babel, and neither was it condemned to the Curse of Babel and thus could still speak the language of all men and animals, plants and spirits." Kleist tilted his head, his expression not changing, his eyes still focused on something beyond her. "By God's new design, the little Mandrake and his children now had something to offer Man, and those who avoided death by its shriek — For who could stand to hear all the knowledge of the world at once? — struck bargains with God's study, which now knew more than the masterwork, and magicians down through the ages kept mandrakes in exchange for their souls — or portions of them."

Dieter's eyes focused back on her. "Before Etrius became one of our kind, he and the others of his coven explored the legends of the Damned. Etrius followed them back to their very beginning, finding the spot where Caine slew Abel. And at that spot he found the Mandrake root. Not *a* mandrake root, but *the* Mandrake root, the first truly thinking creation of God, a creature older than Man — and without a soul, for Abel had not made that bargain with it.

"Etrius kept it, feeding it his blood and nurturing it so that it became a creature of flesh instead of wood, a homunculus. After he had joined the Kindred, he continued to feed his companion, and it grew strong on the blood of the Damned, the master using other magics and Disciplines to give it what he could."

Kleist set down his book then and reached into the pocket of his jacket, pulling out a bundle of skin that Ilse first took to be a sleeping squirrel, but once Kleist folded back the rabbit pelt, she saw that it was Etrius. Etrius, no bigger than a doll, dressed in tiny pants and a sweater lovingly crocheted from the finest embroidery silk.

"Oh, my goodness," Ilse breathed, seeing the bright and beautiful aura of the tiny creature, the quintessential spark of the souls of the men she had loved.

The tiny man snored, warm with life, and she reached out to touch him. He yawned and squirmed, reaching about as if looking for the rabbit pelt, then found her finger instead. He pulled it to himself, still sleepy, and started sucking on the end, like a baby would its bottle. Finding it dry, he smacked his lips sleepily, yawned, and opened his eyes.

"Lisle!" he cried, his voice as tiny and high-pitched as a cartoon mouse's. "You're back! Oh, Lisle!"

The colors of his aura flushed with love, brilliant rose, without the faded shades of Etrius' own or the tints of feeling for Astrid. Passionately he kissed her finger and hugged her hand. On instinct, Ilse picked him up and cradled him to her cheek like the dove in the dream-memory.

"Oh, my God," Ilse said, tears beginning to run down her face.

The tiny creature only hugged her, licking the tears of blood from her cheek, and Kleist already had his damnable sketchbook open, fingers slashed and dabbling blood across the page. Ilse didn't know whether to tear it from him or to thank him.

"Etrie has been helping Dieter with my memoirs," said Etrius' voice, and Ilse turned. Etrius stood at the far end of the table, Astrid on his arm, her eyes blazing like a wildcat's. "I'm sorry I didn't tell you all this earlier, but there's so much to tell."

"It will be my masterwork," Kleist said, still sketching.

"The first of many, I'm sure, Dieter." Etrius nicked his ring finger on one fang, holding it out over the table despite what Cassandra said about drinking in the library. "Here, Etrie — I have a treat for you."

The little homunculus pushed away from Ilse's face, looking towards Etrius, then back to her, a pained expression over his tiny features. He continued to clutch Ilse lovingly, but giving yearning glances to the rich vitæ on the Councilor's finger.

Ilse understood and just gave a sad smile and set him on the table. "Go ahead. I'll still be here."

With a last happy smile and a look that promised he would be back, Etrie ran down the length of the table, joyful as a small child, grabbed Etrius' finger and began to nurse.

Etrius smiled fondly. "Etrie contains my youthful innocence and a certain measure of my exhilaration and exuberance. They were portions of my soul I was sure I would lose anyway, so it seemed better to give them to one who needed them so much."

Astrid smiled with malice behind him. "We've located Carl Magnuson. Or really, Etrius has, though it took a great deal of magic. He's in Berlin, a captive of the Ventrue."

She disengaged Etrie from Etrius' finger, and Ilse saw the power she held over both of them. "That's enough, Etrie. Now take this to Ilse." She handed the little homunculus a folded sheet of notepaper, and it ran with it down the table towards Ilse, whether to get away from Astrid or back to her or some mixture of both, Ilse wasn't sure.

Ilse received the paper and an enthusiastic hug from the tiny man, but before she could open it, Astrid smiled again. "Your Carl is being held by Kurt Westphal, whom you already dealt with in London — his address is on that paper. It would be so very nice if you could fetch Carl back and bring him to the Brocken, where Etrius has the rites planned for *Walpurgisnacht.*"

Etrie seemed to forget that Astrid had been the one to say this, or perhaps had a short attention span for things unpleasant, for he hugged Ilse again, crumpling the notepaper in his exuberance. "Oh, Lisle, it will be wonderful!" he piped. "When we have Carl back, then Etrius will have what he needs to do the spell, and we shall all be one — me, Carl, Etrius! We shall all be a living man, and you shall be alive as well!"

Ilse looked at the Councilor and his tiny homunculus. "You'll become one with Carl?"

Etrius nodded. "Etrie has an immortality surpassing Caine's, but he has no soul. I have a soul, but if I return to life, I shall no longer be immortal. And there are other complications. One of my descendants, the man who now calls himself Thadius Zho — and I now know you know of him and of your history with his soul — sold the souls of *his* descendants to the Dark Lord, Charnas." Etrius made the same gesture against evil. "Only the fact of my existence has kept the demon from collecting those souls, for I was, and am, Zho's elder, but the longer I have existed, the more children and grandchildren each of his heirs has had. I could have returned to life many times since and restored the life of the House by finding any mage of my bloodline and getting him to agree to the merging of our souls and magic in his mortal body. But to do so would be to give up my immortal body and the claim it held by blood over the children of Zho. They would have been damned the minute my vampiric body suffered the Final Death."

The Councilor's face turned even more grave. "The one hope was to find a mortal mage of Zho's tainted line and join with him at the same time he joined with Etrie. I — we — would become an immortal creature that would not ever die, at least not until the next world, when God has promised immortality for all. The chain of ownership of souls would go into a loop — Etrie owning me, I owning the tainted heir, the heir owning Etrie — the three of us joined in a trinity. Zho's compact with the Dark Lord would thus become null and void, every part of it shattering as impossible and unenforceable, and the souls would be free of the demon's claim, at the same time as those others of my immortal bloodline were freed from the Mark of Caine.

"Carl Magnuson is that man, the outcast mage, the tainted heir. We can all save each other from death and damnation." Etrius smiled at Ilse, his mismatched eyes glowing with hope. "Winter will end, and the spring of magic will return."

"And I shall draw its sunrise," said Kleist behind her.

Ilse turned, and the Toreador paused in his sketch, his eyes seeing a scene not in the present. "I have bound myself to Councilor Etrius and will thus share in his masterwork. I had done it so that I might more fully understand my subject, but to be a participant in the man's great work is an honor beyond measure."

Ilse looked back to Etrius, and he smiled at her again. "It is a gift we can offer to everyone. Once House Tremere has risen and magic has returned, Caine's curse can be washed from the brow of all who wish to return to the light."

Astrid looked at Ilse, smiling slightly. "You can see now why it is so important that you recover Carl Magnuson." The Councilor's consort put a hand on his shoulder, light but possessive as a claw, and Ilse understood; Astrid did not so much fear her return to mortality, as she feared losing Etrius. Ilse could see the shadings of it in the woman's aura, but they were complex and confused. She could not be certain whether they signified love of power or love for the man himself. Or whether, for Astrid, there was any difference. But whichever passion it was that drove her, Ilse could tell that Astrid would fight fiercely to protect whatever she considered hers — and if that meant sending a rival into danger, all the better.

"Best wishes, Ilse," Astrid added, still smiling. "After all, so much depends on it."

❧

The rest of the night was spent in transit on the way to Berlin, where Kurt kept his primary base of operations. Kurt dialed the numbers he needed to reach before sunrise on the portable phone in the car, glad as always for the modern methods of communication. He left messages for several Kindred in the United States and called personally to both Gustav Breidenstein in East Berlin and Wilhelm Waldburg in West Berlin, explaining the situation to each of them as best he could. He was once again locked in the paralyzing sleep brought on by the sun's rise fully an hour before they reached his haven at the Europa Center complex.

Long before he faded into sleep, plans were already being solidified in Berlin. While it was rare for the two princes to work together, they could do so when they had to. For the first time in a week, Kurt drifted into slumber with a feeling that he had accomplished something.

Thursday, April 29, Berlin — The Knights of Europa

When the sun had set once again, Kurt stepped from his private suite and into the main living room of his apartment. Zho and Carl Magnuson were involved in heavy debate when he walked in. Both were arguing their cases in Latin, a language Kurt could barely remember studying. Rather than interrupt them, he stepped to the windows and opened the curtains, allowing him to view the city in all its glory. He smiled, happy to once again be in familiar territory. In the distance he could see the Kaiser Willhelm Memorial Church and not far away, the home of Wilhelm Waldburg in the Charlottenburg Palace. From his penthouse in the Europa Center complex, he could see almost all of West Berlin from one window or another.

Jackie came into the room, and Kurt watched her reflection as it approached him, her face set with unfamiliar lines and her red hair pulled back in a ponytail. She was dressed in blue jeans and a dress shirt. He knew what she was going to say before she even spoke. He held up one hand and murmured. "Not here, *mein Leibchen*. In my office, please."

Her reflection nodded and turned away. Kurt followed soon after, heading into the wood-paneled room where he took care of all his business. The hairs on his nape were standing on end, and his stomach felt tight with a flood of butterflies. He felt his face grow stony and willed his features to soften. Here, with this one person, he would not be an Archon, nor would he allow himself the comfort of falling back on his vampiric nature. Here he would be simply a man.

"Kurt, I —"

"You are leaving me." There was no question in his mind. He knew her too well.

"Yes." Her voice was heavy with emotion, and he reached automatically into his jacket pocket, offering her a handkerchief. She accepted gratefully.

The silence stretched on for several moments, neither speaking, simply staring at each other. For Kurt, the time was spent memorizing every aspect of Jackie. What went through her mind was a complete mystery. He could not see past the fact that she was leaving. Finally he broke the silence, no longer able to hold his tongue. "Will you ever be back?" He hated the pleading sound in his voice, but could not hold his emotions in check.

"I don't know, Kurt. I just don't know." She looked away from him, clutching her arms to her sides and moving a distance away. "I've tried to understand that your job makes demands. I've tried to —" She started trembling then and Kurt moved towards her, wanting nothing more than to stop her suffering, to offer whatever comfort he could. She stepped back again, shaking her head. One tear slipped from her eye, running down her cheek and dangling like a gem at the edge of her chin before falling to the ground. "No. Don't touch me. The thought of you, or any of your kind, touching me is enough to make me sick. And I don't ever want to feel that way when I think of you, Kurt. I just can't stand to be a part of your world anymore."

Kurt backed away from her, acknowledging her wishes and feeling rather ill himself. The one person he could count on was abandoning him, and try though he might, he could not make himself forgive the slight. "I did not want this, Jackie. I have never wished you harm. You must know that."

"Of course I know that!" Her voice was halfway filled with laughter, halfway broken by tears. "I've been with you for fifteen years, Kurt. I didn't stay only because your blood keeps me young. Damn it, I love you!" She walked over to the door, looking back only once with an expression that hurt him more than ever the sunlight could. "I — I don't know if I'll be back. Good-bye, Kurt."

Kurt watched her leave, watched the door close behind her, and sat perfectly still. A thousand different feelings lashed though the very center of his being, and he felt paralyzed. When the tears started falling, he stopped his breathing with a concentrated effort. If he allowed himself to breathe, he would make sounds unbecoming of a Ventrue in his position.

Feeling a flood of hot, human emotion unlike any he'd experienced in a long time, he pushed back his chair, prepared to go after Jackie and beg for forgiveness, beg her to stay with him. He'd offer to quit his position, do anything he could to have her by his side. She was, he realized, the very reason he existed, the center of his being. He pushed open the door, prepared to call out her name.

The words would not come, his mouth defied him. His will slipped away, and from deep inside a growing numbness, he cried out in utter silence, trying his best to defy the alien presence that filled him.

NO. WHAT MUST BE DONE IS MORE IMPORTANT THAN YOUR WOMAN. LEAVE HER BE. YOU CAN ALWAYS GET HER BACK LATER. He felt the passions that fueled him fade along with the echoes of the command that consumed him. In seconds, he was once again in complete control, just as he liked it. He ignored the butterflies in his stomach and forced his body to relax. There was work to be done. Jackie Therman was only a human, after all. She would come back after him when he willed it. But that was for later. Right now he had to concentrate on the present danger. The Tremere had to be stopped.

Kurt stepped back into his living room, where Zho and Magnuson looked at him quizzically. Whatever they had been arguing was apparently settled. Kurt smiled politely. "Shall we get on with the business at hand, gentlemen? I believe we have much to discuss."

"Certainly, Kurt." Zho looked at him with a deep regret obvious on his face. "Let's get to it."

"Right, mate. First thing to discuss is why you sucker-punched me last night." Magnuson's face was set and determined. Kurt doubted he could Dominate the man's will at this point, not that he had intentions of doing any such thing.

"I really am sorry for that, Herr Magnuson, but I could see no other alternative. If I'd approached you under normal circumstances, without knowing what the Tremere have said about me, there was the very real threat of you calling out an alarm, or worse still, turning me into something of questionable origin." Kurt gave his best smile, shrugged apologetically, and offered his hand. "For formal introductions, my name is Kurt Westphal. You may call me Kurt, if you like."

"Well. I have to say I've seldom been apologized to as eloquently, Kurt. You may call me Carl." The man smiled and accepted Kurt's hand. He was taken aback to how similar and simultaneously different Carl was to Zho. The smile was as bright and friendly as Zho's (when the mage was employing what Kurt tended to think of as his "real" smile), but there were less lines on his face and fewer years. Kurt believed he understood where at least a little of Ilse Decameron's volatile emotions a few nights before had come from.

"Thadius? Have you discussed the situation with Carl?"

Zho stood and walked over to where Kurt was standing. "Yes, we've been discussing little else. By the best calculations either of us can come up with, Etrius plans on attempting his ritual on Walpurgis Night."

"*Walpurgisnacht?* April thirtieth? But that's tomorrow. Why would he pick a night when demons are supposed to cavort with the witches?"

"Actually, Walpurgis Night is also known as Walburga's Night, after St. Walburga of Heidenheim. The Church chose the last night in April as one of her special days for feasting, and in so doing followed along with the Catholic tradition of the times. Long before it was known as Walpurgis Night, April thirtieth was known as Waldborg's Eve, a pagan celebration in honor of Waldborg, the fertility goddess. What better time to bring his plans to fruition?"

"You've lost me, not that the feat is difficult at this time. Suffice to say the day has significant potential for magickal rites?"

"That'll do very nicely, I think," Carl answered, throwing Kurt again for just a second as he heard the unexpected British accent added to the voice he associated with Zho and coming from the wrong mouth in addition. The more he pondered the situation, the more he realized how many similarities existed between the two men — similar posture, almost identical facial expressions, even small gestures when they spoke. It was disorienting, to say the least.

"Well, then, it seems the easiest way to handle this situation would be to keep you in Berlin for the next few days, yes, Carl?"

Zho spoke again, "An easy enough concept, but you may rest assured, Etrius will do everything in his considerable power to ensure that Carl is exactly where he wants him to be."

"Besides which, I've only your word and Zho's to back up this little theory. No offense, Kurt, but I've really got no reason at all to believe either of you."

"What do you mean?"

"Oh, come on now, Kurt. I hardly know either of you." Much like Kurt had seen Zho do in the past, Magnuson started ticking off reasons for his arguments, lifting one finger for each point he made. "The first time I saw you, you had your fangs bared, and you were chasing after Ilse Decameron. The second time I saw you was last night, and to bolster my confidence, you punched me in the head. The only time I've seen Thadius over here was when I woke up this morning. And to top it all off," — he gestured with his free hand, indicating Zho — "he's admitted to having sold the souls of all his descendants to a major demon. All of his descendants, which, by the way, includes me." He held forth the four fingers he'd raised in his argument, waggling them to make certain his point was clear. "That's four strikes against you, mate, and in cricket and baseball alike, that's an out and then some."

Kurt looked to the other man in the room, and Zho raised his hands in apparent defeat. "Don't look at me, Kurt. I've been having this argument for several hours in numerous languages."

Kurt opened his mouth to protest, but closed it again when a sharp knock came at the door. He waited a moment, fully expecting Jackie to open the door before he remembered that she'd left. Fighting off a wave of depression, he stormed across the room and opened the door himself. Charnas stood outside, dressed once more in his traditional leather biker outfit and carrying a bottle of Dom Perignon. "Hi, Kurt! I know how much you've missed being here in Berlin, so I thought I'd bring you a homecoming gift." The imp's smile was electrifying, and Kurt found, much to his own amazement and disgust, that he was almost glad to see the demon. "Can I come in?"

In a flash, Zho stood behind Kurt, placing a hand over his mouth and speaking in his ear. "That is far too open an invitation, Kurt." The man took his hand away and looked to Kurt expectantly.

"You have a suggestion, then, Thadius?"

The mage nodded, smiling icily at Charnas, who, Kurt noted, was no longer smiling in return. "Oh, most definitely. I'd recommend you allow him into your home with the following stipulations: *One*, he may come in only this one time; *two*, he may touch nothing, and he must leave the bottle outside; *three*, he must state the truth and only the truth in every statement he makes while on your premises."

Kurt contemplated the man's words and nodded. "Agreed. You may only enter my home this one time, you may touch nothing during your time in this apartment and must leave the champagne bottle outside, and you must tell nothing but the truth while you are here. If you are willing to accept these terms, you may come into my home."

Charnas bowed formally, his grin returning as he spoke. "I most humbly accept the conditions you have stated, Herr Westphal." He threw the bottle across the hallway, where it exploded in a cascade of green glass and foaming liquid. As he crossed over the threshold, Charnas lifted off the ground and walked gracefully on the air. "Well, I'm awfully glad you made it here in one piece. I'd hate to think of anything happening to any of you. By the way, Kurt, how's Jackie?"

"I — she's not here."

Charnas positively gloated, his voice a silken purr, "I know."

"You miserable little piglet."

"I could get her back for you. Just say the word, and it's a done deal."

"Enough, Charnas!" Once again, Zho was livid, his single eye burning with an fierce inner-light. "Why are you here?"

"Well, Ilse Decameron found me out. She looked me right in the face and gasped and called me a fiend. Well, far be it from me to overstay my welcome, so I just discoed on down to Berlin-town and decided to let you know what was what."

"I imagine the story is a tad more complicated than you let on, imp." Zho's voice was filled with contempt.

"Hey, I did nothing that Carl over there wouldn't have done. I fulfilled my part of your orders to the letter."

"Ignoring the intent, no doubt."

"Precisely," the demon smiled. "What can I say? I like to improvise."

Carl stood up from where he'd been sitting and walked over to where everyone else was congregated. "Would you care to introduce me to your friend?"

Thadius opened his mouth to speak, but Charnas beat him to the punch. "Certainly, Carl. This is Thadius Zho, your great-great-great-great-great-great-great-great-grandfather," he gestured grandly to the mage. "This is Kurt Westphal, Archon to Clan Ventrue, and all-around hero-type. And I..." He paused long enough to bow again. "I am Charnas the Imp, servant to Thadius Zho and the cuter aspect of Charnas, Lord of Misrule, *et cetera, et cetera*. Tragically misunderstood, but always willing to please."

"Pleasure, I'm sure." Carl did not sound at all certain about the pleasure aspects, but he was polite enough, especially considering the circumstances.

"Not yet, you sweet thing, but I can fix that." Charnas warped and changed before Kurt's eyes, appearing ever so briefly as Ilse Decameron. Just as quickly, he was himself again.

Kurt stepped away, once again pulling himself under control. He was angry, angry with himself, with Jackie and even with Charnas. Mostly, he was angry with himself, for letting Charnas get under his skin and for letting Jackie leave him. His concentration was almost non-existent, but there was nothing he could do about the situation, save step away for a moment and calm down. The task ahead was too important to botch.

Behind him, the three others in the room were talking, Carl asking questions and Charnas and Zho giving him answers. A soft, feminine voice spoke beside him, "Kurt, I am so very sorry for your loss. If I — If I can be of help to you, you have but to ask."

Kurt turned, surprised to see Jing Wei and embarrassed to admit that he'd forgotten she was with them. He studied her face, taking in her beauty and feeling a modicum of pleasure brought on by her presence. She smelled lightly of sandalwood, but her normal traditional attire was gone, replaced by one of his dress shirts that was almost as large as a dress on her.

"Hello, Jing Wei. I appreciate your kindness, but now is not the time for such considerations. Perhaps after tomorrow has passed, and assuming we are both alive at that point."

"You could call her back to you. You know that you could. Why did you let her leave?" The part of her question that bothered him was that she actually sounded puzzled by his actions.

"'If you love something, let it go. If it comes back to you, it's yours. If it does not, it never was.' Or something like that. I've never much cared for that silly little saying, but it fits well enough how I feel about Jackie ."

"You love her then?"

"Oh, my, yes."

"Then you are a very lucky man, Kurt Westphal. Love is hard to come by in our existence." Her voice was soft, barely above a whisper.

"Only if the love is returned, my dear. If it is not returned, then I am truly among the Damned."

Jing Wei rested her head against his shoulder, and he brought his arm around her waist, pulling her close, grateful for the simple contact. "May the love be returned one thousandfold."

❧❧

Two hours later, Kurt was back in his offices, attending to the mundane business he had set aside for the last few weeks. Much could be handled by others in his absence, true, but he preferred to handle it himself whenever possible.

That, and the tasks helped him keep his mind off Jackie. They distracted him from the knots of writhing demons that seemed to course through his chest and stomach, worrying at him with teeth sharper than razors. Were it not for the lack of bloody wounds, Kurt would have thought he was dying physically instead of simply feeling his heart, his soul, die.

The water clock on his desk, a miniature version of the massive original below him in the depths of the Europa Center's main mall, let him know that the time for sleep would soon be upon him. In other rooms throughout the apartment, Magnuson, Zho and Jing Wei all rested or worried, whichever seemed appropriate. Magnuson was sleeping, his mind no doubt overwhelmed by the magnitude of his situation. Kurt had checked on him before retiring to his office and had heard the steady rhythm of his breathing, the slowed pulse of his heartbeat.

The night was growing old, only a few hours before dawn, when the voice assaulted Kurt for the second time. *EMBRACE HIM.* The sheer force behind the words caused his body to twitch.

He spoke softly, a whisper that could not hope to escape the sound-proofing of his office. "Who are you?"

EMBRACE CARL MAGNUSON. STOP THE TREMERE BEFORE IT IS TOO LATE. The words were like hammer-blows against his psyche, lightning strikes that electrified his soul and demanded his submission.

"Who are you? Answer me, damn your soul!" He focused all of his senses, closed his eyes, and stopped breathing, preparing himself to capture every nuance of the voice. "Are you Democritus?"

DO NOT DEFY ME, MY CHILDE.

"Are you Camilla, my grand-sire?" There was no answer, but the absence of communication was not an answer. He sensed, or possibly only imagined that he sensed, a masculine essence to the voice that rang through his brain. "I have served the Ventrue faithfully, but I defy you! I will not follow the orders of a voice that has no name, no meaning to me. Once again, who are you?"

The presence slammed against him, an oppressive weight that pinned him in place and sought weaknesses in his defensive armor. Kurt felt his body spasm, felt himself fall from the plush chair behind his desk and roll across the floor, his muscles dancing in a *gran mal* seizure. Negative suns ignited behind his closed eyelids, and the taste of his own blood filled his mouth. He dared not think, save to focus against the attack. He was only dimly aware of the chair falling across him, and the splintering wood in his hand was no more substantial than the wind. Faint distractions, hardly worth noticing when compared to the storm that ripped across his mindscape.

EMBRACE THE MAGE! DO NOT RISK ALL THAT WE ARE!!

The images in his mind, the super-novae that pulsed across his close-eyed vision with each lashing that the presence delivered, revealed at last what Kurt had already suspected. The face of a man, his image reversed like the nebulous explosions that formed his separate parts. Three weeks after his Embrace, Kurt had seen the man for only the briefest of moments, a graceful figure dressed in a fine silk suit, his long dark hair pulled back and braided, his beard and mustache perfectly trimmed. The man had looked at Kurt and smiled, and in that moment, Kurt had wanted to weep in adoration. Bindusara, the Philosopher of Alexandria. Surely there were few among the Ventrue who did not want to gain his attention, few who did not desire his respect. Bindusara knew more of the Kindred and their ten thousand year history than most vampires could imagine. He was hated, feared, reviled, revered, loved and envied by most of the clans, and he was virtually idolized by the Ventrue. The greatest mind among the clan, and Kurt was trying to struggle against him.

Almost before he had finished accepting what he fought against, the conflict was over. He waited, fearing a return of the storm that had nearly destroyed him. After the previous few seconds, the silence was almost more than he could stand. He opened his eyes. The deep red carpet of his office spread out before him. The weight of his chair shoved against his neck, an unpleasant burden that he shrugged aside, listening in satisfaction as it rattled and crashed against the wall behind him. Kurt unclenched his fists, releasing the broken fragments of his desk that he had apparently ruined when the seizures struck. Where his face had rested moments before, a pool of black stained the carpet — his blood. Kurt felt the partially severed section of his tongue flap against his canines and grimaced in pain.

He stood, his muscles groaning in protest. The room tilted threateningly, and he was forced to grab the edge of his desk to maintain his balance. A heavy splinter of oak rammed into his hand, and he savored the pain, something physical to remind him that he was alive. After a few moments, when the room had once again settled back into focus, he righted his chair and sat down, hard.

Bindusara. He had defied Bindusara, and he suspected the Scholar of Alexandria would not forget the slight. "I —I did not mean offense. I simply could not allow one I did not know to command me, milord."

There was no response.

"What if you had been one of the Tremere? An enemy of the clan?"

There were no answers to his questions.

"I — I cannot do this thing you ask. Please, I do not want to make another suffer this damnation."

The silence continued for several seconds. Then, EMBRACE THE MAGE, CARL MAGNUSON. WE CANNOT RISK THE VENTRUE CLAN AND THE CAMARILLA.

Kurt shook, his body demanding that he follow the commands of the Methuselah. He closed his eyes again, focusing on the voice and preparing himself for the worst. After all that had happened in the last week, all that he had endured, all that his Jackie had suffered through, he could not do what was demanded of him. "Anything else, Bindusara. Anything but that. I will kill him if I must, but I cannot damn him. I will not damn him."

EMBRACE HIM.

"No."

YOU MUST. The voice struck him again, a vicious dagger driving between his eyes. Kurt felt the desk in front of him press against his legs, and then the weight was gone. A distant crunching sound reached his ears.

"N-No! I will not do this. Anything but this!"

Again the silence, and again he waited before opening his senses to the outside world. The oak desk was turned over, belly-up like some poor animal bludgeoned to death. His legs felt scraped and bruised from where he had apparently lashed out to strike the lectern in another seizure. His skull pounded, a steady keening agony accented only by the echoes of Bindusara's voice.

DO NOT DEFY ME, KURT WESTPHAL!!!

"I must. What you ask of me, I cannot do. Not and live with myself. Better that he die. Better that you kill me."

Kurt trembled with fear, waiting for the next attack. Every sound, even the spasmodic movements that still ran through his tortured nerve-endings, caused him to whimper. He had never before felt abuse like that which Bindusara had so easily dealt him. When consciousness faded from his body with the rising sun, he was still waiting.

⇒⇐

The moon reached its zenith before Kurt was once again

ready to deal the people and the matters at hand. More phone calls were made, to both of Berlin's princes, to Gilbert Duane in Miami, Florida, and to J.Oswald Hyde-White at the inn he called his home. With Gilbert Duane's assistance, he managed to wrangle a promise of aid from the Malkavian elder of Berlin. First, Hyde-White and his madmen would keep the Tremere of Berlin occupied with a dozen distractions, and second, the Malkavians would use their influence with the Nosferatu to locate the potential sites where Etrius and his clan would attempt this great ritual, if such a ritual was to be performed. The princes started making calls of their own, each approaching the connections they had in the elder Kindred network throughout the world to ensure that no gross violations of the Masquerade would go unpunished. There was no guarantee that the Tremere would attempt a global attack against the Masquerade, but if they did, the Ventrue would stand ready to stop them. If need be, the Ventrue would have to work a few charms of their own to have systematic blackouts of satellite reception across the entire planet. Not an easy task, but one that could be accomplished. The wheels were set in motion to assure that Etrius and his Tremere could not possibly accomplish their feat by means of assaulting the mortals of the world with the truth of the vampires in their midst.

Finally, a last phone call to Democritus, one that explained in detail all he had learned and all that he hoped to accomplish before the end of the following night. The Ventrue Justicar gave him compliments for a job well done and promised that there would be rewards in the future. Kurt made all the right motions and said all the proper words, but did so with less enthusiasm than most would have expected from him. Democritus himself asked if there was anything wrong, and Kurt admitted that he was tired, rather than boring the man with details of his shattered heart.

Then Kurt spent almost an hour pondering who had

commanded him to stay and handle the task at hand, rather than go after the woman he loved. He could swear that he had been in contact with someone, some ancient influence that forced his will into submission and attempted to Dominate him. Only his sire, to the best of his knowledge, had control enough over him to literally force him to watch as his reason for living walked away. Yet the Justicar had asked him if there was anything amiss. Surely the man was not that heartless, especially to one with whom he was pleased. Then if not Democritus, who?

For the first time since his Embrace, Kurt found himself pondering the intricacies of the Kindred society with something akin to fear. Democritus was almost surely Blood Bound to his sire, and his sire before him to the one who had given her the Embrace. From Democritus to Camilla to Bindusara to…? He had no idea who Bindusara's sire was; for all he knew the man was Embraced by Ventrue himself. Was it possible that each had Bound their childe as surely as Democritus had Bound Kurt? If so, could the Blood Bond that ran through the lineage allow each to control not only their own get but the childer of their get as well?

Kurt scribbled a note to himself, intent on solving the mystery at a later time, then stood to leave the room. As he walked around his desk, he reached over and picked up the note. He tore the note neatly in eight parts, burying half of them in his wastebasket near the door and carrying the rest in his pocket. He made a mental note to dispose of each piece separately and promptly forgot what he had done. He paused before leaving his office, wondering what he had been up to for the last hour. He was tired, and apparently the strain he was under was making him absent-minded. The important thing now, as always, was to protect the interests of the Ventrue clan. The best way to accomplish that was to stop Etrius and his plans.

By the time Kurt returned to the living room, Carl and

Zho had once again settled into discussing their mutual ancestor and how best to approach the problem that Etrius presented. As Kurt approached, Zho commanded Charnas to be gone, and the imp left with a sneer and several obscenities. Jing Wei stood by the window, staring out at the darkness, but her posture told Kurt that she was listening to every word being spoken.

"I see that Charnas has once again worn out his welcome. I must apologize for disappearing so abruptly, but I had a few phone calls to make." The two men looked up at him, and Jing Wei turned away from the window, offering him a small smile. "Have you decided whether or not to risk believing us, Mr. Magnuson?"

"Well, I don't see as I have much say in the matter either way, Kurt. I'm here now, aren't I?"

"Let's stop beating around the bush, shall we?" Kurt dropped all pretenses of a smile, his anger winning slightly, and the need to make his point known only emphasizing the need to get this finished once and for all. "Of course you have choices. If you did not have choices, I could have rectified this matter already."

"How so?"

"Thadius and I decided that we'd reason with you. I am reasoning with you because I abhor physical violence and have no warm place in my heart for kidnapping. Thadius feels that he and you are linked by mystical bonds — a point I won't argue, as one look at the two of you next to each other is enough to convince me that he is accurate in his beliefs — and for that reason alone, he would wish you no harm. Certainly he has already had the chance to choose his own fate. Why would he rob you of the same option?"

"You mean aside from selling my soul to a major demon?" Kurt acknowledged that what Zho had told him and what he had told Carl were two different stories, thought about questioning the man about his divergent tales, and mentally shrugged the matter off. Instead he focused on the attitude the younger mage was tossing his way and forced himself to calm down as much as possible.

Kurt paused a moment, stepping over to a silver-plated humidor set on the oak bar against the wall and extracting a package of brandied tobacco from its depths, followed by a pipe. He delayed a moment longer, filling the pipe's bowl and tamping down the loose leaves. "I will be blunt now. If I wanted to stop Etrius without your consent, I could have drained you of your blood and fed you enough of my own to make you a vampire. By so doing, your usefulness to Etrius would be non-existent. Or perhaps it would have been possible to Blood Bond you to me — a very simple process that would effectively make you my slave — and through that bond, perhaps I could even gain a certain level of influence over Councilor Etrius of the Tremere. An opportunity that most of my clan would kill for, Carl. Make no mistake about that."

Kurt lit the pipe and pulled the smoke into his mouth, letting the sweetened fumes run past his lips in tiny trickles. Normally he preferred to smoke only after he was done with an assignment, but this night he felt the need for his nostalgic habit and the comfort it gave. The two mages before him both stared apparently taken aback by his abrupt change in tactics. That was good; it meant he was achieving his goal. "I could simply have broken your neck last night instead of taking the time to ensure your safety. That would have ended the problem again. It would also have delayed Etrius' plans by at least a few decades."

He noted, with no small satisfaction, the slightly shocked smile on Jing Wei's angelic face. He believed he might have even surprised her, because such direct comments were just not the norm for him, and everyone who knew him in the least knew that he seldom laid his cards on the table without at least a little restraint. "Do not, for one instant, Mr. Magnuson, assume you have no control over your destiny. As a rule I try to avoid taking away another person's options. I respect my own freedom far too much to take away another's without just cause."

"I appreciate that, Kurt. But you've got to understand that you're putting one hell of a weight on my shoulders and asking me to make a decision that will affect the rest of my life. And you're asking me to make that decision with nothing to go one but the words of one demon-dealing mage, one imp of the aforementioned demon and yours." Magnuson stood, walking over to the bar to see if there was anything worth noticing. He pulled a rather dusty bottle of Louis XIII out and looked towards Kurt. "May I?"

"Of course. Forgive my ill manners. I only keep the liquors to offer others, I'm certainly not capable of drinking them, and then I forget to offer them when I finally have guests for the first time in a decade. Help yourself."

"Thank you."

"You have my word as well, Carl." The mage turned from opening the lead-crystal decanter, looking over at Jing Wei. She smiled, moved closer, and took the bottle from his fingers. Kurt stepped behind the bar and rinsed out one of his brandy snifters, remembering with fond regret that Jackie was never the most efficient of housekeepers. Jing Wei poured three fingers worth of the amber liquor, looking to Zho with a questioning glance. He nodded, and she poured another for him. "I had time to study the library at the chantry while waiting for Kurt and Thadius to arrive. There are many tomes in that library, and several refer to similar magics being employed over the centuries. House Tremere has a long and distinguished history, both as a vampiric clan and as a Hermetical order. Make no mistake, the magics employed would have been easy to research and easier still to accomplish."

Jing Wei handed over the glasses to each of the men and turned to look deeply into Magnuson's eyes. "I have seen the images of you, of Etrius, in the presence of a beautiful woman, images older than you and I combined. The woman in those paintings and wood-cuttings bears a remarkable resemblance to Ilse Decameron.

"Did I not step back when asked? Did I not leave you and Ilse together, when you knew even then how I felt for you? I did this because your mutual love is old and powerful. I would not dare to stand in its way." She stepped away from Magnuson, and Kurt could see the hurt in her eyes before she quickly looked back to the window.

No one spoke. Magnuson looked perplexed by her words and unsettled by her confession. Kurt could empathize. The two mages stared at their snifters, and Kurt stepped over to where Jing Wei stared out the window, facing the east and fighting back the emotions she had just exposed. Once again he placed an arm around her waist as she rested her head against his shoulder. This time, he offered what little comfort he could share, and she took it greedily.

"Why do you risk the wrath of your clan, Jing Wei? For the love of a man?" He spoke in whispers, sharing closed murmurs between old friends.

"No, Kurt. I risk much because Etrius is only one of the Seven. Not all agree that becoming human again is a good thing, and even among those who do, there is no surety that now is the proper time. The Comte de St. Germain would not have this happen, and while he is not a part of the Council, his word is normally well-received. Thomas Wyncham is one of the Seven Councilors as well. He would rather the clan wait for final confirmation from Tremere himself."

"Etrius does this without the permission of Tremere?"

Jing Wei smiled, shaking her head. "Who can say? Etrius is in charge of protecting Tremere, and Tremere has not been present to make his feelings known personally. At least not that I am aware of."

"Have you told this to Ilse Decameron? Perhaps she could urge the truth from Etrius." As soon as the words were out of his mouth, he regretted speaking them.

"Perhaps you can ask her yourself, Kurt. She should be here soon." He noticed the edge of frost that had crept into her voice and hugged her waist by way of apologizing.

"Here? At my home?"

"She or another of the Tremere. They will be looking for Carl Magnuson."

"You think Etrius will send Ilse?"

"Oh, yes. He loves her. Besides, who else would he trust?" She stared out the window again, and a slight smile crept up her face. "And who else would Astrid Thomas, who is Etrius' consort, want sent into danger?"

⇒⋇⇐

Ilse turned the Key in the lock of Lady Sarah's umpteenth china cabinet. Ten thousand rooms, a hundred thousand doors, and a million closets and cupboards — the old woman had made certain that the Rite of the Iron Key would have a different, unknown door to use for all the days of a Kindred's unlife.

It was with delight and trepidation that Ilse knew those would soon come to an end.

"House of Shadows, House of Secrets, open out to the lost and forgotten, the barrens and backways, the shadowed byway and hidden hall, the forgotten gate, walled away..." A crumpled photograph of the Brandenburg Gate in her other hand, Ilse pulled open the door, leading out onto a deserted street, a section of the Berlin Wall and the Gate in the distance.

Ilse held the door open, slipping the photograph into her pocket and placing the Key back onto the silver chain about her neck. She then took out her compact and gazed into the mirror, beginning the Rite of Presentation. It was an abbreviated form of the Rite of Introduction, the classic ritual of Tremere courtesy, but instead of paging every Tremere in a city, the Rite of Presentation instead allowed the invoker to contact the chantry Regent, or other high-ranking officer, and that officer alone. It was an invaluable tool for the many cryptic missions a Tremere agent was sent on and entrusted to only the clan's most proven emissaries, but it was a rite that Ilse was very grateful for at the moment, especially when she was able to cross it with the other half of the charm of the Mirror of Hathor.

Ilse finished whispering the incantation, the words of the Sator Square said forwards and back, then began the invocation: "Salutations and greetings, Maxwell Ldescu, Magus of Berlin! I am known as Ilse Decameron, childe of Houdini, childe of —"

Yes, yes, yes, I know all that. The voice came through in her head, quick and amused, and the image in her mirror changed, becoming that of a man, young and handsome, with dark red hair, laughing hazel eyes, and a friendly white smile. *This is Maxwell Ldescu, Magus of Berlin, childe of Schreckt, et cetera, et cetera, and I've been waiting in front of the Mirror since nightfall. Ilse, do you have the door open?*

"Yes," she whispered.

Which one is it?

"Sulfur and Mercury combine to bring a feast for the Dawn."

The reflection paused, and his chuckle echoed inside her head. *I'm guessing that would be Lady Sarah's Cinnabar Breakfast Room.*

"I cannot say. It must remain a secret."

Quite so, he replied. *I know where that opens up. I'll see you in a moment.*

The image faded, and Ilse stood there in the doorway of the china cabinet, one foot in the House of Shadows, the other on an empty street, the Mirror of Hathor held open in her hand, the second half of the charm guarding both her and the Midnight Palace from prying eyes.

She hardly had time to look about before a black Mercedes Benz pulled up in front of the alley. The door opened, and Ldescu climbed out of the driver's side, followed by two women.

"Ah, the illustrious Ilse." He smiled and nodded, head cocked. "I've seen your work and your image, but I must say, it's a pleasure to be working with you and meeting you in the flesh, especially on such an important mission." His handclasp was warm and friendly, even though his skin was as cold as her own.

"Thank every god for the Rite of Presentation and the Mirror of Hathor, not to mention the House. The Ventrue have got the phones bugged, and it's rather hard to throw a countercharm when you're dealing with the entire European satellite system, not to mention malicious computer hacking."

Ilse stepped away from the door to the House of Secrets, allowing the panel to swing closed with a rattle of antique china, leaving nothing more than a boarded-up door covered with posters for forgotten political rallies and concerts. "I'd imagine so." She shut her compact, slipping it back in her pocket.

A woman with a long, oval face, beautiful as a cameo, with luminous, golden eyes and red hair dyed black, matched by a short-skirted dress and stockings, stepped up behind Ldescu almost soundlessly.

"My apprentices," Ldescu said, gesturing to the gold-eyed woman. "Lydia Van Cuelen—," and then to the next figure as she stepped out of the shadows, looming, "— and Sabine Lafitte. Ladies, I give you the illustrious Miss Decameron."

Sabine was a statuesque woman with a heavy-jawed, masculine face, offsetting and confusing the issue with a black crepe spaghetti-strapped party dress, cross earrings, shaved off and penciled in eyebrows, basic black dog collar (with tag), ruby lipstick and slicked back, butched black hair with two strands pulled forward over one eye — either a failed attempt at spit curls or a calculated touch to pick up the line of the spaghetti straps and penciled-in eyebrows. To finish the effect, she wore thigh-high black boots with five-inch stiletto heels, making her tower over the already tall Ldescu by a full head and giving her the general appearance of a transsexual of mixed success or a former member of the East German Women's Olympic Basketball Team.

Either of which might actually be the case.

Ldescu smiled, looking Ilse in the eye, and she heard his voice in her head: *Don't let Sabine's appearance put you off. She's the heart of kindness and the soul of dependability.*

"It is a pleasure to meet you, Miss Decameron," said Sabine, extending her large, black-nailed hand.

"It's a pleasure to meet you," Ilse returned, revising her opinions again. Sabine had a heavy French accent of some provincial sort to offset her obviously Germanic bone structure. Alsatian? Possibly, but Ilse hardly had the time for speculation. She turned back to Ldescu. "Have you ascertained where the Ventrue are holding Carl Magnuson?"

The Magus nodded. "A citadel of sorts. He's being kept in Kurt Westphal's penthouse in one of the hotels of the Europa complex, and, with the shops and restaurants below, there's more than enough Elysium set up as baffles to any concerted Kindred strike force." He grinned, showing a great number of white teeth. "So we're not going to use Kindred. At least, not alone. Our Brujah allies have some interesting allies of their own, and we should be able to cause a sufficient distraction without breaking the Masquerade — or, should I say, without *us* breaking the Masquerade — and get us to the penthouse to rescue Charles the Great. I mean, Carl Magnuson."

"What?" Ilse asked, blinking. "Charlemagne?"

Ldescu beamed. "I haven't the faintest idea if it's true, but it's an engaging idea, isn't it? The coincidence in names is a wonderful stroke of luck, and one of the few things of use my first master taught me is that it doesn't matter if you believe if something is true. If you're a magician, and you tell people, they'll believe it." His eyes danced with mirth. "Especially if they want to believe, and with stories like *that*, let me assure you, there are people who always want to believe. So play along."

Ilse knew well enough about playing along, though did stop to consider the idea. Charlemagne? Her history was terribly rusty, and besides the fact that he was king of the Franks, Ilse didn't know a thing about him. She supposed he'd had a queen, but she hoped it hadn't been her. After all, there were probably a dozen Carl Magnusons in the Berlin phone directory, or at least one or two.

Ldescu put his arms around his apprentices, pulling them forward. "Come along, girls, and you as well, please, Miss Decameron."

"Call me Ilse."

"Call me Max."

They drove down the street until they came to a phone booth. Ldescu pulled against the curb and stepped inside, then paused, one hand on the door. "Lydia, how many minutes would you say?"

"Fifteen at the most. the Europa Center is in the middle of everything."

"In a short while it most certainly will be." Ldescu smiled at some personal irony, then picked up the pay phone, deposited a *Deutschmark*, and began dialing. "*Hallo?* Herr Sosa? Maxwell Ldescu. It appears we shall be needing that favor I mentioned. Yes, yes, certainly. We shall be meeting you a block away. Yes, and thank you. To the return of the Golden Age!"

He hung up, the phone chiming as it swallowed the coin, and he glanced over his shoulder, beaming. "I think a New

Age is indeed upon us. This spirit of cooperation is wonderful." The Magus gave no further explanation, only led them down the sidewalk until a few minutes later, a couple stepped out of a sidestreet and turned, striding purposefully towards them.

The man was huge, at least seven feet tall she was certain, a dancing partner for Sabine and then some, with gargantuan muscles and shoulders so broad it looked like he had football pads permanently attached, swaggering down the sidewalk, blond hair flying, chest and square jaw both thrust forward. The dags on the sleeves and skirt of his knight's tabard fluttered in his wake. His chainmail clanked with each stomp of his enormous jackboots, and on his mammoth chest he had an equally gigantic bear, rampant, Prussian blue on white.

Taking three steps to every two of his to keep up was a woman with spiked blond hair, dressed in the same tabard as the man, but with lighter mail underneath. in place of the greatsword on his back, she had a short sword at her waist, a quiver of arrows and an ivory bow, a fantastic and beautiful piece that belonged in some museum or magician's stronghold, for Ilse could see the magical power that crackled around its aura, even without focusing her sight. And once she did, it was hard to disguise the pale red glow of rage from the auras of both individuals. Angry Kindred — Brujah.

Before Ilse could attempt to read intentions from the couple, Ldescu strode forward an extra pace to meet them. "Ritter Kotlar! Ritter Geiger! Heil!"

"Heil, Magus Ldescu!" the man boomed, a Wagnerian bass worthy of one of the Giants from *Das Rhinegold*. "Is this the one?"

"It is indeed." Ldescu gestured to Ilse as they came to a stop. "Ilse Decameron."

The giant came down on one knee, genuflecting. "The Final Reich offers its services to the servants of the First Reich." He looked up then, blue eyes blazing. "Are you certain that this man is Charles the Great?"

Ilse drew herself up, hoping her *Hochdeutsch* was haughty enough to pull it off. "How can you even question such a thing?" She waited several beats, then let the affected indignation drain from her face. "Of course. I am forgetting, you have never met him. Once you have met Carl Magnuson — Charles the Great — you will never question him again."

Knight Kotlar seemed satisfied with this, and Ilse realized she'd taken a page from Charnas and had deceived without telling a single untruth.

"Are the Knights assembled?" Ldescu inquired.

"Yes, Magus Ldescu," Kotlar responded. "*Die Ritter* are waiting outside the complex."

"And Herr Anvil?"

Geiger responded, "He is there as well, along with Sosa and the Talon from the East."

"Excellent," said Ldescu. "Well, then, let us proceed."

They followed the two anachronistic Brujah and soon arrived at a square outside the Europa Center Complex, where a pavilion had been set up, blue and white, with the Berlin Bear blazoned across everything. People in tabards and armor — mostly human from their auras — wandered about, polishing medieval plate and chainmail and patching bits of it up with duct tape. A few of them sharpened swords while two men sparred with mockups made from rattan and foam, bystanders taking pictures.

Ilse joined them, using Kotlar as a walking wall to keep herself out of sight, then went into one of the pavilions and put on the medieval leather armor and tabard she was given. Ldescu and Lydia did as well. Sabine looked like a Gothic Valkyrie by the time they were done, holding a war spear in one hand, a shield on the other, and with a horned helmet borrowed from the opera on her head.

They were then joined by the three Brujah from Etrius' *Kaffeeklatsch*. Anvil was wearing full chainmail, along with a pot helm, and carrying a wicked-looking cast-iron flanged mace. Yuri, who Ilse supposed was the one referred to as the Talon from the East, had a Cossack's spiked helm and a scimitar at his belt, while Hector Sosa was dressed mostly in leather reinforced with duct tape, a bastard sword in one hand and a skateboard in the other.

The Knights, Ilse realized, were somewhere between the Society for Creative Anachronism and the Society for Creative Anarchism, at least when the Brujah got involved. Once Kotlar had reviewed his warband and given a brief rallying speech, concerning Jews, infidels and other demon-spawn (including vampires) opposed by Martin Luther and the Society of Leopold (making Ilse realize there was at least one muddled vampire hunter among the group surrounding them, not to mention Neo-Nazis) she and Ldescu suddenly had an honor guard of creatively and esoterically armed humans and Kindred.

Bold as brass and twice as noisy, they marched straight for the doors of the shopping complex, the guards holding the doors open for them, either not wanting to trouble the Knights or else, with that peculiar German sensibility, deciding that any large group of persons in uniform must have gotten official approval from someone, so they shouldn't be bothered. Or, more likely, they were walking right into a trap, but the Tremere and their allies would not be the first to drop the Masquerade, especially if they had vampire hunters in their midst.

They marched right along the central walkway of the indoor shopping mall, past tourists, natives, fountains and vendors' carts, the vault as huge and impressive above them as a cathedral, until at last someone chose to drop the Masquerade.

The person was a bag lady who appeared out of nowhere — fangs bared, flowered hat askew, and chainsaw buzzing —, and she swung it into a man in full chainmail, sparks and blood flying and horrible screams of flesh and metal filling the air. Kotlar's enormous greatsword came out at once, and before Ilse could even register, the bag lady's head was separated at the neck and launched high in the air. The chainsaw landed on the walkway, still buzzing, the chain launching it forward till it caught on the short mall carpet, buzzing and chattering as it spun in circles. The head then landed on the rim of one of the planters, bursting like a ripe melon, followed a moment later by the flowered hat.

Whether this was merely strange irony, or some Toreador had actually decided it would all begin at the drop of a hat, it didn't matter. Large numbers of heavily armed Kindred appeared, fangs bared and concealed weapons no longer concealed, many of them Nosferatu or obviously insane, and it was definite that at least one vampire had used his or her power of Obfuscate to cloak the gathering of vampires, for it was impossible that all of them had been Masquerading as shoppers, even the ones pulling large caliber weaponry out of their shopping bags. All told, a small army had turned up to make a show of their obedience to the wishes of both of Berlin's Ventrue princes.

The battle was then joined, and chaos ensued, Ilse flanked by Ldescu on one side and Anvil on the other, the Knights' careful phalanx falling apart into two separate lines of charging crusaders.

There was a scream, and a Nosferatu launched himself from one of the upper balconies, completely nude and monstrously deformed, but with patagia flaps under his arms like a flying squirrel. Geiger drew her bow and plugged him with three arrows in a careful grouping before he landed in one of the fountains.

Hector Sosa then raced forward on his skateboard, sword upraised, swinging at a man and beheading him in the same manner as would a knight on horseback. Bullets flew everywhere, and the sound of automatic gunfire mixed with the clash of steel, making it seem like several time periods had collapsed into one, vampires with machine pistols versus knights in armor.

The Knights, humans though most of them were, were still doing quite well against their supernatural opponents, a severed head Final Death for almost any creature. Indeed, lopping heads off seemed to be their particular specialty, and, with a whoop and holler and a bit of acrobatics, Sosa bobbed and weaved, spun once on his skateboard, then leaped high in the air, taking the head of his opponent of the moment, a Malkavian woman on rollerblades, and sending her spurting headless corpse, still standing, down one of the wheelchair access ramps. He and a human Knight then both raised the heads of their vanquished opponents and howled in triumph, knocking them together like wine goblets.

Inspired by this, Ilse supposed, Sabine screamed like one of the Valkyrie from Wagner's *Ring* cycle, and her spear began to glow. With the might worthy of Odin's daughters, she threw it to fly straight through the hearts of three men, one after the other, and pinning them to an information kiosk, the lights shorting out behind them.

They now had a distraction to end all distractions, and Ilse ran, Ldescu at her side, Anvil charging before them, using his mace to beat in the head of anyone so unfortunate as to get in their way, until they raced through the doors of the Europa Hotel. The doorman stood and stared, as did the clerks at the front desk.

Anvil began to make for the stairway, until Ldescu grabbed his sleeve. "No, they're waiting for us there." At the Magus' behest, they went straight to the elevator, pressing the button just as Kotlar, Geiger and a portion of the Knights made it into the hotel lobby.

Ldescu looked to the blond giant and pointed to the staircase, just as the elevator arrived. Kotlar nodded, and Ldescu waited politely while an elderly matron got out of the elevator, a frightened-looking pug dog in her arms. Then he,

Ilse and Anvil stepped in, the Brujah holding his bloody mace and snarling as the doors closed.

"The penthouse, if you please," the Magus said, and Ilse fit her picks into the lock at the top of the control panel, jimmying it quickly and pressing the button beside it, marked in aristocratic gold.

He placed a hand over the seam of the doors, fingers outlined in a blue glow as the elevator climbed. At last they got to the top, and he took his hand away, the doors still shut. "Open Sesame," said the Magus, and at that key phrase, the charm of locking broke and the doors slid open.

Anvil was the first to step out into the apartment and the white plush carpeting. "All right, Westphal!" the Brujah screamed. "It's payback time!"

⤞⤝

Kurt Westphal looked at the collection of Kindred who had just entered his haven and shook his head, stunned almost speechless by their sudden appearance. "Anvil? What in God's name are you doing here?"

"You owe me, Westphal, and I'm gonna take the payment from your hide." Anvil stepped further into the room, waving his blood-spattered mace about for emphasis. Behind him, Ldescu walked into the room with his usual confidence, and Ilse Decameron trailed just behind the Tremere elder, looking greatly relieved when she spotted Carl Magnuson on the couch.

Kurt ignored Anvil for the moment — hardly the easiest task he'd ever managed — and looked directly at the Tremere primogen of Berlin. "Ldescu. You at least I had expected to be smarter than this." Kurt grinned and shook his head. "You had best pray with all of your soul that whatever the Tremere are attempting succeeds. If not, you will surely find yourselves the subject of a massive Blood Hunt."

"I can't imagine why. I've done absolutely nothing, save be seen in the presence of a large group of men in armor." Ldescu flashed a counter-smile, cold and calculating. "How was I to know they were anarchs set on sacking the city?"

"Please, don't insult my intelligence. If only for old times' sake, let's not be offensive." Kurt moved before the Tremere, smiling even broader than before. "Who the hell do you think you're fooling? It was not all that long ago that the Tremere were not permitted in this city, Max. I suspect you may have brought that malediction back upon your clan." Kurt dropped the smile. "And none too soon as far as I am concerned! You disgust me, Ldescu. To think I have ever considered you an ally... I am appalled by your actions!"

Ldescu stared deeply at Kurt, searching for something that he apparently wasn't finding. "Dear God, you're serious." He actually sounded surprised. "You actually feel betrayed by me."

"Of course I do! You've set back relations between our clans by a hundred years with this preposterous action. In all the times of battle between the princes of Berlin, who listened to you when you begged for leniency on the part of the Camarilla? Certainly you know how many favors I called in to keep this town safe? You cannot be stupid enough to think my task was easy. And now you orchestrate a gross violation of the Masquerade. Regardless that they are mostly humans and a few anarchs, the Inquisition would surely come in force if the Ventrue did not stand ready to drive the memories from every citizen in the city, and you expect me to think this was simply an accident?" Kurt grabbed the Tremere by his lapels, staring in the man's face. "Get out of my sight, you pathetic fool! Leave this town immediately! The Blood Hunt will be called!"

Ldescu staggered back, as Kurt released his grip and pushed. The pleasant smile he normally sported when around Kurt was gone, and a murderous rage suffused his face. "You arrogant little dog! I'll see your ashes scattered to the four winds."

Anvil decided to remind Kurt of his presence with a swing of his mace. Despite doing his best to keep an eye on the Brujah, the mace connected. The man moved in a blur. Jing Wei cried out, "Kurt! Behind you!" at the same time the mace impacted with Kurt's left shoulder. He spun a half-circle, staggering back against the bar. Anvil stepped forward, grinning as if certain that he could not fail.

The Brujah moved in for the kill. "You've had this coming a long time, you bastard." Anvil snarled with vicious delight.

Kurt locked eyes with him, reached out with his mind and demanded the ex-primogen of Miami's obedience. *Stop where you are!* Anvil froze in place, eyes going wide with dawning terror. *Drop your weapon.* Anvil's hands opened, and the mace fell to the ground with a thud. Kurt grabbed the bottle of Louis XIII off the top of the bar and smashed the leaded crystal bottle against Anvil's face. The amber liquor mingled with blood from Anvil's wounds and ran down the Brujah's body as well as flowing into his eyes. The man clutched at his face and screamed as the alcohol spilled into his lacerations.

Kurt cocked his fist back and struck with all of his undead strength, sending the man reeling backwards to crash into the coffee table a few paces away. Magnuson leaped back, crying out as the man thrashed on the ground. Zho stared down at the fallen Kindred, his expression unreadable.

The Brujah roared as he finally got to his feet, his face broken and bloodied. "I'll kill you, Westphal! I'll tear your heart out!"

Kurt reached into his jacket and pulled out his lighter, striking the flint even as he displayed his prize. "Will you, Anvil? By all means, come for me. I am ready." The silence that followed was complete, save for the sound of Zho's subdued laughter.

Dieter Kotlar and Erika Geiger chose that moment to make their appearance along with two others dressed as preposterously as they were. All four had bloodless wounds and abrasions on their bare skin. Kurt recognized the others are Brujah, but could not immediately place their names.

Ilse apparently decided that enough was enough, because she stepped over to Ldescu just then, shaking her head. "Max, this has gone far enough. We've got what we came for — let's leave."

"No. Kurt has offended me, and he must pay the price." The Magus' voice was cold, a razor running across a tombstone. "I've still got ashes to scatter." His eyes never left Kurt, and the stare was a presence he could not ignore.

Anvil turned his head sharply at the mention of ashes.

Magnuson was the one who stopped Ldescu from carrying out his threat. Kurt was bracing himself for whatever the man would do, when Magnuson stepped forward and grabbed the Tremere by his arm. Ldescu looked away from Kurt, and Kurt breathed a sigh of relief. "Listen, Mr. Ldescu, isn't it? Don't you think it would be better if we just left? I'd rather not be around if things get messy. I'll go with you, and everything will be just fine. Right, Kurt?"

Kurt looked at the mage, at the polite desperation on his face — a look he was certain that only the British could manage properly — and nodded. "Yes. I imagine that will be sufficient for the present time."

"Right then, wot say we be off then?"

Ldescu stared at Magnuson, then turned his face towards Kurt again. For just a second, Kurt thought the man's face softened. "Yes. Let's leave." He looked past Kurt, to where Kurt knew Jing Wei was standing. "You. Come with us. You have much to explain."

Zho spoke up, moving from his position against the arm of the couch and shaking his head. "No. Jing Wei stays here. She has my protection."

"And who are you to presume so much?" Ldescu's voice dropped dangerously, and Kurt resisted the urge to seek shelter behind the bar.

"I am Thadius Zho. You know my name, and you know what I am capable of. Don't cross me."

Ldescu sneered, but his voice was far less threatening when he spoke again. "You may keep her. For now."

Kurt looked to where Ilse stood her hand reaching for and finding Magnuson's. "Ilse."

"Yes, Kurt?"

"I could have killed him, just as surely as you could have let me kill the one I love. We are even. My life boon to you is paid."

Ilse looked at him, her green eyes pale and unreadable. "Sparing a life is not the same as saving one." She paused. "Yet I will consider the debt paid. Carl's life for Jackie's."

She left the rest of the thought unsaid, but didn't need to. If Kurt were ever responsible for Carl's death, Ilse could kill Jackie, and in the cruel world of Kindred society games, this would be considered nothing more than right and proper.

Their eyes stayed locked for several more heartbeats as the Brujah and Tremere gathered together and left Kurt's haven. Ilse nodded once before she and her mortal mage left, softly closing the door behind them.

Kurt stepped over to the couch and sat down, his body finally giving in to the need to tremble. "I hate interruptions. I truly do."

>≡<

Following the Tremere was easy. Having finally met Carl Magnuson in person, Zho could now locate him virtually anywhere. At least that was what the mage told Kurt, and he had no choice but to trust the man. There was simply no way around the fact that the Tremere had caught him off-guard. One minute talking with Jing Wei about the possibility of Ilse Decameron showing up at his apartment, the next having not only Decameron, but Maxwell Ldescu and that buffoon Anvil showing up. Looking around one last time as they prepared to leave, Kurt wondered just what in God's name he was supposed to do now that his haven had been uncovered.

"Are you certain you can find the Tremere, Thadius?"

The mage smiled, and beside him Jing Wei smiled as well. "Oh, yes. Between Jing Wei, Carl and myself, we've narrowed it down to one of two locations, anyway. And there's only one of the two spots that would work for what they want to do. They needed a place where life is celebrated; the other is better suited for death."

"Which did they choose?"

"A spot in the Harz Mountains, the Brocken, a place of great power from long ago."

"Well, where else were they considering, especially that would be in the opposite direction?" The Brocken, where devils and demons were said to dwell....

"Best you not know, Kurt. The more you know, the more enemies you're likely to make." The mage's eye twinkled with amusement, and Kurt couldn't help but wonder if his leg was being pulled. Just the same, he kept his mouth shut on the subject.

"Well, then, let's be off." Kurt looked around his apartment one last time, wondering what the chances were that he'd ever see it again. He did not feel good about the odds.

Going through the complex, Kurt spent a few minutes on each floor making certain that the Ventrue he'd called upon could block the memories of anyone who had seen too much. They would remember the Final Reich causing an uproar, but there would be no memories of vampires or bloodshed. Best to bring a little order to the confusion around him and better still to cause the Brujah grief simultaneously.

❧

Outside the Europa Center, the streets were almost

completely empty, save for a few of the vampires that Kurt already knew. He stopped beside one slender man who was almost awkwardly tall, dressed in tattered jeans, a T-shirt bearing the image of Alfred E. Neumann and a top hat. He carried a black lacquered cane and an opera cloak that had seen its best days a few years back draped over one arm. In the fist of that arm, he carried a bloody chainsaw. Kurt nodded and watched as the man picked up a broken bastard sword left behind by the Knights who had invaded the building. "Hello, Ozzy."

"Kurt, when you said they planned to violate the Masquerade, I had no idea..."

"Yes. I really didn't expect the Reich to assist them myself. The damnable Tremere seem intent on destroying a thousand years' worth of secrecy." He looked over his shoulder towards Jing Wei. "No offense, my dear."

"None taken, Kurt."

"We believe we know where the Tremere will show themselves, Ozzy. In the Harz Mountains, at the Brocken. Can we count on you for assistance?"

"The Brujah tore three of mine apart, Kurt. One of them took Druscilla's head away from her shoulders." He paused, motioning with the chainsaw hidden halfway under his opera cloak. "Persia has not stopped crying since she heard about it. Yes, you can count on the Malkavians. Even without the destruction of our own, Gilbert Duane has spoken well of how you aided him in the recent attempt to discredit him. For that reason alone you would have our help." The cultured voice had changed in the last few seconds, and Kurt was now standing next to a slightly broader man, better dressed and a few years older. While he knew he still spoke with J. Oswald Hyde-White, he knew also that he was speaking with Dr. Henry Jekyll. Ozzy was decidedly an interesting individual, and almost always enlightening in one way or another, but Kurt dearly hoped his Mr. Edward Hyde persona stayed quiescent for the next few nights. Hyde was too unpredictable and far too violent.

"Thank you, Ozzy."

"You are certainly welcome, Kurt. But please, call me Henry."

"Henry it is. Will you spread the word? Can you meet with us in Frankfurt tomorrow night? Early tomorrow night?"

"Consider the situation taken care of. My best to your lovely lady, Jacqueline."

"I — I'll tell her, Henry. Have a good night."

Kurt moved on, taking Zho and Jing Wei with him. Charnas had disappeared again, for which Kurt was grateful. Emergency visits with both Gustav Breidenstein and Wilhelm Waldburg were necessary, as was a phone call to Democritus. All three were civil, but only barely. Had it not been for his importance in handling the Tremere problem, Kurt had little doubt that he would be completely ignored. After the discussion with his sire, the two princes were asked to join forces yet again, in an effort to remove the danger to the Masquerade brought on by the minions of Etrius. Gustav, with his well-known bias against the Tremere, was more than glad to assist under the circumstances. A few hours later, after meeting with both princes and discussing the situation with select members from both the primogen of the East and the primogen of the West, Kurt and his associates departed for Frankfurt.

The night seemed to go on forever, a silence stretching further and further between them all. Kurt had no desire to talk to anyone save Jackie, and that was not likely to happen.

Friday, April 30, The Brocken — *Walpurgisnacht*

The sun set, and the other members of Council of Seven arrived at the Vienna chantry, or at least two of them did: Abetorius and Xavier de Cincaō.

Xavier de Cincaō was a stunning man, hard-muscled and lean, with dark skin and dark hair, but startling crystal-pale blue eyes. A Spaniard of partially Moorish descent — or a Moor of partially Spanish blood, depending on how you looked at it — he stood naked to the waist, whether in preparation for the coming ritual or because this was his usual mode of dress, Ilse was unsure. Beside him, almost draped over him, was a Peruvian woman of feline grace and matchless beauty, who made Ilse think of jaguars and deadly jungle cats. As she'd arrived with him by way of the House of Doors, she was no doubt also bound to the South American Councilor by ties of blood.

Abetorius, the Councilor who ruled Istanbul and little else, came in by the front door with no fanfare or retinue. He was, in two words, bitter and jaded, and these emotions were writ into his face with lines centuries deep. He'd dressed in the clothes of a mystic or holy man, though he did not look in the least serene or contemplative — the word *tormented* would probably more easily apply. He seemed willing to go along with

Etrius' experiment for the same reason he'd no doubt gone along with Goratrix's before: It was simpler than suicide, if just because someone else had already done the planning and the preparations. Atop his shoulder he had a small familiar of some sort, a miniature gargoyle with leathery wings and scaly green skin, and though it didn't move much more than one made of stone, it still possessed more life and animation than its master.

Of the other four Councilors, Grimgroth and Thomas Wyncham were opposed, while Elaine de Calinot had abstained. Meerlinda, the Preceptor of North America, had sided with Etrius, but was said to be off arranging things with Melsinde, the mistress of the *Hexenhaus* and leader of the ancient circle of witches who held the Brocken, the greatest node of magical power in Europe. This, it turned out, was the Melsinde that the Hermetic wizard, Aries Michaels, had mentioned to Carl at Etrius' *Kaffeeklatsch*, and the white-bearded gentleman seemed to have been instrumental in formalizing relations with the *Hexenhaus* coven, as the Brocken was crucial to the success of the ritual.

Michaels was busy talking with Etrius, while the rest of the Kindred of the Vienna chantry were lined up in the Grand Hall preparatory to the wizard's Unlocking of the Gate.

"Why is the Brocken so important?" Ilse asked Carl, standing next to her. They'd hardly had a moment to speak with one another since his rescue, the English mage closeted with Etrius or Etrie or Master Harry or Dr. Dee behind one door or the other of the House of Secrets.

Carl grimaced, "The Brocken's the bloody biggest magical site in the world if you want to do a fertility rite, or at least for Hermetic magic and witchcraft, and that's about all I know." He shrugged. "You Tremere may be able to do your magic wherever you please, but us mages have to be a bit pickier, and we're the one's picking up the other half of your spell."

"So you're going along with the rite?"

"Of course, love. You think I'd want to disappoint all these people? Eh, that's right, let's call off the wedding and upset all these nice vampires who went out and bought new suits and dresses just for the occasion." He chuckled, sparks dancing in each mismatched eye. "Listen, Ilse, whatever else may have happened, being kidnapped by Westphal cemented one thing — my ancestor, Zho, is a twit, and I almost like the demon he admits he sold my soul to more than I do him. At least Charnas doesn't apologize in between the 'I've made every mistake a man can make, so listen to me' speeches. Zho's also half-blind, and I mean more than just because he gave his left eye to a demon, along with your previous incarnation's life and my soul, not to mention my six brothers' souls, my dad's, and a substantial portion of the bloody family tree's. Zho went on and on about how if Etrius dies, Charnas gets my soul and the souls of all my other relatives without bothering to think that our mutual umpteen-great-grandad has been practicing magic a mite longer than either of us. Etrius noticed this complication too and came up with a little twist around it."

Carl grinned, his odd eyes still laughing. "Etrius is going to unite with me at the same time as I unite with Etrie, since the Mandrake at the heart of the homunculus is both immortal and quite a bit older than any other person on God's good green earth, at least as is supposed to be here. And if we do this rite right, it'll both save my soul and resurrect the lot of you, and the only bad thing — if you can call it bad — that will come out of it is that Thadius Zho will get his comeuppence, and the Lord of Misrule will take back Zho's immortality and whatever other perks he sold me and the rest of his descendants out for, including his imp's own purple little self. It may not be the kindest thing to do to Zho, but it's no more than the dirty rotter deserves. Besides, I rather like the idea of being an immortal mage in a world of magic, especially since once I do the trick of merging with Etrie, I get the next world's model for a body."

Ilse nodded and, since Carl seemed willing, gave him a hug. The changes that would come about were frightening, but more than that, were wonderful and bewildering.

Aries Michaels was got up in full Hermetic regalia and began his invocation in Latin, Ilse translating in her head: "House of Secrets, House of Shadows, House of Mystery, House of Fear — Open the Doorways of the Forgotten, the old and ancient magics from when the world was young and the portals between the Death and Life."

After her shock at realizing Michaels' invocation was an ancient variant on the Rite of the Iron Key — a formula the Order of Hermes had no doubt preserved even after House Tremere seceded — Ilse also realized that the Unlocking of the Gate was also the beginning of the great rite, preparing the Kindred for the resurrection that was to come. The doors at the end of hall swung open, but instead of leading to the grand ritual room, they now opened out onto a mountainside. The Kindred filed forward, Ilse with Carl beside her, until he dropped aside as they passed through the Gateway, emerging out onto the top of the Brocken.

The witches' mountaintop was a marvelous thing, covered with grass and spring wildflowers, poppies and gentians, glowing in the light of the enormous bonfire at the crest of the hill, a cleared dancing ground to one side, a Maypole with ribbons and maidens' crowns to the other.

Ilse proceeded up the hill alongside Dieter Kleist, who was frantically scribbling in his notebook with a pencil, chronicling everything he saw, and there was much to see. Witches and Hermetic wizards had obviously been busy all day, the air sparkling with magic and the lines of spells, ribbons set down to create the boundaries of thaumaturgic figures, and other patterns cut into the very turf.

Around the ritual ground, almost encircling it, was an immense hunting lodge, beamed and half-timbered, brown on white, with runes and hex signs formed by the placement of beams and crossbeams. Gables and dormer windows abounded, with elaborate wooden gingerbread trim and stained-glass jewels. Rippled diamond panes in all the windows reflected the firelight, giving the *Hexenhaus* the appearance of some epic Christmas confection left out and allowed to go to springtime, grass and wildflowers sprouting in the cracks of the slate roof after the frosting snow had melted.

The third Councilor, Meerlinda, was there to greet them. She was a grave, beautiful woman apparently in her late thirties and reminded Ilse of a younger, thinner version of Cassandra, who, Ilse considered, might actually be a descendant, as there was a strong resemblance.

But the resemblance was stronger yet to Melsinde, their host. The great witch appeared to be nothing more than a simple peasant girl, pretty, but hardly a raving beauty, with sun-browned skin and long, lightly curled chestnut hair, scarcely more than seventeen and just entering the first flush of womanhood. She was dressed in a grass-stained cotton gown and apron embroidered with wildflowers, a crown of their living counterparts in her hair. Ilse was certain that if she looked with the Monocle of Clarity, she would see a far different story and likely one that would drive her mad. She wished she could covertly take a picture of the woman, but knew the witch wouldn't take kindly to it. Instead, Ilse sneaked a glance at Dieter Kleist's sketchbook, who, in honor of the occasion, had brought out a huge tome filled with Bristol board, easily three feet across. For Melsinde, he had begun a portrait of the Triple Goddess, Hecate, Trivia of the Crossroads, naming her a dozen times in the margins and depicting her as Mother, Maiden and Crone, with flowers, nuts and leaves twined in her hair.

Once they were all standing before the crest of the hill, Melsinde raised her wand to the assembled company. "Good friends, sweet lovers and valued allies, *Das Hexenhaus* and my Circle bid you welcome to the Brocken this Beltane, and thank you for gracing us with the opportunity to enact this great rite and usher in the next age of the world. The doorways to the memories of death and decay are closed—" She gestured back to the *Hexenhaus*, and two witches, kirtled in brown and green, pulled the doors at the center of the crescent of the lodge shut, closing the Gateway to the House of Secrets and Vienna, "—and we entreat Venus and her nymphs to bestow their blessings on us, calling for the Venusberg to lend us Her power on this night. The pathways of light and life are open, we salute the changing moon, and let us dance to the return of spring!"

Melsinde turned about, dancing up the hill with her wand, and music started up, fiddles and zithers, woodwinds, and even a few accordions — yes, Ilse had to remember, whatever else, she was in Germany — but she'd hardly expected one the world's greatest rites of magic, and the legendary Witches' Sabbat, to begin with a polka.

Nonetheless, the rhythm was infectious, and pretty soon everyone had lost their clothes, including the Hermetic magicians, who, in preparation for this eventuality, had already painted themselves with magical seals in woad. Ilse cast aside her dress, and, wearing nothing more than her silver necklace and the Iron Key, danced with Carl, feeling alive for the first time in ages. The Witch Queen called the tune, and Ilse switched off, taking a turn with Etrius, then Xavier de Cincaõ, then others, most of whom she had never even met. Witches and magicians flew, actually flew, in on broomsticks, rakes, or milking stools. Some of them rode on horses or goats, and there was even one woman on a sport bike, all of them disrobing and joining the dance, a few in aerial choreography.

Melsinde then came to the center of the ring and clapped her hands, naked but for the flowers in her hair, and the music and dancing stopped. "Who shall come with me?" she asked. "Who will be the Beltane King? Who will come with me to sample the delights of Venus and reconsecrate spring?"

It seemed any number of the males, and no few females, were ready to take her up on the offer, but she spun about until she came to Etrius, whose sole clothing was his chain of office and his steward's key. "I choose you to be my companion on this night of nights! Come and be King of May!"

It was elaborately rehearsed, but unless Ilse had known better, she would have thought the choice was as spontaneous as it seemed. Melsinde took the Councilor by the hand, a young woman with a young man, but both of them ancient souls, and the music started up again, a wild and discordant tune of the dying of the year. The witch grabbed him close to her, spinning and waltzing him about until he fetched up against the Maypole, and the music stopped again.

"With briars I bind you," the witch queen called, "with briars and nettle and the thorns of winter. You are the old king, and you must die to make way for the new."

From her daisy chains and dandelions, Melsinde somehow produced a rope of thorns, wrapping it around the Councilor, binding him tight no matter how greatly he struggled or how loudly he screamed. The witch then silenced him with a kiss, coming back a minute later, her mouth bloody.

Melsinde clapped her hands, and the music started up again, a slow dance tune with a dark edge. The witches and warlocks skipped forward, seemingly at random, but then taking up the maidens' crowns that hung in a wreath just above Etrius' head, unwinding the ribbons, men going clockwise, women dancing widdershins, over and under, the music weaving its spell as the ribbons wove a prison of both magic and thread, binding Etrius to the pole as the bonfire blazed higher. Ilse knew that he would be cast upon it once the rites were done.

Meerlinda, Xavier de Cincaõ and Abetorius then signaled the Tremere to order, and Ilse linked hands with the two Kindred nearest her, Master Harry to her left, Dr. Dee to her right. Together they began the Chant of Union, hands linked, moving in a circle, widdershins around the outer perimeter of the ritual of the mortal witches and magicians. The Chant was usually only performed at the opposite side of the Wheel of the Year, Samhain, what mortals knew as Halloween, but it was done now, calling through the blood of each of Clan Tremere and through the blood of each of those bound to them. Allies from other clans were joined into the circle, including Anvil, Smudge, and Kleist — his notebook set aside for once — and the light from the witches' bonfire gleamed in the eyes of the Kindred as the clarion call went out invoking the power of the night, and unifying the minds of those of the blood of House Tremere.

The cry rose and fell, and then the voice of Etrius rang forth, at the center of the ritual: *WE CALL YOU TOGETHER IN THE NAME OF TREMERE!*

WE CALL YOU IN THE NAME OF MAGIC! cried Meerlinda.

WE CALL YOU IN THE NAME OF POWER! cried Abetorius.

WE CALL YOU IN THE NAME OF UNITY! cried Xavier de Cincaõ.

WE CALL FOR THIS MEETING TO DISBAND! cried the souls of Thomas Wyncham and Grimgroth as one. **WE HAVE NOT CALLED YOU! THIS IS NOT THE WILL OF TREMERE!**

SINCE WHEN HAS IT EVER BEEN? came the voice of another soul. Goratrix, the wicked Councilor who had authored their vampirism with his impious experiment and who had abandoned the clan to join the Sabbat and start his own line. *TREMERE IS AN OLD, DEAD FOOL, AND THE ONLY WISDOM HE EVER TAUGHT IS THAT POWER IS ALL THAT MATTERS.*

There was no response from the soul of Tremere, though there had been occasionally in years past, and then there was a pause as the souls of the Tremere reached out to one another, not in unity against the tainted souls of the Sabbat, as when they usually joined in the Chant of Union, but just to familiarize themselves for this extraordinary event.

I AM LISTENING, came one last voice of power. Elaine de Calinot, the Councilor of Africa. *PLEASE, CONTINUE.*

ETRIUS HAS CALLED YOU TOGETHER TO DESTROY THE CLAN! cried the united voice of Grimgroth/Wyncham. **DO NOT LISTEN TO HIS LIES!**

There was a dark chuckle from Grimgroth. *IF THE COWARD WISHES TO DESTROY THE CLAN, THEN FOR ONCE, HE HAS MY SUPPORT.*

Etrius replied, *I DO NOT CALL YOU TO DESTROY YOU — I CALL YOU TO SAVE YOU! WE HAVE DEVISED A RITE WHEREBY THE CHARM OF GORATRIX CAN BE BROKEN AND EACH OF US MAY LIVE AGAIN. FREE TO WALK AGAIN IN THE SUN! FREE TO LOVE! FREE TO LIVE!*

YOU SHALL LOSE EVERYTHING! cried Wyncham/ Grimgroth. **YOU SHALL BE WEAK AND MORTAL! YOU SHALL DIE!**

YOU SHALL NOT! MAGIC WILL RETURN TO THE WORLD, AND THE OLD CHARMS WILL WORK AGAIN. WE HAVE THE AID OF OTHERS TO ASSURE THIS. THE WORLD SHALL HAVE MAGIC, AND WE SHALL BE MAGES AGAIN!

LISTEN TO ETRIUS, said Meerlinda and de Cincaõ as one. **HIS COUNSEL IS WISE, AND HIS SPELL IS SOUND, FAR MORE SOUND THAN GORATRIX'S. ETRIUS HAS DEVISED A METHOD TO WASH AWAY THE STAIN OF INNOCENT BLOOD, TO EXPUNGE THE MARK OF CAINE. HE COULD DO THIS FOR HIMSELF ALONE IF HE WISHED, BUT HE INSTEAD OFFERS THIS GIFT TO ALL. DO NOT BE FOOLS AND REFUSE IT.**

ALL, EH? came the thought from Goratrix. *WHAT LITTLE CHARM DID YOU DO, ETRIUS?*

I STOLE THE EYE OF SAULOT, said Etrius, *AND I DID NOT DESTROY ALL OF MY MORTAL DESCENDANTS.*

Shock rippled through the web of spirits, even the Sabbat, who had not yet been cast out of the gestalt. *I HAVE FOUND ONE, A MAGE, A SEVENTH SON OF A SEVENTH SON, AS I AM A SEVENTH SON OF A SEVENTH SON AND THE SEVENTH OF THE COUNCIL OF SEVEN. WITH THIS MAGE TO LINK TO, AND WITH THE EYE OF SAULOT AS THE EYE OF THE PYRAMID, WE CAN DO THIS GREAT WORK. I HAVE ALSO GAINED ANOTHER TOKEN OF POWER — THE MANDRAKE, THE **FIRST** MANDRAKE, GOD'S STUDY FOR US ALL, WHO PREDATES THE RACE OF MAN AND WHO WAS WATERED WITH THE BLOOD OF ABEL, THE BLOOD OF THE FIRST INNOCENT, THE FIRST AND GREATEST OF THE WORLD'S SACRIFICES.*

WHAT, EXACTLY, DO YOU PROPOSE, ETRIUS? Elaine de Calinot's voice was calm and mild, tinged with curiosity.

THE MANDRAKE IS NOW THE CORE OF MY HOMUNCULUS AND THUS ALSO HOLDS MY BLOOD, AND THROUGH ME, THE BLOOD OF CAINE AS WELL AS ABEL. THE EYE OF SAULOT IS MY SOUL GEM AND CONTAINS BOTH MY BLOOD AND THE BLOOD OF SAULOT.

MY MORTAL DESCENDANT, CARL MAGNUSON, SHALL DRINK MY BLOOD UNTIL THERE IS NO MORE. ALL MY POWER SHALL FLOW INTO HIM, YET MY SOUL SHALL FLOW INTO THE GEM WHICH WAS THE EYE OF SAULOT, THE HEALER. CARL SHALL THEN PERFORM A RITE OF TRUE MAGIC, TAKING THE GEM AS HIS THIRD EYE WHILE MERGING WITH THE LAST OF MY BLOOD, THE FLESH THAT CLOTHES THE MANDRAKE ROOT. THE SYMPATHY SHALL MAKE US ALL ONE, AND WE SHALL BE REBORN AS A NEW CREATURE, IMMORTAL AND WITH ALL THE POWERS OF THE THREE. THE BLOOD OF CAINE WILL BE

UNITED WITH THE BLOOD OF ABEL, AND THE MARK OF CAINE WILL BE WASHED AWAY BY THE BLOOD OF THE FIRST MARTYR AND INNOCENT. BY THE ANCIENT LAWS, THE POWER WHICH RESIDES IN MY BLOOD WILL BIND TOGETHER ALL WHO HAVE TASTED IT, AND THE CHARM OF LIFE WILL COME TO EACH PART OF ME, EACH WHO IS OF MY BLOOD. AT DAWN THE NEXT DAY, WE WILL AWAKEN AS MAGES, ALL OF US, ALIVE AND WITH ALL THE POWER WE HELD BEFORE, AND MORE. MAGIC AND LIFE SHALL RETURN WITH SPRINGTIME.

There was a long pause, then Elaine de Calinot inquired, IF YOU CAN DO THIS THING, WHY DO YOU NEED ASK OUR PERMISSION?

BECAUSE HE'S ETRIUS, said Goratrix, and if there was a way for soul to sneer, his did.

BECAUSE IT IS RIGHT TO ASK, AND BECAUSE THE CHARM WILL NOT WORK IF YOU OPPOSE ME. A PYRAMID THAT WILL NOT SUPPORT ITSELF WILL CRUMBLE, AND A BODY THAT FIGHTS AGAINST ITSELF WILL DIE.

TRUE, YET I SHALL STILL ABSTAIN, said Elaine de Calinot, BUT I WILL BE INTERESTED TO SEE THE RESULTS NEVERTHELESS.

I SAY YEA, said Meerlinda

AS DO I, said Xavier de Cincaõ.

Abetorius' voice was long in coming. AYE HERE AS WELL.

I SAY **NAY**, said Grimgroth. YOU BETRAY US ALL, ETRIUS. YOU, WHO HAVE SET SUCH A GREAT STORE BY YOUR LOYALTY.

I SAY NAY AS WELL, said Thomas Wyncham.

DO I GET A VOTE? Goratrix chuckled with dark humor. IF I DO, I VOTE TO JOIN ETRIUS IN HIS EXPERIMENT, AS HE DID IN MINE. IF IT SUCCEEDS, THERE WILL BE

*LITTLE ROOM FOR VAMPIRES IN HIS NEW WORLD,
AND IF IT FAILS, THERE IS NOTHING TO BE LOST BY
THE SABBAT. IT WILL MAKE FOR AN AMUSING
EVENING.*

WHAT AN EASY WAGER, said Elaine de Calinot. *AND
YOU CALL ETRIUS THE COWARD, GORATRIX. YOUR
SOUL QUAKES IN TERROR AT THE THOUGHT OF HIM
SUCCEEDING AND YOU STILL REMAINING IN YOUR
GRAVE.*

Goratrix did not respond, but then the power filtered down
along the chain, each soul making its decision, and the gestalt
came to a resolution: **YES. WE SHALL DO THIS THING.**

The chain then broke, and Ilse opened her eyes.

And to what a sight. The Brocken had been transformed,
and the field of wildflowers glistened in the moonlight, each
flower seeming to glow from within as they had in the
memories in Etrius' dream, the whole mountaintop transmuted
into something pure and primal, burgeoning with life and love
— the Mountain of Venus, the Venusberg. The witches had
summoned it, a place of legend superimposed atop the
Brocken. The *Hexenhaus* become the Palace of Venus, a manse
of living wildflowers. Nymphs and satyrs danced and frolicked
with the witches and magicians in the dancing circle. It was
beautiful and wonderful —

Then a shot rang out, and one of the nymphs screamed
and fell into the bonfire, wailing.

The music stopped, and everyone turned to look. Atop the
easternmost gable of the Mansion of the Moon was a man in
a tie-dyed straightjacket, a deer rifle raised to pick off another
of the revelers.

Melsinde raised her wand, and it was as if time itself had
stopped. The witch queen, though still appearing as the simple
peasant girl, now glowed with the power of the Goddess, no
longer in her benign and beautiful phase, but a terrifying figure
of rage, hair floating in a cloud about her, her eyes burning

with silver flame. *"The circle has been profaned!"* she cried, then looked to the madman on the roof. *"And the transgressor will pay..."*

She looked about, as if seeing something beyond the house and the mountaintop, even magically transformed by the glamour of the Venusberg. ***"All** of them will **pay**..."*

➤❖◄

The meager forces Kurt Westphal had managed to gather surrounded the lodge, watching the proceedings in stony silence. Ozzy Hyde-White stood beside him, leaning against the chainsaw he'd collected the night before; it was the first time Kurt had ever seen him without his cane. There were another dozen or more Malkavians with them, easily spotted by the tie-dyed straightjackets that each of them wore — the Straightjacket Dancing Club of West Berlin, known to Kindred and kine alike as a dangerous group to toy with. Another dozen Ventrue stood with them, armed with a variety of weapons. Despite his wishes, the Nosferatu had opted not to show themselves. Outside the influence of the powerful ritual, Zho and Charnas waited for Kurt's return. The powerful chantry of the Brocken was well-guarded against the forces of evil, and there was simply nothing to be done for them.

Kurt was almost amused by the knowledge that neither of his companions could enter the area. Thoughts of *Faust* and the man's deal with Mephistopheles had haunted him since his realization that they were headed into the place where Goethe had set his play. To find that demons were not permitted actually relieved him while also leaving his forces lessened. At least he still had Jing Wei, though at the moment all she could do was give the signal for them to start the attack.

Ozzy looked over to Kurt, "It's an impressive lot of us out here, Kurt, but there are members of the Tremere Council of

Seven in there, and for all we know Tremere himself. How in the name of Caine do you expect us win against those odds?"

Kurt stared at the light creeping from below them in the amphitheater where the ceremonies were just beginning, shaking his head. "If it comes to actual fighting, Ozzy, I shall strongly suggest retreating. All I need from you and yours is a distraction. A very big distraction. I'll take care of the rest." He spoke with a confidence he did not feel. The thought of breaking into the crowd below was terrifying him.

"You're sure you want to go this alone, then?"

"Yes. But if I should fail, Ozzy, I'd greatly appreciate your replacing me. The Soul Gem of Etrius must be ours if we're to stop this madness."

"I won't let you down, Kurt. We've both got too much at stake in this affair. I don't think I could hope to stop the Dancing Club now, anyway. They want revenge for what happened last night, and they'll take it with or without me."

Jing Wei spoke up, her voice commanding and urgent. "Now, Kurt. You must attack now."

"Well, no time like the present. Let's get this show on the road."

While the noises of revelry came from the crescent-shaped building, they sounded too distant for the short space that separated the celebrants and Kurt. He hoped the sound was muffled in both directions, because the piercing whistle that erupted from Ozzy's mouth was close to deafening. The Malkavian called out to his companions, demanding a game of "Hide and Seek" for the benefit of the Tremere.

A few moments later, the cries began from inside the lodge. All around Kurt and Ozzy, the Kindred they had gathered began spreading out, the tie-dyed maniacs moving among the trees and disappearing into the darkness. From time to time one would appear, only to disappear a second later. Hide and seek, indeed.

The mages and Tremere within the oddly distorted field

of sound began looking around, and one frail girl pointed to a straightjacketed Malkavian. The man she'd pointed to exploded in a blaze of blue flames, a walking screaming funeral pyre that fell after only a few seconds, but continued to writhe for what seemed like an eternity. The Malkavians moved forward as one, rifles, submachine guns and even a flame thrower sending arcs of ammunition and tongues of flame into the area around the heart of the witches' ritual. Vampires fled the burning fires, giving in to the Rötschreck, and the mages and nymphs scattered as well, fleeing from the deadly hail of bullets and liquid fire.

Ozzy nodded to Kurt, and both of them plunged forward towards the heart of their enemy's camp. Even as they moved, Ozzy White blurred for a second, seeming to grow in size and bulk. His already wild hair grew shaggier still, his face became brutal, and his laughter was several octaves lower than usual. Mr. Edward Hyde became the dominant personality, and the words he spoke as he looked at Kurt sent icy chills running down his spine. "Master Therion sends his regards, Westphal. Let's stomp a few Tremere, what say you?"

Kurt poured on the speed, barely keeping pace with the madman beside him. The sound of Hyde's chainsaw screaming into motion was a battle cry that could not be ignored. Tremere and mage alike turned to see what demon was barreling their way, and several fled from the maniac even as he cut down the first creature too stupid to get away from him.

The path the fleeing people cleared was easier to maneuver through, and Kurt saw the object of his desire within seconds — Etrius stood bound to a pole, covered with seemingly countless ribbons connected to wreaths. Against his chest, the Soul Gem gleamed redly in the light of the bonfire. The ancient vampire was powerless, and Kurt ripped the chain of office from around his neck with ease. In the chaos surrounding them, Etrius' screams were buried beneath a thousand other sounds.

Never pausing to think about what he had done, Kurt pivoted around and ran back towards the area he had just left. His foot caught on something as he moved, and he fell to the ground, nearly dropping his prize at the same time. He looked towards his feet, and there he saw the form of Etrius, only far too small to be the true Councilor of the Tremere. The tiny form looked upon him with dread, and Kurt seized it in his hand before regaining his feet. It called out to him, but he could not hear the words, would not hear them. Small hands pummeled against his finger with little effect, and Kurt increased his pace again, hurdling the prone form of a naked young man. He did not allow himself to think of the wetness he slid across as he landed on the other side of the body.

He bolted around the side of the lodge, slowing and stopping only when he reached Zho, where the man waited in the shadows. There was no preamble. Zho held out his hand, and Kurt set the Eye of Saulot in the mage's grasp. He presented his second prize and watched as Zho's single eye blazed with greed.

Zho then writhed in pain and fell to the ground, mouth stretched in a silent scream. Behind him stood a second Zho, a grim and brooding image of the mage. Kurt looked down at his fallen ally, only to see Charnas where Zho had been. The real mage reached down and grabbed both the small man and the necklace of office from the imp's hand.

"For the last time, Charnas. Never imitate me again."

Before the demon could reply, a voice cried out, filled with enough sorrow for a thousand years, a voice that sounded as lost as Kurt had felt since Jackie walked away the night before, one word distorted by grief: **"EETTTRRRRRIIIIIIEEEEEE!!!!"**

And that's when all hell broke loose atop the Brocken.

➣€

The Inquisition had told of the Witches' Sabbat being a place of chaos, damnation, and horror, and with the crazed vampires storming the ritual grounds, it had become just that. The madness network of Malkavian dementia had somehow allowed them to pierce the glamour which Ilse had been told hid the true peak of the Brocken from campers and hikers, and Ilse knew with a horrifying certainty that Crowley was responsible. The madman knew magic and hated both vampire and mage alike — whichever he truly was.

"Play with Mr. Hyde, witchy-girl!" roared the maniac, all his teeth pointed like a barracuda's. "See what Talbot's chainsaw can do to rich witch-bitches like you!"

"Play with fire!" Ilse screamed and grabbed handfuls of hot coals with her mind, hurling them straight from the bonfire at the man and his top hat and billowing opera cloak.

A vampire's vulnerability to fire was legendary, but so was the ability of the mad to ignore everything but their own crazed world, and the Mr. Hyde creature continued on his course. The coals landed in a line, blazing like fallen stars on Hollywood's Walk of Fame, creating instead a Walk of Flame, a trail of hellish breadcrumbs before the *Hexenhaus*.

Ilse fell backwards, tripping over a root, holding up one hand in a desperate gesture of warding, for she had no talismans or tools save the Iron Key about her neck, but then Lazarus stepped into the madman's path. While naked as the rest of the participants in the ritual, the Miami primogen had retained his serpent-headed cane, and he blocked the madman's chainsaw with the ebony wand, holding it in the manner of a quarterstaff. Etheric flashes and sparks flew up as the two weapons clashed, the enchanted wood holding against the chattering blade. The serpent's head came alive and spat venom.

Ilse rolled out of the way, seeing Sarah Cobbler play a Gandalfesque Zorro, cutting a pentagram into a man's chest with an elaborate flick of her sharpened foil. The cloth of the tie-dyed straightjacket fell away in a star, and the wound began to smoke. The man screamed, mouth open in a rictus of pain and terror, then he began to be eaten away from within until nothing was left but a husk of ashes and glowworm fire.

Xavier de Cincaõ and Aries Michaels had linked arms, eyes as intense and postures as choreographed as if they were doing the tango, weaving some spell in the air about them. de Cincaõ's woman had disappeared, and in her place a huge jaguar leaped straight onto the roof of the Witch House, bounding up the slick slate shingles to score open the face of a woman in another of the tie-died straightjackets. The woman's flamethrower tumbled down the roof, spitting arcs of fire into the air.

Sarah Cobbler rushed in to join Lazarus, and as Mr. Hyde's enchanted chainsaw shattered the Englishwoman's fencing foil into so many bits of metal, the Tremere elder swung his cane around, and the serpent's head connected with the Malkavian's shoulder. The chainsaw fell from the psychopath's hands as his right arm withered and hung useless, and then the brute seemed to shrink in his clothes, becoming a tall, skinny young man, still in a top hat and opera cloak, and he took a step back. "Oh, dear," said the new personality, who Ilse took to be Jekyll. "This has gotten a bit sticky."

He turned and ran, leaping astride one of the tethered goats and flying it off over the gables of the *Hexenhaus*, rope and stake dangling behind, the hijacked goat bleating in terror. Several witches and magicians took off after him, and then came the scream: "*EETTTRRRRRIIIIIIEEEEEE!!!!*"

Etrie. The homunculus. The Mandrake root that would save the souls of Carl and all his family, not to mention the world.

The scream came from Councilor Etrius, still bound to the Maypole, and Ilse looked around, seeing the altar table and the tiny throne, which had held the homunculus only moments before now overturned. Carl lay on the ground before it, horribly wounded. He was aided and guarded by Meerlinda, while beside them, Melsinde floated in the air, blazing with the power of the Goddess, the air crackling around her as the bullets intended for the Queen of the Witches turned to rose petals and fell to the ground.

Despite the rose petals, Venus was not a peaceful goddess, and her aspect in Melsinde was even less so. "I want *blood!*" the Witch screamed, the wind rising up and whipping her hair. "I will have blood! *NOW!*"

A storm gathered above Her, the elements reflecting Her mood, lightning crackling in the dark air. She pointed at one man, and only the fact that he still had clothes on identified him as one of the enemy. Lightning stabbed the ground before him, but the witch's weather control had not missed, only served to underscore Her wrath. The man looked up, fangs bared, but the Goddess' eyes blazed and he fell to the ground, screaming in terror.

A pack of mænads descended upon him, maidens of unearthly beauty, ripping him apart with tooth and claw, drinking his blood. The mænads then filled a drinking horn with the vitæ and brought it back to their Goddess. The cup rose up into the air and roses sprouted where the blood spilled as she drained it.

Melsinde snarled then, casting the chalice aside, and the roses came alive, twisting and twining over each eave and gable of the Mansion of Venus, a Sleeping Beauty hedge-wall of briars and thorns that snagged and caught, trapping invaders and spearing thorns through the hearts. The trapped Kindred screamed as their thorny prison wove tighter, then screamed no more, staked, and the briar hedge began to drain essence from them, blood red roses blooming on every vine as the bodies withered away into mummified corpses and skeletons. Those Kindred not already caught by the thorns fled in terror, the ones within the circle of brambles taking the last refuge they had left — the Witch House.

"Into the Manse!" screamed the Goddess. "Bring me their hearts!"

Seeing Carl lying upon the ground, Ilse was filled with a fierce blood fury. Then she saw a target worthy of her anger — Thadius Zho. The dark mage, the man who had murdered her, ran back around the side of the witches' lodge, fleeing the questing tendrils of wood and thorn, his imp capering and turning cartwheels at his side.

Ilse ran forward, her hands curved into claws, intending to rend him as fiercely as the mænads had rent their victim. The rose canes parted for her as she reached them, the tendrils of thorns whipping up one after the other like an archway of swords and falling closed in her wake.

She slammed the door open that Charnas and Zho had taken and followed the stench of sulfur and lavender, her senses heightened to a fever pitch. She heard screams throughout the corridors of the witches' dark and twisted lodge as the magicians and sorcerers found their intended victims and those who had profaned the sacred mysteries met their fitting end.

At last she came to a door painted with a linden tree and doves, without a lock, yet barred against her. She slammed against it with the full force of her mind and fury, the bar giving way, and then strode through, slamming it behind herself and sealing it with the hex sign Astrid and Cassandra had used.

Zho and Charnas were there, Etrie clutched in the mage's hand.

"Lisle!" cried the tiny creature. "Lisle!"

"Give him to me," Ilse growled.

"You might as well, Thadius," Charnas said, sitting atop a dresser. "After all, you're gonna die pretty soon, or at least wish you could. This House hates you, and you don't have a bolt-hole — unless you want to make another bargain and give me your soul."

"I do not want another bargain, Charnas."

"You don't? Why not?" The imp flipped over on the

dresser-top to lounge on his stomach, then cradled his chin on his interlaced fingers and grinned. "You got immortality, didn't you? What, you don't like the idea of immortality as a heap of little bloody pieces after Ilse gets through with you, not to mention what the witches outside want to do or that *nasty* Goddess of theirs. Hell hath no fury—"

"Shut up, Charnas!"

"It's gonna *hurt*..."

The mage collapsed to the floor, the pride and anger draining out of him at the imp's horrible truths. The homunculus pried himself from Zho's hand and ran across the floor to hug Ilse around the ankle. At the touch of the tiny arms, Ilse felt her fury ebb somewhat, or at least gentle as she did not want to harm the sweet little creature, the repository of Etrius' innocence. She reached down and picked him up, cradling him in her hands to protect him from any possible harm.

Ilse then saw Etrius' chain of office clutched in the mage's other hand, the Eye of Saulot still set in the center stud. "Give me the Soul Gem, Thadius."

"No," he said softly.

"Give it to me."

"*No.*" He spoke with quiet desperation, opposing her with the last of his power and will.

Ilse felt the blood fury return. "Do you wish to destroy everything? Everyone's last chance for happiness?"

"Gwyneth — Ilse — No, please, you don't understand..."

The blood burned behind her eyes, and she saw the dark marks on his soul. "Of course I don't understand. I may have loved you once, but I don't know what could have possessed me to do anything so stupid. Now give me the gem. Carl may be dead, but if not, there's still time to finish the rite and save him along with everyone else."

"No, you don't understand." The dark mage looked up, his one blue eye pleading, the green pentacle on the patch in place of the other eye a mockery of the men she'd loved. All of them. Even Zho. "The rite you would do — It would not lead to the world's salvation, but its destruction." He pointed to Charnas. "The imp would gain everything. All of you would become alive again, yes, but House Tremere would still be linked by blood, and Etrius would be at the Eye of the Pyramid, but younger than me. Charnas would gain not only the souls of my heirs, but those of Etrius as well. An entire House of mages." Thadius Zho's weathered face was stricken, and in it she saw the face of the man she had loved. "Charnas would destroy the world."

"Oh, please, Thadius," the imp said, leering down at him from the top of the dresser, "how many times do I have to tell you? I'm not the type of demon who likes destroying worlds. I prefer the phrase 'remake in my image.' And who's to say that would be a bad thing? I mean, look at this one. Anyone could do a better job. And if that anyone were me? Well, at the very least, it would be more amusing."

Etrie stood up in Ilse's hand then. "But we already thought of that!" he squeaked. "I would be joined with Etrius and Carl, and I'm older than you, Thadius, older than Etrius, older than any of the men of this world!"

Zho blinked his one eye, a horrified light of realization dawning in its depths. "You mean…"

"That's right!" howled Charnas. "You really screwed the pooch this time, Thadius old boy! The magic midget is one hundred percent correct. Might as well tell you now so I can enjoy watching you squirm before the witches play Stretch Armstrong with you." He cackled with delight, then pointed to Etrie. "That little critter is the Mandrake. *The* Mandrake, the oldest thinking critter on the planet, though, unfortunately for him, without a soul. Oh, well, that's God for you. All these little oversights we demons can take advantage of. But *if* Etrius and everyone do their little rite, it'll not only work the way you knew it would, it would also cut me and the Lord of Misrule right out of the loop —

previous claims and all that — and the only consolation prize we'd get is that since our contract with you would be null and void, we'd just clear it all out, give you back your eye, give Ilse here a life she wouldn't need, and take back everything we ever gave you, including your immortality and my own cute little self." Charnas giggled, then shoved Zho with his fingertips. "But hey, we could still be together. You'd die, your sins would drag you down to Hell, and when and if your soul gets put on the auction block, I intend to be right there in the first row and at the top of the bidding." The imp fluttered his eyelashes. "And you thought I didn't like you."

Zho clutched the chain and the Soul Gem and stared up at Ilse. "Please, Gwyneth, I would take it all back if I could, but I can't. I never meant to hurt you — I never meant to hurt anyone — I only wanted to save my soul."

"At the price of ten thousand innocents," Charnas put in. "I don't know about you, but that's the way I like seeing souls saved."

"It was just one…"

"I know. That's how it starts. Just one. Like potato chips."

Seeing the imp's childish cruelty and Zho sitting there, Ilse remembered herself in the baths, the words she had had with Merrill, and half the anger and fury drained out of her.

Charnas looked up and beamed. "Ooh, boy, I think someone just had a moral epiphany." The imp looked at Ilse. "Just realized you're no better than him, didn't you? Sucks, doesn't it?"

The fury returned, but not for Zho. "Go away, Charnas."

"What, and torment you no longer?" The imp whined. "Aw, c'mon, it's my job!"

"What—?" Zho began.

Ilse blinked away a tear of blood. "I have sins on my conscience too, Thadius. Things I should not have done, and I didn't even do them to protect my soul." She paused, her throat catching. "That's why the rite was so important. It would have made up for some of the things I've done."

"And you can still do it!" Charnas beamed. "Sacrifice ten thousand to save one, sacrifice one to save ten thousand. Hey, Hell doesn't care. It's all the same to us. And the law of potato chips always applies."

Ilse tried to ignore the imp, but couldn't block out the poisonous truth he spoke. If Carl and Etrius did the rite, with the knowledge that it would send Thadius to Hell, then their souls would gain that taint. The Mark of Caine, the sign of a brother's murderer. And looking at the one remaining eye of Thadius Zho, Ilse realized that they were just that — brothers. Brothers in spirit. If one was damned, then all were damned.

She knew what she had to do. All her death she had done what was best for the good of the clan, whatever were the wishes of the Council, and not what she knew in her heart to be right or true. She now saw where that path of power led.

Ilse set Etrie on her shoulder, letting him hang on to the silver chain which held her Key, then walked forward, holding out her hand. "Give me the necklace, Thadius."

He clutched it. "It's my life."

"I know," Ilse said, "but you owe me that much. Repay this one sin on your conscience. Do what is right."

Hand trembling, Zho slowly lifted the chain of office, then set it in her palm, dropping his head into his hands.

Charnas applauded sarcastically, still grinning. "Ooh, a good deed. An angel got its wings. Makes you feel warm all over, doesn't it?"

Ilse ignored the imp and went to the central stud of the necklace, examining the catch, then slipped her nail under the seam and pried it open. The Soul Gem tumbled out into her palm, round as a marble. The Eye of Saulot, the mystic third eye of knowledge and healing.

Ilse dropped the chain, then raised Zho's head up, flipping up the patch to find an empty, torn socket hidden behind the ugly green pentacle. Before he could raise his hand to hide his maiming, Ilse slipped the Eye of Saulot into the socket, where it fit as neatly as a glass eye.

Zho winced, lids clenched tight, tears running down his face, then opened his eyes, both of them. His right eye was still blue, but the left was now red, a gemstone, the Soul Gem. As Ilse watched, the color reversed, red changing to green, ruby to emerald. He blinked, and then he had the two mismatched eyes she remembered, the eyes that all of her men had had.

Ilse took the Key from around her neck, the Iron Key to the House of Secrets. "You are of the blood, Thadius. You can escape into the House Between the Worlds. It will hide you, for mysteries are neither good nor evil, and it keeps all of them." Her throat clenched, and she swallowed. "Go, and when you have redeemed your soul, return, and we will do what must be done."

He took the Key and stood up. "You were always too good for me, Gwyneth."

"I'm Ilse now," she said. "Go. Please, go."

He nodded once, and Ilse sat down on the bed of the witch's room. As Zho ran off to lose himself in the rambling corridors of the Witch House and then the House of Secrets, Charnas glanced back and leered. "Damned if you do, damned if you don't. Isn't this a great game?"

Ilse only wept, and Etrie, on her shoulder, hugged her, whispering in her ear, "It's all right, Lisle. I love you, and Etrius loves you too. He will understand."

Ilse looked at the discarded chain of diamonds on the floor and only hoped he would.

Both Etrius and Carl.

And she hoped that Paul, whoever or wherever he was, would understand as well.

Epilogue

And so it ended, with a prolonged scream that trailed down to a final echoing whimper. No sooner had Etrius called out with a voice of unspeakable agony, then everyone went crazier than before. The Kindred he'd brought with him were forced to flee from the woman/goddess who ruled the *Hexenhaus* and her pack of savage women. The witch-woman called to her minions and stalked the remaining vampires as if leading the Great Hunt of legend. The Tremere ran after Zho, completely ignoring Kurt, save to push him out of the way. The stunning flowering masses that surrounded the *Hexenhaus* built a net of vines and thorns that snared many of the Kindred from both sides of the battle, draining them of blood and sending them into torpor.

And while everyone ran their own ways, Kurt climbed through the tangled prison of foliage and thorns, snapping the vines that tried to attack him and gaining several small wounds.

At the center of the clearing before the witches' place of power, he found Etrius, still tied to his pole and crying tears of crimson sorrow. Looking at the man, Kurt knew that he had made a hideous mistake. This was not the face of an enemy. This was the face of a good man, a true kindred spirit. In Etrius he saw not a powerful member of the Tremere's Council of Seven, but rather a man who wanted more than anything else to simply be human again. A man who wanted to be free of his own Damnation.

"I am so very sorry, my lord. I did not understand." The bonds that held Etrius were strong, but hardly enough to stop Kurt. He had the advantage of leverage and could pull them away easily, where Etrius had well and truly been pinned in place. The heavy strands of thorns that imprisoned the Tremere elder tore into Kurt's hands, but gave way before he surrendered to the pain.

The Archimage of Clan Tremere fell free from his bonds and would have fallen to the ground if Kurt had not reached out to catch him. Etrius was nearly bloodless, likely having burned away his own vitæ just as Kurt had done in Crowley's haven.

Looking upon the man whose dreams he had ruined, Kurt could do no less for Etrius than Ilse Decameron had once done for him. He bared his fangs and slashed his own wrist, offering the blood in his body to Etrius. The man drank deeply, and Kurt made no protest. Etrius stopped himself before he would have done permanent harm to Kurt, and Kurt was saddened. Surely if anyone had the right to take his life, it was this gentle soul.

Numb in mind and body both, Kurt stepped away, going to sit among the fading beauty he'd helped destroy. The plants faltered, withered away, and left only weeds where once a magical forest had been. The beautiful and deadly rose bushes became simple wild roses again. He watched the passionate blooms fade and die and felt their loss as trenches cut across the scarred field of his soul. For a very long time, he sat and stared, hearing and seeing everything around him, but simply beyond caring.

While he sat, the Tremere returned. He heard Ilse

Decameron's voice and Etrius' and Carl Magnuson's as well, but he did not listen to what he heard. For a time he lost himself in memories of Jackie, bittersweet thoughts that filled him with agony and despair....

Eventually, he became aware that someone stood directly before him. After wishing the person would leave him be — until he realized his wish would not come to pass — he looked up from where he sat and stared into the face of Etrius.

The man gazed down at him and reached out with a hand that was surely strong enough to shatter rock. Kurt did not flinch, accepting that this one had the right to decide his fate. The hand clasped his arm and gently urged him to stand. When he was upright, Kurt lowered his head, unwilling to face the kind eyes that stared into his own.

"Ilse has told me all that she knows," Etrius said. "She has told me of Thadius Zho's ignorance of certain facts, and that you, too, had your reasons for stopping my actions."

"Again, my lord, I am truly sorry for what I have done to you."

"I have already forgiven you, Kurt Westphal." Kurt looked up, surprised by the words. "Will you now forgive yourself?"

"I — I don't know that I can, Lord Etrius." Kurt's eyes burned, and his vision grew red and blurred with the sting of his tears. "God help me, I don't know that I can!" His voice broke on the last word, and a jagged sob cut through him. Etrius reached out to him and held him in a powerful embrace, supporting him when all the foundations of his life had been shattered. Kurt wept openly, with no consideration of his place in the Ventrue and no thought of anything but the losses he had suffered and the damage he had caused.

When he was able to see and think again, he pulled away from the Tremere Councilor, ashamed of what he had done. Etrius stared at him again, with eyes that were too kind for one who had suffered so much. "If you would like, you may visit me in Vienna, Kurt. We can discuss what has happened and perhaps even find you a place among the Tremere."

I...I might well take you at your word, my lord. I shouldn't be surprised if I find myself in Vienna soon. Thank you."

Etrius nodded and gave Kurt's shoulder a farewell squeeze. "Melcinde will likely be back soon. I would be away from here before then, Kurt Westphal."

Then the Archimage turned away, and a woman Kurt remembered glimpsing in the witches' circle rushed up to him. Her dark hair was tangled with leaves, and her eyes glistened with welling tears. Etrius slipped his arm around her comfortingly; perhaps she was his consort. Kurt watched with the Councilor with a painful envy in his heart of that comfort, now denied him. In the distance a group of Tremere waited for Etrius, turning and following behind the Councilor as he walked towards an east-facing doorway of the *Hexenhaus*. Kurt nodded to Carl Magnuson when the man waved a good-bye, and nodded again to Ilse Decameron as she acknowledged him. As the last of the Tremere walked through the threshold of the door, the lodge where they had come to celebrate began to fade, changing into the trees that had been standing atop the Brocken for centuries.

And then Kurt turned away from the Brocken himself. The sun would rise all too soon, and he had need of shelter from the morning's light. Perhaps another day he would seek death, but not this one. For now he sought after the only thing that seemed to matter anymore — Jackie was out there alone, facing a world that was far too dark and unforgiving to be faced alone. He would find her, and from there only time could tell where his path might lead.

About the Authors

James A. Moore has been writing professionally for the last five years, and has been compared to both Stephen King and Dan Akroyd on numerous occasions...Sadly, the comparisons have all been to their looks and not to their talent. Jim's work has been seen in Marvel Comic's *Clive Barker's Hellraiser* and *Clive Barker's Night Breed* comics as well as in numerous supplements for White Wolf's *World of Darkness* games. Jim has served two terms as the Secretary of the Horror Writers' Association, and lives with his wife, Bonnie, in the suburbs of Atlanta, Georgia.

Kevin Andrew Murphy is one of the Wild Cards authors and has published stories in a number of anthologies. He's also an avid gamer and has written supplements for various roleplaying games, including *Mage*. He has his B.A. from U.C. Santa Cruz in Anthropology and Creative Writing, and his Masters in Professional Writing from the University of Southern California. This is his first novel.

The Most Glorious Dream

CHANGELING

Caught between harsh reality
and a paradise lost,
not quite human,
not wholly faerie —
an outcast.
You live in fear of the crushing weight of reason
and the chaotic terror of madness
in a waking dream all your own.

The last of the Storyteller series
and the beginning of a new age.
Over 250 full color pages.
Changeling: The Dreaming, in June from White Wolf.